CW01360215

MAGDEBURG

MAGDEBURG

HEATHER RICHARDSON

LAGAN PRESS
BELFAST
2010

Acknowledgements

Thanks to Sara Maitland, for her wisdom and encouragement; to Patrick Ramsey for enabling this book to come into existence, and Hazel Orme for her sensitive and thorough editing; to Alex Morgan, Marion Kleinschmidt and Patrick Fitzsymmons for being such honest critical readers; to the Lancaster friends who kept pushing me and asking the right questions, especially Rosalind Stopps, Val Waterhouse, Annia Lekkia, Laila Farnes and Tony Murfin; to Andrew Mattison for allowing me to make the acquaintance of a matchlock musket; and most of all to John, Isaac and Leon, for putting up with it all over the last few years.

Published by
Lagan Press
Unit 45
Westlink Enterprise Centre
30-50 Distillery Street
Belfast BT12 5BJ
e-mail: lagan-press@e-books.org.uk
web: lagan-press.org.uk

ARTS COUNCIL
of Northern Ireland

© Heather Richardson, 2010

The moral right of the author has been asserted.

ISBN: 978 1 904652 73 1 (pbk)
978 1 904652 88 5 (hbk)
Author: Richardson, Heather
Title: Magdeburg
2010

*Dedicated to my parents,
Tom and Evelyn Hutchinson*

The substance of peace lies in forgetting
—The Treaty of Westphalia, 1648

Author's Note

The Thirty Years' War (1618-48) can be viewed as a power struggle between the Catholic Holy Roman Empire and a coalition of Protestant German princes, but this is, of course, an oversimplification, given that the war involved armies and monarchs from all over Europe and Scandinavia. Allegiances shifted many times during the course of the conflict, and the armies of the two factions were made up of men from many nations and religious backgrounds. The three main historical figures in the background of this novel are the Holy Roman Emperor, Ferdinand II, General Tilly, one of his most experienced commanders, and the King of Sweden, Gustavus Adolphus. Ferdinand was a devout Catholic, and determined to use his power to roll back the Reformation. Gustavus Adolphus, as committed a Protestant as Ferdinand was Catholic, was seen by many as the saviour of Protestant Germany, arriving with his army to rescue his co-religionists when they were in danger of being overwhelmed. Both men were in the happy position of finding that the demands of their religious faith coincided with their ambitions for their earthly kingdoms.

The biblical quotations used have been translated from Luther's version of the Bible, first published in 1534.

1620

CHRISTA'S FATHER LIFTED HER FROM HER bed and carried her out of the room. She rested her head on his shoulder, still half asleep. Her baby sister began to cry, a thin wail that filled the house. 'Where are we going, Father?' she mumbled.

He shushed her and carried her down the stairs, past the looming bulk of the printing press in the workshop and out of the front door into the close. It was still dark, but the sky was beginning to lighten. She asked him again where they were going, and this time he answered her: 'We're going to the city walls, child. Don't be afraid.'

Christa wasn't afraid. Her father was big and warm, and he held her very tightly in his arms.

The city was quiet. Every house and place of business they passed was shuttered and silent, except for one bakery. Through the doorway she saw the baker's apprentice stoking the oven. The air was sharp with ripening yeast.

They reached the walls and climbed the steps to the top. Christa clung to her father, grasping the rough wool of his cloak. There were other men on the walls; the watchmen. In the grey half-light they looked like the bad spirits in the stories Helga, the new servant-girl, told her. One of the men held up a lantern and peered closely at the two of them. 'You're early again, Herr Henning,' he said. 'It's a cold morning to have the little one abroad.'

'Let me walk,' her father said. Christa could feel that he was trembling, and for the first time she felt fearful.

He walked the whole circuit of the walls. Christa turned her head so that she could see the great dark plain that surrounded the city. As the sky paled she made out the wide ribbon of the river.

After a time he stopped suddenly and stood gazing down into the city. The inner side of the wall was topped with a wooden fence no higher than his belt, and he leaned against it until it creaked. Christa hid her face in his cloak so that she didn't have to look. They were so high up, and the stones of the city streets so very far below.

'You should step back, Herr Henning,' the watchman said. 'The fence is hardly strong enough to bear your weight.'

'Christa, my love ,' her father whispered, 'this is a wicked world for a motherless child.'

'Yes, Father.' She knew her mother was dead. Helga had told her the worms were feasting on her.

The men had gathered close to her father now. She watched them over his shoulder. They were as motionless as a picture in a book, like the ones he printed in his workshop. Christa turned her head back towards the city. The streets were still in shadow, but the rising sun glowed pink on the twin spires of the cathedral. 'Beautiful,' she said.

Her father frowned. 'What's that?'

'Magdeburg is beautiful, Father.'

He set her down. The stones of the wall were cold under her bare feet. 'Beautiful?' he said. 'That's a big word for a little girl.'

She wondered if he was angry with her, but he crouched so that he was face to face with her and touched her hair. 'Yes, our city is beautiful.'

'Please will you move away from the edge, Herr Henning?' the watchman said. 'For the child's sake, if not your own.'

He covered his face with his hands. At first Christa thought he was coughing – his whole body shook with strange gasps – but when he fell to his knees, still sobbing, she understood that this was something more. She knelt beside him, and put her arm across his back. It seemed very pale and tiny against his broad shoulders, and she wondered how a child like her could ever mend a great broken man like him.

One

ON THE MORNING OF HER BEST friend Gertrude's wedding Christa called Helga. She told herself to be calm, and not to let the woman's sourness taint her joy. 'Stay with Elsbeth, and be sure she has some dumplings at the usual hour or she'll forget to eat.'

Helga folded her arms under her bosom. 'It's a grand day of it you'll all have, feasting, and me here with that one.' She nodded at Elsbeth, who was now installed on her usual seat by the window, poring over a book.

'Crowds and disorder distress her – it would be cruel to take her to the wedding. At home she'll be in peace with her books and prayers.'

'Why must she spend her days reading? The cat has more understanding than she has.'

Christa bit down the anger that swelled in her — in truth she'd often thought the same about her little sister. 'Elsbeth takes in more than we can comprehend,' she said. 'Now do as you are bid.'

Helga flounced away and began to clatter the breakfast dishes together.

'I'll ask Frau Schwarz to put something aside for you,' Christa said, in an attempt to mollify her.

Helga's mouth twisted, as if she'd tasted something bitter. 'Crumbs from the rich man's table.'

Christa had neither time nor the appetite for a quarrel. She left Helga to sulk, and went to her room to get ready.

Her brother was waiting for her on the stairway and caught her arm. 'Have you some money?' he whispered. 'Just a couple of *Taler*.'

'What do you need it for today?'

'A little brandy for Klaus.'

'Before he goes to the church?'

Dieter shrugged. 'If he's sober he may not be there at all.' He nudged her playfully. 'Come, sister. The bravest man needs a quart of courage for his walk to the gallows.'

Might Klaus bolt? Gertrude would be humiliated before everyone she knew, and ruined. 'One *Taler*. No more. And make sure he's at the church.'

Christa went on up to her room and smoothed her hair. She opened the chest and took out her money bag, which she kept hidden in the pocket of an old apron. She didn't think Dieter would dare to search through her clothes, but Helga … It was all there. She took out a coin and packed the bag away.

Dieter was waiting for her downstairs. She slipped him the coin as they left the house and made the short walk across the close to Gertrude's home. The door into the family's shop stood open. Inside, the workbenches had been pushed against the walls to make space for the wedding feast and the floor was clear of the usual clutter. Only the press stood where it always did, too heavy to move. There was no one in the shop, but the house echoed with footsteps and voices. Christa and Dieter walked through to the kitchen. Frau Schwarz was stooped before a cupboard while two maidservants sliced a haunch of ham.

'Christa, Dieter,' said Frau Schwarz. She tugged out a battered pewter bowl and straightened.

'How is the bride?' Christa said.

'Not well. She has always been so delicate.'

Poor Frau Schwarz had blinded herself as to the true cause of her daughter's sickness. It was unthinkable that a bastard grandchild should even now be growing in Gertrude's belly.

'Perhaps she took too much *Bratwurst*,' Dieter suggested.

Frau Schwarz blinked rapidly. 'Gertrude has never cared for it.'

'No?' Dieter was suppressing a grin.

Christa scowled at him. 'It's time you went to get Klaus.'

Dieter made a little bow and sauntered out.

Frau Schwarz rubbed at the bowl with her apron.

'I'll go up to Gertrude,' Christa said.

'Look at this.' Frau Schwarz held up the bowl. 'So dented. It's hardly more use than a sieve. Yes, my dear. Tell her I will bring her a bowl.' She gestured at an earthenware dish on the floor, which was splattered with a greenish substance. 'She's not even dressed. Lotte has been urging her on this last hour, but she pays no heed.'

Christa ran up the stairs to Gertrude's room and met Lotte outside the door. 'She's in a fierce temper, Miss Christa,' the maid whispered, 'and the hour's nearly on her.' Christa patted the old woman's arm and went into the bedroom.

Her friend was sitting on the edge of the bed dressed only in her shift and a petticoat. 'Gertrude,' Christa remonstrated gently, 'you must be at the church soon.' Gertrude's new gown lay beside her on the bed. Christa lifted the skirt and shook it out. 'Come, now, step into this.'

'Oh, Christa,' Gertrude groaned, 'I am dying.'

'You'll be wed first.'

Gertrude pulled a face, but forced herself up from the bed and allowed Christa to ease her into the skirt. 'Not so tight,' she snapped, as Christa fastened it about her waist.

'If it's loose the bodice won't go over it' Christa helped her into it. 'One breath in,' she said, and began to pull at the laces.

'Oh, God!'

'That's blasphemy.'

'It was a prayer. Oh, God, deliver me from this evil woman who will kill me by lacing my dress too tight ... Don't make the knots too small.' She gave Christa a sly smile. 'Or Klaus will never undo them.'

Christa felt a little pang of ... what? Not jealousy. Gertrude had changed in so many ways these last few months. Once they had gossiped together — about newlyweds who would not leave their bed so great was their delight, or the frightened bride who had rushed home to her father's house at midnight, dressed only in a blood-spotted shift. Each time a young woman got married they would study her closely for signs of difference after the wedding night. But now that Gertrude knew the secrets of what went on between men and women she would only smile and look away if their talk ventured towards such matters. Gertrude was her closest friend, though – a sinner, too – and they had shared everything until now. 'He'll manage,' she said, and thought, *As he has before.* 'We must hope he's not too drunk,' she concluded.

Gertrude stiffened. 'Why would he be drunk?'

'Dieter wheedled for money so that he and Klaus might toast your good fortune.'

'You gave it to him?'

Christa shrugged, glad to have ruffled her. 'I find it hard to resist him.' She paused, but some spiteful impulse urged her on. 'And once you had a fancy for him.'

Gertrude flushed. 'I was only a little girl.'

'It was not so long ago. I used to think you and he would wed some day.'

'Dieter is a wicked boy. No girl with any wit would wed him.'

Christa pointed at Gertrude's belly. 'But he wasn't as wicked as Klaus.' Her heart beat a little faster at her own boldness.

Gertrude's face was scarlet now. 'Stop.' There was a catch in her voice and her hand flew to her mouth.

'Are you taken badly again?' Suddenly Christa was ashamed of her mean-spirited thoughts and words.

Gertrude shook her head. 'It's not my condition that sickens me.' She pulled the fabric tight across the front of her skirt so that her belly seemed more swollen than it was. 'I wish that Father had not asked Pastor Ovens to conduct the ceremony.'

Christa felt her own face redden. 'Is he not a pleasant man?'

'Pleasant?' Gertrude squawked. 'Perhaps on the surface, but underneath …'

'He's a godly man at least.'

'Oh, yes. Very.' Gertrude sounded even more miserable.

'He preaches so well. Not like Pastor Helmholtz. Even Elsbeth would fall asleep during his sermons, and she's the godliest of us all.'

'Since he has been lodging with us … Oh, Christa, you should see how he looks at me and at Klaus. It is not … kind.'

Christa sat down beside her friend and put an arm around her shoulders. 'Your father and mother showed great charity in taking him in when he first came here and he has given them good return. Remember how he smoothed things with Klaus's family when you realised …' Christa sought the softest words '… when you knew you had need to marry?'

Gertrude sighed. 'I cannot explain things as easily as you can. What I mean is, when I talk, he frowns. And if I laugh …' She shuddered. 'And he never stops eating. My father says he's like a locust. But when he picks up his spoon he regards the food as if it were poison and tasted of gall or wormwood.'

'What does your mother say of that?'

'Nothing. She fears him as I do. But she would happily throw his platter at his head.'

'The poor man.'

'No, Christa!' Gertrude exclaimed. 'You cannot harbour sympathy for Pastor Ovens. He is like a big black crow.'

Christa blushed deeper now. 'I pity him because the Papists drove him out of Mannheim and he has neither church nor home. It is nothing more than that.'

Frau Schwarz's voice rang out from the bottom of the staircase: it was time they were gone. Christa picked up a damp washcloth, dabbed Gertrude's face and rearranged a stray ringlet. 'There now,' she said. 'The beautiful bride.'

The Johanniskirche was the neighbourhood church of the printers' quarter. A crowd had gathered at the front door to await the bridal party. Herr Schwarz led the way, pushing through the throng, with Gertrude, Christa and Frau Schwarz struggling to follow. Gertrude grabbed Christa's arm as a foul-smelling old man toppled against her.

Christa pushed him away, and the bystanders parted to let him fall. 'Who is he?' she asked.

'Not from my side of the family,' Frau Schwarz said sharply. She flailed at those closest to her. 'Make way! You will get no food or drink until my daughter is wed.' The crush eased a little and at last they forced their way to the church door. Pastor Ovens was nowhere to be seen. Klaus was there, thank God, but he resembled a corpse, his dark hair lank against his ashen face. He made a sharp contrast to Dieter, who stood at his side, holding his arm to steady him. The winter sunlight brought out the red gleam in Dieter's blond hair and his face was flushed as it always was when he had been drinking. He smiled at Christa and Gertrude.

There was a dark flutter of movement at the side of the church and Pastor Ovens stepped forward, his hands clasped tightly around his catechism. He was dressed completely in black, apart from a plain white kerchief tied loosely around his neck. His stern gaze swept over the crowd. Christa's face burned as his eyes took her in, but she didn't look away. He was handsome in a forbidding way — Dieter and Klaus looked like boys beside him.

'Dearly beloved,' Pastor Ovens began. It seemed he favoured the old-fashioned ritual, with vows exchanged at the church door. 'We are gathered here …' He rattled through the service. His voice was quieter than it was when he preached inside the church. Christa was sure those at the back of the crowd wouldn't hear him. The air was heavy, in spite of the chill weather. She felt sweat prickle in her armpits and at her waist where her bodice fitted tightly. Gertrude's face looked clammy.

Pastor Ovens stopped abruptly. 'Come now into the Lord's house, and hear His words.' He turned and rapped on the door. There was a long pause. People shifted from one foot to the other, coughed and muttered to their neighbours. Pastor Ovens knocked again. They heard a thin squeak, and then the door opened. A wild-eyed man with no eyebrows peered out. 'Let us in Helmut,' Pastor Ovens snapped. 'What do you think you're doing keeping me standing here like a pedlar?'

'Forgive me, Father,' the man said. 'I was afeard it was the Calvinists.'

'There are no Calvinists here. And do not call me "Father". That is a popish title.'

Helmut cringed as if Pastor Ovens had made to hit him. He pulled the door wide. The crowd pressed forward, and Christa found herself pushed to the front of the church. She looked round for Gertrude, but couldn't see her in the crush.

By now Pastor Ovens was at the altar, staring down on the congregation, a sour look on his face. Christa understood now why Gertrude had become so set against him. He did not seem like the same Pastor Ovens who enthralled her each time he preached.

Gertrude, Klaus and Dieter emerged at last from the throng, Gertrude clinging to Klaus's hand. Pastor Ovens noticed and frowned. Klaus shook her off. Once again Pastor Ovens waited for silence. Christa saw his chest swell as he took a deep breath.

'"At that day",' he declared, '"such a song will be sung in the land of Judah; We have a strong city; its walls and defences are salvation." When you hear these words, good people, the words of the prophet Isaiah, do you think of your own city?' Christa thrilled to his words. She sensed that everyone around her was equally rapt.

Pastor Ovens continued: 'Do you think of Magdeburg, the spotless virgin, unbroken and undefiled, despite the assaults of her enemies? How many times has the seducer we may call War tried to woo her, to force himself through her pure gateways to pleasure in her riches? Too many times, but always, by the grace and mercy of almighty God, she has withstood him. So, good people, you are proud of your city. But remember these wise old words. Pride struts before it tumbles.' Pastor Ovens paused, looking from face to face. Christa both hoped and dreaded that his eyes would meet hers, but he seemed lost in his own world. She held her breath, waiting for him to go on.

'The seducer approaches again,' he said, more softly, and it seemed to Christa that the whole congregation leaned forward to hear him. 'Yes, he approaches near, but now he is attired in the false glamour of his consort, the Whore of Rome. Will you resist him, good people? Or will you lie down and offer yourselves in exchange for the baubles of popery? Trust not in your own resolve. Only the Lord has the power to preserve your city and, of more importance yet, the chastity of your soul. For hear what Isaiah says: "He puts down them that dwell in the heights; he degrades the high city, yes, he knocks it to the ground until it lies in the dust."'

Christa resolved to study the Book of Isaiah when next she was reading her Bible. She and Elsbeth could read it together, and perhaps some of Elsbeth's goodness would reflect on her.

'And will you be saved?' Pastor Ovens asked. 'Listen to Isaiah, good people: "Your vices have separated between you and your God, and your sins have hid His face from you, that He will not hear. For your hands are beflecked with blood, and your fingers with vice; your lips have spoken falsehoods, your tongue has composed wrongs."

'But what do these words signify on a day such as this? On a happy epithalamic day, where two young people are come to be joined as man and wife? Where is the vice in this day? Let us turn to the teaching of Paul, in the seventh chapter of his first letter to the people of Corinth.' His voice sounded louder now. '"It is good for a man not to touch a woman." Strange words, you may think, and more fitting for a papist priest than a Lutheran.' He glared at the bride and groom. Christa followed his gaze. Klaus's pale face reddened, and he swayed. 'Yes,' Pastor Ovens repeated. '"It is good for a man not to touch a woman. Nevertheless, to avoid *whoring*..."' he waited as the word echoed around the church '"... let every man have his own wife, and let every woman have her own husband."' He closed his eyes. 'Satan,' he hissed, 'is the father of fornication. When a man and a woman roll like animals in their stinking bed of lust, Satan lies with them, their pander, their *Zuhälter*. His forked tongue licks up each drop of licentious sweat that leaks from their depraved skin. They are his meat and drink.'

The church was hot. A shaft of sunlight now shone directly on Pastor Ovens. His black clothes looked shabby in the brightness. Christa's heart was thundering in her ribcage. 'Verse thirty-four,' he continued, his voice calm again. '"There is a difference also between a wife and a virgin. The unmarried woman careth for the things of the Lord, that she may be holy both in body and spirit: but she that is married careth for the things of the world, how she may please her husband." Yes. Let me repeat. "There is a difference also between a wife and a virgin."' He pointed at Gertrude. 'And what of this wretched child? Neither a wife nor a virgin.'

Frau Schwarz gasped, and a tremor seemed to grip the congregation. Christa was ashamed now of how Pastor Ovens's words had stirred her, and felt a rush of anger.

Pastor Ovens turned to Klaus. 'And what of you, vile worm? Partner in sin. Despoiler of virtue. You are loathsome in the sight of the Lord!' He gazed up at the ceiling. When he spoke again his voice was gentler. 'This city, your beautiful city, is a shining beacon of truth in the Stygian darkness of idolatry. You call her the Maiden City, do you not? Chaste. Unbroken. When I first came here, cast out from my own church by the emissary of Satan I will not name, I walked in through the Brücketor gate. Above me, I saw a statue. Not a loathsome papist statue, but the very image of this city, the maiden herself. She carries a virgin's garland. There are words written on the garland, are there not? And what do those words say? Can you answer me?' He glared down at Gertrude and Klaus. 'You!' he boomed. 'Can you answer me?'

Gertrude's face had taken on a greenish tinge. Klaus opened his mouth and tried to say something. Pastor Ovens leaned closer. 'Speak up, child,' he said quietly.

'"Who shall take it?"' Klaus croaked.

'Yes!' Pastor Ovens shouted. '"Who shall take it?" Who shall take the virgin's garland from our city?' He pointed at Klaus. 'And you — you dared take this poor maiden's flower of purity.' Klaus was trembling now. Even Dieter was pale, standing bolt upright, straight-faced for once. 'On your knees!' Pastor Ovens roared. Gertrude and Klaus obeyed. Christa felt her own legs weaken, but somehow she remained standing.

'Repent. Repent while you still may.' Pastor Ovens's voice sounded like a chant now, low and mesmerising. 'Satan is nipping at your heels. He tugs at the very hem of your wedding clothes. Can you feel his fingers slipping beneath that finery to the filth beneath? Repent, dear brother and sister in Christ. Repent, dear children. For though you are mired in sin, yet the Lord will wash you clean. Repent. Repent. Repent.'

'I repent,' Klaus cried. 'Dear God, dear Lord Jesus, I repent.'

Now Pastor Ovens fell to his knees. 'Thank God, thank God.' He raised his eyes and held out his arms to Gertrude. 'And you, my child? Submit to your husband in this. Be led by him. Be led to the waters of Jordan. Repent, my daughter, repent!'

Gertrude glanced at Christa, her face showing her anguish, then turned back to Pastor Ovens. 'I …' She lifted her hand to her mouth, then bent over and vomited on the church floor directly in front of the clergyman. She tried to stand but the tangle of her skirts held her down.

Christa and Frau Schwarz leaped forward to help her to her feet. Pastor Ovens shuffled back, still on his knees, but his robe was splattered with bile.

'It is done?' Frau Schwarz barked.

'Done?' said Pastor Ovens, dully, as he struggled to his feet.

'They are married, yes?'

'Yes, but my sermon is not finished.'

'Never mind that.' Frau Schwarz nodded at her husband. 'Jörg! Help me.'

Herr Schwarz pushed forward and put his arm round Gertrude's waist, moving Christa out of the way as he did so. Gertrude clung to him, and he half carried her out of the church.

Christa and Frau Schwarz helped Gertrude upstairs to her bedroom where Lotte held a cloth dampened with lavender water to her brow. Gertrude was calling for Klaus, but they had lost him in the chaos of the church. 'He'll find his way back,' Christa said, trying to soothe her friend. 'Dieter will bring him.' She prayed he would. At least her brother's pockets were empty. If he and Klaus wanted more drink they would have to come to the wedding feast.

Frau Schwarz said nothing, but Christa could feel her fury. There were voices in other parts of the house, and heavy footsteps running up and down the stairs. 'Will I stay with Gertrude so you can tend the guests?' Christa offered. 'Or I could be downstairs if you'd rather stay here?'

Frau Schwarz shook her head. 'We will all go downstairs.'

'Ach, Mother!' Gertrude wailed. 'I can't show my face.'

Frau Schwarz took hold of her shoulders. 'You are my only living child. This is your wedding day. We will not hide up here.'

They paused. There was a series of thumps, as if a heavy box was being dragged steadily down the stairs. Frau Schwarz took a deep breath and opened the door.

The main room was half full of people, but most were pressed around the windows, looking out into the close. Christa peered about for Klaus and Dieter and spotted them among the few men who were at the table. Klaus was crouched on a stool, clutching a tankard. Dieter was nudging him, as if he was encouraging him to drink. Both young men looked up as Christa and Gertrude walked across to them. Klaus smiled weakly at his wife.

'Why is everyone staring out of the windows?' Christa hissed to Dieter.

'They're watching the casting-out of a demon,' he replied, deadpan.

Christa and Dieter pushed their way to one of the windows. Down in the close Pastor Ovens held himself stiffly. His face bore a strange expression. Christa wondered that she had ever thought him handsome, but at the same time she felt a twinge of compassion. It could not be comfortable for a man of his dignity to be standing so exposed. A large trunk lay on the ground beside him. Herr Schwarz and Herr Pflummer, the paper merchant, were a step away from him. Herr Schwarz was talking intently to the other, whose arms were folded. 'Herr Schwarz has put Pastor Ovens out?' She forced herself to smile up at Dieter. 'Would you ever have thought it?'

'He had no choice. Pastor Ovens impugned the family's honour.'

Dieter's face was serious. Christa had never heard him speak of honour before.

It was well into the afternoon when Christa noticed her father standing in the doorway. He was frowning. She nudged Dieter. 'We should go to Father.' Dieter glanced up, then shrugged and turned back to his friends. It was clear he had no intention of interrupting his merrymaking.

When her father saw Christa coming towards him his face softened a little, but she could see that something was worrying him. 'I'm glad I've found you,' he said. She could smell beer on his breath. 'I need you to run home and prepare for a guest.'

Christa did her best to mask her disappointment. 'A guest? Today? Who is it?'

Father looked around to check that no one was listening, then leaned closer to her. 'Pastor Ovens.'

'But why?'

'After that sermon Jörg had no choice but to send him away, yet he still feels beholden to the man. He can't see him sleeping in a ditch.'

'So he is to stay with us? For how long?'

'How should I know? Not long, I hope.'

'What about Elsbeth? You know how change disturbs her.'

He rubbed his forehead. 'She spends her life at prayer or with her books. Perhaps she can be encouraged to keep to her room.'

Christa felt a flare of irritation. Her father was too willing to do a kindness, even at the inconvenience of his family. 'So we must lock her out of sight?'

'That was not what I meant!' he snapped, and then shook his head. 'Jörg asked me to take in the pastor because everyone else refused him.'

'Let me explain to Herr Schwarz how things are with Elsbeth, and then—-'

He held up his hand to cut her short. 'Elsbeth's … strangeness is family business. We do not discuss it with anyone.'

Christa knew she would gain nothing from further argument. She looked back across the room at her friends. Dieter said something that made Klaus laugh. Gertrude seemed shocked. Why should Dieter stay to enjoy the celebrations when she was chased off to bring order to the house? Her father touched her arm. 'You must go now.'

Christa nodded, then stopped short. 'Where is Pastor Ovens to sleep?'

'He will have to share Dieter's room.'

Christa couldn't stifle her laughter. 'Dieter! And Pastor Ovens?'

'Well, what else do you suggest? That I put Andreas in with Dieter, and ask a man like Pastor Ovens to sleep in a journeyman's bunk?'

'It might inspire another sermon. "He has set me in dark places, as they that be dead of old."'

'Don't be frivolous, Christa. Run home now. I'll bring him with me when I leave.'

'Don't come too soon — I shall have much to do with us having been out all day.'

'We cannot be long. The poor man's hiding in the alley, being talked at by old Albrecht. Even Frau Schwarz would say he deserved better than that.'

Christa left the house. Pastor Ovens in their home! A few hours ago she might have been in a flutter at the idea, but now a slow anger burned. He had shamed Gertrude and was now the cause of her having to leave the feast early. As she made her way across the close she tried to remember what food they had in the larder. She wasn't sure that they had the makings of a decent meal for a guest, and by now the market would be closed.

Andreas was cleaning the press when she got back to the house. Printed pages hung from the racks on the workshop ceiling and fluttered as Christa closed the door behind her. 'I didn't expect you back so soon,' Andreas said, picking up a letter block and wiping it with a rag. His hands and the cloth were stained black with ink.

'Pastor Ovens is to stay with us. I'm to prepare for his arrival.'

'Then God be with you.' His mouth twisted into a smirk. She hated that look. It suggested he knew more than she did.

She ignored his comment and walked through to the back kitchen. It was empty, and the fire was down to its last embers. She ran up to the first floor, and paused for a moment at the door, calming herself. Elsbeth became flustered when people rushed in without warning. Oh, poor Elsbeth ... How long would Pastor Ovens stay? Christa took a deep breath and quietly opened the door.

There was no one there. The little hearth was cold, and the room was so chilled that Christa could see her own breath cloud the air. The fire that had warmed them at breakfast time must have burned out hours ago, and Helga hadn't troubled to relight it. The table was still littered with their breakfast plates and the remains of a midday meal. Christa climbed the next flight of stairs and went into the bedroom she shared with her sister. Elsbeth was kneeling at the side of the bed, her face turned upwards, eyes closed, lips moving. Christa stood still, watching her. She was such a fragile child, with those skinny little fingers clasped in prayer, and that pale face so drained of colour that the skin seemed to gleam. 'Elsbeth,' Christa said, hearing the clumsiness of her own voice in the quiet room. 'I need your help. We must tidy the house.' She decided to save the news of their visitor for later.

Elsbeth's lips stilled and she opened her eyes. She smiled at Christa a little sadly, and stood up. Christa led the way downstairs. 'Have you seen Helga?' she said.

'Not since this morning.'

Christa bit back her anger. Helga had been told to care for Elsbeth, but had clearly decided that as there would be no one to check on her she could go out. No doubt she'd planned to scurry back at nightfall, chase Elsbeth to bed and hide the dirty dishes until the morning.

Down in the main room she told Elsbeth to sweep the floor, while she cleared the table. She heard Andreas's footsteps on the stairs, and opened the door to him. 'Please help me,' she said. 'Would you straighten the furniture?'

Andreas nodded and set to work. Christa glanced at his hands, but thankfully he'd washed them. His fingernails were still black, and the lines on his palms were inked like a woodcut, but at least he wasn't leaving marks on the chairs as he pushed them into place. Elsbeth was dreamily sweeping the crumbs into a pile near the hearth.

Christa heard the main door open downstairs. 'They're here, and not even a fire lit!' she said, half to herself.

Andreas spat into his hands and ran his fingers through his hair to smooth it as the door opened and Herr Henning ushered Pastor Ovens into the room. Dieter followed sullenly. He was dragging a small travelling trunk. 'These are my daughters, Christa and Elsbeth,' their father said. 'You may have seen Christa at the wedding today.'

Pastor Ovens made no reply, but bowed his head slightly in Christa's direction. He looked at her intently, without a trace of a smile. She dipped a curtsy, feeling her face burn. Elsbeth tugged at her sleeve and Christa took her hand reassuringly.

Their father continued with his introductions. 'And this is Andreas, my journeyman.'

Pastor Ovens turned his fearsome stare on Andreas, and Christa was gratified to observe that he, too, seemed uncomfortable under such scrutiny. 'Shall I take Pastor Ovens's things to his room, Herr Henning?' Andreas said.

'If you please. Up to Dieter's room.' Dieter glared at him.

'Father, Elsbeth and I should go to the kitchen,' Christa said. Pastor Ovens was staring at the heap of crumbs before the hearth.

'Of course, my dear,' said Father. 'And tell Helga to bring up a jug of beer.'

Christa decided not to mention Helga's absence. It might make their household appear ill-managed in the pastor's eyes. 'Yes, Father,' she said, and fled with her sister.

They sat at the table, heads bowed as Pastor Ovens said the grace. After a few minutes he paused, and Christa opened her eyes, but he was merely drawing breath. The prayer continued. Someone's stomach rumbled, and Christa's lips twitched with the effort of holding back a laugh. She looked up again, and saw that Andreas's eyes were on the food. Steam rose from the pot of soup and dumplings. He looked from it to the bread, then the cheese, and bit his lip. He must have realised she was watching him, because his face reddened.

Pastor Ovens seemed to be reaching the high point of his prayer. His voice was growing louder with every word. Only his and Elsbeth's eyes were still closed. At last he stopped speaking. 'Amen,' he said, in a whisper. 'Amen.'

Christa ladled out the soup and dumplings. For the first few moments there was no sound but the clatter of spoons in bowls. Christa remembered what Gertrude had said about Pastor Ovens's gluttony and watched him covertly. Sure enough, his bowl was emptying faster even than Andreas's, although from his expression he took little pleasure in the meal.

Elsbeth's soup was untouched. 'Eat, sweetheart,' she said gently.

Elsbeth picked up her spoon and dipped it into the bowl, but seemed unable to lift it to her mouth. She was trembling, and taking quick, shallow breaths.

'My daughter is unused to strangers in the house,' her father said. Christa was irritated by the note of apology in his voice.

Pastor Ovens stared at Elsbeth. 'Is she a simpleton?'

'Indeed not,' Christa said, before her father had a chance to reply. 'She can read and comprehend better than many a grown man.'

'Christa, my dear, perhaps it would be a kindness to take Elsbeth to her room.' Herr Henning's face was damp with sweat.

Christa wondered if he was angry with her for speaking out. 'Yes, Father,' she said, and urged Elsbeth to her feet.

In their bedroom she did her best to soothe her sister by reading to her from a book of rhymes. How dare Pastor Ovens think her a simpleton? She was a strange child, to be sure, but with a gift of understanding about her, and goodness too. At last Elsbeth seemed calmer. 'Please leave me be, Christa,' she said. 'I will pray for a while, then ready myself for sleep.'

Christa kissed her and made her way downstairs. As she descended she could hear her father's voice. He was still talking when she took her place at the table.

Pastor Ovens said little, and it seemed that the less he said the more Herr Henning felt he had to talk. 'Ah, here's Christa,' he said, as if he was glad to have a fresh topic. 'A very good girl.'

'Is she?' Pastor Ovens said, fixing her with that cold stare again.

Christa ignored Dieter's grimace, and Andreas's insufferable smirk. 'I endeavour to be,' she said, struggling to keep her voice soft and modest.

'As all good Christians must.' Pastor Ovens reached for the last crust of bread and chewed it slowly.

Anger flared in her again. Christa turned to Dieter. 'How did Gertrude fare when you left her?'

He met her gaze and she saw that he understood her. 'A little better, but heart-sore at the day's turn.'

'And who could blame her? Poor Gertrude.'

They fell silent. Father coughed, and Andreas shuffled in his seat. Pastor Ovens steepled his fingers and looked at the ceiling. Christa wanted to say more to him, but she could not shame her father by showing ill-manners to a guest.

'I think it is time for the table to be cleared,' Father said, nodding at her. 'Helga will help you.'

'Helga is nowhere to be found,' Christa said sharply, no longer caring what Pastor Ovens thought of them. She began to gather the plates.

'Fräulein,' Pastor Ovens said, 'do you think I spoke harshly to your friend today?'

Christa could feel the eyes of all the men on her. She steadied her voice. 'I do, sir.'

'Christa, you must not—' Father began, but Pastor Ovens held up his hand to silence him.

'Do not let loyalty lure you into sin, Fräulein.' Pastor Ovens paused, as if he expected some reply from her. When none came he went on: 'Had I the opportunity to conclude my sermon, I would have continued with the words of Paul to the people of Corinth. "Let the husband act with friendship unto his wife, and likewise the wife unto her husband." So, you see, my just admonition would have been followed with words of consolation.' He looked at each of the men in turn. 'In this the preacher must model himself on the workings of the Almighty, who first breaks the human heart in order to restore it, reshaped by holiness.'

Christa glanced briefly around the table. They seemed not to know how to arrange their faces, apart from Pastor Ovens, who glowed pink with fervour. Her father's mouth hung open, Dieter was glowering and picking at a splinter on the tabletop, and Andreas looked sulky and childish. The room felt very hot to her, unbearable, and the silence continued. She could feel Pastor Ovens's eyes on her as she lifted the dirty plates.

'To bed when you've finished,' her father said.

'Yes, Father,' she said demurely, and left the room.

Elsbeth was already asleep when Christa went up. The room was quite dark, so she felt for the candle and lit it. She put on her nightclothes and had just knelt to pray when Dieter tapped on the door and poked his head into the room. 'What do you think you're doing, Christa Henning?'

'I don't know what you're talking about.' Christa scrambled into bed, pulling the covers around her. 'And be quiet. You'll wake Elsbeth.'

'Giving him encouragement. We'll never get rid of him now.'

'I don't understand.'

Dieter smirked. 'You should have heard him after you'd left.'

'Pastor Ovens?'

'Oh, yes, dear sister. He wanted to know all about you, and poor Father knew what game he was at, yet could not stop himself boasting.'

Christa hoped that Dieter would not notice her confusion. She considered all the strategies she could use to persuade her brother to say more, but she knew it was hopeless. He was clearly aware of how keenly she wanted to hear what Pastor Ovens had said, so he would not tell her. 'Please, Dieter,' she said, more in despair than hope, 'what was he asking?'

Dieter affected a yawn. 'It is too late to discuss such things. I'm away to bed. I may hope the good pastor doesn't mistake me for you in the dark of the night.'

Christa wished she could find some clever words to cast at Dieter.

'He's old,' he said. 'Nearly thirty. And he has children — three of them. His first wife died.' Dieter contorted his face until it looked like one of the gargoyles on the cathedral. 'In *childbirth*.'

'Stop it. That's not funny.'

'He's looking for a wife. Andreas was furious.'

'Good. Andreas is a pig.'

'At least Andreas has a job. Father would never let you marry Pastor Ovens. The country's full of preachers without churches.'

'I wouldn't marry Andreas. He's too dull. And I don't like his eyes. He can marry Helga.'

Dieter grinned at her. 'Father will never let you marry anyone. You'll have to stay here to look after him and Elsbeth until you're a hundred. You'll be buried in an old maid's grave, and they'll write on your headstone, "Untouched by any man."'

'I hate you. I hope Pastor Ovens preaches at you all night.'

Dieter laughed. 'You could always do as Gertrude and have Pastor Ovens plant a baby in your belly. Father would have no choice but to let you marry.'

'Get out!' Christa hurled her pillow at Dieter, but it fell short of the doorway, which amused him still more. He grinned and left, pulling the door closed after him. She waited until she heard his footsteps retreat along the corridor, then retrieved her pillow.

Two

THE REGIMENT HAD BEEN ORDERED TO set up camp on the water meadows outside the town of Saalfeld. Sergeant Lukas Weinsburg had spent the days since they had come working with the other men of Captain Gebwiler's company to ready their muskets after the winter. They were resting today, it being Sunday. The captain was concerned for the pack horses. Those that had survived the cold months were scrawny and listless. They needed more than meadow grass to fit them for the march north. The night before he'd charged a half-dozen of the wildest lads with finding feed for them. They'd come back from Saalfeld with bloodied knuckles and half a sack of stale oats. It wasn't much, but it might put a little sparkle back into the horses' eyes. Lukas's belly was empty. Sometimes he envied the animals. At least they had grass to take the edge off their hunger.

Lukas had no fondness for Sundays. Some might welcome a day of rest, but to him inaction was torment. He and Katherine shared the little food they had in the cramped quarters of his ragged tent. It was ill-designed for a woman in her state, with the child in her belly near ready to be born, but she seemed determined to remain there with him, even though he had found her lodgings with a widow in the town. When they had finished eating, Lukas sat in the sun outside the tent to keep company with the other men. One of the Croats had come by a jar of rum, and they passed it round discreetly. Lukas was just taking a gulp when a young priest appeared from between the tents opposite. The lad seemed not to know where he was. Lukas set the jar down and wiped his mouth. 'Are you lost, Father?'

'Yes, I ...' The lad was staring at him as if he beheld a monster.

My scars, Lukas thought. 'Don't be afraid of my battle-marks. They will do you no harm.'

'We are here to say prayers with Colonel von Breuner,' the young priest said, 'but Father Tomas sent me away while they dined. I lost my way in the camp.'

'To hell with Father Tomas!' shouted Corporal Baxandall, the wildest of the lads. 'Will you wet your throat with us?' Matko the Croat laughed, although it was doubtful he had understood his friend's words. The pair conversed in a mixture of soldiers' Latin and profanity.

The priest came closer. He looked at the jar of rum and chewed his lip. 'Thank you, no.'

'Go on, Father,' Baxandall said. 'We'll not tell your master.'

The boy glanced upwards. 'My master will know whether you tell Him or not.' He cleared his throat. 'You must not call me "Father". I am not ordained.'

'Why are you dressed as a priest, then?' said Baxandall.

He blushed. 'I am a lay brother in the seminary. I help to teach the younger ones there.'

'And what is your name then, if we are not to call you "Father"?' said Lukas.

'I am Götz Fuhrmann.'

'Sit down, Götz Fuhrmann.' Lukas waved at a powder box to the side of the tent door. 'It's too hot to be standing.'

Götz sat awkwardly, catching his heel in his robes. Baxandall sniggered and Lukas shot him a silencing look. 'Will you be a priest one day?' he asked.

'I would like that, but Father Tomas says I need to test myself in the world first.'

'By playing schoolmaster to seminary boys?' Baxandall's voice was more contemptuous. He nudged Matko, who laughed.

Götz looked uncomfortable. 'I must earn my keep.'

'Then earn it like a proper man and fight for your faith.'

'Is that what you're doing, Baxandall?' Lukas said.

'When the Protestant King of Sweden pays his men as much as the Holy Roman Emperor, I'll fight in defence of my faith.'

Götz looked puzzled. 'You're a Protestant? Fighting for the Emperor?'

'This year the Emperor is my master. Like as not I'll take a different coin next spring.'

'Don't look shocked, Götz Fuhrmann,' Lukas said. 'I fought with the Elector of Saxony's men for a season, and he's as firm a Lutheran as you may find.'

Götz seemed nonplussed, but soon collected himself. 'It's a fair wage, is it, that you get if you sign for a soldier?'

The men laughed and looked at Lukas. He smiled bitterly. 'The wage sounds well enough but payment is another story.'

'What do you mean?'

'We are paid only when our masters do whatever rich men must when they need money. A soldier can wait a long time for what he's owed.'

'So how do you live?'

'We beg and we borrow,' Lukas said.

'Or we take,' Baxandall added.

'Perhaps you'd be better staying in the seminary,' Lukas said. 'At least there you eat every day.'

Götz leaned closer to Lukas, lowering his voice so that the others could not hear him. 'I've heard that soldiers can make their fortunes with the booty they take.'

Lukas nodded. 'Indeed we can, but we usually lose them as smartly as we find them. And why would you want a fortune, young Götz? Do not priests take a vow of poverty?'

'It's hard for a poor man to become a Jesuit.'

'Have you no family to pay you in?'

'None living. I was reared by the sisters, then schooled by the Jesuits when I showed promise.'

'Aye, you sound book-learned, not like us,' Lukas said. He glanced at Baxandall. 'Especially not like him.'

'Whoring and fighting give me more delight than all the books in Germany,' Baxandall fired back.

Lukas watched the colour rise in Götz's face. 'You don't hear talk like that in the seminary, do you?'

'Sergeant,' one of the other men said, 'why don't you ask him to read the picture you came by in Schweidnitz?'

Lukas nodded. 'I've found no one to explain it to me yet. Will you do me this favour, young Götz?'

'I must find Father Tomas.'

'I will be your guide through the camp if you will be my guide through the words on this paper.' Götz nodded and Lukas ducked back into the tent.

Katherine was sitting on a blanket. 'Will you be talking out there all day?'

Lukas searched among his things for the red coat he'd taken from a dead man in Schweidnitz two winters ago. 'You can sit outside with me, if you wish.' He found it and took a folded sheet of paper carefully from the pocket.

'I don't like their talk. And Baxandall makes my flesh creep.'

'Keep away from him, then.' He'd never told her what Baxandall was capable of, but she seemed to sense it. He was glad she had that wisdom. 'Many of the other women are out taking the air. You could pass some time with them.' She didn't reply so he shrugged and stepped back out into the sunlight. 'Here,' he said, unfolding the paper and handing it to Götz. 'What is it about?'

The men crowded round as Götz studied the woodcut of three men tumbling out of a castle window, with a few words printed below it. The young lad had acquired an air of power, Lukas thought, perhaps because he alone could translate the marks on the paper into words. '"A Swift Cure for Tyranny",' Götz read aloud. '"Our Brethren in Bohemia Protect their Precious Liberties."'

'What does that mean?' Baxandall said.

'It celebrates the heretics of Prague. They treated the Emperor's emissaries most shamefully.'

Lukas took the page back and looked at it more closely. 'They threw them out of the window?'

'Yes.'

Baxandall started to laugh. 'That would have been good sport.'

Götz frowned at him. 'You have a strange notion of humour.'

Lukas tucked the paper into his pocket, while Baxandall and his cronies continued to mock Götz. Whatever power the boy had possessed as he read to them had dissipated.

Another soldier was walking towards them, carrying a musket. 'Here, Sergeant Weinsburg,' he called. 'Take a look at this piece, will you? I thought it was damp, but I've dried it and it still chokes like a man on the gallows.'

Lukas glanced at Götz, then back at the musketeer. For some reason he did not want the boy to think worse of them than he already must. 'It's the Lord's Day, you heathen. You should not be labouring at your weapon.'

'Lord's Day be damned.' He stopped short, noticing Götz in his lay brother's robes. 'Forgive me, Father.'

The other men laughed and Götz blushed again.

'Give it here,' Lukas said, and took the weapon. He glanced at Götz. 'What do you think, my young friend? What ails the gun? Would a prayer help it?'

Götz reached out for it. He held it inexpertly, and Lukas had to warn him not to let the smouldering end of the slow-match fuse hang too close to his robes. In spite of his awkwardness, when the boy spoke his voice was clear, with barely a tremor. 'God our Father and Maria our Mother, bless this weapon in the hands of these thy righteous defenders. Smooth their path, confound their enemies, in the name of the Father, the Son and the Holy Ghost.'

The soldiers chorused, 'Amen.'

'Would you care to test it, Götz?' Lukas said.

'I do not know how,' he stammered.

'I can show you.'

'Look at him,' said Baxandall. 'He's as coy as a virgin.'

'Happen he's that too,' one of the other soldiers said slyly.

Somebody laughed at the back of the group, but Lukas silenced him with a glare. 'Forgive us, Götz,' Lukas said. 'We're not used to polite company.'

Götz handed the gun back to its owner. 'You said you would help me find my way back to Father Tomas,' he said.

Now Lukas heard desperation in his voice. 'Come on, then,' he said, slapping Götz soundly on the shoulder. 'I'll set you back on the path to righteousness.'

Lukas was working alongside Captain Gebwiler to pack the weapons and supplies for the march north when a boy came from the town with a message. 'I've news for Sergeant Weinsburg,' he said.

Lukas set a bushel of shrivelled apples on a cart. 'I'm the man you're looking for.'

'Your woman's pains are on her, may Our Lady be good to her.'

'Is the child born?'

'Not when I left.'

Lukas found a coin in his belt-bag and handed it to the messenger. 'Send word to me when it's over.'

'She's crying out for you. And the old wives want you there, so you won't hold them guilty if things turn bad.'

'Do as I say or I'll clap your ear.'

The boy took a step back, his eyes still on Lukas. 'You'll be away soon.'

'Captain says we'll be here a few days more. Tell her that.' Lukas turned back to his work and didn't look up again until he was sure the boy had gone.

'You chose a good time to father a child, Weinsburg,' Captain Gebwiler said. 'You had the pleasure of her, and now you can stay away while she's laid low and the babe is filling the house with its gurning.'

Lukas nodded.

'Will you wed her by and by?' Captain Gebwiler was known for his strict living. His wife and children travelled with him to keep him safe from sin. Even Baxandall had married a foreign trollop in the hope of advancing himself in the captain's eyes.

'It's hard to be a soldier's wife,' Lukas said.

'Harder to be a soldier's bastard.'

'The babe may not live to know its stain.'

Captain Gebwiler raised his eyebrows. 'You've a cold heart in you.'

Lukas shrugged. 'She was merry enough before the child was in her. But ... I don't think I was the first to play in her garden.' He felt a pang. He knew he'd been Katherine's first man.

'Ah. You'll hardly wed her, then.'

'I never spoke of marriage, but she lay down for me readily enough without my promise.' *You're damned, Lukas Weinsburg*, he thought. *You talk like a lawyer.*

Captain Gebwiler slapped him heartily on the back. 'A wise man won't marry a whore, but be sure to do right by the child. Send the woman money for its care.'

It was evening when word came that the baby was born and lived. Lukas drank his daughter's health with the other men. Darkness was falling by the time he crossed the bridge into the town. He walked slowly towards the lodgings, the warm haze of the brandy changing to thirst and a thumping head. He needed another drink before he could face Katherine, so he stepped into the first tavern he came to and demanded beer, with a pour of rum. The tapster served him in silence as the two other customers stared. Lukas drank quickly, and pushed his empty tankard across the table.

'You'll get no more in here,' the tapster said.

'Why?' Lukas said. 'Does my money not suit you?'

The man squared his shoulders. 'The wrecking your sort do costs me more than I earn from your drinking.'

Lukas felt the dull throb of anger. 'There'll be a wrecking right enough, if you won't serve me.'

The other two customers stood up. Lukas held the tapster's eye, but he was aware of the others. He couldn't tell from the way they held themselves if they would slip away from the fight or join it.

The door was pushed open and another man came into the room. He walked quickly to a table and sat, his head dipped.

'Find another drinking place,' the tapster said to Lukas.

Inside his head Lukas could see his hands on the man's throat. His rage was mounting and it would have to come out. But not yet. He made to leave. The newcomer looked up at him. It was the young lad from the seminary who'd lost himself in the camp. Götz … Fuhrmann? 'Give him his drink, Justus,' Götz said. 'I know him. He's a sound man.'

The tapster muttered something and snatched up Lukas's tankard. Lukas walked over to Götz and sat down. 'I'll stand you a drink for that.'

The tapster brought their beer and a jar of rum.

'Thank you.' Götz sipped.

Lukas offered him a dash of rum. Götz accepted and sipped again. 'You'll be away soon?'

'In a day or two.'

'What brings you to the town alone?'

'My woman has given me a daughter today.'

For a moment Götz was silent. Then he said, 'Poor child. To be born when this war has the country in ruins. Is she healthy?'

'I've not seen her yet.'

Götz seemed to consider this, but whatever his thoughts were he kept them to himself. He drank his beer and signalled to Justus for more. As their tankards were refilled Lukas realised that his anger had faded and thanked God for it. He couldn't see Katherine and the child with that sin in him.

Lukas had no idea of the hour. They seemed to have been in the tavern for ever. He was telling Götz war stories, bragging about the men he'd killed and the booty he'd won, and the boy was lapping it up as thirstily as he had the drink. At last the tales ran dry and Götz laid his head on the table. Lukas looked around the tavern. They were alone — even Justus was nowhere to be seen. 'Here,' he said, shaking Götz, 'I must go back to camp.'

Götz raised his head. 'What about the child?'

'Child?'

'Your daughter. Were you not to see her?'

Lukas slumped in his seat.

Götz struggled to his feet. Justus appeared from the back room, eyes bleary with sleep. He gathered up the money Lukas threw on the table.

Lukas and Götz supported each other out through the tavern door. The sky was past its darkest and Lukas reckoned there were less than two hours until daybreak. 'Keep quiet,' he whispered to Götz. 'I don't want to be held by the night-watch.'

'I doubt they'll notice us,' Götz said. 'They'd rather sleep than work.'

They staggered through the town. More than once they lost their way in the ill-lit streets, but at last they found the house where Katherine was lodging. The windows were shuttered for the night, but Lukas could make out a chink of light in one of the upper rooms. He tried the front door, but it was bolted, so he banged on it with the flat of his hand.

Götz leaned against the wall, breathing deeply, as if he had just run a race. There was no sound from the house.

Again Lukas banged on the door. The window above them was opened, and the shutter pushed back. 'Quiet down there,' an old voice called. 'There's a wee one sleeping here.'

'And I'm her father,' Lukas roared. 'Let me in or I'll wake the street.'

A shutter banged open directly opposite the house. 'You've already done that, you bastard.' The man's voice sounded thick with sleep and anger.

Lukas felt an answering rage quicken in him. 'Come down here and say that again. I'll soon put you back to sleep.'

Götz put a hand on Lukas's arm. 'This isn't the time for fighting, my friend.'

They heard muttering and thumping from the house across the street. The man whose sleep had been interrupted was obviously on his way downstairs. Before he appeared, the door of Katherine's lodging house was pulled open, and Lukas felt Götz push him inside.

The landlady had a blanket draped round her shoulders and held a stub of candle. The flame was tall, and flickered in the draught, but she seemed oblivious to the hot wax dripping on to her skin. 'You were in no rush,' she said to Lukas. 'She was calling for you until she'd no strength left.'

'Is she well?'

The old woman grimaced. 'She had a hard time. But she's living.' She turned and led the way upstairs.

'I should stay down here,' Götz said. 'It might not be right …'

'Right be damned.' Lukas took his arm. 'I'll not make it up these stairs without you to hold me.'

The two men followed the old woman up to the second landing. She opened a narrow doorway and stepped through. The room was cramped. Lukas had to stoop to avoid hitting his head on the ceiling. Katherine was sleeping on a ragged mattress, the baby tucked in beside her. 'This place stinks,' he said, covering his nose with his hand.

'It's your lady who stinks, sir,' the old woman said, with a certain satisfaction in her voice. 'As I said, she had a rough time and is badly torn.' She leaned closer to Lukas and whispered, 'If I may be plain, sir, she can hold nothing in, neither her soil nor her water.'

Lukas recoiled from her foul breath and the meaning of her words. 'She'll mend, won't she?'

'Time will tell. You'd best leave money for a surgeon before you go.'

Lukas remembered the coins he'd paid to the tapster. His

pockets were light now, unlike his conscience. He made no response.

'The infant looks healthy,' Götz said, crouching beside the bed despite the stench.

Katherine stirred, and opened her eyes. For a moment she looked peaceful, but then her face tensed as if with pain. Götz stood and moved back, nudging Lukas towards the bed. Lukas ignored him and stayed where he was. 'Katherine,' he said simply.

Katherine looked down at the baby. 'I am tired.'

'Of course.'

'I wanted you here.'

'I couldn't ... I asked the captain but ...' He stopped. 'I'm a soldier, not a midwife.'

'Let me rest.' Katherine laid her head on the mattress and closed her eyes.

'I'll come back before we're away,' Lukas said, but she made no reply.

The landlady led them down the stairs. 'Shall I send for the surgeon? Or the apothecary?'

'I'm owed pay. Send for the surgeon, and I'll settle with you later.'

She shook her head. 'The money first.'

'Haven't I paid you for her keep?'

'Enough for the midwife, and your woman's bed and board until Easter Sunday. No more.'

'You call that pile of rags up there a bed?' Lukas felt the anger build in him again, but now it was bitterly shot through with guilt.

The old woman pulled open the door to the street. 'You think I'd put her on my best mattress, with the blood and filth running out of her?' She pushed them both outside before Lukas could reply.

The sky was light enough now for them to see their way as they walked. Lukas waited for Götz to speak. What would he say? Words of condemnation? Pieties best fitted for those who knew nothing of life? But Götz kept silent, and Lukas's conscience gnawed at him even more sharply.

When they reached the town square Götz stopped. 'I'll say goodbye, then.' He pointed to the far side. 'The seminary is beyond the church.'

'And what will Father Tomas think of you creeping in with the dawn?'

Götz smiled bashfully. 'The gateman is my friend. He'll not tell.' He hesitated. 'When will you march?'

'A day or two. No more.'

Götz nodded. 'God be with you.'

'Remember me in your prayers.'

The two men parted. Lukas crossed the bridge, stopping to quench his thirst with the river water. He made his way through the meadow to his tent. The other men were still asleep. He eased off his boots and lay down on his side, tucking the boots between his knees, in case some thief should try to make off with them. Once they were on the march and passing through strange parts a local villain might chance his luck. Lukas closed his eyes. The tent spun. He was a father. The Katherine he had seen lying in that filthy room tonight was not the sweet, wicked girl who had warmed his bed this last year or more. He thanked God he was a soldier, and could march away.

The weather had changed. A northerly wind blew in, and with it a dull grey sky and scuds of chilly rain. The blossoms in the orchards around Saalfeld were battered and limp. It was as if winter had returned to chase spring away.

The army was nearly ready to march. Lukas had dismantled the tent and bound it up with a length of thin rope. He was carrying it to one of the baggage wagons when he saw Götz walking through the camp. The lad was dressed in breeches and coat instead of his seminary robes. He was holding a letter, and had a bag slung over his shoulder. 'Have you come to watch us on our way?' Lukas asked.

Götz stopped. 'More than that, I hope.'

Realisation dawned. 'Are you running away to the war, young Fuhrmann?'

'Not running away. Here's a letter from Father Tomas, asking Colonel von Breuner to take me.'

'It's a strange world when a priest turns soldier.'

'But I'm not a priest yet. It is a rule of the Jesuits that before they take a young man he must prove himself in the world. This is to be my experiment. Perhaps I'll make my fortune too and then Father Tomas will be more than pleased to see me return.'

'You'll find Colonel von Breuner over there, where the standards are flying.'

Götz walked away.

Lukas was glad the boy had made no enquiry after Katherine and the baby. He had not been back to the town. The guilt of his neglect tormented him like hunger. He'd tried to pacify it by sending more money. The little he'd been able to cadge from the other men would hardly be enough for a surgeon, but it was better than nothing. Even Captain Gebwiler had contributed, and he, too, was waiting for his back-pay. So, he'd sent money but no message. When he thought of finding his path back to that cramped room, with its heat and stench, something stronger than guilt held him back.

Three

CHRISTA'S FATHER ALWAYS SAID YOU COULD read the state of the world from the prices in the market. If he was right, then the war was nearly upon them. The early lettuces were selling for the usual sum, but the price of bread was rising fast. When Christa complained to the baker he sent her to the miller, who directed her in turn to the farmers. The price of grain was moving upwards, because while bread must be eaten quickly grain would keep. It was happening with cured meats, salted fish, wine and brandy, too. Anything that would last through weeks of siege sold for twice or three times its normal price. Father doubted it would come to a siege — the King of Sweden and his army would be at Magdeburg before midsummer — but he warned Christa to buy a little extra of whatever dried goods she could find at market. It seemed to her that the victuallers were prospering – which was odd in Lent.

The printers and booksellers were doing well too: the people of Magdeburg had developed an appetite for the freshest words in these uncertain times, and Christa's father — with some help from his elder daughter — had devised a scheme to supply their need. It was this that had forced him into his best clothes on an ordinary market day. He stood in his bedroom with Dieter and Christa, waiting as Christa re-read the letter of petition he had written. 'Well,' he said, before she was halfway through it, 'will it persuade the council?'

Christa held up her hand to quieten him and read on. It was a bold request her father was making. He was asking the councillors of Magdeburg to grant him the right to publish a weekly newssheet, compiled of all the tidings that came to the city postmaster from every end of the country and the empire beyond. Further, he had asked that he should be the only printer permitted to produce such for the next five years, on account of the extra costs he would incur. 'It sounds well, Father.'

'Well enough to win them over?'

'Who knows? We must pray so.'

Father turned to Dieter. 'Will you look over it, son?'

Dieter shrugged. 'Christa has blessed it. That's usually enough for you.'

Christa heard the bitterness in his voice, and their father frowned. She handed the letter back to him.

'Herr Schwarz won't like it,' Dieter said, 'or the other printers hereabouts.'

'This is business,' Herr Henning said. 'They'd have done the same if they'd been sharp enough to think of it first.' He winked at Christa. His high spirits seemed restored, and she thought she understood why. The notion of besting their neighbours in business held a sweet excitement.

Dieter sighed. 'Well, shall we go? I suppose you want us to sell a pamphlet or two while you bow and scrape in the *Rathaus*?'

Herr Henning hid the letter in his coat and they left the bedroom. Christa half expected to find Pastor Ovens lurking outside the door. He seemed to be everywhere in the house. Her father's bedroom was one of the few places they could be sure he wouldn't enter.

They tramped down the stairs to the main room. Elsbeth was in her usual seat by the window, and Pastor Ovens had taken over the table with his papers. After a week or so of restlessness she had become accustomed to his presence.

As they crossed the room Herr Henning muttered that he had business to attend to in the town.

'Will you, by any chance, be visiting the *Rathaus?*' the pastor enquired, his eyes on Herr Henning's apparel.

'I may pass that way.'

Christa wondered what had prompted their lodger to take an interest. He usually found matters of trade dull and — as he put it — *worldly.*

Pastor Ovens rested his fingertips together as if he were about to pray. 'I have heard from … certain acquaintances that the King of Sweden has dispatched one of his most robust and devout soldiers to assist and defend us. Falkenberg, I believe his name is. I should be pleased to know if there is truth in this intelligence.'

Herr Henning smiled, although Christa sensed he was hiding a degree of nervousness. 'You may trust that I will remain alert for all tidings of the war.' He bowed and led Christa and Dieter from the room.

Pastor Ovens showed no sign of leaving them. For nearly a month he'd been eating their food and contributing nothing but prayers and a certain disturbance to Christa's mind. He preached sermons here and there, but if he received a *Taler* or two from the listeners he didn't throw it into the Henning family coffer. He was an encumbrance; there was no doubt of that. Christa knew this, yet when he singled her out for attention over the dinner table, or chanced on her alone in the back kitchen, she felt a strange excitement that was almost like fear. Sometimes he would stare at her as she answered his questions in a way that made her feel she was being tested. Without understanding why, she wanted to convince him of her worth. Dieter teased her about him, and she was aware of her father's sharp eyes on her when the pastor was nearby.

Now she and Dieter moved through the print shop. He lifted a bundle of pamphlets from a bench and threw it onto the loaded barrow. Christa checked the stock that Andreas had selected for the day's trade.

Helga was leaning against the door frame. 'Poor lamb,' she said to Andreas, watching as Christa packed some books he had forgotten onto the barrow.

'Now, Andreas,' Herr Henning said, 'busy yourself with a run of that song about the Swedish king, then tidy the shop.'

'Very well, *mein Herr*.' Andreas sounded humble, but his face was flushed and angry-looking. He, too, had taken notice of his master's fine clothes.

The journey from the printers' quarter to the new marketplace in front of the *Rathaus* didn't take long. Christa and her father quickly unloaded the stock, but it was clear that his mind was not on the best arrangement of their merchandise. 'You should go, Father,' Christa said. 'The earlier you get there the sooner your petition will be heard. Dieter and I can manage here.'

He patted his pockets as if to reassure himself that the letter was still there. 'I hope to be back before noon.' He left them and made his way towards the *Rathaus*.

There were no customers for the first half-hour, but that did not concern Christa. There was a rhythm to the market, like the movement of the seasons. At first, the food vendors were busiest — the people of Magdeburg liked to be assured that they would eat well that day, Lent or no Lent. Only then would they turn to the other goods on offer. Christa passed the time in making sure that their books and pamphlets were well displayed, while Dieter bit his nails and kept an eye open for pretty girls.

A pair of matrons stopped at their stall to study a devotional pamphlet. 'It's a fine text,' Dieter said, smiling at them. 'Very improving.'

'*An Admonition to the Young, to Guard Themselves against the Sin of Disobedience*,' one of the women read aloud. She looked coolly at Dieter. 'And have you taken its words to heart, young man?'

Dieter fluttered his eyelashes. 'Alas, I am very disobedient. I should be taken firmly in hand.' He offered her his most charming smile.

She blushed and started to laugh. Her companion nudged her sharply and she stopped short. 'How much is it?' She fished for coins. Dieter took them and gave the two women a mocking bow as they moved away.

'Dieter Henning, you are shameless,' Christa said, snatching the money from him and stowing it safely in her skirt pocket.

He shrugged. 'It shifts the stock. You should try it with the men.'

'I sell more than you do without such antics. Anyway, men don't like girls who talk so freely.'

Dieter laughed. 'Who told you that? I like a girl with a wicked tongue.'

'You're such a sinner.'

'I know. I'm relying on a good woman to save me. But not just yet.'

'You're the same age as Klaus, and he's a married man.'

'More fool him.' For a moment Dieter seemed lost in thought, then pointed at a man making his way to the stall. 'Here's your chance, sister.'

The man was dressed as richly as a merchant and walked with a limp. His face was very red, especially his nose, which glowed like a hot coal. She smiled. 'Good morning, sir. Would you care for something to read? We have—'

'Enough of your patter!' the man snapped. 'I can see for myself what you have. If I couldn't read the titles there'd be little point in us dealing.' He had spoken without looking at her.

Christa glanced at Dieter. *See?* she wanted to say. *It doesn't work.*

'You just haven't got the trick of it,' he whispered, and sauntered out from behind the stall towards a farmer's fair-haired young wife who was selling eggs from a barrow.

The merchant had picked up a copy of Luther's *Three Treatises* and was turning the pages. Christa tidied some pamphlets, watching him out of the corner of her eye. She could tell by the careful way he handled the book that he thought well of it, although he was wily enough to keep his expression bland. After a few moments he said, 'Did your master print this himself?'

'My father did, sir. Paul Henning, master printer. His mark is on the title page.' She still felt a flutter of pride each time she read her father's name on one of his publications.

'How much are you after for it?'

'Four *taler*, sir.'

'Hmm. The quality is fair.'

'The best in Magdeburg.'

The man set the book down. 'I've seen better at that stall there.' He waved his hand vaguely at the other side of the market.

She knew he was putting on an act in the hope of gaining a better price. Her usual response would have been to shrug and smile, but his manner put her out of temper. 'Then away and buy it there,' she snapped.

The man stepped back. 'You're a bold little hussy.'

Christa felt herself flush. 'Is it bold to be honest? If you've seen better elsewhere, then you'd be as well giving your money to them.' The man's face grew even redder. He turned and limped away.

Dieter returned from the farmer's wife, with a clutch of eggs tied in his handkerchief. 'If you scare them all off we'll be begging at the street corner before Christmas.'

'He was a time-waster. You'd learn to spot them if you ever spent more than five minutes here.' Even as she said it she knew it was not true. If she'd used her wit she could have made the sale. She pointed at the eggs. 'Did you sweet-talk your way to those?'

'I did a trade. Let me have something to give her in return.'

'A song-sheet?'

'No.' Dieter checked that there was no one close. 'She's a Papist. Have you anything …?'

Christa nodded. 'Of course.' Father conducted a discreet trade in songs and pamphlets for the tiny Catholic population of

55

Magdeburg. Christa slid her hand under a stack of hymnals and slipped out the top sheet of a slim pile of paper, then checked what was printed on it: a woodcut of the martyrdom of St Ursula. That would do well enough. The Papists loved a murdered virgin. She rolled the sheet into a tight scroll and passed it to her brother. He took it and sauntered back to his new lady-friend.

The *Rathaus* clock chimed the hour. She wondered how her father was faring with the city councillors.

Christa was kept busy for the rest of the morning. Dieter wandered off, claiming he was taking the eggs home in case they got broken and promising to return. She was still on her own at noon when she saw her father walk through the thinning crowd of shoppers. He was trying not to smile. 'Well?' she said, already knowing the news was good.

'Our petition has been granted.' He was bouncing up and down on the balls of his feet. 'This is very good, Christa,' he murmured. 'A print run of three hundred, once a week. Two *Gulden* for an annual subscription.'

'Will people pay that?'

'Oh, yes, they'll pay for news in these times. So, allowing for costs and a little variation in our sales, we should make a profit of near four hundred *Gulden* a year.' He looked around. 'Where's Dieter?'

'Running an errand. I'd expected him back by now.'

Her father deflated. 'He'll take no delight in it. And Andreas will only moan about the extra work.'

'Could we not give Andreas a little more in his wage? That might cheer him.'

'But what about your brother? What's to be done with him?'

Christa squeezed her father's arm. 'I am pleased, Father. You may content yourself with that.'

The market was emptying. The stall-holders were packing away or selling off fresh goods cheaply. Christa left her father tidying the stock into neat piles and made a quick circuit of the square, filling her basket with enough vegetables to make tonight's soup. When she got back to their stall the red-faced merchant was examining the *Three Treatises* again. She held back, fearing that the sight of her might cost her father the sale. Then she remembered the four hundred *Gulden* profit they would make from the newspaper. She strode forward and set the basket behind the stall. 'You have returned, sir,' she said, as pleasantly as she could.

'Evidently,' The merchant scowled at her. He turned the pages of the book, opened his mouth as if to speak, then seemed to reconsider. 'Three *Taler*, did you say?'

'Four.' Christa smiled at him.

The man held the book firmly, but made no move to reach for his money. 'I'll give you three.'

'Four *taler*,' Christa repeated, without the smile this time.

He hesitated.

Christa knew her father was watching, for all that he was busying himself with packing the stock. Christa stretched out her hand. The man could either give her the money or the book. She was not minded to play this game any longer. At last he loosed his moneybag from his belt and counted out four *Taler* on to the stall.

'Thank you, sir,' Christa said, scooping the coins into her hand. 'Come back another day.'

The man grunted and limped away, the book clamped under his arm.

Her father was staring at her with a mixture of admiration and disapproval. She giggled. 'I don't have Dieter's charm, but I made the sale, did I not?'

'You are sharper-tongued than your mother ever was.'

Christa didn't reply. She found it hard to understand the grief that was still in her father. Sometimes she thought it strange that she couldn't feel it. Now her memories of her mother were so confused with the tales she'd heard from him and the Schwarzes that she couldn't be sure she remembered anything about her at all. Her mother had stood in this marketplace; she had cooked meals in their back kitchen. She had slept and given birth and died in the bed where Father now slept, and he still missed her. But she didn't seem real — even when someone compared Christa to her and found the daughter wanting.

They finished packing the stock and began the walk home, Herr Henning pushing the barrow. In spite of his triumph at the *Rathaus*, he was quiet and Christa felt uncertain. Was he thinking of her mother, or merely saving his breath for the labour of transporting the stock? As they turned into the alley that led to the printers' quarter he said, 'It's as well you have more edge than your mother did.'

'I had thought you didn't much like me for it.'

He shook his head and smiled sadly at her. 'Your mother was made for softer times than these, Christa.' He stopped and set the barrow down, then glanced around him before he spoke. 'The rumour Pastor Ovens heard is true. Falkenberg is expected any day, and a squad of soldiers with him. By all accounts he's a firebrand.'

'But what difference will it make to us?' Christa was puzzled by the concern on her father's face.

'It means the Emperor's army is coming this way, Christa — they say old General Tilly is at its head — and the King of Sweden is sending Falkenberg to ready us. We may be besieged again, and it might cost us all of our wealth to rid ourselves of the problem.'

Christa patted his arm. 'Think of the newssheets we'll sell! We'll get more subscriptions than we could ever have dreamed.'

He smiled. 'You have a good head on your shoulders, Christa Henning. Keep that four *Taler* in your own purse. It was your hard words that earned it, and you might need it sooner than you think.'

Four

A MONTH OF COLD NIGHTS ON an empty belly had crushed the joy of the march out of Lukas. At first Götz had been full of questions, but soon the unfamiliar effort of the day-long marches had silenced him. The trees were in full leaf, and the crops were green in the field, but they'd been forced to celebrate Easter with nothing stronger than river water and a mouthful of stale bread.

Today, as always, Colonel von Breuner rode far to the front of them with the cavalry. Lukas could just see his standard way ahead, a scrap of bright colour against the greens and browns of the landscape. The infantry battalions came next. A good number of the men still carried pikes, but most were armed with muskets. There had been none to spare for Götz, and Lukas was glad of it — the lad would most likely have blown his own head off. Each evening Lukas taught Götz about the parts and workings of the musket. He wouldn't trust the boy to fire one, but at least he could be put to work cleaning the weapons. He had given him a short dagger: Götz couldn't do much more than wave it around, but it made them both feel better.

The wagons creaked along at the rear, loaded with baggage and the women who accompanied their menfolk to war. There was little food to carry, with supplies so short. The men's eyes were sharpened by their hunger. They scanned the country they marched through for anything that would make a meal. The rumour was that they were headed for the city of Magdeburg, which had lately been besieged by General Tilly, and they tormented each other with speculation on the food and booty to be claimed there.

It was past midday when their progress was stopped by shouting from the back, and the crack of pistol fire. 'What's happening?' Götz said.

'I don't know. Stay here.' Lukas ran down the flank of the march, his musket banging against his back. The last of the wagons was toppled, and a gang of three ragged men was rifling through the bags and boxes. The two young baggage boys who'd been steering it were doing their best to beat the men off with their sticks, but one of the raiders had a pistol, which he fired wildly towards them. Another of the men let out a shout as soon as he saw Lukas draw near. The three grabbed what they could, leapt over a ditch and were soon out of sight.

Lukas stopped to right the wagon. 'They stole our bread,' one of the boys told him. 'There was little enough of it.'

Out of the corner of his eye Lukas saw a movement in the direction the raiders had gone. He swung round, one hand on the hilt of his short sword. Götz was clambering over the ditch. 'Where are you going?' he shouted.

'To get our food back,' Götz yelled over his shoulder.

You fool, Lukas thought, jumping over the ditch after him. The raiders were halfway across the field, but Götz was running at full pelt after them. The ragged men were slowing now. Lukas guessed they hadn't reckoned on being followed so far. Most likely they were weak with famine, but a starving man could be a mean fighter and one had a pistol, although it would need to be reloaded before it could be fired at them. Lukas had his musket, but it, too, must be loaded and the slow-match wasn't lit. He hadn't thought he'd need it so soon. If he stopped now to prime his weapon Götz would be on his own against the three of them. Lukas kept running.

One man had stopped, and was standing doubled over, his hands on his knees. The bundle he'd grabbed from the wagon was on the ground by his feet. His companions kept going, shouting to him. Götz ran on past him, still chasing the others. By the time Lukas reached him, the man had caught his breath. He was holding a cudgel but there was no sign of the pistol. One of the others must have it.

He eyed Lukas. The bundle lay between them. Lukas didn't dare take his eyes off his quarry to study it more closely. From its shape he doubted it held food. Probably clothes or blankets, which could be sold or exchanged for victuals. That was how it was on the march. Every possession, every tiny item of booty, could be translated into food. 'Give me a chance,' the man said. 'I was an honest man once, but there's no work to be had with this trouble in the country.'

'I'll give you your life and nothing more. Now go.' Lukas was hungry, but the other was starved. His face was yellow with it.

Across the field there was a crack of pistol fire. They both looked round. Götz and the other men were a good two hundred yards away. All three were still on their feet. At a sudden movement Lukas whirled round. The cudgel was swinging towards him. He ducked, and pulled his short sword from its scabbard. The man took another swing at him, and Lukas brought the sword up to meet his assailant's arm. It felt to him like a light enough parry, but it sent the cudgel flying and brought the man down, clutching his arm. Lukas watched, sword still at the ready, as the man gasped on the ground. 'You've broken my arm,' he said unsteadily.

'You should have gone when you had the chance.' Lukas sheathed his sword, picked up the bundle and the cudgel, and loped towards Götz and the other two.

There appeared to be a stand-off. Götz had his little dagger in his hand and was holding it as far away from himself as he could. One of the other men was swinging a wooden stave at him. Neither was giving ground. When the man with the stick came too close Götz would spring forward, and the man would back away a pace or two. His companion was struggling to reload the pistol. When he saw Lukas approaching, he fumbled, spilling powder round the muzzle, and dropped the priming flask. Not a soldier, that was for sure. Lukas wondered where he'd stolen the pistol. Götz glanced over at him and smiled, but turned back as the man with the stick tried to strike his head.

Lukas set down the cudgel and the bundle, then slung his musket off his shoulder. The man with the pistol snapped it shut. Its joints must be full of powder, Lukas thought, so with luck there'd be little in the chamber. He held his musket as if he'd been given the order to present arms. Götz and his opponent were dancing around each other now, each trying to prevent the other from intervening. The man with the pistol raised it, pointing the barrel towards Lukas. His hand was trembling. There was a snap, a great curl of smoke, and a few beads of shot flew from the barrel. Götz yelped, even though he wasn't in the line of fire.

Lukas walked closer to the man, raised his musket, then flipped it over so that he was holding it by the muzzle. He lifted it high and brought it down hard on the man's head. There was a thud as it met hair and bone. The man crumpled on the ground at Lukas's feet. Strangely there was little blood coming from his head, but a thin trail ran from his nose and ears. It had always been a mystery to Lukas that some men would stand and be taken. Perhaps there came a point when they knew there was nothing else for it.

Götz's adversary turned and ran with one small sack, ignoring the curses of his companion with the broken arm. Götz made to run after him, but Lukas grabbed him. 'Let him go.'

'He's stolen our goods.'

'Aye, but he'll take his story with him of how we fought back. Killed one and injured the other. That's the sort of name we want.' He stooped to lift the pistol from the hand of the man he'd felled. 'Search him quickly, Götz. I doubt he has anything worth taking, but we'll make more use of it than he will now.'

Götz pulled a paring knife from the man's belt and tucked it into his own. He patted the man's pockets. All he found was an empty bullet pouch. He handed it to Lukas. Then they walked back across the field towards the battalion. As they passed the man with the broken arm he struggled to his feet and stumbled off after his companion.

Lukas and Götz climbed over the ditch and rejoined the tail-end of the march. After an hour or so the order came to halt and word came down that the head of the battalion had reached a stream. They were to stop and water the horses. Lukas and Götz walked up the line and restored the bundle they had rescued to the wagon it had been plundered from. The two baggage boys had been joined by a musketeer armed with a short-muzzled pistol in addition to his piece. Clearly those in command had decided that protection was needed. They walked on until they caught up with Captain Gebwiler and the rest of the company. 'I thought you'd left us,' the captain snapped.

They began again to march. Götz kept looking at Lukas, who felt awkward and tried to outpace him, but he couldn't shake him off. 'Listen, boy,' he said at last, 'you'd best learn not to let a little tussle unnerve you. There's men here who'd rip you to shreds for acting the woman.' He looked at Götz to make sure he was listening. There was a smudge of dried blood on the boy's earlobe — a stray fragment of shot from the raider's pistol must have found its mark. 'You have your first battle scar,' he observed.

Götz touched his ear. 'I'd forgotten. Now I think of it, I remember feeling a sting.'

'Please God you get no worse.'

The next morning Lukas woke with the familiar ache of hunger, a weary pain that came from never having enough. It was late in the afternoon when a message came down the line from Colonel von Breuner. The scouts had discovered a well-provided village an hour's walk away. A party of them were to make for it, and persuade the inhabitants to support the Emperor's army. Captain Gebwiler selected Lukas, Baxandall, Matko and a handful of the others. Götz looked imploringly at him, but the captain shook his head. 'You'd be an encumbrance.'

'I helped Sergeant Weinsburg get our goods back from those raiders yesterday,' Götz said. 'I was a help, wasn't I, Sergeant?'

Lukas didn't reply.

Captain Gebwiler raised his eyebrows, and Lukas felt a tremor of concern for Götz. The captain wasn't accustomed to being spoken to in such a way by a new recruit. 'Join us then,' he said at last, 'but don't come crying to me if some farmer blows your head off.'

The raiding party — all except Götz — were equipped with pistols. Götz carried the empty sacks they hoped to fill with food. The men loaded their weapons and set off down a path through woodland. 'Mind how you talk to the captain,' Lukas said quietly to Götz. 'He'd have you flogged for insolence in a flash.'

Götz walked on in silence.

A few minutes later Lukas said, 'I'd have thought you'd have had enough excitement for a while. You looked winded by what went on yesterday.'

'Will there be fighting today?'

'I doubt the villagers will give up their food gladly.'

'But all those other houses we've passed needed little persuasion.'

'We were many and they were few. They didn't dare protest. The bigger the settlement, the more trouble they give.'

'Why doesn't the whole battalion go, then?'

'It would take too long for us all to push through this forest. The noise would give the villagers time to hide what they have. Now save your breath.'

Dear God, the boy could talk. Lukas wondered if he could be persuaded to take a vow of silence. That would hardly fit him for the Jesuits, though. They never stopped.

'Yesterday, what we did …' Götz said.

'What about it?'

'Did I do well enough?'

Lukas considered this. The few stolen bags had hardly been worth risking their lives over, and no seasoned soldier would have bothered with the chase. But the lad had courage – which would earn him either glory or a grave. 'You did well enough,' he said at last.

'One thing weighs on me. That man whose head you struck. Are you sure he died?'

'Yes.'

'So if I hadn't given chase, he'd still be living.'

'And getting fat on our bread. If he hadn't tried to steal from the Emperor's men he'd still be living. Don't shed any tears for a thief.'

'While I was in the seminary I used to dream of what it would be like to be a warrior — like Hector or Achilles.'

'I don't know them.'

Götz sighed. 'That fight with those men, it was not what I had expected. But it was … exciting.' He looked at Lukas. His eyes were shining. 'Did you not find it so?'

Exciting was not the word Lukas would have used. But there was something about a fight that offered … release. 'You'll get all the excitement you could wish for, by and by,' he said.

Captain Gebwiler raised his arm to signal that they keep silence. Lukas could see sunlight ahead where the trees thinned.

At the edge of the woods they stopped. It was a fair-sized village right enough. There was a church and several comfortable-looking houses, as well as the usual ramshackle dwellings of the feckless or unlucky. Beyond the village half a dozen ewes were grazing on a hill with their lambs at their sides. Lukas's mouth watered at the memory of roasted meat.

Captain Gebwiler gathered them round him. They were to stick together until it was established whether or not the villagers would resist. If all went well they would work their way from house to house, taking food and light booty. Likewise with the livestock. Anything a man might readily carry — chickens, a lamb, a piglet — should be slaughtered and brought away. Any half-fit horses should be ridden back to the battalion. If the villagers tried to fight back, the Emperor's men would humble them and take what they wanted. 'But do no harm unless you must,' the captain concluded. 'Save your strength for the real battles.'

They broke cover and marched into the village. Two old men were sitting taking the sun outside a low wooden house. They stared at the intruders, but didn't move. Captain Gebwiler carried on to the grandest house and drew his men to a halt in front of it. 'Sergeant Weinsburg, Corporal Baxandall, go in and see what you can find. Keep your pistols at the ready.'

Baxandall was all for kicking the door in, but Lukas held him back. 'It's probably unlocked.' He tried the latch and the door swung open. The main room was empty, but a fire burned in the grate.

Baxandall walked to a side table, picked up a jug and sniffed it. 'Milk,' he said. 'Should we drink it, or must we take it out to the captain?'

'We may drink it. There'll hardly be enough for the rest of them.'

Baxandall took a long swallow, then handed him the jug. Lukas didn't much like the taste of milk, but it would quieten his hunger until he found something better.

There was a noise from the back room. Lukas put a finger to his lips and crept to the door that led deeper into the house. He pushed it open sharply. A middle-aged man was holding open a window. Beside him stood a woman, with both hands on the sill. They stared at Lukas, frozen in the act of making their escape. 'There's no need for that,' Lukas said. 'We want food and drink, and any small thing of value. We'll give you no trouble so long as you're honest with us.'

The man of the house was so frightened he couldn't speak. It was left to his wife to talk. 'There's little enough. We've been making contributions to Colonel Heberle all winter.'

Baxandall edged his way into the room. He and Lukas stood and stared at the couple for what seemed to Lukas a long time. He could hear noises from outside in the village street. The squealing of pigs. Men shouting. A pistol shot.

'My husband was the mayor, two years ago,' the woman continued. 'Herr Minck, he has been mayor these last years, but has been dead of the plague since February, so my husband ... well, he was mayor before, so... what else could we do?'

'Food. Drink. Gold,' Baxandall said softly. The woman looked into his face and shrank back half a step. She opened a cupboard and lifted out a bowl of wizened turnips, with the earth still stuck to them. Lukas tipped them into his sack. He followed the woman round the room, taking each meagre ration she produced.

'What about valuables?' Lukas said, when she had finished.

'There's nothing left.' The loose skin hanging beneath her jaw trembled as she spoke.

'My friend here will go through the house. If he finds you've lied to us he'll be angry.'

The woman looked at her husband, but there was no help from him. 'Next to nothing. I have a few trinkets. Shall I fetch them?'

'I'll come with you.'

She nodded, and Lukas followed her up the stairs, which led directly into a bedroom. The bed was high, and covered with a heavy brown quilt. Lukas wondered how it would feel to sleep in such a bed. It would be soft, he imagined, and warm. He felt drowsy just to think of it. The woman's breathing had changed, interrupting his thoughts. She was staring at him, alarm on her face. 'Take no fear of me, good wife. It's your jewels I'm after, not your virtue.'

She went to a corner of the room and reached up to the low beam where the ceiling met the wall. 'There's little enough left. No gems. There was a pretty ruby ring that I had from my mother, but it had to be given up.' She felt around behind the beam and pulled out a small linen bag.

Lukas took it from her and emptied it onto the bed. A woman's silver belt-buckle, six brass buttons and a small pile of coins he didn't recognise. 'What are these?' he said, picking up one of the coins.

'From some foreign country. I don't know where.'

'And this is all you have?'

'As God is my witness.'

Lukas felt very tired. The urge to lie down on the bed, to feel the softness of the brown quilt on his skin, was almost overwhelming. His eyes were heavy.

There was a shout from outside the house. Lukas shook his head to clear it. He grabbed the woman's pathetic treasures and walked quickly to the back window to see what was going on. There were other, smaller, houses behind this one, and beyond them the grassy hillside. Götz and another soldier were out there, running frantically in pursuit of a lamb, which was determined not to be caught. The older man was yelling instructions at Götz, as if he thought the lad was a sheepdog. Whichever way they ran, the animal outpaced them. The rest of the sheep had scattered.

Lukas and the woman returned downstairs. Baxandall and the man of the house were watching the performance with the lamb as well. 'Why don't they shoot the damn thing?' Baxandall said.

'There'll be less of it to eat if they blow a hole in it. Let's go.'

They lifted their sacks and left. 'You took your time up above with the woman,' Baxandall said. 'The old man's ears were wagging at every creak of the floorboards.'

Lukas was about to mention how inviting the bed had looked, but remembered just in time that he was talking to Baxandall. He didn't want to put ideas into his head. Instead he said, 'I've more interest in eating than wenching. We need to do better than this.' He held up his sack. Their meagre loot had barely made its mark.

Out in the street one of the men had taken possession of a stout little pony. He was trotting it up and down, swinging his sword around as if he was charging into battle. Some of the rest of the party had stopped to watch and laugh. 'Get off that beast before you break its back!' Captain Gebwiler roared, and the man dismounted to the jeers of his companions. They returned to tying a half-dozen slaughtered piglets to a stout pole for carrying back to the battalion. No villagers were about.

'I'll away and help Matko wring those chickens' necks,'

Baxandall said, pointing at a hen-house where Matko and another Croat were working their way through the fowls.

Lukas let him go. Captain Gebwiler had hold of the pony now, and called Lukas over to help load it with what they'd found. 'We should gather the men and go back,' he said. Lukas sensed his disappointment. The few pigs and chickens would not feed a battalion, still less an entire regiment. This village had been wrung dry too many times already. Lukas walked back between the empty houses to the field where the sheep had been. Götz and the other man had the lamb cornered. As Lukas got closer Götz pounced on the lamb, but it slipped from his grasp and ran away up the hill.

'Leave it,' Lukas said. 'Captain says we're to go back now.'

Götz looked sadly in the direction the lamb had run. 'I would have enjoyed a bite of roast lamb.'

'You'll make do with boiled pork. And you'll be lucky if you get a mouthful of that.'

The men gathered around Captain Gebwiler, and burdened the pony with more bags. The beast snorted and tried to back away, but the captain had a firm grip on its bridle. One man rolled a keg of liquor out of a house. 'There's a barrel of wine too,' he said, 'but we'd never manage it through the forest.'

Baxandall sauntered up, carrying a sack heavy with freshly killed chickens. Lukas could see feathers poking through the loose weave.

Captain Gebwiler made a quick headcount. 'One man down.' He ran his eye over them. 'Corporal Baxandall, where's your Croat friend?'

Baxandall looked around. The other Croats were there, but not Matko. 'He was pulling the necks of chickens ten minutes ago.'

Captain Gebwiler turned to Götz. 'You're quick on your feet, boy. Away and get him.'

Götz beamed with delight to be trusted with this small order and ran to the hen-house. Captain Gebwiler began to lead the pony towards the forest. The rest followed.

Lukas heard the slap of Götz's footsteps running back. The boy stopped just short of them. His face was white. 'What's wrong, lad?' Lukas said.

Götz stared at him. His mouth opened, but no words came. Captain Gebwiler handed the pony's reins to one of the others and came back to see what was afoot. He took one look at Götz's face and set off for the hen-house, signalling for Lukas and Baxandall to follow. As they approached Matko stumbled outside. He was breathing hard. When he saw them he looked alarmed briefly, then laughed and walk towards them . He said something in his own language, clapping Baxandall on the back. Then he spoke again: 'We go?'

Captain Gebwiler took hold of Matko's arm. 'Sergeant Weinsburg, away and see what so disturbed our new recruit.'

Lukas climbed the ramp into the silent hen-house. He had to stoop to get through the door. A girl lay on the floor. Her skirts were pushed up over her face. Lukas saw the bare legs, the smear of blood on her thighs. She was motionless. He moved closer. When he was beside her he knelt and pulled her skirts down. Her face was dark, like a hanged man's, and her tongue poked out through her lips. Lukas knew she was dead, but even so he leaned down to listen for her heartbeat. His stomach churned as he felt the childish flatness of her chest under his cheek. She was as warm as the living. He stood and slowly made his way outside. Captain Gebwiler and Baxandall both had hold of Matko now. The Croat was sweating, his tongue darting over his lips. 'There's a girl-child, Captain. Ravished and killed.'

Captain Gebwiler flushed red with fury. He tightened his grip on Matko and shook him. 'There are rules. We are the Emperor's men.'

Matko turned to Baxandall and spoke rapidly in his own language. Baxandall listened for a moment or two. 'He says that after I left him he heard a sound in the rafters and found the girl hiding. He thought there'd be no harm in a little fun. But then she cried out, and he took fright.'

'I didn't know you were so well acquainted with his tongue,' Lukas said.

Baxandall shifted his weight from one foot to the other. 'I was always a quick study with words.'

Captain Gebwiler and Baxandall marched Matko back to the rest of the party. Lukas walked on ahead and took a length of rope from the pony's back. The rest of the men stood silently while Lukas pinioned Matko's arms to his sides. At a signal from Captain Gebwiler they began their walk back to the regiment, taking a different path, which would bring them out further along the road, Lukas and Baxandall flanking Matko.

Götz squeezed past them as they made their way through the woods. His face was still drained of colour and his eyes were full of fear and questions.

When they rejoined the march Captain Gebwiler sent a baggage boy forward to tell Colonel von Breuner what had happened in the village. When they'd gone a mile or so further up the road, the boy came running back. 'Well?' Captain Gebwiler said. 'What instruction did the colonel give?'

'Colonel says you have his trust to make good enquiry, and if you are satisfied you may hang the man on your own authority.'

'Very good.' Captain Gebwiler's face was grim.

'He also says, sir, that on no account is the march to be delayed, and if the man's to be hanged he may wait until we make camp tonight.'

Captain Gebwiler nodded and sent the boy back to his wagon. They marched on through the afternoon and early evening. No one in the company spoke, but Lukas sensed that news of Matko's crime was moving from man to man. Götz marched beside Lukas, but didn't look at him. Matko was seated on a wagon now, his legs bound too, in case he took the notion to flee. To Lukas the day seemed endless, but he reckoned that to Matko the sands must be running fast through the glass.

An hour before sunset Captain Gebwiler gave the order to pitch the tents and make fires. As soon as that was done they must gather to hear the case against Matko.

Götz helped Lukas with the tent. 'What will happen?' Götz asked. 'Will Matko be hanged?'

'Most likely.' He saw the stricken look on Götz's face. 'Don't you think he merits it?'

'Aye, but ... Will he have the opportunity for repentance?'

'If the priest can stir himself to walk down the line.'

'I shouldn't like to see him lose his soul, for all he's done wrong.'

Before long a steady drumbeat summoned them to the little patch of grass that was to play the part of the courtroom. Matko stood alone, still bound. The rest made a wide circle around him. No one wanted to stand too close to him, not even the other Croats. 'Do you understand why you're here, Matko?' Captain Gebwiler shouted.

Matko looked up when he heard his name and gazed blankly at the captain.

'He doesn't understand you, sir,' Baxandall said.

'Does anyone here speak in his tongue as well as ours?' The captain looked at Matko's compatriots, but if they understood him they gave no sign of it. He turned to Baxandall. 'You seemed to understand him well enough when first I questioned him.'

'I can speak a little of his language,' Baxandall said grudgingly.

'Then tell him he must plead for his life.'

Baxandall spoke haltingly to Matko. His friend listened and shrugged, muttering a few words in return. 'He says she was willing enough, and he meant no harm.'

'God help any man who has to depend on Baxandall to argue for him,' Lukas muttered to Götz.

Captain Gebwiler called Götz forward. 'Tell us, Private Fuhrmann, what did you see when you looked in the hen-house?'

Götz took a breath so deep Lukas thought the whole regiment must have heard it. 'Matko was there, sir.'

'And what was he doing?'

'He was ... he was lying on his face and ... squirming. Sir.'

Some of the men sniggered. Captain Gebwiler glared at them, then turned back to Götz. 'What do you mean by that, boy?'

'His — his bare arse was bouncing up and down.' Götz's face blushed a deeper red than Lukas had ever seen it before. The laughter was louder. Even Matko's face wore a half-comprehending smirk.

The captain ignored them all. 'Was the girl beneath him?'

'I couldn't tell you for certain. I didn't stop to look closely.'

'And did Matko see you looking in at him?'

'He didn't notice me. So I came away, sir, and then you all went up.'

'But why did you run to us in such alarm?'

Götz frowned. 'I can't say, sir. But I knew that what he was about was wrong.'

Captain Gebwiler dismissed him, and called Baxandall forward. 'What about you then? You were with him in the hen-house.'

'I left when the fowl were all slain. Matko said he would look for eggs, so I went on.'

'Ask him how he discovered the girl.'

Baxandall spoke to Matko, and received a long, agitated reply. 'He says she had concealed herself and came out saying words to him, which he couldn't understand but he knew her meaning well enough. Then she took fright, thinking of her reputation, and Matko feared he would be condemned, as he is a foreigner, in spite of being the Emperor's true servant these last ten years. So he tried to hush her, but he was too strong and she too frail. And that's the end of it, sir.'

'If she had been a full-grown woman I might have believed his story. But she was a child, was she not, Sergeant Weinsburg?'

'There was not a sign of womanhood about her,' Lukas agreed.

Baxandall shot him a bitter look.

'Your life is forfeit, Matko, for all you've served the Emperor well. I'm sorry for it. It's hard enough to find good soldiers in this weather and I can't afford to lose any to the rope.' He slowly looked around the circle of men. 'Remember this day. I will tolerate no wickedness in our company. Now, find a priest post-haste and we'll make an end of this business.'

Another of the baggage boys raced up the line. While they waited the rope was made ready. When Matko saw what they were doing he shouted at Baxandall, a non-stop torrent of incomprehensible words, but he was dragged towards a wagon that had been emptied for the night.

Götz stayed close to Lukas. 'I've never seen a hanging before,' he said.

'Never? I hadn't thought Saalfeld so genteel.'

'Oh, there were executions, but Father Tomas would never permit us to attend. Some of the others sneaked out to watch, but I never did.' He was silent for a moment. 'Do you think I must stay to see this?'

'Aye. We must all stay and learn the lesson.'

The baggage boy came back down the line, accompanied by a man dressed like a merchant fallen on hard times. He didn't look like a priest, but he pulled a dirty chasuble from his pack and tossed it over his shoulders. When he got to the wagon where Matko was he sat down beside him, and waved away the men who had been keeping guard. Only Baxandall stood near, but Matko sent him away with a solid German curse. He turned back to the priest and shrugged apologetically.

'I don't see how the priest can shrive him when he won't understand a word he says,' Lukas muttered.

'That doesn't signify,' Götz said. 'The priest can hear his confession even if he doesn't comprehend it, and absolve him too.'

'Is that so?'

'Aye. The priest is only the instrument. God Himself is listening, and He is the great translator.'

'I'm a lucky man, with a wise friend like you to instruct me.'

The priest had finished with Matko. Captain Gebwiler called for their attention. 'There are to be no merciful interventions. If any lads have been paid a coin or two to speed Matko on his way, you've gained money you won't have to work for.' He nodded to the men who were standing guard over the prisoner.

They closed in on the wagon, taking hold of him and pulling him right onto it. Captain Gebwiler ordered the wagon be pulled to a well-grown tree. Another boy was ordered to shin up with the end of the rope and lashed it to a thick branch. The noose was left dangling, while the other end of the rope was thrown down into the hands of the Blickle brothers, who were the weightiest men in the company. They stretched the rope taut, to ensure that it would hold fast. Matko was forced to his feet and the noose placed round his neck. He struggled, shouting a mix of his own language and soldiers' curses. The priest was standing close to the wagon. He was reading from his missal, but he could scarcely be heard.

At a signal from Captain Gebwiler a whip was brought down on the horse. It leapt forward, but only by a couple of feet. Matko and the men who'd been holding him lost their balance. With his feet and arms bound Matko struggled to regain his footing. The noose had tightened round his neck, but only enough to quiet his shouts. Captain Gebwiler yelled at the lad who had been charged with the horse. The boy whipped it again, and it sprang clean away, pulling the wagon after it. Matko was dangling from the branch now, bucking wildly. His face was turning a congested red, and his eyes bulged as he stared at the circle of men watching him die. The branch creaked as he struggled. The leaves rustled as if a breeze was blowing through them, but the air was still.

Lukas felt Götz move closer to him, so that their sleeves were touching. The boy was trembling. Lukas felt an almost fatherly urge to put an arm round him, but he restrained himself: it would do Götz no good to show weakness before the others. 'Keep your eyes on the spot where the rope is tied to the branch,' he whispered. 'It'll be easier for you that way.' He knew well enough how a hanging could linger in a man's mind. There were images that once let in could never be purged. He'd spare Götz such memories if he could.

The creaking of the branch and the rustling of the leaves

seemed to grow louder. It should have been stopping, or at least diminishing, but it wasn't. He glanced at Matko. The man was still fighting death, his arms straining to be free of the pinions. Lukas turned to Götz. 'Don't move from here,' he whispered. Götz opened his mouth but Lukas moved before he could speak. He ran towards Matko, aware of voices behind him, but they weren't as loud as the creaking of the tree. He could smell the shit leaking out of the dying man. Part of his mind recoiled from the thought of embracing that filth, but he forced himself to jump up and wrap his arms round Matko's waist. He felt Matko's body jerk as the extra weight pulled the noose tighter. Good God, the man was solid muscle, in spite of a winter of hunger — no wonder he'd fought death. Lukas felt hands pull roughly at him, dragging him to the ground. No matter. Matko was done.

Lukas shook the men off and stood up straight. The stench of Matko was on him. His gorge rose and he forced himself to keep it down. The captain was striding towards him, white with rage. 'Explain yourself, Sergeant Weinsburg,' he barked. 'I said there were to be no interventions.'

'In all conscience, Captain, I couldn't let him suffer any longer.'

'You disobeyed me.'

'I did, sir. I was sorry to do it.'

'You deserve a flogging.'

'Yes, sir.' Lukas's skin prickled into goose pimples.

Captain Gebwiler's face was red now. 'Look at the state of you. A flogging would likely kill you.' He looked round the rest of the men. 'The penalty for this disobedience is that Lukas Weinsburg is stripped of his rank and becomes again a common soldier.' He turned back to Lukas. 'Now get out of my sight.'

Lukas walked back to Götz. He wanted to wash off the smell of Matko. The company were occupying themselves with making camp for the night. 'Can you see to our fire?' he said to Götz, then went to the stream that flowed along the valley bottom. When he got there he pulled off his jerkin. There was a damp mark on it. He sniffed, then splashed it with water. Pray God the sun would shine tomorrow and dry it out. He took off his shirt. One cuff was stained brown, so he plunged it in and rubbed until it was as clean as he could make it. When he had dealt with his clothes as best he could, he washed his face and upper body. The water was icy. He wished he could plunge into the stream and let it wash away all the filth that clung to his skin, but the hour was too late for such indulgence. The sun had set, and there was no warmth in the evening air. He pulled his damp clothes back on and walked up to the camp.

Götz had made a fair enough start on the fire and Lukas threw a few more sticks on it. Some of the women had set to plucking the chickens and the scent of woodsmoke made Lukas's mouth water, even before the cooking had begun. 'We'll eat tonight, thank God,' he said, half to himself.

'What's that, *Private* Weinsburg?' It was Baxandall, hunkered at his own fire. His little wife was stirring a pot.

One or two of the other men laughed. 'Why'd you do it, Weinsburg?' one said. 'I didn't think you cared much for Matko.'

'Neither I did. But it went on too long. We'd show more kindness to a dog turned savage.'

'Why, you're a true Christian man, Private,' Baxandall said. 'You're a mirror to us all.'

Lukas felt as if the day's happenings were gathering inside him. There'd be anger, sooner or later, but not today. 'You were supposed to be his friend,' he said. 'He might have expected you'd give him the mercy.'

'And if I'd tried it the captain would have had the flesh from my back.' He spat into the fire. 'I might have known he'd grant you favour, even when he's demoting you. No doubt you'll be up again as quickly as you were down.' He turned away.

Lukas watched him for a moment, but he had done for now. It must be a low day indeed when Baxandall had no appetite for a quarrel.

The meal was faster eaten than it was cooked. There was little enough food when it was shared among the whole company. They had to pacify their hunger with the brandy they'd found in the village. Lukas and Götz sat by their fire, drinking. 'So how did you enjoy today's lessons, little scholar?' Lukas said. He could hear the slurring in his own voice, and supposed he must be drunk.

'What sort of question is that?' Götz was stumbling over his words too. 'How do you think I enjoyed it?'

Lukas heard fear behind the boy's outburst. 'Aye, it was a daft question, right enough. But pay heed to what happened, if you don't want to end up swinging like Matko. I've seen men hanged for less. Obey your captain.'

'Like you did?'

'I'm a fool. Don't follow my lead.'

Götz uncorked his flask. 'There's a little here yet. Will we share it?'

'Let us make it the *Brüderschafttrinken*.' Lukas wondered at the impulse that had made him offer that to the boy. He had known some men in this company for most of his soldiering life, but he would never have dreamed of taking the drink of brotherhood with them.

Götz was as delighted as a child presented with a gift. 'In truth? Are you sure it is not that the liquor has hold of you?'

'Likely it has, but let us drink and be brothers from this day on.'

They shared the final drop of brandy. 'Here's to you,' Götz toasted him.

'And to you. You may call me by my Christian name from now. I was baptised Lukas.'

They shook hands and sat in silence. The little ceremony seemed to have distracted the boy from all that had occurred earlier. Lukas wished it had had the same effect on him.

At last Götz yawned. 'I'm away to my bed.'

Lukas stayed by the fire. One by one the men crawled off to their tents, until he was the only one left. He watched the last of the embers glow in the night breeze, then closed his eyes and dozed where he sat. The leaves rustled in the trees around him, and the branches creaked.

The sounds stayed with him when he finally made his way to his tent. Götz was sprawled flat on his back, snoring, but still Lukas could hear the trees. Rustling. Creaking. As if nothing would ever silence them.

Five

'PLEASE COME WITH US, GERTRUDE. THERE'LL be more sport if you're there,' Christa begged.

'You expect me to climb onto the city walls with this belly?'

'Oh, let's leave her behind,' said Dieter. 'She'll only moan and spoil our fun.'

'Klaus! Are you going to let him speak of me like that?'

They all looked at Klaus. 'Go or stay as you please, wife. I need some air after a day's labour.'

Gertrude pouted and flounced from the room – or attempted to: the weight of the child in her rather spoiled the effect. She banged the door behind her.

'Are you going after her?' Dieter asked his friend.

'I am not,' Klaus said. 'She treats me as if I'm a servant to be ordered about. I must show her that I'm the master.' Christa turned away to hide her smile. She couldn't imagine Gertrude deferring to Klaus.

It seemed Dieter had had the same thought, for he laughed. 'You'll pay for it later. Come on. Let's go to the walls while the light is still good.'

The three walked down the stairs and out through Herr

Schwarz's workshop. Work had finished for the day, and Herr Schwarz had retreated to his bedchamber to doze. Dieter peered around the workshop as they passed through it. 'So, all this will be yours when the old man is watching the grass grow from beneath it?'

'Yes. Lucky for me that I wed into a family with no sons.'

'By God, you'll earn your inheritance with that one for a wife.'

'Dieter, don't blaspheme,' Christa said.

Her brother looked at her quizzically. 'There's no need for piety now — your dear Pastor Ovens is not in earshot.'

Christa blushed, and forced herself to think before she replied. Pastor Ovens had prepared for her a series of daily Bible readings, and this morning the appointed chapter had been the words of King Lemuel's mother in the Book of Proverbs: guidance for a good wife. One line in particular had stayed with her: *She opens her mouth with wisdom.*

'I speak in all sincerity,' she said, doing her best to sound modest. 'If Pastor Ovens has guided me towards a more righteous way of thinking …'

'Ach, hold your tongue,' Dieter said, and led the way out into the close and through the covered alley to Gelsenkirchenplatz. The evening air was still warm, and the streets were busy with late shoppers and early revellers. Some of Falkenberg's soldiers loitered on the corner of Breiterweg and Silberstraße. They were a coarser crew than the garrison soldiers. One shouted at Christa, but she did not understand the meaning of his words. Dieter covered his mouth to muffle his laughter. 'What did he say?' Christa asked.

'Don't ask, sister. Keep your innocent mind unsullied.'

'You should defend her honour,' said Klaus.

'Have a bit of wit. There's half a dozen of them, and they're armed with pistols and swords. It won't do Christa's honour much good if I end up on the cobbles like sausagemeat.' He looked at the soldiers. 'It must be a grand thing to be in the army, don't you think? You can drink and swear and do as you please, and there's no one to clip your wings.'

'And you have to march across the country from end to end, and likely as not be killed in a battle,' Christa said.

'We could be dead of plague next week.' He nudged Klaus. 'Don't you like the notion of soldiering, Klaus? We could run away from work and nagging women and be men of the world.'

'I'm happy enough where I am.'

The crowds thickened as they drew closer to the city wall and the Brücketor gate. Dieter stooped down and gathered up a handful of stones. 'What are those for?' Christa asked.

'You'll see.'

They pushed their way to the steps. A soldier was sitting at the bottom of the flight, picking his teeth. He nodded for them to go up if they pleased. Dieter went first, followed by Klaus and Christa.

The walkway that ran along the top was as crowded as the street below had been. Soldiers were patrolling, but they had to push their way through the citizens who were squinting at the army that had besieged their city.

It took Klaus and Christa a moment to find Dieter in the crush. When they saw him he was leaning on the ramparts, gazing out over the river and the land beyond it. Many of the citizens had gardens and orchards outside the walls, on the island that divided the river into two channels, and on the far side of the Elbe. The ground should have been green with spring growth, but it had been trampled into the earth. The Imperial soldiers had made camp beyond the reach of the city's cannon. The standards fluttered, their colours rich in the evening light.

When General Tilly and his soldiers had first arrived, Christa had felt a childish excitement, as if they were no more threatening than a travelling fair. For those first few weeks the citizens could still come and go, so long as they paid a fee to the Emperor's men. It was different now. The army ringed the city with its tents, and the gates were shut fast.

'My God,' Dieter said. 'There are even more of them now than there were yesterday.'

'How many are there, do you think?' Klaus said.

'I don't know. Thousands?'

Christa tried counting, but soon gave up. Dieter pointed towards the camp. 'Look. Some of them are coming closer.' A group of perhaps a dozen men were marching in close formation from the camp in the direction of the Brücketor gate. They were carrying a red and yellow flag.

The soldiers had noticed too. They forced their way to the edge of the outer rampart and waited. When the Imperial party was nearer a shouted order travelled around the wall. 'Parley party. Stand down.' The soldiers stepped back from the outer ramparts and continued with their patrols.

'Will they open the gates to them?' Christa asked.

'No,' Klaus said, with so much certainty that he might have been a councillor. 'The gates will not open until the city is relieved.'

'Listen to you,' Dieter said scornfully. 'Of course they'll open the gates. How else will they exchange their pleasantries?'

The Imperial party was nearly at the Brücketor gate now, their parley standard hanging limp as they reached the shelter of the walls. The citizens jeered at them, shouting insults and obscenities. Dieter handed Klaus some of the stones he'd lifted from the street. 'Come on,' he said. 'Let's see if your aim has mended.'

'I'll wager six *Pfennigs* that I can hit the one with the broad-brimmed hat before you do,' Klaus said.

'Six *Pfennigs*? That's hardly worth breaking sweat for.'

Klaus looked sullen. 'My father-in-law has me on servants' wages.'

'My father keeps us on no wages at all.'

'He feeds and clothes us,' Christa said.

Dieter sneered at her. 'Trust you to take his part. He gives you some of all you make in the marketplace.'

'He does the same for you when you stir yourself to work.'

Klaus elbowed them away to give himself more room and threw the stone. There were a few cheers as it arced through the air, and a groan when it fell short of the Imperial party. 'Ha!' said Dieter.

'Now it's my turn.' His missed the soldier in the broad-brimmed hat, but hit the standard-bearer on the shin. The crowd on the walls laughed as the man rubbed his leg. Klaus grabbed another stone and hurled it down into the men below, Dieter followed, and soon missiles were being tossed from all along that part of the wall. One struck the man in the broad-brimmed hat as he cursed at the citizens. He yelled and lifted his hand to his nose as blood poured down his coat. The crowd on the walls cheered wildly, even when the soldiers from the garrison pushed their way towards them, shouting at them to stop.

One soldier grabbed Dieter and Klaus by their ears as if they were schoolboys. 'Throw one more and I'll have you in jail. Don't you see they're carrying the parley flag?'

'Can we not have a little fun with them?' Dieter's face was red with the pain from his ear.

'You'll have all the fun you want when the King of Sweden comes to chase them off. Now, get off home to your mothers.' The soldier noticed Christa watching him. 'Forgive me, *Mädchen*. Do these two young fools belong to you?'

'I'll take them down now.'

The soldier let go of Klaus and Dieter, and Christa dragged them back to the steps.

'You owe me six *Pfennigs*,' Klaus said.

'Are you mad? It was my stone got him.'

'Be quiet, both of you,' Christa said. 'Half the town was throwing stones at them. You'd never know whose hit home. Keep your money in your pockets.'

They climbed down the steps and walked back to the printers' quarter. 'Is there any food in the house, sister? I'm half starved,' Dieter said.

'There's soup left over from earlier.'

'Oh,' he said gloomily, and scuffed his shoes through the dust on the street. 'And some beer, I hope?'

'Not for you. I'm to save it for Pastor Ovens's prayer meeting tonight.'

'I'd forgotten about that. Why is Father allowing it?'

Christa had persuaded him to let Pastor Ovens hold his meeting in the house. He hadn't been happy. He was letting his impatience with the clergyman show now, and with a crowd in his home he'd feel obliged to confine himself to his bedchamber. Christa had argued with him to convince him that the meeting was God's work, and it was the first time that she and her father had been at odds. It scared her a little, and she felt an uncomfortable glow to have done God's will.

'Klaus,' Dieter said, 'have you any money?'

Klaus shook his head. 'I'm not drinking tonight. Gertrude's in a bad enough mood as it is.'

They turned down the alley into the close. Klaus bade them goodbye and went into the Schwarzes' house. Christa steeled herself to try once more to steer Dieter to a more godly path. 'Why don't you come to the meeting?' she said casually.

'Don't be stupid.'

'You're on the road to hell, Dieter Henning.'

Dieter stopped dead and faced her. 'Listen to yourself. You sound like a schoolgirl rhyming your lessons to please the master. There's no need to repeat everything that overfed crow says because he's taken a shine to you. This is the man who shamed our friends in front of the whole town and you reckon him a godly man? I might not be the finest Christian in Magdeburg, but at least I stick fast to my friends.'

'I have been a loyal friend to Gertrude,' Christa said, stumbling over her words. 'And, yes, it was cruel what Pastor Ovens said at the wedding ... but it wasn't untrue. They had committed a most grievous sin.' Her heart was thudding in her chest. Was this how it felt to be righteous?

Dieter stared at her. For a moment she thought he was going to hit her, but instead he strode in through the open door of the workshop. She waited for a moment, then followed him and heard his footsteps hammering up the stairs. Andreas and her father were cleaning the press. 'What's wrong with your brother?' her father asked.

'We disagreed.'

'He owes you money, I suppose. You must stop lending to him, Christa.'

'It wasn't over money.' Christa noticed Andreas watching her. 'I need to make things orderly for the gathering tonight. You will say a word of welcome to them, won't you, Father?'

He frowned. 'I would rather you took no part in this, Christa. It's one thing to offer a little hospitality, hand round the beer jug, but to participate …'

'It's a prayer meeting, Father. What can be wrong with prayer?'

'The praying is well enough. It's who you're praying with that worries me.' He lowered his voice. 'Pastor Ovens's friends are headstrong, Christa. They would sooner see us martyred than come to reasonable terms. Are there men of business among them? No, not one. They have no notion of compromise.'

'Do you forbid me to attend, Father?' There was no challenge in her voice, and she hoped she looked calm, but she was in torment.

'Would you heed me if I did?'

'Of course.' She held her breath.

He sighed and rested his hands on the edge of the press. Christa noticed the tiredness in his eyes.

'Master,' Andreas said hesitantly, 'if Miss Christa is present she can tell you what occurs. It might be as well to know which way the wind blows.'

'And if the councillors hear of it and question my presence you may say I'm just a weak-minded girl.'

Her father smiled. 'No one who knows you would believe that excuse, daughter.' He sighed again. 'Attend the meeting if you must. But only open your mouth to pray — and listen to what else is said and by whom.'

'Yes, Father.'

'Master, may I attend also?' Andreas had adopted his most wheedling voice.

Christa's heart sank.

'Yes, indeed, Andreas. I will trust you to take care of my girl.'

Andreas smiled at Christa. *Sneak*, she thought, and did not return the smile.

Christa was surprised that Pastor Ovens was not to preside at the meeting. That role fell to a captain from Falkenberg's force who arrived with a dozen other men Christa had never met. Some were garrison soldiers, others townsmen of the lower sort. Pastor Ovens fluttered from guest to guest, looking ill at ease. He tried to make jokes with the soldiers, but they fell flat. Andreas stood by the fireside, watching. Christa and Helga poured the beer. When Helga went back to the kitchen Christa took a seat in the corner of the room. The captain glanced at her. 'Run along, *Mädchen*, this is men's business.'

Christa coloured. She stood up, looking imploringly at Pastor Ovens.

'Ah, no, Captain,' Pastor Ovens said. 'This young woman is a most devout and determined creature.'

The captain ignored him, and gestured for Christa to leave.

'Begging your pardon, sir,' said Andreas, in his ingratiating voice again, 'this is her father's house, and he desires her to be here. A guest should respect the wish of his host, should he not?'

There was a glint of anger in the captain's eyes. 'The father may attend if he wishes, but not his daughter.'

Pastor Ovens stared at his boots, and the other men shuffled awkwardly. Christa looked at Andreas. His eyes were bright and frightened. She couldn't believe he'd stood up to a captain. He met her gaze as if to say, *I tried my best.* 'Very well,' Christa said. Her throat was dry but she spoke clearly. 'In that case you may take your meeting to some other place. Admit me or be off with you.'

The captain walked across the room. He stopped less than an arm's length from her and stared straight into her eyes. He smelled of stale tobacco. 'Your father has you well spoiled.'

'He's reared me to say my prayers.'

Pastor Ovens coughed in the way he did when he wanted attention. The captain glanced at him as if he were an annoyance.

'The girl is of our mind, Captain. Discreet and trustworthy too.' His voice sounded higher than normal, like an old man's.

'So you are to blame,' the captain said, turning to face him. 'You assured me that this was a fit place to meet.'

Pastor Ovens squirmed and flushed bright red. Christa felt a flare of hatred towards the captain and was ashamed for Pastor Ovens. Or was she ashamed *of* him?

'We should continue here,' one of the townsmen said. 'Time is slipping past and we'll hardly find anywhere else at this hour.'

'Very well,' the captain said. He walked back to his seat. 'Get on with your praying, Pastor,' he said, snapping his fingers at Pastor Ovens. 'You're fit for nothing else.'

The prayers were quickly said. The captain looked around the room. 'Some of our leaders have been parleying with the enemy. They're of a mind to agree terms. It is our determination that we should hold fast until relief comes.'

'How far off is the King of Sweden?' a townsman asked.

'No more than a month.'

Christa doubted they could last so long without fresh supplies of food from the countryside. She longed to speak, but didn't dare.

Pastor Ovens coughed and waved his hand to engage the captain's attention. 'Will the council be persuaded to stand firm?'

'That is where we must play our part. What sort of men are our councillors?'

'Rich,' said a soldier.

'Fat,' said another. The men laughed.

The captain nodded. 'Aye, right enough. Rich and fat, but don't forget they fancy themselves pious too. They want to preserve their fortunes and their souls.'

'So,' Pastor Ovens said slowly, 'we must make them see that refusing to surrender is the will of the Lord. And, moreover, that it will cost them less than submission.'

'I rely on you and your fellow clergy to address their spiritual obligations,' the captain said. 'As for their earthly concerns, we need to persuade the merchants and guildsmen against compromise.' He turned to Andreas. 'Your master has the ear of the council, has he not?'

Andreas cleared his throat. He glanced at Christa and, just as quickly, looked away. 'I believe he has a good name with them. More than that I couldn't say. Why don't you ask his daughter?'

'I may as well listen to the yowling of a cat, for all the sense I'd get from a woman.'

The other men laughed, except Pastor Ovens and Andreas. Christa was uncomfortably aware that Pastor Ovens seemed diminished in this company. The captain paid him little attention, the other men none at all.

The debate rambled on and the room was hot, but when Christa went to open the window the captain forbade it, in case unfriendly ears were listening in the close below. Christa's eyes grew heavy. A townsman demanded more beer, and she told him curtly there was none left, which was true. Perhaps thirst would speed their planning.

They stopped talking when someone banged on the front door of the house. Christa rose and opened the window now, glad of the cool night air. The close was dark, but she saw someone move. 'Who is it?'

'Dieter, of course,' her brother hissed. 'Why the devil is the door barred?'

'I'll come down and let you in.'

Dieter must have been leaning against the door, for when she unbarred it he tumbled into the workshop. 'Be quiet now,' she whispered. 'The meeting is still in session.'

'Have the fools nothing better to do than sit around praying?'

Christa smelled drink on his breath. 'Come up quietly.' She took his arm and guided him up the stairs. He stumbled once, but otherwise kept steady.

She had expected him to go straight to bed, but when they reached the first landing he pushed past her into the main room. 'Good evening, friends,' he said, spreading his arms wide. 'Welcome to the home of Herr Henning and his dynasty!' The men stared at him, and he giggled. 'You're a silent breed, I see. Well, you'll not commit blasphemy if you never speak.'

'My brother is tired,' Christa said.

'In his cups, more like,' a soldier muttered.

The captain stood up, scraping his chair back over the floorboards. 'Our business is done.' He signalled to the other soldiers to leave, and they were followed by the townsmen. Pastor Ovens escorted them to the door.

'That looked about as much fun as being hanged,' Dieter said. 'I hope your soul is well mended.'

'Go to bed, Dieter.'

He reeled away from her. 'Of course, sister. No doubt you want a little time with the dear pastor.' He tapped the side of his nose with a finger. 'For private prayer, eh?' He swayed out of the room, laughing softly.

The next morning Dieter lay late in his bed. Christa was glad not to have to look at him over the breakfast table. At first she and her father sat alone. 'So,' he said, keeping his voice low, 'what went on at the meeting? You ran off to bed so quickly last night.'

'Have you spoken to Andreas?'

He nodded. 'He was grumbling about how he and Helga had to put the room to rights this morning.'

'He'd get little help from her.'

'He had none at all from you. You should be more mannerly towards him.' He hesitated. 'He'd be a better man for you than some others.'

'I'm too young yet for that.'

'Yes. But some day …' He looked at her, and must have seen something in her face that warned him to drop the subject. 'He tells me there was more politicking than praying went on last night.'

'We cannot give in to the Papists, Father. We must stand firm.'

He smiled sadly. 'At your age I would have said the same. But if we pay a tribute to them they will go and we can get back to normal. There'll be food on the table again, and trade in the marketplace.'

'So we should give in? And what if they are not satisfied? What if the next time they run low on loot they say to themselves, "Ah, yes, Magdeburg, those feeble creatures won't put up a fight," and come back to plague us?' Excitement swelled in her as she spoke.

Her father lifted his hand to urge her to be quiet, and she realised she had almost shouted. 'You're becoming hard,' he said, with the slightest trace of a tremor in his voice. 'I don't like to hear that from my daughter.'

Christa's face burned. She felt angry and sorry too.

The door opened and Pastor Ovens came in. Had he heard? Dear Lord, the whole house had probably heard. Pastor Ovens murmured a good morning to them both and took his place at the table. They ate and drank in silence. The pastor kept glancing at Christa. When she reached for a piece of bread he stretched his hand forward too, but stopped short of touching her. She felt flustered. She broke the bread into small pieces and put one into her mouth, even though her appetite had vanished. Was a girl meant to feel awkward and a little nauseous when she was admired? Her father was watching them sternly. 'Isn't it time you were off to the market, Christa?' he said.

'Yes, Father.' She was glad of the excuse to leave.

Trade was slow. Food prices were higher than ever, and the ordinary people were saving their *Talers* for bread. It was as well they'd gathered in so many subscriptions for the newsletter, or things would have been even leaner for the Hennings. With so few customers, the morning passed slowly. Christa was wishing she'd thought to bring a stool with her when she saw the dark figure of Pastor Ovens walking through the marketplace. He was glancing from one stall to the next as if he were searching for something. Was he looking for her? She stood very still, not sure if she should call or wave.

When he saw her, he came quickly towards her, smiling. 'Ah, I've found you. I couldn't remember where your stall was set.'

There was something eager in his manner, and she realised she could tease him a little, that he would allow it. The notion pleased her. 'We're always here, Pastor.'

Some passing townspeople acknowledged him with a word and a respectful nod. The weakness she had seen in him last night had vanished. Eventually he leaned over the stall so that he could speak to her without anyone else hearing. 'I had hoped for a word with you earlier.' His robes brushed against the merchandise, disordering her neat arrangements.

'You could join me on this side,' Christa said. 'It would save you bending.'

Pastor Ovens straightened. His face was shining with sweat. 'Very well, then,' he said, and came to stand beside her.

Christa tidied the books and pamphlets. 'You'd be as well to speak now, for I'll be packing the goods away soon enough.' She was surprised at her forward tone. Few in the city would dare speak to Pastor Ovens like that. Indeed, she wouldn't have dealt with him so if they had been in the house – although she didn't quite understand why.

Pastor Ovens coughed and stared down at the stall. 'I wanted to say that I was full of admiration for you last night. That captain was an insolent oaf, and you spoke well against him.'

'Did I?'

'Indeed you did.' Pastor Ovens looked at her now. 'I see that your father has shaped you into the pattern of righteousness.'

'He'd be pleased to hear you say so.'

'You heard last night how some in the city are urging concession. We must stand against it. Could you persuade your father to the same firmness as you have shown?'

'I ... I don't know. He holds his opinions as strongly as I hold mine.'

Pastor Ovens touched her sleeve. 'With God's help, I believe you could convince him.'

Christa was conscious of his hand on her arm. 'I will pray for the grace to move him.'

The clock struck noon. The marketplace was half empty. 'I must clear up,' Christa said. 'Would you like to help me?'

Pastor Ovens looked up at the clock. 'I cannot do that. It would not be ...' He patted his cassock as if he were looking for something. 'I will see you at your father's house.' He stalked away.

Christa began to gather the stock into bundles, but was detained by one late customer looking for a *Pfennig* song-sheet. She sold it to him, even though he would pay only half its value. When he had gone she lifted her bundles onto the barrow and began the journey home. The day was warm, and she wished Pastor Ovens had stayed to help her. Her head was filled with the things he had said. She had never thought of herself as a strong woman, but that was what he had said she was. Hadn't the best of men fine women at their sides, like Martin Luther with Katerina von Bora? She slowed to tread firmly and purposefully across the cobbles. Katerina von Bora would never have rushed or scuttled.

When she got to the house she found Andreas eating bread and cheese in the workshop. 'Why are you down here?' she said, parking the barrow and setting the merchandise on the side-table.

'They're in some twist up there.' He sprayed crumbs as he spoke. 'It would have given me griping in the guts to eat upstairs.'

Puzzled, Christa went up to the main room. Her father, Dieter and Pastor Ovens were sitting round the table, eating and drinking. No one spoke. Only her father looked up to acknowledge her presence. Dieter was red-faced and sulky. Pastor Ovens wore the expression he'd adopted when he'd preached Gertrude and Klaus's wedding sermon. The moment she sat down he excused himself, heading for the upper floor. Dieter left the table without a word, stamped down the stairs and slammed the front door.

'What's wrong?' Christa said.

Her father sighed. 'If I knew that ...' He shook his head and got to his feet. 'How was business today?'

'Slow.' She emptied her purse onto the table and they counted the few coins.

'You may keep it and see what food it will buy.'

'Yes, Father.' She thought about trying to persuade him as Pastor Ovens had suggested she might, but the tiredness in his eyes made her hesitate. Later, perhaps. Pastor Ovens had been sure she would succeed, with God's help. She would pray first. That was the answer. Prayer and contemplation, and then she would talk to him.

Pastor Ovens neither spoke to nor looked at her for the rest of the day. At the table that evening he responded politely enough to her father's attempts at conversation. When Dieter spoke, Pastor Ovens stared at his plate as if he hadn't heard. Christa forced herself to eat. The food left a stale taste in her mouth. Her belly felt uneasy, and she would happily have left the bread and soup, but she knew that hunger lay ahead and didn't dare fast. She was glad to escape to the calm of her bedroom and Elsbeth's undemanding company. Together they read from one of Elsbeth's favourite old books, *Sweet Swans of Song*.

A little later there was a tap on the bedroom door and Dieter came in. He perched on the barrel-topped chest under the window and listened to Christa read for a moment. 'Your paramour seems out of sorts tonight,' he said, when she paused. 'What have you done to distress him?'

'I don't know. I wish I did.'

'The man is like sour milk. He puts a taint in everything.'

Once again Christa felt the strange desire to protect the pastor. So few people liked him, yet he was clever and godly. 'Perhaps his mood will have improved by the morning,' she offered.

'He has only two,' Dieter said, standing and stretching. 'Black and blacker.'

'Are you for bed?'

He shook his head. 'I'm away to see Klaus and listen to his woes.'

'I don't know why you go to him.'

Dieter shrugged. 'His misery is more entertaining than the gloom in this house.' He pulled one of her plaits lightly and left the room.

The next morning she rose early and read the passage of the Bible Pastor Ovens had stipulated. She wondered if he was reading the same words as she was. It gave her a little comfort to think he might be, but when he appeared at the breakfast table his manner was unchanged and he left without a word. There was no declaration of the importance of his day's business, just cursory politeness. Only yesterday he had been questioning her with the intent look he seemed to reserve for her. She found it hard to describe the sensation it aroused in her. It was a little frightening – but most people were afraid of Pastor Ovens so that wasn't surprising – and there was something else: she had felt special to be singled out by a man like him, to feel his attention shine on her like the heat from a fire. Now he had withdrawn his favour, and she felt cold.

When she returned from market the house was unusually quiet. Christa was glad of it. The menfolk were at their labours in the workshop and Helga had gone out, claiming she'd heard of a woman who was willing to sell slices from a side of bacon she'd kept from the winter. Christa had sent Elsbeth along with her, hoping that her sister's quiet presence might inhibit Helga from wasting the afternoon in gossip.

She was in the back kitchen, preparing a thin soup, when she heard Pastor Ovens come in and climb the stairs. Would he sit awhile in the upper room, or would he go straight to his bedchamber? Christa gave the soup another stir, took a few deep breaths, then walked upstairs.

When she came through the door Pastor Ovens was sitting at the table. Immediately he stood up. 'Excuse me,' he said. 'I will not disturb you.'

'Please, stay a moment.' Christa's face grew warm. Pastor Ovens waited. She couldn't tell if she had offended him or not, and swallowed. 'Have I done something to displease you?'

Pastor Ovens pursed his lips. 'Tell me, Fräulein,' he said, 'what is the fate of the blasphemer?'

Christa knew, of course – everyone did – but what could he

mean by such a question? 'A blasphemer is surely damned,' she said, 'unless he repent and beg our Lord Jesus for forgiveness.'

'Yes. That is the judgment of God on the blasphemer. But how would an earthly judge pass sentence on a known blasphemer?'

'I suppose the sinner would forfeit his life.'

Pastor Ovens nodded. 'He would. And rightly, wouldn't you agree?'

'Of course.' Christa tried to remember everything she had said and done in his presence over the last few days.

'You are trembling,' Pastor Ovens said.

'I'm frightened. I don't know what you meant by those words.'

'Sit down.'

In some part of her mind she noted that Pastor Ovens had spoken as if he were the man of the house, rather than her father. When she was seated she looked up at him. He seemed so tall, gazing down on her, with a sour, dusty smell rising from his dark robes. 'I fear that your brother is not among the saved.'

Christa felt sick. Dear God, what had Dieter done? 'Sometimes he … is not as respectful as he might be. But not a blasphemer, surely.'

'Beware that loyalty to your kin does not come before loyalty to the Almighty.'

'Has he said something? Did you overhear …?'

'I have had concerns about his manner since first I came to your father's house. He is too concerned with the things of this world. At first I feared he was, like many a young man before him, on the road to hell.' He stopped as a door banged downstairs. He paused, seeming to listen, then pulled out a chair and sat close to Christa. 'Yesterday, you will recall, I was attending to some business in connection with our present difficulties in the city. I returned earlier than I had anticipated to consult some papers. When I entered the chamber I share with your brother I found him reading the Holy Word of God.'

The smell of him was stronger now. 'Is it not a good thing that he was reading the Bible? Father is always telling him he should read it more often.'

'Indeed, that was my first thought. But something in his manner caused me to suspect him of ... thoughts.'

Christa was amazed to see a blush creeping up his pale face. 'I don't know what you mean.'

'Nor should you. But the Evil One can so poison the mind that even the Word may fuel lust.'

Christa thought of all those times she and Dieter had been made to sit for hours to study the Bible. He had had a knack of finding the lewdness. 'Did you speak to him about this?'

Pastor Ovens pursed his lips. 'He fled the room so I had no chance to do so. Since then I have been considering prayerfully how to proceed. Your father, I fear, seems reluctant to chastise his children — unless, perhaps, he beats you privately?' His lips parted and she saw his tongue moving to and fro against his teeth.

'He only beat Dieter once, and it caused him great distress, on account of his love for our poor mother.'

Pastor Ovens shook his head. 'A bruise is a purer mark of love than a caress or a kind word. So, it seems there is little to be gained from speaking with your father. Which leaves me with two options. I could pray for your brother's redemption. Or I could consult with others more expert in the signs of devilry, blasphemy and witchcraft.'

Christa was chilled. 'Please, Pastor Ovens, don't do that. Let me speak to him.'

'Poor child. I can see how you are led by him. Do not let him carry you with him to death.' He reached out as if he intended to touch her hand, but drew back abruptly. 'I speak not only of the death of the flesh, but of the death of the spirit.'

Christa fought down the panic that was rising inside her. It would be easy for Pastor Ovens to say a word or two to the city judges, whereupon Dieter might find himself pleading for his life in the ecclesiastical court. And Pastor Ovens was unpredictable, for all his seeming admiration of her. If she was over-passionate in her defence of Dieter, he might accuse her too. She must be very careful. 'Please, sir,' she said, as calmly as she could, 'do not mistake my frailty for weakness. Of course I am a poor thing, young and only a woman. But God is my strength. I trust in him. I will go to my brother and implore him to mend his ways. Let me do this, sir. How much better to bring my brother to repentance than to the flames?' She lowered her eyes, but risked an occasional peep at him.

'Very well,' he said at last. He leaned closer to her, so that she could smell his breath. 'For your sake.'

Dieter didn't come back until it was time for dinner. The family ate in silence, and when Christa and Helga were clearing the plates Christa signalled to Dieter that she wanted to speak to him. She bade Helga rest, and while the older woman seemed suspicious at this kindness she was too lazy to follow them down to the kitchen.

'What is it?' Dieter asked, once they were sure they could not be overheard.

'I've spoken to Pastor Ovens. It's you who has so upset him. He said he came upon you reading the Bible for its ... carnal pleasures.'

Dieter snorted. 'If I want carnal pleasures I'll find them in other places. Unlike poor Pastor Ovens. He—-'

'Don't be disrespectful.' Christa surprised herself with her stern tone. It sounded false in her ears, like a child playing at being an adult. 'What were you reading, anyway?'

Dieter looked sullen. 'It was nothing. Good God, that man has a sick mind.'

'I know you, Dieter Henning! Remember how you used to sneak off to read the Song of Solomon? Don't pretend you were trying to mend your soul.'

Dieter sighed. 'I was reading about Amnon and Tamar. Remember how he was mad with love for her, and pretended to be ill so that she would come to him, and then after he had ... he couldn't stand the sight of her?'

'That's the way with men. Frau Schwarz told me. She said a girl must not give way unless she's married or the man will grow cold.'

Dieter's mouth twitched into a smile. 'Frau Schwarz said that?'

Christa shrugged to hide her embarrassment. 'She said it was the sort of thing my mother would have told me, if she'd lived.'

'A pity her own daughter didn't pay her more heed.'

'Pastor Ovens believes you were taking carnal pleasure from the Word of God. He's accusing you of blasphemy.'

'Has he not problems enough of his own without looking for trouble where there's none? Good God, am I to be condemned for reading the Bible?'

'Dieter, he mentioned witchcraft.'

'Witchcraft? He's mad.'

Christa grasped his arm. 'Be serious! People have gone to the flames on lesser words than Pastor Ovens could utter.'

Dieter shook her off. 'My God, I'm sick of this place. Why won't our father drive him out?' He took a deep breath. 'I've a notion to leave Magdeburg.'

Christa stared at him. 'No one can leave the city until the King of Sweden comes to free us.'

'Maybe I'll join the army. Falkenberg is crying out for fresh recruits, and when the Swedes come I could be away from here for ever.'

'You? A soldier?' She couldn't keep the mockery from her voice.

'It's time to grow up.' There was tension now in the way he held himself. 'Things are bad in the world. I can't spend my life getting drunk with Klaus.'

'But the army! It's so dangerous.'

'I'd rather be blown apart by a cannon in defence of the faith than be burned in the marketplace at the word of a lunatic like Pastor Ovens.'

'Have you told Father?'

Dieter shook his head. 'And don't say a word. Not yet. Promise?'

'Only if you promise you'll be careful with Pastor Ovens. Ask him to pray with you. That might help.'

'Very well, then. We'll exchange promises.'

Christa heard Andreas's heavy tread coming through from the print shop and busied herself with washing the plates. He tramped in, and looked from her to Dieter. 'What are you two gossiping about?'

'You,' Christa snapped. 'We were wondering when you will put Helga out of her misery and marry her.'

Andreas scowled. 'I've no more intention of marrying Helga than I have of turning Papist. You shouldn't say things like that. It might put ideas in her head. She'll be harder to deal with if she feels wronged.' He looked at the table. 'Is there not a bite more to eat in this house? I'm half famished.'

'You may get used to that, if the King of Sweden doesn't come soon. There's a spoonful of soup left in the pot. Eat that if you will.'

'Why give it to him?' Dieter said. 'What about me?'

'He works harder than you,' Christa retorted. Andreas scraped around the soup pot, trying to scoop out the remnants. 'Make the most of it,' Christa said, 'I don't know where I'll find food for tomorrow.'

'There's little point in me staying here to watch him eat,' Dieter said. He went to leave, but hesitated at the kitchen door. 'Frau Schwarz was right about men, sister. Their fancy grows cold more quickly than you'd think. You'd be wise to heed her advice.'

She left Andreas in the kitchen and climbed up to her room, needing to think and pray. Her heart sank a little when she saw Elsbeth perched on the window-seat, reading a little book. 'What have you there, pet?' she said, touching her sister's hair.

Elsbeth smiled and handed it to her. 'The meditations of St Mechthilde. Do you think she was a godly woman, even though she was a Papist?'

Christa squeezed onto the seat beside her. 'I suppose she might have been. It's so sad to think of the people living in darkness before our good Martin Luther shone God's light of truth into the world.' She glanced at the open page. A floorboard creaked in the room next door — Pastor Ovens. She shuddered. What would he think of such reading matter? She closed the book. 'I think,' she said softly, 'that you should read this book privately. Others may think badly of you if they see it.' Almost as soon as she had spoken she regretted it.

Elsbeth frowned, her eyes clouded with confusion. 'If it is wrong to read it then I must cast it from me,' she said, and the first tear spilled down her cheek.

'It is not wrong, sweet,' Christa said, putting her arm round Elsbeth's shoulders. 'Don't listen to your silly sister. Here, let me put the book safely away and we will choose another.' She set it on the shelf, and lifted down *The Old and New God* instead. It always soothed Elsbeth when she was agitated.

Elsbeth was asleep at last. Christa knelt to pray, but her mind was stirred with anxiety for Dieter and she couldn't concentrate. If only he could show piety while Pastor Ovens was under their roof. Would God consider her heartfelt wish a prayer? He would hear her, she knew. She must endeavour to deflect Pastor Ovens's attention from her brother, at least until the siege was raised. But what would happen when the Swedish army arrived? They'd be half starved, soldiers and horses alike. There was little enough food as it was, and the meadows around the city were stripped of grass. Would Dieter really go with them? Everyone had been in a fever since the gates had been locked. No one was quite right in their minds. She realised she'd never *seen* the city walls until now. She remembered how she used to love the sense of cosiness as the day ended and the gates were closed for the night. The walls had been like her father's arms round her when she was a little girl, protecting her from the dark and the bad things that hid in it. They had been a comfort — but now they were a prison. The whole city felt airless, as if the very breath were being squeezed out of it.

Six

THE WEATHER GREW HOTTER THAN IT was at harvest-time as the army moved north, and by the time they were a day's march from Magdeburg many of the soldiers would have been glad of a splash of rain to wash the dust off them. The spring vegetables were wilting in the fields so they could find no nourishment there.

Lukas was sweating with a light fever. His throat pained him each time he swallowed, and he couldn't breathe through his nose. The illness had run through the company. One man had fallen down with it just outside Hettstedt. Captain Gebwiler had ordered him laid on one of the wagons, then forced the village pastor to take him in. Half a dozen other men begged to lie down in the village, but Captain Gebwiler told them they'd be hanged before he'd let them away for no more than a head cold. They continued their march, but two of the sick managed to lose themselves as they passed through a forest. Lukas envied them a little. Perhaps they were lying down now in the cool shade of the trees with a stream flowing nearby.

Götz was one of the few who still had his health. He had offered to carry Lukas's satchel for him, but Lukas had refused brusquely.

Götz took the rebuff with composure, but Lukas could feel the boy watching him like an anxious nursemaid.

The sun was dipping low in the sky, but the order came down the line that they were to continue until they reached Magdeburg, and to hurry if they wanted to make camp while it was still light. There was some muttering among the men. Lukas's mind was empty of everything except the effort of placing one foot in front of the other. His legs were heavy but his head was unpleasantly light. Only the thought that he could sleep at the end of the journey carried him onward.

By the time they saw the spires of Magdeburg ahead the sky was darkening and they knew they would not get there that night. The city was built on the wide floodplain of the Elbe, and a man would see it in front of him for hours on the march. He could walk and walk, and never seem to get closer. When it was truly night and they couldn't see the ground under their feet Captain Gebwiler ordered them to find a spot to lie down and rest. It was the very thing he had declared he would not allow, but none felt inclined to protest. He instructed them that they would rise and continue as soon as the sky lightened. The tents would not be pitched to save delay in the morning.

Lukas lay down close to the others, resting his head on his satchel and tucking the stock of his musket under his coat to keep it from the damp. Götz tapped his arm. 'Will you take some wine before you close your eyes?' he asked.

'Have you no water?'

'None. I'll away off and hunt for some, if you will, but the river's a good half-hour from here.'

'I'll let my mouth gape and gather the dew.'

Götz laughed. Lukas heard him open his flask and drink. The thought of wine made his head throb. He'd near enough have sold his soul for a draught of water, cold from a spring. Götz corked his flask and Lukas heard him lie down. He hoped the boy wouldn't be too restless. It was taking him a while to learn the soldier's art of sleeping where he fell. As the air cooled, the nightly chorus of coughing began. Lukas closed his eyes. It wouldn't keep him from his sleep.

They staggered to their feet before dawn. Lukas thought he was a little better, but his head spun from hunger. Götz begged a half-cup of water from one of the baggage boys and Lukas took a cautious sip. His throat was as raw as it had been yesterday, but perhaps it would mend.

The march got on its way. Magdeburg seemed to float on the morning mist. It looked further away than ever. They were pressed forward by the thought of General Tilly's siege camp. There'd be food there, although the price would be high. Lukas still had the scant treasure he'd pocketed in the village where Matko had killed the girl. It wouldn't buy him much.

As the sun rose higher in the sky, the city walls glowed red. The many steeples were sharp against the blue of the sky. 'It's beautiful, isn't it?' Götz said.

'Aye, and packed with heretics.'

'If they have food in their larders, I'll be happy to sup with them.'

'What would Father Tomas think of that?'

Götz reddened. 'I'd say he'd content himself, so long as I persuaded them back to the true religion while we dined.'

'Well, I'll let God deal with their souls as long as they hand over their plenty to feed us.' Perhaps when they had taken the city he should try to find some way to send a little money to Katherine and the child. He quickly dismissed the notion as impossible. Even if he could find a trustworthy person to carry the gift, they would more than likely be robbed before they were anywhere near Saalfeld.

Their pace slowed as the morning wore on. Captain Gebwiler's horse walked so lethargically that the men on foot were overtaking it. Lukas glanced up at the captain as they passed him. His face was pale and greasy with sweat. He must have succumbed to the same fever as the rest of them.

The sound of the siege camp reached them before they could make out the standards fluttering in the wind. As they drew closer they saw that the land around the city was covered with thousands of tents. Some were clearly the campaign homes of aristocratic soldiers, as elegant and robust as miniature castles. The well-moneyed regiments had supplied their men with sturdy enough shelters, but the majority were obliged to take their rest under whatever they could improvise. Lukas's tent had seen him through the last two summers of campaign, and had room enough for himself, his musket and accoutrements. He had let young Götz share it with him since they had left Saalfeld. There was hardly space enough for the two of them, and he would have to find something more commodious if they were to be fixed for a time at Magdeburg. Some of the other men would have room for Götz in their tents, but the boy was so green and they were so coarse that Lukas was disinclined to allow it. True, Götz no longer blushed each time he heard a curse, but he was too innocent yet for this game. A week or two in the siege camp would harden him, that was certain.

They halted at the fringes of the camp, and waited while Colonel von Breuner and his party went forward to seek out General Tilly. No sooner had the men set themselves down than a group of sutlers appeared, pushing little carts piled with food and liquor. Some of the low merchants who had accompanied the soldiers from Saalfeld intercepted their rivals. Lukas and Götz watched as words were exchanged. After a few moments the merchants retreated. 'They look long in the face,' Götz said.

'They'll have tried to make an accommodation, but those siege sutlers could buy and sell them a dozen times before Matins.'

'We could wait until we get our daily ration, I suppose.'

Lukas looked at the food carts. In truth he was beyond hunger, but he'd a yearning for something salty. 'Go and ask how much they want for a slice or two of bacon.'

'Should I take the moneybag?'

Lukas shook his head. 'They'd take one look at your fresh face and rob you blind. Find their price and tell me.' Götz hesitated, then walked over to the sutlers. Lukas watched as the boy pointed at the bacon. His mouth watered at the thought of it. Raw or cooked, there was nothing like a morsel of bacon.

Götz turned from the cart and came back. 'They want a *Reichstaler* for two slices.'

'A *Reichstaler*? Dear God. I haven't seen one these last twelve months.' He struggled to his feet.

'Where are you going?'

'My face may drive a harder bargain with the sutler than yours.'

'Shall I come with you?'

'No. You bide here a while.' Götz bit his lip and sat down.

Lukas made his way to the cart.

'Good day, friend,' the sutler said. 'You look as if you've a fierce hunger on you.'

Lukas stared at him, but did not respond. He pointed at the side of bacon displayed on the cart. 'I'll give you five *Kreuzer* for three slices.'

The sutler's lips twitched as if he was about to laugh. Lukas fixed him with a glare. 'If I sold it you for that I'd be robbing myself. I told your young page there that I'd need a *Reichstaler* for two slices.'

'You're a thief.'

'A thief with bacon.'

'I'll give you a *florin* for three slices.'

'One slice.'

'Two.'

'There's no dealing with you, sir.'

Lukas looked again at the bacon. The fat glistened. The heat had drawn a sweat from it. He could smell the aroma of woodsmoke rising from it. 'A *florin* for a slice, then. But make it a thick one.' He searched in his moneybag for the coin, watching carefully as the sutler sliced the bacon. They made their exchange and Lukas carried his prize back to where Götz was sitting cross-legged.

'I suppose you struck a better price than I did,' Götz said.

'Aye. Don't take a huff over it. When you're as ugly as I am you'll make sharper deals.' He took out his pocket knife and cut a sliver of bacon from the slice. 'Here, try this.' He held it out to Götz. The boy took it and chewed. 'Don't rush it down.' Lukas cut another sliver for himself.

'How did you win your scar?'

'Found myself on the wrong end of a dragoon's sabre.'

'Did it ... hurt?'

Lukas laughed and cut another piece of bacon for Götz. 'What do you think? I was lucky not to lose my eye, or fall with wound fever.'

'Aye, God be praised for His mercy.'

'Maybe God did have a hand in it. My scar keeps me honest.'

Götz frowned. 'How so?'

'I daren't commit any wrongdoing, for the witnesses need only say, "He was a man with a great scar from his eyebrow to his jawbone," and I would be found out.'

'Then God be praised for scars.'

By the time they had finished eating Lukas could feel a little of his strength returning. Colonel von Breuner's party returned and they were ordered to another part of the field, closer to the city walls. Lukas watched as Captain Gebwiler was helped back into the saddle. The company tramped through the camp, past tent after tent. The place was as crowded as a town on a fair day. A few platoons of soldiers were being drilled, but most were lounging in front of their tents, drinking and shouting greetings or insults to the company as it passed. Some had tobacco pipes in their mouths. The smell of the smoke made Lukas's stomach churn.

They found their place where the land sloped down to the river. There was a good quarter-hour's walk between their pitch and the bank. An island lay a little upstream of them. The Emperor's flag flew from the remains of a dilapidated fort that stood at the near end, and the earth round about was pitted with holes where cannon shot had landed. It looked as if a bridge had once crossed the river there but now it was gone. Lukas was close enough to see the enemy soldiers and citizens on the walkways that topped the city walls. Some townspeople shouted down at them, but he couldn't make out what they were saying. At least the company was not within musket range.

The fever weakness came over Lukas again. Götz urged him to rest, and set to pitching the tent, but he was obliged to leave off when the call came to assist with raising Captain Gebwiler's canvas. Lukas lay down with his head on his satchel and watched his fellows make short work of it. The captain himself stood by a baggage wagon, leaning against it. A lieutenant was at his side, with the captain's wife a little way off. Once Captain Gebwiler swayed, and would have fallen if the other man had not held him. As soon as the tent was pitched and furnished the captain walked to it unsteadily and disappeared inside, his wife following.

Götz came back to Lukas and continued his work on their own tent.

'How did the captain look close to?' Lukas asked.

'Badly.'

'Pray God he mends.'

'Amen.'

Götz soon had the tent ready, and Lukas crawled inside. 'Should I see if there's to be rations given out today?' Götz called.

'Aye, do that,' Lukas said. He closed his eyes. The noise of the camp was dulled by the canvas. He'd rest here awhile, then go down to the river's edge. The sound of the fast-flowing water would ease him.

He woke feeling sluggish and unrested. There was shouting outside and Götz pulled open the entrance to the tent. 'We're ordered to assemble. They've appointed a new captain.'

'Is Captain Gebwiler dead?'

'No, but he's not fit to lead us. They've sent a Captain Sadeler.'

Lukas rubbed the crust from his eyes and shuffled out of the tent, dragging his musket. His throat was sore and parched again. The company was lining up in uneven rows.

Captain Sadeler was watching the men with his hands on his hips. 'Come on, you crowd of bumpkins. Call yourself soldiers? I've seen more order in a herd of pigs fleeing the butcher's knife.' He waited until they had settled into their lines. The musketeers were at the front, with their weapons on their shoulders.

Lukas stood at one end, alongside Baxandall. He'd have preferred a truer comrade at his side. The pikemen were behind the musketeers, and the unarmed lads like Götz at the back.

'Poise your muskets!' Captain Sadeler shouted.

Lukas swept his down in one smooth movement, resting the stock on the ground in front of his feet and holding the barrel steady. The other men did the same. Captain Sadeler walked slowly down the row, looking closely at each weapon. Twice he stopped and ran his finger up a barrel. He reached the end of the row and looked hard at Lukas. 'Your name and rank?'

'Weinsburg, sir. Private.'

'How long have you served the Emperor, Weinsburg?'

'Fifteen years, sir.'

'Fifteen years, and still a private?'

'I was a sergeant, sir, but torn down to private.'

'For what fault?'

'I gave the mercy to a hanged comrade, sir.'

Captain Sadeler seemed to consider this, then said, 'Draw forth, Weinsburg.' Lukas whipped the ramrod out of its keeper and held it with the end just inside the muzzle of his musket. His arm was shaking with exhaustion, and the ramrod rattled against the metal. Captain Sadeler made the sign to ram home and Lukas let go of the rod. It slid smoothly inside the barrel without obstruction. The captain moved on to Baxandall, and went through the same procedure — the questions, then the ramrod test. Baxandall's gun was as clean as Lukas's. Captain Sadeler passed on.

No one was exempt from his questioning. Lukas felt the lightness in his head worsening, and wondered when they would eat. If the captain continued in this way it would be nightfall before he had finished.

Halfway along the line a man's ramrod lodged three-quarters of the way down the barrel. He made to push it home, but Captain Sadeler knocked away his hand. 'This weapon is clogged,' he said.

'Perhaps it got fouled on the march, sir.'

'Six lashes.' He indicated for his lieutenants to take the musketeer. They came forward and waited for the man to hand his gun to the comrade next to him, then pulled him from the line. Lukas couldn't remember his name. He was one of those who had been recruited in Saalfeld.

'May I speak, sir?' the man said.

Captain Sadeler had already turned towards the next man in the line. 'Mind yourself,' he said, not looking back. 'I'll tolerate no insolence.' He glanced at one of the lieutenants. 'Hold him steady until I'm done here.'

The inspection continued for another hour. Thankfully, Captain Sadeler seemed less interested in the pikemen. They fell so quickly in a battle that it was scarcely worth learning their names. He ignored the unarmed boys altogether. At last he ordered them to gather round and observe the penalty that would befall any man who failed to cherish his musket.

The man spoke a quiet word to the lieutenants. They looked at each other, and loosened their grip on him a little. He walked steadily towards the wagon that Captain Sadeler indicated. The rest of the company followed. Lukas and the other musketeers were at the front. When they reached the wagon the man turned and addressed himself to Captain Sadeler again. 'Sir, I have a plea, if you would hear it.'

'You want mercy?'

'No, sir.'

'What, then?'

'Would you let me take my shirt off? It will be torn off otherwise and I have no other.'

Captain Sadeler was silent for a moment. 'Aye, very well. A soldier needs a shirt on his back.'

The man nodded his thanks, pulled off his shirt and threw it to his comrades. He turned and leaned his hands against the strut of the wagon, bending his head and spreading his feet wide apart. His back was pale and unmarked. In the short time he'd been a soldier he'd never fallen foul of Captain Gebwiler. The lieutenants tied his wrists to the strut. Lukas looked behind him for Götz. He could just see his dark hair in the press of unarmed lads at the back, and was glad that the boy had not come closer. Captain Sadeler ordered the tallest and broadest of the pikemen forward, and signalled for him to be handed the lash. 'Be at your mightiest, friend,' the captain said. 'Do not hold back or you'll be the next for it.'

The pikeman nodded, then delivered six swift hard strokes to his comrade. The man bore up well, not crying out. Captain Sadeler ordered him untied, and dismissed them all. Several musketeers stepped forward to assist the man, and took him to apply a poultice to the lash-licks.

Lukas looked round for Götz, and found that the boy had crept forward to his side. 'Are you still minded to be a soldier, young Götz?' he said.

'Do you think I have the stomach for it?'

'You'll not know that until you've lived through a battle.'

'I'd be little good in a battle without a weapon.' He pointed at Lukas's musket. 'You have me making shot for you nearly every night. Is it not time you taught me how to make fire too?'

'Not yet.' Lukas walked towards the tent, with Götz trotting after him.

'When, then?'

Lukas sat down in front of the tent and reached inside for his satchel. He pulled out his rag and the flask of gun oil. 'First I must be satisfied you have learned how to clean the weapon,' he said, handing the musket to Götz. 'You saw what happened today. A fouled piece will earn you a beating at drill, but in the battle it will earn you a slow, hard journey to eternity if the damn thing blows up in your face.'

'Have you seen that happen?' Götz slid out the ramrod and wrapped the cloth around one end.

'I've seen a novice musketeer have half his face ripped away when the barrel burst on him. It took him a week to die.' He watched Götz dab a drop of gun oil onto the cloth. 'Not too much there, young Götz. There's little enough left, and scarce a *Pfennig* in my pocket to pay for more.'

'Will we get our food ration today, do you think?' Götz said, using the ramrod to force the rag up the barrel.

'We may pray so.' Lukas looked up at the walls of the city. 'I wonder have they much in there? They seem lively enough on the battlements.'

'Is there no word of them reaching amity with us?'

'None that I've heard. A hard-headed lot.'

'We'll teach them reconciliation,' Götz said, and pointed the musket towards Magdeburg. 'Bang! There — I've softened them.' He smiled at Lukas. 'Wouldn't I make a grand musket-man?'

'Aye, if your words were shot, you'd be a fierce lad right enough.'

One of the baggage boys came trotting towards them. 'You are Götz Fuhrmann, are you not?' the lad said. Götz nodded. 'You're to attend Captain Sadeler this minute.'

'Why does he want me?' Götz said.

The boy shrugged and ran off on some other errand.

'You'd best do as you're bade,' Lukas said. 'Don't look so afraid. If you'd done some wrong he'd have seized you by now, not given you warning to flee.'

'Will you walk up with me?'

Lukas sighed. 'We may pray that you show more boldness under fire than you do when you're told to attend the captain.'

Götz smiled weakly and smoothed his hair. 'Aye, but the worst the enemy can do is kill me.'

They made their way to Captain Sadeler's tent. The captain was seated at his table with a number of papers spread out before him. He grinned when he saw Götz. 'Young Private Fuhrmann,' he said. 'It's a rare day when the post carries a letter for a humble prentice soldier.' He held up a letter and turned it to show the seal. 'From the Jesuit seminary in Saalfeld, no less.'

'It's there I was educated, Captain,' Götz said.

There had been an odd note in his voice, Lukas thought. He glanced at him and saw that that the boy's face was paler than the paper the letter was written on.

'Well, if you're to be in the habit of receiving post, be aware that it's the custom to tip the lad who carries it, which good deed I have done on your behalf.'

'Thank you, Captain.'

Captain Sadeler wiped his nose with his free hand. 'Hold on to your thanks. I'll be docking it from your pay.'

Much difference that will make, Lukas thought. They'd none of them been paid since they'd begun the march north.

Captain Sadeler threw the letter onto the table and returned to his papers. Götz picked it up and he and Lukas left.

The day's ration of bread and beer had been brought while they had attended the captain, and the men were waiting in an orderly fashion for their share. Götz ran back to the tent for their tankards, while Lukas took a place in the line. When Götz returned he handed them to Lukas. 'I'll away back and read this letter, if you're willing to carry our rations.'

Lukas agreed and watched Götz walk off. There was no eagerness in the lad's step.

When their bread and beer had been doled out, Lukas returned to the tent. Götz was sitting outside, with the letter in his hand. The seal was unbroken.

'You seem disturbed, Götz,' Lukas said. 'I'd have thought that a letter from home would please you.'

'I need something to strengthen me before I open it.'

'Well, here's food and drink.'

'Is there nothing stronger?'

'Here,' Lukas said. 'Take a swallow of beer. I'll away and see if I can find you some liquor.'

'We've no money to pay for it.'

'Aye, but we'll take the city in a day or two. Some of the sutlers will give me credit on expectation of repayment when my pockets are full of Magdeburg gold.'

Lukas walked to the part of the camp where the victuallers traded. Little business was being transacted, with most of the army owed back pay, but he soon found a man willing to give him a skin of brandy on promise. The sutler added Lukas's name and company to a long list he had scraped onto a slate. 'If you're killed before you repay me I'll come for satisfaction from your companions,' the man said.

'I'll endeavour to live, then,' Lukas said, 'and save them the inconvenience.'

When he got back to the tent Götz had retreated inside it. Lukas crawled in through the opening and handed him the brandy-skin. Götz took it but would not meet his eye. The letter lay on the floor.

'What was the news from Saalfeld?'

Götz took a long swallow of the brandy and wiped his mouth. 'Not good, alas.'

Lukas waited. Götz drank again. He held out the skin to Lukas. Lukas took a drink and waited for the liquor to scald the emptiness from his belly. 'Tell me, then. There's little to gain from silence.'

'The letter was from Father Tomas. You remember him?'

'I recall you talking of him.'

Götz nodded. 'I had been fearing he would find me.'

'I don't understand, Götz. You came with his blessing. This time was to be your ... What was the word you used?'

'Experiment.'

'Aye, your experiment. The better to prepare you for the priesthood, and a chance to earn the loot to pay for it.'

'I did not have Father Tomas's permission to join Colonel von Breuner's battalion.'

'But you had papers. I saw them in your hand the day we left Saalfeld.'

'I wrote them myself. They were false.'

Lukas fought to suppress a smile. Poor Götz looked so contrite. He slapped the lad cheerfully on the shoulder. 'So, what does your old master require of you? That you come home and be beaten? Or does he tell you that you may never cast your shadow in Saalfeld this side of Judgment Day?'

Götz shrugged, his eyes downcast. 'He will welcome me in a spirit of forgiveness if ever I return.'

'Well, that's not so bad. Why are you still in such low spirits?

At last Götz looked up at him. In the dim light of the tent the lad's eyes seemed bigger and darker than usual. 'There was plague in Saalfeld not long after we left. He would have written before, but no one could leave the town to carry the letter.'

Lukas felt a sudden chill in his gut. 'And are many dead of it?'

'A dozen or so. It could have been worse.' He took a loud breath. 'Your Katherine was taken.'

Lukas heard the words and understood them. He felt strangely empty, and wondered why that should be. When he closed his eyes he laboured to recall Katherine's face, and found he could not. Words gathered slowly in his mouth, provoked by some puzzle in Götz's news. Something did not make sense. He waited patiently as the words arranged themselves. He could see Götz's face and knew that the boy was talking to him, but his ears were filled with the hiss that sometimes came in the silence after battle. The puzzle was clear now. The words resolved themselves into a question. 'What would your Father Tomas know of Katherine? Why would he be concerned to tell you of her death?'

Götz drank more brandy and passed the skin to Lukas. 'When it was discovered that I was gone he made enquiries about the town. He heard reports that we had been seen drinking, and that led him to the house where Katherine lodged. She had mended somewhat, and was attending to the child.'

'The child is dead too, I suppose.'

'Every grown person in the house was taken when the plague came, but the baby lives yet, God be praised for His mercy.' Götz reached forward and picked up the letter. 'As Father Tomas tells it, the whole town considers it a miracle.' He unfolded the letter. 'Would you like me to read to you what he says?'

'No.' Lukas's voice sounded angry to his ears, but it was not anger he felt. There was nothing. He crawled out of the tent and walked through the camp, finding his path in the gaps between tents. The brandy-skin was still in his hand, and he drank as he walked. After a time he realised there were fewer tents. The ground beneath his feet might have been pasture at one time, but the scrawny horses that were tethered at intervals about the place had eaten the grass. There was forest in front of him. All that was left of the nearest trees were stumps, and those further into the forest were being stripped branch by branch. As he walked closer a pair of foreign soldiers — Russians, he thought — came out carrying a heavy bough between them. The wood looked damp. Lukas doubted it would burn well unless they gave it time to dry out. Pathways had been trodden through the forest, and Lukas followed one until he came to a place where the trees seemed untouched. He sat down on a fallen sycamore, and waited for his heartbeat to slow. All he could see around him was forest. The camp, and the city beyond, were hidden by the trees. He finished the last drop of brandy. For a moment he thought of throwing away the skin, but it could be traded for something, perhaps a slice of cheese.

Now that his body was still, the twisting in his brain began. He was not good with thoughts. What would he gain from forcing them towards Katherine? That time was gone. More liquor might help, or a good fight. If only the taking of the city would begin. He looked back through the trees towards the camp. Some men who were tired of soldiering came to the forest and slipped away, living by their wits until they found their way home. That was not his way. The war was his home.

As the days went by they fell into a routine of drills and preparation. They sharpened their skills, and there were no more floggings. There was word that Captain Gebwiler had rallied, but a day later that he was failing again. Lukas took to his bed early each night, and drank less than usual, and presently he began to feel more like himself. Some days they got their rations, and some days they had none. Götz prided himself that he knew which sutlers had the best supplies for the cheapest price, but Lukas had little enough left to pay for them, and Götz hadn't a *Pfennig* with which to bless himself.

They'd been there about a week when Captain Sadeler gathered the musketeers around him. 'General Tilly has ordered a party to approach and deliver a letter inviting parley. We are tasked with guarding them. I will lead, and the rest of you form a line at either side of the colonel's party. Keep your eyes on the walls. Don't trust those heretic sons of whores.'

Götz helped Lukas strap on his bandolier of powder flasks and ran to relight the long cord of slow-match. Lukas could manage without such assistance, but it seemed to please the lad to act the apprentice. Before they marched off he took out his shot-making tools and handed them to Götz. 'Refill my spare shot bag while I'm away, in case the citizens get a taste of my lead.'

Captain Sadeler led them across the camp towards General Tilly's headquarters. They passed all manner of tents and gatherings. Some of the sutlers had set themselves up in sturdy wooden huts, with soldiers and their women queuing outside for beer, rum or tobacco. There looked to be a row brewing outside one such establishment, where two tawdry girls were cursing each other. Lukas and the other men slowed a little, the better to watch the goings-on. 'Eyes forward!' Captain Sadeler barked. 'The Emperor doesn't pay you to watch cat-fights.'

At that moment a woman trotted up on a pony and harangued the girls with language even looser than theirs had been. She was dressed like a lady in a green velvet dress, but the fabric was worn and dirty. There was a suspicion of paint on her face.

When they reached General Tilly's tent they waited in tight lines, muskets steady on their shoulders. At last the parley party emerged. The old general himself was not among them. Instead, the party was led by a richly clothed man who was clearly convinced of his own superiority. Captain Sadeler ordered the musketeers into position, the general's standard-bearer took his place, and they set off for the city.

The land they walked over had once been cherished. It was still possible to make out the foundation lines of garden walls, and the odd late daffodil bloomed in corners where the earth hadn't been hard trampled. The fruit trees were gone, torn down for firewood, and likewise the fences that had marked out the orchards. Lukas wondered how the people behind the city walls were provisioned. The talk in the camp was all of the wealth hoarded by the citizens, but gold was of little use without bread. The siege had held for more than two months now. They must surely be hungry, but there seemed no sign of them capitulating.

A rough bridge had been constructed from the camp to the island, and then to the city. The parley party crossed, and marched to the gate they called the Brücketor. There they waited for some minutes, while the citizens on the walkway above shouted abuse. Lukas scanned the top of the wall. He could see the garrison soldiers, but their muskets were pointed skywards. It wasn't them he feared — they would have been ordered not to fire unless they were first attacked. The civilians were a different matter. One up there now was ranting about the sons of Satan, and declaring that Jehovah would smite them. Others were less holy in their language. Lukas's eye was caught by a movement immediately above him. A group of women were leaning over the parapet and waving. 'Hey, little lads!' one shouted. 'We'll not open our gates of paradise for you.'

'We only let real men in,' another added. They cackled like a tree of rooks.

Captain Sadeler turned to the men. 'Pay no mind to the whores. Be sure their sons aren't levelling a weapon at you while you're diverted.'

'Here's all you'll get from us,' the first woman shouted. She had unlaced her bodice and bared her breasts. Every man in the party stared up at her, including Captain Sadeler, and two of the others emptied a bucket over them. The party stumbled back, but not before they'd been splashed with cess. The sharp reek filled Lukas's nostrils.

'Hold the line!' Captain Sadeler shouted. 'We'll put manners on those bitches soon enough. Now hold firm and watch the walls, not a whore's dugs.'

The gate opened, and a party of councillors stepped out, led by a grey-faced man wearing the chain of the *Bürgermeister*. He sniffed the air and kept his distance. The jeering from the walls grew louder. General Tilly's man stepped forward and pulled a letter from his coat. 'You are advised again to offer us terms. Your obstinacy benefits neither party.'

'If it was only we elders who had the decision we should have terms by sunset.' He waved a hand at the city. 'But they would tear us apart in the marketplace if we dared it.'

'It would be the better for you if you could persuade them.'

'Each time we try they are fiercer set against it.' He slipped the letter inside his coat. 'But we will try again, and pray for God's protection from our fierce-hearted citizens.'

The councillors withdrew and the gates were closed again. The parley party gathered itself for the return to camp. 'Guard the rear until we're out of range,' Captain Sadeler ordered. The musketeers positioned themselves in a horseshoe shape around the general's party and walked backwards, facing the city. There was a sharp crack of pistol-fire from the parapet above the Brücketor gate. The big Slav musketeer, whom they all called the Bear, stumbled and fell, clutching his thigh. The rest of the musketeers tucked their weapons under their arms and prepared to make fire. Captain Sadeler gave the order. They were not quite out of range, but because they were firing upwards towards the parapets their shots did not carry as far as they might have done on the flat. One or two skimmed the lower part of the walls with a puff of brick-dust, but most fell uselessly into the ground. The parley party, meanwhile, had fled to the bridge and safety. There was more jeering from the citizens on the walls, and a few stones flew down. Lukas and Baxandall helped the Bear to his feet. He was bleeding badly, but at least it was not that wild pumping of blood that would have meant the end of him.

They had just got him steadied when Lukas reeled from what felt like a fierce punch to the head. As he fell he heard another pistol crack, and understood that he was hit. He wondered that the sound of the shot should only reach him after it had found its mark. Someone was pulling at him, urging him to his feet. He scrambled up and tried to open his eyes, but they were so full of blood he could see nothing. He rubbed them with his sleeve. They were retreating now, heading for the bridge and the camp. The citizens of Magdeburg were still shouting after them, but Lukas could no longer distinguish what they were saying. The mockery in their tone told him enough.

When they reached the river Lukas wished he could stop to scoop some water over his face, but they were disordered enough without breaking ranks. Blood was still seeping from his wound, half blinding him, but at least he could walk without assistance. The Bear was being supported by Baxandall and one of the other Slavs. His head was lolling to one side, and his breeches glistened with blood.

As soon as they were over the bridge and out of full sight of the city Captain Sadeler ordered them to lay down the Bear and attend to his wound. A lad rushed out from one of the tents and offered a bundle of rags to staunch the bleeding. Captain Sadeler knelt beside the injured man and bound up his wound. Someone had found a stretcher, and he was loaded on to it. Baxandall and the Slav took an end each, and they all resumed their journey to the camp.

Lukas followed in the rear. The first pain had been succeeded by a fierce burning. The ball had grazed him, he reckoned, but the powder must have scorched his skin.

Word of their trouble had reached the company, and they were met by a press of them. Götz was near the front. He ran up to Lukas, his face pale, his eyes red-rimmed. 'I heard someone was hit badly,' he said.

'It was not me, thank God.' Lukas gestured at the Bear. The stretcher had been laid on the ground.

'But you're hurt.'

'A head wound will bleed so.' Lukas bit his lip to help him resist the urge to touch his burnt face. 'Be a good lad — see if you can find me an onion. And an egg.'

Götz looked perplexed. 'But—-'

'Do as I say. Ask for credit if you must.'

The lad ran off into the heart of the camp. Lukas made his way to their tent and sat down. He felt strangely clear-headed as he always did when he was hurt. The burning of his skin was real enough, but he was somehow detached from it. A few men sat round the Bear. Lukas could see that the bandage on his leg was already soaked through. If the bleeding could not be stopped there was no help for him.

A few minutes later Götz returned, triumphant. 'I could only get a sparrow's egg, but here's an onion.' He handed them to Lukas.

'Now get a cup from the tent, and my other shirt.'

Götz brought them to him. Lukas cracked the egg into the cup, then took his knife from his belt and began to chop the onion into fine pieces. He dropped them into the cup, then mashed everything together with the knife handle. 'This is the best cure for a powder burn,' he said. His eyes were streaming with the tang of the onion.

'Do you eat it?' Götz peered at the mixture. His eyes were even redder now.

'No. Spread it on the skin.' He handed the cup back to Götz. 'I'll lie down here. Cover the burn on my face with that, then tie the shirt round it to make a poultice.'

Lukas lay flat and turned his head so that the injured side was uppermost. Götz dabbed on the paste. The boy had a gentle enough touch, but the mixture burned like the fires of hell on his raw skin. This was a healing pain, though, and worth enduring. Götz made a clumsy bandage with the shirt, and Lukas sat up to put it to rights. 'This is a trick worth remembering, Götz, if ever you're burned. Keep it in place for a day or so. Old women will tell you all sorts of odd cures, and some might soothe your hurt, but this is the only one will cleanse it of harm. It's not the wound that kills, but the following fever.'

Götz nodded gravely. He looked at the Bear. 'What of him? Will he live?'

'Likely not. You may pray for him.'

Around them, small groups of the men stood talking, shaking their heads. The womenfolk were crying. It was hardly the Bear's fate they were mourning. He'd only joined them on the road a month ago, not long enough for him to be considered a true brother. 'Is all well in the company, Götz?'

'It happened while you were gone.'

Lukas understood. 'Captain Gebwiler?'

Götz bowed his head.

'Is he buried?'

'The priest had to run off to give the Rites to Colonel Kehraus's eldest son. There's a bad run of fever going through the younger ones. He said all the burying is to be done at the one time this evening, otherwise he'd be talked hoarse.'

They were silent for a time.

'What do you think of the soldier's life now?' Lukas said at last. 'Don't you wish you had stayed in the seminary?'

'It's too soon to say. I've seen nothing of war yet.'

'You have, though. This is war. Marching and making camp. Going hungry. Getting a lump of yourself torn away by a stray shot. That's all war is, in truth.'

'It appears somewhat different in my books.'

Lukas could think of nothing to say to this. The boy had told him tales of a faraway war that had seemed to be over no more than one man bedding another's wife. He had liked some well enough — the great wooden horse had been a grand trick, although Lukas doubted any citizens would really fall for such a scheme — but most of it seemed nonsense. Such books were of little benefit to a young soldier. An hour spent learning the workings of a musket would be time better spent.

The men who had been gathered round the Bear were dispersing. 'He's dead, then?' Lukas called over.

'Aye,' said one, 'and the priest not yet here.'

Lukas stood up and signalled to Götz. They walked over to where the Bear lay. Someone had covered his face with his kerchief. 'Intercede for him, Götz,' Lukas said, and bowed his head.

Götz spoke a brief prayer.

When Lukas opened his eyes, Baxandall was beside him. He had a spade in his hands. 'Come on,' Baxandall said. 'Captain Sadeler says we're to go and help dig today's graves.'

Lukas and Götz took spades from the back of a wagon. Yes, Lukas thought, this was the truth of war. Marching. Hunger. Burying the dead.

Later the men gathered together to honour Captain Gebwiler in drink, which was plentiful in the camp, and cheaper than food. They made one fire and sat round it. Some told tales of skirmishes and ambushes, but Lukas sat and listened, with Götz by his side. Götz had a jar of some fierce spirit on credit from a Polish sutler, which they shared. It burned Lukas's gullet, but he forced himself to drink his share.

A man laughed as he recalled the morning he'd woken to find a woman snoring in his tent. 'I'd been that full drunk I couldn't mind if I'd taken my pleasure with her or not. And I'd scarce got my head cleared and the woman awake when Captain Gebwiler announced a tent inspection. I'd little wish to be flogged for a sin I couldn't recall committing.'

'Keep that in your mind, young priestkin,' Baxandall called across the fire to Götz. 'Don't be caught with a whore in your tent, or your back will pay the penance.'

'What happened then?' Lukas said, to the tale-teller.

The man laughed again. 'I poked my head out the front of the tent to see how near the captain was. There was a baggage boy walking past, so I called him in to help me. We unpegged the back of the tent, and when Captain Gebwiler drew near I pushed the woman out into the lad's hands. Then I stood at the front, engaging the captain in conversation, though my head was spinning like a windmill in a gale. As soon as Captain Gebwiler's head was inside the tent, the lad took the woman by the hand and trailed her back to her sisters.'

'You did well to fool him,' said Baxandall. 'There's not many who did.'

'Aye, well, he was a fair captain,' the man said.

The rest mumbled agreement, all except Baxandall.

As the hour passed the talk grew coarser. Then came the singing, a fight or two, and tears. In the grey light before dawn Lukas was the only one still in front of the fire's embers. He had drunk himself sober. The wound in his head was throbbing with each beat of his heart. He wasn't sure if it was the dregs of the fever that had taken hold of him on the march, or a new one let in by his injury. From where he sat he could see the spot where the Bear had lain. The ground was dark with blood.

There was movement from the tent behind him. Götz was stirring. He heard the boy yawn and groan. Götz had poked his head out of the opening and was resting his head on his arms. 'Did you not sleep at all?' he asked.

'I was tired right enough, but my mind wouldn't settle,' Lukas told him. 'Don't get that Polish drink again. There's no peace to be had from it.'

'Aye, it gave me strange dreams. My head's not so bad, though, considering.' Götz crawled out of the tent and came to sit beside him. 'You look weary. Is your wound paining you?' His face was pale as ashes in the bleak light.

'It's not so bad.' He looked again at the bloodied place where the Bear had died. 'I'm troubled in my thoughts, young Götz.'

'You mourn for our captain, I suppose.'

'Not that. Not just that. I was thinking of Katherine. I did wrong, leaving her in such a way. If it had been me who'd taken the shot the Bear took yesterday, then I'd have died with that sin on me and no repairing it.'

'Have you made your confession since you left her?'

'There's little time on the march for such.'

'You must speak to the priest, and soon.'

'Aye. I will. But ...'

'What?'

'I'll do my penance and be absolved, but the wrong is still not put right. I brought Katherine to shame. My child, who you tell me lives yet, is a bastard. I should have wed Katherine while I could.'

'What prevented you?'

Lukas laughed bitterly. 'Myself. I'm a soldier. I've no wish to play the husband.' How would it feel, he wondered, to know there was a family waiting for him at the end of the season's fighting? Or to have a wife and child with him here? Someone to tend his clothes and seek food for him. It was a pretty enough picture, but he knew he wouldn't tolerate it for long. He remembered Katherine's moods, her weeping, the foul stench in the birth-room. The wrong was done, and she was dead. In truth he didn't know that he would have put it right if she had lived.

'You could write to the nuns who have care of the child,' Götz said. 'Tell them you'll make amends when next you're in Saalfeld.'

'I cannot write.'

'But I can.' Götz smiled modestly. 'I'll scribe it for you.'

'How would I pay for a letter to be carried to Saalfeld? We've barely enough to feed ourselves.'

Götz's smile cooled. 'It seems you have a brave lot of excuses not to right the wrong.' When Lukas did not reply he went on, 'You must learn to endure a troubled conscience.'

Day was fully broken now, and the sun warmed them. Men were stirring, crawling from their tents with curses. Lukas stood and stretched, trying to ease the ache that ran through his whole body, right to his bones. He looked across the river to the walls of Magdeburg. The bastard who'd clipped him was doubtless in a soft bed, with a bellyful of beer and a woman curled close to him. He was maybe the same bastard who'd thieved the Bear's life. Lukas felt the old anger wake in his chest. He thought of the whore who'd bared her breasts, mocking them, and felt a sour pang of lust. He pushed it away, disgusted that he could be aroused by a drab who wore the taint of a hundred men on her. Somehow his shame drew in the dull guilt he felt about Katherine and the child, which fed his anger.

'If thoughts were *Pfennigs* you'd be a rich man, Weinsburg.'

Lukas jumped and swung round. Captain Sadeler was watching him. 'I was wishing ill on the man who killed the Bear.'

Captain Sadeler nodded. He had kept to his own tent last night, but from his bloodshot eyes he'd drunk as much as the rest of them. 'We may get our revenge in time. The Swedes are on their way, and General Tilly will want the city taken before they're upon us.'

'Surely the citizens will have the wit to capitulate.'

'They're a stubborn breed.' He walked on.

Lukas closed his eyes and let the anger pulse through him again. It was stronger now, as if it knew its time was near.

Seven

THE ROOM WAS STIFLING, BUT GERTRUDE refused to open the windows. 'There's so much fever — I'm almost afraid to breathe in case I inhale some air that has harm in it.' She fanned herself with a pamphlet and shifted in her seat. 'Ach, I can't get comfortable at all.'

'Shall I fetch you a pillow?' Christa stood up from the bench she was sharing with Elsbeth and made to walk out to the staircase.

'Don't bother. It makes no difference. Sit down and talk to me. Why do you never come to see me?'

Christa's skin and undergarments were damp with sweat and she wished she was out in the marketplace, or in her father's workshop, or some other cool place. 'It takes half the day to find food, and Father is all nerves when I go out in case the Emperor's men start the bombardment again. I tell him we must not give in to them.' In truth there was more that made her keep her distance. As her friend's belly swelled with the child in it Christa felt increasingly uneasy in her company. Something about the bringing forth of children sickened her. She feared it was a sign of some lack in her nature. Surely a good Christian girl should long for the blessing of fruitfulness?

'The Emperor's men are thoughtless brutes,' Gertrude said. 'My head pounds when they fire those cannon.'

'No one is buying in the market. Is your father finding it the same?'

'I never listen when he speaks of business.' Gertrude moved around on her seat again. 'I wish you would tell your brother not to be always tempting my husband away from home.' Her lip trembled, and Christa could see that she was about to cry. 'It's not very nice being here alone, my mind full of all that lies ahead of me, and my husband coming in late with the smell of drink on him.'

'Dieter won't heed me. I scarcely see him myself.' That was no lie. Dieter preferred to be anywhere other than at home. He slept late, in spite of their father's strong words, and spent his days God knew where. He came home only to eat and sleep, and sometimes not even that. Christa had heard that many of the young men were being drilled by Falkenberg's officers so there would be a reserve to defend the city. She didn't know if Dieter was of their number, but he had changed. He neither smiled, joked nor teased now.

Gertrude pulled a handkerchief from her bodice and dabbed her eyes. 'I suppose he's running around causing trouble. All the young men are, so my father says. Up on the walls, shouting at the Emperor's men, swaggering around as if they were soldiers.'

'I don't think Dieter has much interest in the Emperor or anyone else.' Christa thought of his threat to join the Swedish army when the soldiers came. What sort of soldier would he make? He'd never obeyed an order in his life. She felt a sharp stab of anger that he could even think of leaving. It would be she who had to tend Elsbeth, she who had to intervene between Father and Andreas when they squabbled, she who had to get work out of Helga. She glanced down at Elsbeth, who was as composed as she always was, her eyes downcast to keep out the distractions of the world.

Sometimes she thought Elsbeth truly was one of the blessed. The anxiety of the times, the gnawing hunger that could never be stilled, the tension in the house seemed to pass her by. If she had her way she would spend every moment in their bedchamber, reading her books and praying. Christa had brought her along today in the hope that a little air and exercise would persuade her to take some soup later on. Elsbeth seemed to be the only person in Magdeburg who didn't care whether she ate or not, and Christa feared she would weaken herself.

Frau Schwarz bustled into the room, carrying a bundle of clean laundry. 'Ah, girls, you can help me with the mending. Jörg's shirts are nearly in pieces.' She handed one each to Christa and Gertrude. 'What about you, little Elsbeth? Has your sister not taught you stitching yet?' Elsbeth smiled vaguely. Frau Schwarz clucked disapprovingly. 'Christa, you must get this girl fit for something. How will she ever keep house if she cannot mend her husband's shirt?'

Christa touched one of Elsbeth's plaits. She didn't like it when Frau Schwarz spoke sharply to her sister. Elsbeth was too gentle and shy to reply for herself. 'I think she'll marry a man so rich that he throws his old shirts away,' she said.

Elsbeth laughed. Christa guessed she hadn't understood the joke, and was just happy to have been kindly addressed.

They worked quietly at the shirts. In fact, they weren't badly worn, and there was little to be done. Gertrude was the first to finish. She folded her father's shirt and set it on her lap, then sighed and tapped her foot. 'I may as well do some more while I have a needle threaded,' she said. 'Christa, would you run up to my bedchamber and fetch the shroud from the trunk that sits under the window?'

Frau Schwarz hesitated, her needle half pulled through a shirtsleeve.

Christa ran upstairs.

Gertrude and Klaus's room was better furnished than the bedchambers in the Henning household. Frau Schwarz had insisted that the bride and groom must have new linen, and had stitched a coverlet made of silk fragments, assembled in a pattern that made Christa's head spin. It felt strange to be in her friend's room, standing close to the bed where Gertrude and Klaus lay together. She wondered again at the mystery of what went on between husband and wife. As a little girl she had thought they would lie side by side, that there was nothing more to it than that. She was wiser now — Dieter had dropped enough hints for her to guess that other things were done.

She froze at a sudden movement under the bed. As she watched, a skinny grey rat scuttled across the floor, squeezed through a gap in the wainscot and vanished. There were more of them than was usual for the time of year, and they had grown bold. Even in the broad daylight of the market they would run about. The gossips said it was because so many dogs and cats had disappeared — the rumours of what had befallen the unfortunate creatures made Christa's stomach heave.

She shook her head to clear her thoughts, then went to the chest below the window and opened it. The coarse linen of the half-made shroud was on top of Gertrude's other garments. She lifted it out, closed the trunk and went downstairs.

Frau Schwarz watched her carry it to Gertrude. 'Thank you, Christa,' Gertrude said, shaking it out and smoothing an unstitched seam.

'Why do you do this to me, daughter?' Frau Schwarz said. Her voice was weak and trembling. 'Do you not think I'm tormented enough by what lies ahead of you? How can you sit there stitching your shroud more merrily than you mended your father's shirt, and me with my heart breaking?' She ended her sentence with a sob.

'I am preparing myself for my final end, Mother. You taught me yourself that a good Christian should keep themselves in readiness for the grave.' Gertrude wore a smug little smile. Christa knew of old how her friend liked to provoke her mother.

'Christa wouldn't do such a thing in front of her poor father, would you, Christa?' Frau Schwarz looked hopefully at her.

'I have not made a shroud.'

'Well, why would she?' Gertrude snapped. 'She won't be dying in childbed before midsummer, will she?'

'Oh, sweet Lord!' Frau Schwarz wailed. 'Preserve my only living child from the great danger of childbirth! "The ropes of death ensnared me: and the pains of hell took hold of me." Dear Lord, I beseech you, deliver my daughter from this peril!'

Elsbeth raised her head. 'The final trump might sound tomorrow. We should all make ready.' She turned to Christa. 'We'll have no need for shrouds then, will we?'

'No, sweetheart.' Christa stroked Elsbeth's hair, hoping that Judgment Day was some way off. 'Pastor Ovens says it's a vanity for women to make their shroud ahead of their time,' she said absently.

Frau Schwarz stopped sobbing. 'Pastor Ovens?' she said sharply. 'Pay him no heed, Christa.'

The room seemed suddenly hotter than before. Christa tried to take a deep breath, but there was little air to be had. 'He is a fine man,' she said. Frau Schwarz and Gertrude glared at her. When they didn't speak she went on, 'He is standing firm against our enemies.'

'What does he know about anything?' Frau Schwarz said. 'He's not even from Magdeburg.'

'How can you say he's a fine man?' Gertrude said. She threw down the shroud and stood up. 'You were at my wedding — have you forgotten how he spoke to me and my Klaus?' Her lip trembled and she walked awkwardly from the room, tripping over her skirts. Christa could hear her footsteps on the stairs up to her bedchamber.

Frau Schwarz walked to where the shroud lay and picked it up. 'You are supposed to be her friend,' she said coldly.

'I'm sorry.' Christa stood, and motioned to Elsbeth to do the same. 'But he is principled. A man of God.'

Frau Schwarz followed Gertrude upstairs. Christa waited for a moment to see if either of them would return. When neither did, she took Elsbeth's hand and they made their way downstairs and out through the workshop.

'Ach, are you girls going so soon?' Herr Schwarz called, as they made for the door. He was working the press, but he had long perfected the art of projecting his voice above the creak of machinery.

'Gertrude was a little ... tearful,' Christa said, not wanting to damn her soul with a full-blown lie.

Herr Schwarz sighed, and paused. 'And I suppose her mother was as bad? I'd hoped that having a son-in-law would shield me from the strife of a house full of women — and the good Lord knows I've endured it for many a long year — but young Klaus has run wild this last while.'

'The young men are all agitated, in their different ways.'

'Aye, the old ones too ... those who have no proper business to attend to.' He turned back to the press. Christa pulled Elsbeth out into the street.

'Shall we go home, sister?' Elsbeth said. She chewed her lip.

Christa knew that she was afraid of being abroad in case the bombardment started again. Even so, she said, 'Not yet. I've heard tell of a man off Petristraße who has salted herring for sale. Let's wander by there and see what we can find.' She linked her arm with Elsbeth's and set off.

The house where the man lived was old and cramped, more wood than brick, but the ground in front of it was swept clean. The door was half open, so Christa knocked and called in. When there was no reply she pushed it wide and they stepped inside. The room was empty. A few sticks lay in the fireplace, but no flame had been set to them. The air stank of fish, and she felt her stomach tighten with hunger.

Christa called again, and this time a man emerged from the back room. 'Who are you?' he said, his eyes glancing from her to Elsbeth. 'What is it you want?'

'I heard tell you had herring for sale.'

'It's all away.'

'You must have some. A little held back.'

'I've none.' He turned to a cupboard and lifted a pistol from inside it. 'I must ready this piece, for there's ones who would rob a man who has earned some honest money.' He nodded towards the door. 'I tell that fool of a wife that she must keep the door closed and barred, instead of letting all walk through the place, as if it was the old times.'

'I have money,' Christa said. 'And I am sure by the smell of this place that you still have some herring.' She untied her purse from her belt.

The man looked at it as intently as if he could weigh it with his eyes. 'You know how it is with fish. The reek lingers.' He was silent for a moment, still gazing at the purse. 'How much have you?'

'You have some left, then?'

'I asked how much money is in that purse.'

It was bad bargaining to reveal what she had to spend, but the man could set whatever price he chose for the herring, and they both knew it. 'The best part of a *Gulden*,' she said. 'But that will be no good to you, since you've no fish to sell me.' She began to tie the purse back to her belt.

'Hold on, girl,' the man said. 'Let me see your money first.'

'But there's no herring left, you say.'

'I might have a scrap, for the right price.' He motioned for Christa to empty the purse onto the table. When she had done so he pushed the coins into a straight line, counting them under his breath. 'Have you something to wrap it? I've not a thing here.'

'I have this.' Christa took a square of waxed sackcloth from her skirt pocket and handed it to him. 'But don't be wrapping it up before I see it.'

'Never worry. I'll not rob you. I'm a Christian man.'

'No doubt you are, but I'll look at what I'm buying before our dealing is done.'

The man grunted, and went into the back room. Christa touched Elsbeth's cheek. 'You will have herring for your dinner, sweetheart,' she whispered. 'We shall make a fine fish soup.'

The man returned, carrying the waxed cloth. He held it out for Christa's examination. The scrap of fish was no bigger than an oak leaf. It was darker than any herring she'd seen before, and curled dry at the edges. Even so, her mouth watered. 'Will that do, *Mädchen?*'

the man said. He stopped short and drew the fish away from her. 'Now that I think of it, I should put it by and save it for my missus. It was meant for her, and she'll likely chew the ear off me for selling it, especially if she hears I got less than a *Gulden* for it.'

Christa looked sharply at him. His tale about his wife had been lies, she knew. 'You have seen what money I have. There's no more, so you may save your patter. Keep your sad story for the next fool to walk in your door.' She prayed he would not hold out for a higher price, for she had nothing more to offer him.

The man looked unconcerned. 'Aye,' he said. 'And the next fool might have more money than you.'

Elsbeth stepped forward and touched the man's arm. 'Jesus is watching us.'

Briefly the man was dumbstruck, his mouth hanging open. Then he looked at Christa. 'Is this some trick?'

'She's a godly child, sir.' Christa tried to hide her own astonishment. Elsbeth so rarely spoke outside their home and she'd *never* spoken to a stranger before.

'We must pray to be worthy of His love and compassion.' Elsbeth clasped her hands and prayed, her lips moving silently.

'Here,' the man said, thrusting the herring into Christa's hands. 'Take it and be off with you.' He swept the coins off the table and into his pocket.

Christa led Elsbeth, who was still praying, out of the house. When she glanced back at the man he touched a finger to the side of his head and made an ugly face. Christa put her arm round Elsbeth's thin shoulders and squeezed her. 'Let's go home to Father.'

The marketplace had been all but empty when they crossed it not half an hour ago, but now it was bustling. A parade of soldiers was progressing across it, with the lower sort of townspeople behind them, faces blazing with eagerness for trouble. Christa grasped her package of fish in one hand and Elsbeth's arm in the other as she pushed her way through. There was always the danger in a press like this that sly fingers would ease the precious food out of her grip without her knowing it.

When they had forced their way to the edge of the crowd she stopped to see what had caused the stir. The citizens were made quarrelsome by hunger, these days, though there was drink for those who had the money to buy it, which led to more fights. The parade across the square, though, seemed a different matter. An odd mood hung in the air that she'd never felt before. But with the throng so thick she could see nothing.

Elsbeth tugged at her arm. 'What goes on, sister?'

Christa turned to the woman beside her, who seemed respectable enough. 'What is it has everyone gathering here?'

The woman's mouth twisted, as if she were trying to cover a smile with a pious expression. 'It is witchcraft, God bless us. Three men accused.'

'And what harm have they caused?'

The woman shrugged. 'Ach, the usual. Sickness. Children failing. Rats everywhere. Somebody's chicken, I heard, dropped dead for no reason.'

Elsbeth threw her arms round Christa's waist. She was trembling.

The woman leaned closer to her. 'It is said they were secretly Papists too, and casting spells for the Emperor's victory.'

'Secret Papists?' Christa looked at the faces in the crowd. Could there be secret Papists among them, even now?

'Aye. Thank God the good Pastor Ovens found them out.'

The shock of hearing his name spoken by a stranger made Christa tremble. *Dieter.* Christa tried to ask the woman what sort of men had been denounced, but she was prevented by an unearthly sound, like the baying of hounds, from the gathered people. Three men were marched up the steps to the courthouse door. Christa's heart beat faster as they came into view, terror gripping her that she might see Dieter's face among them. But, no, they were old. Their hair was grey, not golden-red. *Thank God*, she thought. *Thank you, dear sweet Lord.* She felt light-headed with relief, then immediately contrite because the men stood in peril of life and soul. She looked more intently at them, trying to frame a prayer in her head. One was familiar. The mottled red nose was obvious even at this distance. He was her rude customer, the one who had tried to barter her down on Martin Luther's *Three Treatises*. Could he really be a secret Papist? She had thought ill of him at the time, but she would never have wished this fate on him.

The constables and soldiers forced him and the others through the doors to face the first stage in their descent to hell. Christa was unsure whether she should pray for mercy, repentance or simply a swift death for them. *Thy will be done*, she prayed silently at last. God would know what to do.

The doors closed, but the crowd was slow to disperse. Christa sensed their reluctance. It was a diversion, after all, and she shared their unwillingness to leave. There was a hectic sort of joy here, a means of forgetting the empty larder at home, but Elsbeth was near collapse with fear. She had no choice but to go. The package of fish sweated in her hand. The wax had melted in places, and her skin felt thick with it. As she tried to push her way towards home, she heard a voice say that the three men would be executed the next morning. Another contradicted him: such a business, he said, would have to be conducted with a full council and the bishop to boot; since half the council had left the city before the gates were sealed, and the bishop had never got back in after his visit to Bremen, there was little chance of them being assembled to hear the case. The two men argued, and everyone else judged themselves expert enough to join in. There was only one matter of interest to them, which was that they did not miss the great sport of a burning.

It was the deep of night, but Christa could not sleep. Two days had passed since she and Elsbeth had bought the pickled herring. The soup she'd made had long gone, but hunger made her imagine she could still smell it in the house, even in her bedroom, so far above the kitchen.

The Emperor's men had kept up the bombardment since dawn, and only sunset had silenced them. However, the night hours were no longer a time of silence in Magdeburg. People kept indoors, but the air crackled with their fear. Only the rats were made lively by hunger. If she listened hard Christa could hear the scritch-scratch of their claws on the street outside.

The weather had been so still and dry that for weeks now she had heard the night sounds of the soldiers. Sometimes there was laughter, or voices raised in a quarrel. A drum might be beaten long enough to wake them all, then fall silent. There were musket shots too, as the Emperor's men made fire at the soldiers of the city garrison who patrolled the walls. Perhaps moonlight had glinted on a brass button, or some careless lad had held up a lantern, or the dawn sky offered a soldier's silhouette. It was rare that a night shot hit its mark, but the threat meant no one could rest.

The weather had changed. It was still unseasonably hot — more like August than May — but a hot wind had sprung up this past day. The sounds from the enemy camp came in gusts now, swooping over the walls and away again, like a flock of starlings at sunset.

The house creaked around Christa, in its usual windy-night manner. Sometimes there would be whistling when a blast licked its way along the eaves. Then the wind would change direction and a hollow note would echo down the chimney. A shutter rattled at the window of some other house in the close, perhaps the one that shielded Klaus and Gertrude's bedroom. Were they awake too? Christa hadn't been to the Schwarzes' house since the last disagreement. She knew she should visit, and had even thought of taking over a drop of the fish soup to help build Gertrude's strength, but something had held her back. There had been little enough for the Henning household. Still, she should visit. Make her peace. Maybe that was why she couldn't sleep. She lay on her back, her eyes open in the darkness. Perhaps if she turned towards Elsbeth she would be lulled to sleep by her sister's warmth and steady breathing, but she was certain she had heard some other noise in the house. She didn't know how far off daybreak was, but she was sure it was too early for anyone to be moving about. Too early even for her father to be up at his prayers. When the wind dropped briefly Christa held her breath and listened hard. Yes, there was movement. A creak on the stairs, and a dull thud as if something had bumped down on the floor.

It must be Dieter. He had been at home tonight, and not gone out. Was he downstairs, searching for some scrap of food? Might he be running away? Christa felt sick at the thought of rising in the morning and finding him gone. She slipped out of bed and tiptoed towards the door. He couldn't go. The garrison soldiers and Falkenberg's men had as little food as the rest of them – they'd take no new recruits until the King of Sweden came to raise the siege. Still ... someone was afoot in the house.

She opened the bedroom door quietly and waited. From each of the rooms around her she could hear breathing: Elsbeth's soft snore behind her, the familiar night-breath of her father in his room, and Helga's grunts from her cupboard bed along the corridor. Nothing from Dieter's room. Carefully she crept to his closed door and laid her ear against it. There was a creak from inside, as if a sleeper had turned over. Christa recoiled, wondering if it were possible that her presence had somehow disturbed Dieter and Pastor Ovens. *Thump.* There it was again. Somebody was downstairs.

The wind picked up. As it played its notes on the angles of the house Christa crept down the stairs. Any sound she made was lost in its keening. She reached the landing on the first floor. The door to the main room was closed, and there was no chink of light at its edges. She went on down to the ground floor and the hallway that lay between the back kitchen and the workshop. When the wind subsided for a moment she could hear Andreas in his narrow bed against the near wall. As the next gust hit the house the kitchen door opened a fraction, then closed again. It had been loose in its frame for as long as Christa could remember. The moon must be shining in through the window, because each time the door moved the darkness in the hallway was sliced through with a pale light. And there was that sound again – as if a window were being pushed open. It was coming from the kitchen. She could hear the rasp of wood on wood, and a grunt such as a man would make when straining at his work.

There was a sudden rush of air and the door opened wider than before, then banged shut. Christa rested her hand on the door handle. What if it wasn't Dieter? It might be some half-starved vagrant, driven to housebreaking by hunger. She should wake Andreas, but he was always so slow to stir. Whoever was in the kitchen would be long fled by the time Andreas was on his feet. Christa took a deep breath and opened the door.

Pastor Ovens was looking out of the open window. His little travel trunk was on the bench that sat close by. For a moment he didn't notice her. Instead he continued to peer outside, glancing at his trunk as if he was trying to work out the best way to transport it and himself through the window. Then something made him look back. He flinched when he saw her, bringing his hands up to his chest as if he feared for his heart.

'What are you doing?' Christa asked.

'I ...' He swallowed hard. 'I ...'

'You are leaving?'

'I am.'

Christa tried to understand what she was seeing. 'But why now, in the depths of the night? If you wished to go you had only to say.' It was discourteous of him, insulting to her father; to them all. She was about to say as much, but stopped short. What if he was going because of Dieter? He might be planning to denounce him this very morning. The three men she had seen brought to the courthouse had still not come to trial. They were waiting, even now, in some dark cell under the city. Did Pastor Ovens intend Dieter to join them? *Tread carefully*, she thought.

Pastor Ovens seemed to have gathered himself together. He looked her up and down. She felt her face burn, and thanked God that the moonlight from beyond the window was dim enough to offer her a cloak of modesty. The stone floor felt cold under her bare feet.

'I intend to crave admittance to the retinue of Falkenberg.' He touched the white kerchief at his neck. 'I believe I have done both him and his master, the Swedish king, good service in promulgating God's will for the city. He will not, I hope, deny me.'

'I don't understand. Could you not have waited until the morning? Must you really creep away like this?' Christa thought of how Dieter would laugh at the idea of the pastor heaving himself out of the kitchen window. Lord, Dieter would split his sides when he heard of it.

'By morning it may be too late,' Pastor Ovens said. His voice sounded different now: there was no fervour, no deliberation.

The wind blew in through the window, making her shiver. 'They mean to attack, then?'

'Of course. What else have these past days been leading to? And the King of Sweden is still more than a week's march away.'

'Then we must stand and fight, mustn't we?'

He made no reply.

'I've heard it said that Falkenberg will lead us,' she went on. 'That is what he has promised. Is that why you are going to him? So that you can help him in the fight?'

'Yes,' he said. 'You have it right.' His voice was thick and he gulped air like a man with pleurisy. 'Would you be so good as to hand my trunk through the window after me?' He turned and pulled up his robes, the better to climb out. Dieter would have roared with laughter at the sight of him. Christa watched as he hauled himself over the sill and let himself drop into the alley. He reached back into the kitchen, and she lifted the trunk out to him. She staggered under its weight, even though it was small. Full of books, no doubt. He nodded to her, and walked quickly away, the sound of the wind drowning his footsteps. Christa closed the window. The end was coming, and he had gone.

She heard the workshop door creak open. Andreas must have awakened. She called his name, in case he was poised in the hallway with a cudgel in his hands to beat off a housebreaker. 'All is good, Andreas. It is only I.' The kitchen door swung open.

'What's going on?' Andreas had the cudgel so it was as well she'd spoken.

'Pastor Ovens has gone.'

'Good. We're well rid of him. Your father will say so too.' He glanced around the kitchen. 'What has he taken? Any food he could lay his hands on, at a guess.'

'No! He has taken nothing, I'm sure of it.' Even as she spoke, Christa realised that she was not at all sure. 'Would he steal from us?'

'He has sucked us like a leech these last three months.' Andreas tensed, and gave Christa a hard look. 'You knew he was going, didn't you? You aided him.'

The idea was so ridiculous that she laughed — and stopped as she realised the insult in Andreas's words. He started to speak again, but she could not bear to listen and pushed past him into the hallway. She would have taken the stairs at a run, but she feared to wake the rest of the household. She needed time to compose her thoughts. It would be daybreak by and by, and there would be no more sleep for her this night, she knew, but if she could at least lie down in her bed, with the rhythm of Elsbeth's soft breathing to soothe her, she might calm herself for the questions that the morning would bring.

Eight

THE WIND DROPPED AN HOUR BEFORE dawn, and it was the silence that woke Lukas. He lay under the motionless canvas. All night it had slapped and cracked as one gust after another had stirred it. There had been a time when he had thought the whole cursed tent might fly away, with himself and Götz tangled up in it. Now all was still. The air stank with their filth. It had been too long since he'd found the means to wash. The river was rank with the waste that flowed from the camp: the piss and shit of men and horses; weapons broken beyond use; chicken bones boiled and boiled again until there was no goodness to be got out of them; the slow and terrible seepage from the burying ground. Everything fouled and ruined made its way to the river, so that it, too, was ruined, and fit for no good thing.

Götz stirred in his sleep and rolled over. Lukas turned his face away from the boy's breath. A man could get drunk again just smelling it. This would be the day. He was sure of it. All of yesterday the cannon had fired at the walls on the eastern side, while at the other approaches the musketeers and pikemen had worked to build redoubts able to withstand the snipers on the parapets above. It had been dangerous work. Men of arms such as himself had taken turns to dig and guard. Lukas preferred the digging, hard as it was. At least when he was bent over a trench with every muscle screaming he could blank out thought. If a shot should come from the walls and blast a hole in him, so be it. He had laboured like a farmer's beast, blind to everything but the clay under his spade. The hours on guard duty were harder: his eyes had burned with the strain of watching the walls, and his nerves were ground to dust between the millstones of boredom and fear.

The digging was done, though his body was still racked with it, like the ache of a bad memory. Today they'd return to the redoubts, giving cover to the powder-men who would spike the walls with small charges to weaken the structure. There was movement now, out in the camp. The men were stirring. Someone pulled open the front flap of the tent and whispered that they should ready themselves. Lukas shook Götz awake, and crawled outside, dragging his musket and accoutrements after him.

It was still dark. Captain Sadeler was walking around the company, accompanied by a boy with a shaded lantern. Now and again he would stop and give instruction to one or other of his junior officers. Lukas checked his musket by touch. He had cleaned it as best he could last night and made up a bagful of ammunition. Powder was plentiful in the camp, thank the Lord. At least the weapons would not go hungry.

Lukas stood to attention as the captain approached him. 'Well, Weinsburg,' he said, 'our payday may have come at last.'

'We're to take the town, then, sir?'

'Aye. The bombardment will commence as soon as the sky lightens. General Tilly wants us in place before then.' He looked around as the men gathered in loose file. 'We're for the Fürstenwall gate. A light cannon was carried there last night. As soon as the gate's breached we're to humble the garrison and subdue the citizens.'

'Are we to take prisoners?'

'The people of quality, yes. Any person who looks as though they might be ransomed.'

'What of the common citizens?'

'General Tilly says we're to give quarter where it's honestly asked for.'

'Is there food in there, do you think, sir?'

Captain Sadeler shook his head. 'Little enough, I'd say. I've heard it rumoured they've been feeding on the best cat and dog stew.' He gave a little laugh. 'But there's gold in plenty.'

'And we may take what we will?'

'Aye.' The captain leaned closer to him. 'What shall we feed to today's prisoners, eh? Does the general expect us to share our ration with them?'

Lukas was shocked by his words. The common fighting men would criticise their betters often enough, and earn a beating for it if they were overheard, but he had never heard an officer complain about General Tilly before. He did not dare reply to Captain Sadeler.

The captain looked about him. 'Where's your young friend?'

'Still in his bed.' Lukas kicked at the tent, harder than he needed to. 'Wake up, Götz, you sluggard. There's a battle to be won.' There was a groan and a mumbled response.

Captain Sadeler motioned for Lukas to come closer to him again. 'Is the boy able for the musket, do you think?'

'He's well enough practised now, but how he'll manage it in the heat of strife I don't know.'

'Aye. He'll polish his skills in the fury, just as we all did.' He eyed Lukas steadily. 'Do well today and you may find your station improved.'

Lukas's mouth dried. 'I hope to earn some honour this day, for the Emperor and for myself.' Captain Sadeler nodded and walked on to the next group of men.

Götz wriggled out of the tent like a sheep escaping the fold. 'What need had you to give me a dig like that?' he grumbled. 'You near broke my ribs.' He stood up and stretched. 'What was the captain saying?'

Lukas gave Götz the gist of Captain Sadeler's instructions. He left out all mention of what mercy they were to show or withhold. Götz would be blooded soon enough. Let him live in innocence a while longer. 'Have you every item ready for your weapon?' he asked.

'I think so.'

'We'll check together. As well to be sure now than to find you're wanting later.'

They ran through a check that everything was to hand. Lukas knew from of old that this was the best way to calm the nerves. Once the action had begun all would be well. It was in this waiting time that a soldier could lose his nerve. Götz, though, seemed easily distracted. Every other moment he looked up at the city, its walls black against the grey sky. 'Do you think they know what is to befall them?' he said, propping his musket, stock down, on the ground.

'If they have any wit they'll understand well enough. Our cannon have been announcing the general's scheme these last days.'

'It must be a strange thing to belong to a place like this.'

'Sometimes, Götz, I haven't a notion what goes on in that head of yours.' Lukas punched his arm lightly. 'And don't use your weapon like a cripple's stick. Sling it over your shoulder like a man.'

Götz did as he was told. 'Don't you ever wonder, though, how it would be to bide in a place where your kin have always been? That's what they're like here. I heard Captain Sadeler say as much.'

'You had lived all your life in Saalfeld, had you not?'

'I don't know where I'm from. My mother and I were travelling when she fell ill and died.'

'But you know your name.'

'Aye. That's a blessing, I suppose. But that's not what I mean. Captain Sadeler said that when a Magdeburg man is laid in the ground his bones will be keeping company with his father and grandfathers, and every generation of his family.'

145

'We're soldiers. We belong nowhere.' Lukas found it hard to attend to Götz's words. His mind was filled with the idea that the captain had put into his head: that this day might be the mending of his fortunes. If he acquitted himself well — did the captain some service, perhaps — he might be a lance corporal by sunset.

One of the other men came close and motioned that they were to muster. The drummer was silent this morning. The citizens of Magdeburg would not be forewarned as to what the Emperor's men were about. Lukas and Götz took their places in the company and, on the signal, marched forward, down towards the bridge. It was light enough now that Lukas could see the faces about him. He glanced back at the camp and saw that the soldiers were still coming. The very ground seemed to be moving, yet there was barely a sound. No drums or fifes. No shots. Not even the heavy tramp of marching men. There was something else — a whisper. Like the noise the wind made when it hissed over a field of wheat.

Company after company poured forward from all parts of the camp. All were marching towards the bridge, and as they converged each one would halt, waiting for their turn to cross. When it was time for Captain Sadeler's men to make their journey, he indicated to them that they should cross as softly as they could.

The silence was cracked open by a volley of shots from the city walls. Quiet as they might be, it was near daylight, and the men of the garrison were not blind. Someone was hit to Lukas's left, but they kept moving, heading for the safety of the redoubt at the Fürstenwall gate. Lukas checked that Götz was keeping up. The lad nodded to him, his eyes bright with excitement, no trace of fear. He might make a good enough soldier yet.

For the next several hours they were entrenched. Before the bombardment began Captain Sadeler had ordered them to husband their shot wisely. 'Don't waste a musket ball on those walls,' he'd said. 'Let the cannon do their work. Make fire only where you have a fair chance of striking home at one of the garrison.'

After that there was no more talking. The cannon made an end of words. Lukas, Götz and the other musketeers of the company stayed crouched in their redoubt, watching as the eighteen-pounders were loaded, fired and loaded again. The walls seemed solid enough, although they were pocked where the cannon balls hit. Brick-powder flew at every strike, and the air was so filled with dust and smoke that the sun was invisible. Lukas could not tell what time it was. The wind had picked up again, and while it brought some relief from the heat of their crush in the redoubt, with every gust it blinded Lukas's eyes with pain. He showed Götz how to tie his neckerchief over his mouth and nose so that he could breathe.

It was almost impossible in the thickened air to take aim at the garrison soldiers who manned the wall. One or two of the company tried, but Lukas held back. Götz would not be restrained, though. The shot fell short of the wall, and he lowered his musket quickly. Lukas felt a pang of sympathy for the boy. His first shot in battle had been inglorious.

Such entrenchment as they endured was the hardest part of storming, Lukas always thought. The men of the cannon had their work to do, and the pikemen had been set to undermining the walls with yet more digging, but the musketeers were forced to stand idle. Lukas could sense the battle-need in them, like molten lead almost at the point of boiling over. It wasn't anger exactly. They were standing so close together, crushed on every side, that it seemed to him they were one man, with this same feeling running through every part of every body.

Lukas had found his own way to live through the waiting time. His thoughts became absent. Neither life nor death was real to him. There was no fear, no hope, no prayer. That would come later, if he lived long enough. His very limbs might have been someone else's. He felt their pain, yet did not feel it. In this trance he could stand for hours without flinching. They all could.

Time stretched on. It might have been an hour or half a day. The cannon fell silent, and a voice cried that the wall was breached.

Lukas felt the tension tighten through the men in the redoubt. Götz was by his side. 'Is it true?' he said. 'Are the walls breached?'

'Wait for our order,' Lukas said. 'When we go, move fast. Don't pause to look for the garrison men on the wall. Caution will kill you now, not haste.'

'Can I stay close to you?'

There was a little fear in the lad's eyes, and that was good, Lukas thought. A seasoning of fear rendered the fight more flavoursome. 'Aye. Keep with me.'

Captain Sadeler pushed through to the front and scrambled over the lip of the redoubt. He surveyed the lie of things, then turned back to them. 'In we go, lads,' he shouted. 'This maiden city is deflowered.' He strode towards the walls, and the rest of the company followed him.

There were shots from the top of the wall, and one man fell injured at Lukas's feet. He and Götz hauled him up and dragged him to the shelter of the wall. 'Stay there, friend,' Lukas said, propping him against it. 'If you're still living at day's end we'll fetch you back to the surgeon.'

'I'll be grand when I get my breath,' the man said, pressing one hand over the wound in his shoulder.

Lukas pulled Götz towards the breach. The cannon had weakened the wall where it met the Fürstenwall gate. While the gate itself was still closed a hole pierced the brickwork, big enough for them to enter four abreast. The pikemen had already laid ladders to help them reach it. There would likely be soldiers from the garrison on the other side, ready to greet them with a bellyful of lead shot. Lukas made sure that he and Götz kept to the middle of the company. The first through the breach would take the worst of it, while any stragglers might be picked off, or at the least marked down as fainthearts. He noticed that Baxandall was in the vanguard, eager to lay his hands on whatever treasures awaited them. Captain Sadeler was more canny, keeping to the centre like Lukas. He was shouting orders that no one could hear in the riot of men.

As Lukas climbed one of the ladders the wind blew hard again.

He had to feel his way up the rungs, his eyes clenched shut against the dust. This was dangerous, right enough. If they were stumbling through the breach half blinded, the garrison men's work would be done for them. The wind would hardly be as fierce inside the walls as it was without. Lukas reached the top of the ladder and forced himself to open his eyes. At first the street below looked deserted, but there was likely an armed man crouched behind every wall and round every corner, and the air was clouded with powder-smoke. It was hard to tell which were the Emperor's men and which belonged to the city.

Lukas scrambled down the rubble the cannon had made. The instant his feet touched the cobbles he turned to find Götz, and they ran for a low wall that was already giving shelter to others of the company. When he was sure they were as well shielded as they might be, Lukas checked his musket and peered over the wall. A garrison soldier was running from one alley to another not fifty yards in front of him so he made fire. The shot took the soldier in the chest, but he must have been equipped with armour beneath his coat because the blow merely threw him back without appearing to harm him. Lukas cursed at the waste of a ball. Had he struck him in the neck that would have made an end of him. The soldier found his haven in the alley before Lukas could reload.

They were caught in their position for a time. Captain Sadeler was of their party now, and so was Baxandall. At last there was a lull in the fire from the garrison men. Some of their company broke forward. One was taken down by an enemy shot, but others ran further into the town. 'Will you go on now, Captain?' Lukas said.

'I'll bide a while yet. Better to be sure that these bastards are quelled than risk our blood.' He looked at the small group crouched behind the low wall. 'You may make your own choice. On this ground you're masterless.' Two more of the company exchanged a glance and bolted out from their shelter. Their run flushed out a garrison man who was shooting from the first-floor window of a building that overlooked the street. Now only Captain Sadeler, Baxandall, Lukas and Götz were left behind the wall.

Lukas made ready his musket. 'I shall find my way in to our friend up there,' he said. 'Cover me while I cross the street.'

'Can I come with you?' Götz said, his own piece already primed and ready.

'Aye. Why not?' The boy was better with him than left here. He'd be of little use in covering the run, so he might as well be at his side. 'Move fast, mind. No stopping to look about you. We go on my signal.'

As soon as they left the cover of the wall the soldier made fire from the window above, but his shot struck the ground and did no worse harm than add more dust to the air. Lukas knew it would take him a half-minute at least to reload, and that was time enough for them to gain the doorway of the house. It was barricaded, as he had known it would be. He and Götz put their shoulders to it, but it wasn't for shifting. There was a window close by, and Lukas used his knife to break open the shutters. The blade was bent beyond help in the doing, but he pushed it back into his belt, not liking to throw away any metal thing. 'Be careful in here,' he said quietly to Götz. 'We've seen one, but there may be more.'

He helped Götz up and through the window, then followed. When they stood inside they paused to let their eyes clear. There was dust in the air, even here, but it was better than outside, and there was no wind to torture them. Lukas looked about the room. All the furniture had been stacked against the front door. There was no sign of food, or of the kind of treasure that would fit into a man's satchel. The floorboards above them creaked, and Lukas gestured Götz towards the bottom of the stairs.

Beyond the city boundary the Imperial cannon were at work again, and in the lull that followed the barrage Lukas fancied he could hear the clatter of brick on brick, as another part of the wall tumbled. The soldier in the room above fired into the street again. Another wave of the Emperor's men must be pouring through the breach. Götz signalled that he was for going upstairs, and Lukas nodded his agreement.

They crept upwards. Lukas let Götz go first. The boy was light-footed, and quick enough that he would have a chance of ducking if the soldier turned on him. At the top Lukas checked that his slow-match was still lit, and made sure Götz did the same. At a nod from him, Götz kicked the door open.

The soldier spun round and raised his musket at them. Götz got his shot off first, but it bedded itself in the wall a good three feet from their target. Lukas pushed Götz aside, out of the way of the soldier's reply, then raised his own weapon. Gun-smoke swirled around the room.

The soldier swung his musket barrel down to use the stock as a cudgel. His chest was armoured with a cuirass, but he had no helmet. Lukas knew that any shot he took would be wasted. This man looked seasoned enough to see it coming, and he'd use the moment of firing as his chance to charge the door. He lowered his weapon. 'Is there food here?' he said.

The soldier grimaced. 'There's been little food in Magdeburg this long while.' He fixed his grip on the barrel of his musket. 'What's your price for giving me quarter?'

'Leave down your weapon.'

The man looked from Lukas to Götz and back again. 'I have your word you'll give me quarter?'

'Aye.'

He laid his musket on the floor. 'It's a piece of shit anyway. No man could get off a straight shot with it.' He nudged the gun with his boot. As he did so, Lukas raised his own weapon and made fire full in the soldier's face. The man fell, clutching his mouth, which looked to be coming apart under his hands. There was a deal of blood on the floor. As the man's body juddered in convulsions Lukas remembered Matko, the little Croat, dancing from the hanging tree. He shook his head to chase the memory away. His victim gave a strangled scream, and as the sound died away his body stilled.

Lukas walked to the window. The street was empty again. The latest wave of the Imperial troops must have moved through. 'We're clear in here, Captain,' he shouted down. Captain Sadeler and Baxandall came out from behind the wall and ran to the house. Lukas turned to Götz. 'We should make a search of the place. Food, drink, anything that can be pocketed and sold, you understand?'

Götz was staring at him. 'You promised him quarter.'

'Stop acting the woman. Look for food. Better yet, search our friend's body.' There was noise below, as Captain Sadeler and Baxandall tore the house apart in the search for anything worth taking. Götz didn't move. Lukas walked across the room and took hold of him. 'You made fire at him.' He dug his fingers into Götz's arm until the boy was helpless with the pain of it. 'You'd have killed him, and thought yourself the big man for doing it. So don't turn priest on me now.' He shook him hard. 'Do you understand me?'

Götz nodded and pulled away.

'Now let's search him.' Lukas knelt down, crossed himself, and worked his way through the dead man's pockets. 'Pull his boots off,' he ordered Götz.

'They're in no state worth having,' Götz said.

'Do as I say.'

Götz stooped and hauled them off. The sole came away from one as he tugged at it. 'They're falling apart, see?'

'Shake them out, then take a feel at the lining.'

Götz obeyed again. A small key dropped out onto the floor. Götz probed the inside of the boot with his fingers. 'There's something in the lining.'

'Cut it free. My blade is destroyed.'

Götz slashed open the lining, then turned the boot upside-down again. A length of gold chain slithered out. 'Treasure!' he said, and looked up at Lukas. 'My first booty.'

You soon forgot your scruples, Lukas thought. There was nothing like the glint of gold to quiet the conscience. Just as well too. 'Don't count on it staying yours,' he said. 'It's as well to give your captain first refusal of all you find. It'll make him sweeter disposed to you. Now, lend me that knife.' Lukas cut the brass buttons off the soldier's coat, and added them to the little pile of treasure. The coat itself had been ruined with blood, but it was badly worn anyway. It would have fetched nothing from the traders in the camp. Götz worked his way over the body, feeling for concealed coins or other valuables. Together they undid the man's belt and bandolier. The powder-flask was well made, and might fetch a few *Taler*.

Captain Sadeler and Baxandall came pounding up the stairs and into the room. Baxandall was carrying a stone liquor jar. 'There's damn all food here,' he said, 'but we can quench our thirst at least.' He offered the jar to Captain Sadeler.

'Let our comrades taste it,' the captain said. 'They've been hard at work.'

Lukas took the jar from Baxandall and gulped a long draught of the brandy. Pray God it would fill him until some food could be found. 'Precious little we got for our labours.' He indicated the items they had looted from the dead soldier. 'There's his weapon too, although he spoke none too well of it.' He passed the jar to Götz, who drank more even than he had.

'Take it, if you will,' Captain Sadeler said. 'I'd rather it was useless in our hands than left here for the enemy.'

Lukas lifted the musket and bandolier, and let Captain Sadeler scrape up the rest of their takings. They finished the brandy and left the house. Lukas could feel the liquor in his blood already. It strengthened him.

They pressed on through the city, short swords at the ready. The ground was thick with men, and the dust and smoke were so dense at times that it was hard to tell friend from foe. They turned one corner and came upon a pair of Magdeburg lads, armed only with butchers' knives. One dived forward and made a cut in Götz's sword arm. Lukas battered him over the head with the stock of the dead soldier's musket until he lay still. When he turned from his work he saw that Baxandall was standing over the other boy, whose throat was cut clean through. Baxandall didn't bother to wipe his sword. Götz looked pale, but there was little blood seeping into his sleeve. 'You may work with your other arm,' Lukas said, and they moved on.

The next house they passed was a tavern. Two men rolled a hogshead of beer out of the doorway and struck off the pivot. There was a rush of men towards it, and more than one fight broke out as they jostled to get their mouths under the tap. Another man staggered out of the tavern, fumbling with his breeches. 'There's sport to be had in there, lads,' he shouted, to no one in particular.

'Shall we take a look, Captain?' Baxandall said.

'Aye, do as you please.'

They shoved their way in through the doorway. Lukas grasped the back of Götz's coat. He didn't want to lose the boy in the crush. The air inside was thick with the bittersweet smell of beer and the stink of men. Götz grabbed a pitcher of beer from another man and drank as much as he could before it was snatched back. Lukas pushed him forward before the other took his revenge. There were men clustered around the door that led to the back room. One noted Captain Sadeler and judged his rank from his clothes and manner. 'Will you take your turn here, sir?' he said, pointing into the room.

The men stood aside to let Captain Sadeler through. Baxandall, Lukas and Götz followed. They saw two women on the floor. One had been stripped naked, and a white-haired old soldier was taking his pleasure on her. He was losing heart, and his companions called to him, some with words of encouragement, others with insults and vulgarity. The girl's skin was very white against the stone floor. Lukas felt a guilty stirring in his blood as he glimpsed her breast, gripped in the old soldier's fingers. The other woman knelt beside the girl, holding her hand. She still had her dress on, but her bodice had been cut open, and her breasts were slack, as if she'd reared many a child. Lukas saw that her face was wet with tears, and her mouth bloodied. The old man had exhausted himself, and the others pulled him off the girl. She struggled to sit up and clung to the older woman. Seeing them now, Lukas recognised the resemblance between them. Mother and daughter, he thought. Perhaps they were the tavern keeper's wife and child. The desire died in him, and he felt only a sense of his own sinfulness. There was anger too — at himself, yes, but at these women also, for making him feel his guilt. He felt a hand on his arm, and turned to see Captain Sadeler's face close to his. 'You may do as you please, Weinsburg. A soldier must have his recreation.'

'Thank you, sir, but no.'

'By God, you're a pattern of virtue.' The captain smirked. 'And what of your young friend, Fuhrmann?'

Lukas turned to Götz. The lad's face was unreadable. He looked as if he might faint if he wasn't got into the air. 'I believe he's too tender in years for such doings, sir.'

Captain Sadeler was still smiling, but there was anger in his voice when he spoke. 'By Christ, someone better prove that we've men in the company.' He turned to Baxandall. 'You'll not act the maiden, will you?'

'So long as I can have the young one, sir, I'll oblige you,' Baxandall said, with a sidelong look at Lukas. He stepped forward to the cheers of the other men, loosened his breeches, pushed the girl back down onto the floor and applied himself to his task.

Lukas looked away. He sensed Captain Sadeler's eyes on him. Some other man pushed past them and set about the older woman. The cheers grew louder.

Lukas found it hard to breathe. His mind was all turned about, with the heat and noise and drink. He felt someone drag at his coat and let himself be led out of the back room, through the main part of the tavern and into the street. The cursed wind was still blowing, but it was better to be outside than in the stale air of that room.

He looked to see who had brought him outside. It had been Götz. The boy leaned against the doorframe. The blood from his wound had dried on his sleeve, and none fresh was leaking out.

They waited until Captain Sadeler and Baxandall joined them. 'What ails you, Weinsburg?' Baxandall said. 'Were you not able for her? If a pretty young thing like that can't stir you I fear you're no man at all.'

'I'd no wish to go where so many others had been.'

155

'Right enough,' Captain Sadeler said. 'She's probably had half the army march through her.' He slapped Baxandall's shoulder. 'Perhaps she'll give us a taste of the French disease to remember her by. That will be a fine memento to give your little wife, won't it?'

Baxandall glowered and pointed at Lukas. 'More likely he feared he'd be shamed like the old boy who went before me. Not up to the job, eh, Weinsburg?'

It seemed to Lukas then that something exploded inside his head. He leaped at Baxandall and grabbed him by the throat. As he tightened his fingers on the muscles and bones, hands tried to drag him away. The rage in him was too strong to be prevented, and he knew he would kill Baxandall before he was done. He'd be hanged, to be sure, but even that fearful thought could not loosen his grip…

Suddenly there was a blow to his head, and darkness. When he came to there was dust in his mouth. He was lying face down on the road, his head pounding with pain. Someone kicked him. 'Get up, you bloody fool,' Captain Sadeler said.

Now Götz was helping him to his feet. Baxandall stood at a safe distance, rubbing his neck. 'You're a fucking lunatic, Weinsburg,' he said. His voice sounded damaged.

Lukas reached up and touched the back of his head. It felt wet, and when he brought away his fingers they were tipped with blood. 'You may thank me for saving you from the gallows,' Captain Sadeler said, wiping the stock of his musket clean. 'Better a grazed scalp than a broken neck, eh?'

'Pardon me, sir,' Lukas said.

'Save your fury for the enemy. Now, come — we've found neither food nor treasure this day.'

Nine

ONCE THE WHOLE HOUSEHOLD WAS AWAKE and gathered around the breakfast table Christa told them of Pastor Ovens's departure. Her father was silent at the news, staring at the meagre breakfast before him. Seemingly he had no appetite. When she said that the clergyman had gone to join Falkenberg, Dieter snorted derisively. 'Do you think Falkenberg would have one such as him? We need useful men now — men who can defend the city with weapons, not words.'

'I doubt he's gone to Falkenberg in the hopes of joining him in battle,' Herr Henning said. 'If the city falls, the likes of Falkenberg will be ransomed.'

Christa thought back to what Pastor Ovens had said to her last night. He was certain that the city would be taken this very day. She tried to steady her breathing. 'Do you mean he left us to save himself?'

Her father nodded, keeping his eyes on her face. 'He has calculated he'll be better placed if he's in the entourage of a nobleman.'

So he had gone to preserve his own life and not considered hers. If she had not discovered him last night he would have run away without a word. She had been led by him to find fault with the dear people around her. He had sown dissension in this house, and she had helped him. As bitter as his desertion was, her sense that she had betrayed her family – in spirit at least – was more so. And then there was the most fearful thought of all: he had fled because he did not have faith that he would be safe in this house. The city would fall today, and the Hennings' home would be no defence against the Emperor's men. When she looked up Dieter was scowling at her contemptuously. 'You picked a fine man to be your idol, sister.'

She wanted to make a sharp reply, but tears stung her eyes. Helga was slouched in her seat, trying to hide a grin behind her hand. Andreas studied the tabletop as if it held infinite interest. Elsbeth shuffled closer to her on the bench, and Christa realised that her little sister had never seen her cry before. She blinked away the tears.

Father stood and rested his hand on Christa's shoulder. 'Wiser heads than yours were turned by Pastor Ovens and his fiery words.'

'Trust you to take her side,' Dieter spat. 'She's been opposing you this past quarter year, nurturing that bastard Ovens, and still you defend her.'

'Your sister could not have known it would come to this.'

They fell silent as the bombardment started. After a short while Dieter stood and went to the door. 'Son,' Herr Henning said, raising his voice above the cannon fire, 'where are you going?'

'We'll not find out what's afoot by sitting here like fools. I'm away to the walls. The soldiers will have the news.'

'Dieter, please, no ...'

Dieter ignored his father and clattered down the stairs. Herr Henning went to the window. Christa guessed he must have watched until Dieter was out of sight, and she thought she understood why. *He thinks he may never see him again.*

Time passed, but it was hard to tell how long. If the church bells were still ringing out the quarter-hours they could not be heard over the thunder of the bombardment. Herr Henning paced the room, stopping each time he passed the window to look out into the close. At length the cannon fire stopped. Now there was only the sound of the wind. It rattled the glass in the window-frame. Elsbeth began to pray out loud, and Christa closed her eyes to join in.

'It's Dieter!' their father cried, rousing them from their devotions. Christa leapt up and ran to the window. Dieter was racing through the covered alleyway as if the hounds of hell were at his heels. She went downstairs quickly to let him in.

He stumbled into the workshop and slammed the door behind him. 'Bar it, for God's sake,' he gasped, barely able to get the words out.

Christa did as he bade her. 'Praise the Lord that you are returned safely,' she said, as tears filled her eyes again.

'Aye. Praise the Lord.' He leaned against the press, struggling to catch his breath.

'What have you seen, Dieter?' she asked, although she feared the answer.

He rubbed a hand over his eyes. 'They nearly got me.'

'Who did? Not the Emperor's men?'

'The walls are breached at the Fürstenwall gate. Maybe in other parts too. I don't know.'

'My God.' Christa thought of the rest of the household waiting upstairs for news. 'We had better tell them.'

Dieter's lips were pressed together as if he feared to speak again.

When they entered the room the first thing Christa noticed was the silence. The bombardment had stopped. She looked at Dieter, but he shook his head and sank onto a seat by the empty hearth. 'The enemy are through the walls, Father,' she said.

Helga moaned and threw herself into Andreas's arms. At any other time Christa might have smiled at her craftiness, but not now.

'Dieter,' said their father, 'is there any instruction from the garrison? From Falkenberg?'

Dieter's face was drained of colour. 'They nearly had me, Father. Two had me cornered, and I thought …' His breath was coming in short gasps.

His father crouched in front of him, placing a hand on each shoulder. 'Gather your wits, son. Have courage.'

Andreas had shaken Helga off and gone to the window. He opened it and leaned out, with Christa beside him. 'Do you see anything?' she whispered.

'No, but ... Hush a moment.'

They both listened. A bell rang somewhere not far off, a hand bell. A crier was calling. 'Can you hear what he says?'

Andreas shook his head. 'I'll away out and see if I can get closer.'

'Be careful.'

He was back within a few minutes. 'We are to stay inside,' he said.

Dieter looked up from his place by the hearth. 'On whose instruction?'

Andreas swallowed. 'General Tilly's.' He looked at Herr Henning. 'The streets are empty, sir. The crier gave General Tilly's promise that if we obey we'll come to no harm.'

Christa felt the fear loosen its grip on her. 'Well, thank God,' she said. 'Perhaps now that the walls are breached there'll be terms reached. Isn't it as you said, Father? We'll pay them a tribute and they'll be on their way?'

'We must pray so,' he said softly.

Dieter stood abruptly and paced over to him. 'You don't believe that, do you?'

He made no reply, but his expression made Christa's spirits quail.

Andreas glanced around the room. 'Where's Helga?' No one had noticed that she had gone.

'Did she follow you into the street?' asked Herr Henning.

'I don't know. I was so fixed on hearing what the crier had to say.'

'If she's gone out there she's mad,' Dieter said. He turned to Christa. 'Don't you even think of going outside. No matter what happens.' She'd never heard him speak in such a tone before. He sounded angry, but there was more to it than that. He began to bite his fingernails as he had when he was a little boy.

The day wore on, and the room grew oppressive, even though the wind was blowing gusts down the chimney. 'Do you think we dare open the window?' Christa said.

Her father nodded, and she went over to unfasten the casement. As she did so the room filled with dust and the smell of burning.

'Can you see flames, daughter?' He was at her side.

The dust stung her eyes, but she peered out of the open window. The close was deserted, and all the other houses seemed shut tight. The sky above the rooftops was white with smoke, the smell stronger now. Some part of the city was alight. 'No flames, Father, but I think there is fire close by.'

He held up his hand to silence her and cocked his head as if he was listening hard. Christa did the same. There were noises in the air, carried on the breath of the wind. Musket-fire. The crackle of burning wood. Shouts. Screams. Her eyes met his, and she hoped for guidance. If there was fear in his heart he hid it well. 'I must make you and your sister safe.' He turned to Andreas. 'It seems the time for concession is past. We cannot stay here cowering like children. We have to defend our city.'

'Yes, sir.'

'Dieter, you will stay here to protect your sisters.'

'But, Father, I can fight! I have been training these last weeks.'

Their father nodded, and patted his arm. 'You may need those skills if your sisters are discovered.'

Dieter's face flushed red with fury. 'I will not stay here while you go and fight. Let Andreas stay.'

Herr Henning turned to Andreas. 'What do you say, Andreas? You may be safer here.'

'If I could fight for my city and protect your family I would do both, sir, but I can only do one. I have lived more years than young Dieter has. Let him stay here, and pray to God the Emperor's men don't get this far.'

Dieter made to protest again, but his father silenced him. 'You must do as I ask, Dieter. On this day, of all days, you must obey me.'

They gathered up every scrap of food in the house. There was half a pot of cold pea soup and a small loaf of stale bread that Christa had been saving. The wine jug was almost empty, but there'd been no clean water for days, so it would have to do. Their father led them down the stairs to the hallway that lay between the workshop and the back kitchen. The door to the cellar was set into the floor, and Andreas heaved it open. Dieter had brought the last candle from the room above. He lit it now and shone it into the cellar.

The ceiling was so low that none of the men could stand upright unless they stayed close to the entrance. Christa took Elsbeth's hand and walked her down the steps. The air was cool and smelled of ink. Something rustled in the far corner. Mice, Christa hoped, not rats.

Dieter set the candle on top of an ink barrel. 'Don't let it burn too long,' their father said. 'Bolt the door after us, and remember to blow out the candle as soon as you are settled. Keep the kindling beside it, so that you may find it by and by.'

'Shall I fetch some bedding from up above, sir?' Andreas said.

'Yes, Andreas.'

Andreas ran back up the stairs. Christa could hear his footsteps thundering through the house. 'Wait here a moment,' their father said, and left them in the cellar. Christa didn't dare speak to Dieter. He was still furious at being made to stay behind.

Andreas returned with his arms full of blankets and quilts. He and Christa piled them together at one side of the cellar, and Christa settled Elsbeth. The child was silent, her eyes downcast as if she were in another world. When their father returned he was carrying a short sword and a small dagger. 'Where did you get those?' Dieter asked, surprised out of his angry silence.

'I have had them this long while. Here, take the sword.' He handed it to Dieter, then weighed the knife in his hand. 'Do you think you could make use of this, daughter?'

At first Christa did not know how to reply, but she saw that she must help him to keep courage. 'Yes, Father,' she said. 'I have gutted fish, so I'm sure I can do the same to the enemy.'

In spite of himself, her father smiled. He glanced at Andreas. 'Never fear, I have weapons for us too.' He took a deep breath. 'We must go.' He crouched and made his way to where Elsbeth sat. 'I must be gone a while, my dear,' he said, stroking her cheek. 'Be a good child for your brother and sister.'

'Yes, Father,' she said, without looking up.

He came back to the steps where the rest of them stood waiting. 'Stay in here until you are sure it is safe to come out. It may not be as bad as we fear.' Christa tried to embrace him but he pushed her away gently. 'Don't, my love. Please.' His mouth was working as if he had no control over it. He nodded at Dieter, and patted his shoulder roughly.

Their father and Andreas climbed back up the cellar steps. Christa looked up at them, silhouetted in the doorway. They stepped away, out of sight, and the door was pushed shut. Christa locked it, but when she went to snuff out the candle Dieter stopped her. 'Not yet,' he said. Footsteps echoed from the room above the cellar and then there was no sound but that of the three of them breathing.

'We should put the candle out,' she said. 'It's the last we have, and God knows when we will have another.'

Dieter sat on the bottom step to examine his sword. 'It is sharp. What about your knife?'

Christa still had it in her hand. She tried its blade on her thumbnail, which it clipped easily. 'Where should I keep it? If I put it in my skirt pocket it will cut the fabric.'

'Tuck it into your sleeve.'

She did as he suggested, and sat down beside Elsbeth on the bedding. 'Come now, Dieter. Spare the candle.'

Dieter stood up, but instead of snuffing out the flame he leapt up the steps and began to unbolt the cellar doors.

'What are you doing?'

He let the doors fall open with a crash on to the stone floor of the hallway. 'I'm sorry. I can't stay here while the city is put to the sword.'

163

Panic rose in Christa's throat like sickness, and she rushed to him. 'You can't leave us here!' she hissed, not wanting Elsbeth to hear. 'For God's sake, Dieter! Father said——'

'Magdeburg needs every man she has. I know I'm untried, but I've as brave a heart as any soldier.'

'Not two hours ago you raced into the house like a hunted hare. You could barely speak for fear.'

Dieter bowed his head. 'None of you will ever believe in me, will you?'

'I didn't mean that, I only——'

'You'll know what I'm made of by the end of this day.' He looked directly into her eyes. 'Will you allow me to go, sister? Will you let me prove myself a man?'

How could she forbid him? Dieter, who never asked permission of anyone. 'Do what you must,' she said, struggling to keep her voice level.

'And you must use that knife if you need to.' His face was shining with sweat, and he wiped his sleeve across his forehead. 'There are worse things than dying, you know.'

It seemed unlike him to be sermonising, but if that was his frame of mind she would not distract him. 'Of course. Damnation is worse than death.'

He stared at her again. 'I was not talking of damnation.' He seemed about to say something more, but stopped. 'Well, then, until I see you again ...'

Christa reached out to embrace him, and he hugged her so tightly that she could hardly breathe. They were shaking so much that she couldn't tell where she ended and he began.

Dieter broke away from her and went over to Elsbeth. He kissed the top of her head, but she was so lost in prayer she did not seem to notice. For the last time he climbed the cellar steps and banged the door shut. Christa locked it. 'I shall put out the light now, Elsbeth. You won't be afraid, will you?'

Elsbeth opened her eyes and smiled dreamily at Christa. 'The Lord is with us, sister. What have I to fear?'

Ten

ON AND ON THEY WENT, FIGHTING when they had to and stealing where they could. The blow he'd taken from Captain Sadeler made Lukas feel as if his head had been cloven open with an axe. They found liquor aplenty along the way; Götz had run mad with it and kept stopping to fire his musket at anyone he saw, friend or foe. He'd brought a man down earlier before his wits had become so befuddled. The garrison were slaughtered — the message was shouted from street to street. Some of the better sort of citizen were attempting to bribe their way out, and Lukas relieved one matron of a fine silver belt for the freedom to pass them. 'She'll be stripped naked by the time she gets to the gates,' Captain Sadeler said.

'Shame she weren't prettier, then, eh?' Baxandall was still lusty as a billygoat.

They were in the heart of the city now. In some places the citizens had barricaded off a street or square, and strove to defend it with whatever weapons they had to hand, but Captain Sadeler led the men on, not pausing to help in the fight. 'Come on, lads, let's away down the alleys. There's little point in picking for scraps where our men have already been.' He conducted them down a narrow side-street that led to a covered alley. There were the remains of a barricade across its entrance, but the citizens who had manned it were dead or fled, and they climbed over it easily enough. The wind blew so fiercely between the high buildings that they could barely hear the fighting. The alley led to a close with tall houses on all sides. Several had signs swinging above their doors. One showed a picture of a book, another the image of an angel with a trumpet to its mouth. Most, though, had words upon them. Lukas considered asking Götz what they said, but he did not want to show his ignorance. One house had been broken open, but he could see little of what was within. There were papers tumbled in the doorway, and the wind was picking them up and tossing them all over the close.

They stopped short when a door banged shut ahead. As they paused, the door opened, then slammed again.

'It's just the wind, is it?' Lukas said. His nerves were ragged now. The quiet of this close had put a fear into him that he had never felt in the roar of battle.

Baxandall nodded. 'Aye. Let's go on.'

They walked into the house. A printing press stood in the middle of the floor. 'Books!' Götz exclaimed. He struggled to sling his musket over his shoulder, and stumbled against a bench.

'Give that lad no more drink,' Captain Sadeler said. 'He can scarcely stand up.'

'I'm grand,' Götz retorted. He stood with his feet wide apart, but he was swaying a little nonetheless. 'Can I take a book? It would be a fine thing to have a brand new book.'

Captain Sadeler walked over to the bench and picked up a pamphlet. 'What's this? Heretic nonsense, I suppose. We'd do better to fuel our fires with it.'

'But look here,' Götz said, lifting a book bound in oxblood leather and opening it. 'This is the first volume of a great work by Homer, translated from the Greek to the English.' He looked from Captain Sadeler to Lukas. 'I told you the tale, Lukas, of the great warriors at Troy. This is what follows.'

'It looks a fair weight to be carrying with you. You already have your New Testament.' Lukas felt a foolish kindness towards Götz. The boy's eyes were alight with his fervour for book-learning when, not half an hour ago, he'd been firing his musket and drinking like the worst of them.

Captain Sadeler was searching through the workshop. 'Take it if you will, young scholar. These are strange times when soldiers carry books in their knapsacks.'

Baxandall threw papers down from the shelves. 'I'd trade all the books in the world for a bite of bread or a handful of gold.'

'Let's try the kitchen.' Lukas walked through to the back of the house. He emptied the cupboards but could find nothing more than a handful of dried peas hidden in a clay pot. Near enough useless, but he tipped them into his satchel anyway. 'Nothing worth taking,' he shouted into the workshop. 'Not even a pewter spoon.'

The other three came through from the workshop. 'Have you tried the cellar?' Baxandall said, nodding towards the trapdoor set into the floor of the hallway.

'We'd do better to start at the top of the house,' Captain Sadeler said. 'Let's away on up, and work our way down.'

They did as the captain ordered. The house offered rich enough pickings. Baxandall found a chest full of good warm clothes in the largest bedroom, and decreed that the best way to carry them was to wear them. 'Here,' he shouted, throwing a faded green bodice at Lukas. 'You're better fitted to dress as a woman.'

'Fuck off.' Lukas knew what Baxandall was about, but in spite of that he felt the temper rise in him.

'Or maybe you'd rather young Götz wore the lady's gown, eh? Perhaps he's more to your taste.'

Captain Sadeler lashed Baxandall in the face with the back of his hand. 'Enough of that. Hasn't he tried to kill you once already today?'

Baxandall stepped back, wiping blood from his nose. 'He's no merriment in him.' He glanced down at his stolen robes. 'Ach, I've stained my new wearings.'

In all they gathered a bag of mixed coins, a fine old-fashioned lace collar, a pair of summer boots that fitted Götz and enough shirts and stockings to clothe them all twice over. Baxandall found a jar of brandy hidden under a loose board in another of the bedrooms, and they sat on the bed drinking it in a rare moment of harmony. Lukas made sure that Götz did not take more than he could bear. He'd no wish to be carrying the boy back to camp.

The brandy gave them another flare of energy, and they clattered down the stairs as merrily as if they were tumbling home from a night at a tavern. 'Here,' said Götz, as they gathered themselves, 'will we try the cellar door? Maybe these good people had a store of beer down there.' He ran to the trapdoor and tried to pull it open, but was toppled by his drunkenness.

Lukas joined in with Captain Sadeler and Baxandall's laughter, and Götz laughed too, spread-eagled as he was on the floor. Their mirth eased Lukas's nerves, and he was heartily glad for the relief. Baxandall and Lukas hoisted at the door, but it resisted. 'Is it locked, do you think?' Lukas said.

Captain Sadeler studied it. 'There's no bolt here.' He looked up at Lukas. 'Perhaps it's locked from the inside.'

Lukas helped Götz to his feet, and the four stood in silence, listening. What with the wind moaning around the corners of the house, and the occasional noise of conflict in the city beyond, they could detect no sound. Lukas felt his skin prickle into gooseflesh. Baxandall went into the workshop, and returned with a pry-bar that would serve to jemmy open the cellar door. He hooked it under the near edge and levered at it until the wood splintered. Lukas searched the kitchen, thinking there might be a hatchet or the like for chopping stove-wood, but any such implements as there might have been had gone. It occurred to him that whoever was hiding in the cellar might have armed themselves. His head was clear suddenly.

Baxandall kept working at the trapdoor, and at last he broke through a big enough hole to let Captain Sadeler feel inside for the bolt. The captain stooped to his task. They all joined to heave the trapdoor open. Steps led down into the darkness of the cellar. 'We need light,' Captain Sadeler said.

Baxandall scooped up a sheaf of paper that had blown in from the workshop. He rolled it into a tight wand and held the slow-match of his musket to it. As soon as it lit he jumped down the steps, flaming paper in one hand and his short sword in the other. Lukas heard movement from the cellar — the rustle of cloth on cloth and a sharp cry of alarm. Baxandall advanced into the cellar, as swift as a cat on a sparrow. 'Come on, lads.' His voice was muffled. 'We'll have some sport here, but bring a proper light, for God's sake.'

'Who have you in there, Baxandall?' Captain Sadeler called.

'Two lasses.'

'Well, bring them out, for God's sake.'

Lukas stood with Götz and Captain Sadeler at the top of the steps, waiting to see these finds of Baxandall's. A sick dread grew in him. He knew already what was in Baxandall's mind.

A young woman – very young, from the look of her – came up the steps slowly, with her arms round a girl-child. The child had her eyes closed and her hands clasped together. In spite of this she never missed her step. Her lips were moving, as if she were praying. At last they were out of the cellar, with Baxandall following, his sword pointed at their backs. He made to speak, but Captain Sadeler silenced him with a raised hand. 'We'd best discover if they have value,' he said, then turned to the older girl. 'Where are your menfolk?'

'Gone to defend the city, sir,' the girl said. She looked at each of their faces in turn. Lukas felt a stir of anger when she flinched at his scars. He knew that women made their judgement too readily. Fuck them all. He stared hard at her. Her pale skin seemed to turn even paler. She was breathing rapidly, and he watched the rise and fall of her chest. Dear God, she looked untouched. Clean. Her hair was plaited into two braids, in the custom of unmarried girls in these parts.

'The city is lost, *Mädchen*,' Captain Sadeler said. 'Has your father any fortune?'

'There is a little money in the house, sir, that you have likely found already. Other than that every *Pfennig* was spent trying to put food on the table since the siege began.'

Was she lying, thinking to save her father's money? If she was, she was a fool. There was no value in hostages whose family had not the means to ransom them back. For a moment Lukas pitied her. 'Have you food hidden anywhere?' he said.

The girl looked directly at him. 'There's a piece of bread down in the cellar, and a drop of wine in the jug.'

'Should I away and get them?' Götz said.

'You'll hardly find them, with no light down there.' Lukas looked back to the girl. 'Have you a lamp?'

'Just the one candle, and that's down there too.'

'Ach,' Baxandall said. 'We'd more likely break our necks trying to find the damn food. Let's take our pleasure here, then move on for richer pickings about the town.' He smirked at Lukas. 'Do you think you're capable now, Private Weinsburg, or are you still afflicted with the droop?'

'I'll cut your throat one fine night, and then we'll see who's limp.'

'Do you want me to show you how it's done?' Baxandall grabbed the girl and began to paw at her bodice. When she resisted him he fetched her a blow to the face that shocked her into obedience. *No man has laid a finger on her until now*, Lukas thought, *neither in lust nor anger*. The child was still clinging to the girl, and Baxandall pushed her away roughly so that she stumbled and fell.

'Be brave, Elsbeth,' the older girl cried out. 'Stand quietly now, there's a good child.'

Baxandall looked from the girl in his arms to the child. 'By God, I have enough heat in me that I could break them both in. What say you, Weinsburg? Do I not put you to shame? Your cock's likely shrivelled away, it's had so little use this last while.'

Captain Sadeler sniggered at Baxandall's wit. 'Ach, Weinsburg, you'll never gain advancement in my company if you don't show yourself a proper man.'

'You could order him to it, Captain,' Baxandall said. 'Then he'd have to fuck her or be hanged.'

Captain Sadeler shook his head. 'I fear the thought of the gallows would make any man wilt.' He slapped Lukas heartily on the shoulder. 'Come now, Weinsburg. Show you're one of us. Is she not fresh enough for you? You like 'em fresh, don't you?'

Lukas felt the blood pulsing in his head. His thoughts were so tumbled that he could not tell anger from fear, guilt from lust, passion from ambition. He must take this girl: that much was clear.

Götz spoke out, his voice stronger than Lukas had heard it before. 'Leave them be. In the name of Jesus and His Blessed Mother, do not harm them.'

Captain Sadeler raised an eyebrow. 'This is no time for preaching, young Götz. If it ain't to your taste I suggest you find some other trade than soldiering.'

'Lukas, don't do this. I beg you.'

'Turn away, Götz.' He wished the boy a hundred miles distant. How could he acquit himself with those condemning eyes on him? His shame made him angry. 'Clear off, will you? Get out of here.'

'We are friends, Lukas. Brothers.'

Lukas went forward and pulled the girl away from Baxandall. As he did so he saw the glint of a blade in her hand. He grasped her wrist instinctively.

'Mind yourself, Weinsburg!' cried Baxandall, with a laugh, backing away from the girl. 'Your cat has claws.'

Lukas twisted the girl round. She had a short knife in her hand. 'Did you think to use this on me?' he said, tightening his fingers on her wrist. He could feel her bones, dainty as a bird's. It would cost him no effort to crush them. The thought stirred him. 'Let go the knife.' He could feel her trembling now. She uncurled her fingers and let it drop onto the floor. Baxandall scooped it up and tucked it into his belt.

'Please, sir.' She was finding it hard to speak, so great must be her fear. 'Do not harm my sister.'

'Be quiet,' Lukas said, twisting her arm again so that she was forced closer to him. He could feel the tension in her. Beneath the fabric of her sleeve her arm was firm, muscled. A strong girl. He felt the fire of lust burn in him, and thanked the devil for it. Yes, he could demonstrate that he was as much a man as Captain Sadeler and Baxandall. He put his hands round her waist, spreading his fingers wide until he felt the curve of her breasts. He pulled her close and put his mouth to her ear. Her hair felt soft against his lips. 'It will go better with you if you obey me. It will all end the same, do you see? I will have my way.'

'I don't understand you, sir.'

Sweet Jesus, she was an innocent. Somehow it made him angry with her. 'Lie down for me now.' He tightened his grip on her wrist again until he could sense the pain run through her. 'Lie down or I'll hurt you worse.'

She nodded. 'Elsbeth,' she said softly, 'close your eyes now. Say your prayers.'

'Ach, for God's sake!' Lukas shouted, and shook the girl so that her head bobbed around like that of a broken doll. 'You think a man can fuck with that child praying in his ear? You stupid bitch.' His voice had risen to a scream, such was the fear in him. Dear God, what if he was incapable? He struggled to calm his mind. 'I'm trying to make it easy for you,' he said, in a quieter tone, 'and you do this ...'

'You've never had the knack of mastering a woman, have you, Weinsburg?' Baxandall said. 'Give her to me and I'll show you the trick of it.'

Lukas ignored him and forced the girl onto the floor. He knelt, pushed her skirts up and felt a jolt of lust at the sight of her bare thighs. Captain Sadeler said, 'She's willing enough.'

The younger girl was praying out loud, and her voice was growing more fervent and frantic. 'In the name of Jesu, take that one out of here, will you, Götz?' Lukas said, without looking up. He couldn't bear the thought of seeing the condemnation in his friend's face. Götz made no reply, but Lukas heard footsteps going out into the workshop and the sound of prayer ceased.

Lukas looked down at the girl. 'Let me have my way now, do you understand?' Her face was the colour of whey, and as frozen as a statue's. She nodded. Lukas pushed her legs open.

'Are you sure she's untried, Weinsburg?' Baxandall said. 'Perhaps she has us all fooled.'

Lukas tried to block their words from his mind as he undid his breeches. The girl was lying very still. He didn't look at her face now, but concentrated on her naked skin and her soft maidenhair. This was a wrong thing he was doing. His very soul knew it, but his body was determined to continue. He tried to force himself inside her, but she was tense as a fresh-strung bow and he could not gain entry. For a few terrible seconds he felt his lust falter, and he was sure he would be disgraced in front of Captain Sadeler and Baxandall. The anger that had been festering in him this long while flared again. He reached down and forced her legs wider, pushing one finger inside her. She cried out and grabbed at his wrist, trying in vain to pull his hand away. Her twisting excited him, even as he understood it was pain not pleasure that moved her. He flung himself down on her, so that he was crushing the breath from her body, and finally made good his penetration. Baxandall and Captain Sadeler were cheering, clapping in rhythm to his thrusts. The noise intruded into his mind and robbed him of his potency. Dear God, he was turning limp even as he neared the end of pleasure. The shame of it unmanned him further, but he kept on with the pretence for a few moments more, long enough to acquit himself in their eyes. The girl would know no better, thank God.

'Off her, Weinsburg, and allow me my pleasure,' Captain Sadeler cried.

Lukas made to pull himself away from the girl but she grabbed his arm. 'Please,' she whispered to him, 'not the others. Please, don't let them.' For a moment, before he could turn away, she was staring him straight in the eye. He shook his head, and stood, fastening his breeches, before he stepped away.

An explosion sounded from out in the city. 'What the hell is that?' Lukas said.

'The fifth so far,' Baxandall replied, watching Captain Sadeler as he took off his buff coat the better to get at the girl. 'You were too caught up in your delight to hear the others.'

The girl sat up and went to cover herself with her skirts, but Captain Sadeler nudged at her with his boot. 'Who gave you permission to rise?' She looked all round the room – for her sister, Lukas imagined. Captain Sadeler placed his foot on her shoulder and pressed her down again. 'Here, Weinsburg,' he said. 'There's blood on her petticoats. She was a virgin, after all.' He made a mocking bow to the girl. 'We impugned your good character, *Mädchen*, but what were we to think when you lay down so readily for a common soldier?' Lukas turned away. He could not bear to look at her any more.

They all froze as they heard footsteps approach through the workshop. Götz appeared in the doorway. He didn't look directly at any of them. 'The city is in flames. We must be away.'

'Ach, for God's sake, Fuhrmann,' Captain Sadeler exclaimed. 'You are only trying to spoil our merrymaking.'

'If you don't come away now you'll be merrymaking in the next world.' He glanced at the girl and then away. 'You'll die unshriven too, with sin on your souls.'

Captain Sadeler uttered a string of curses and pulled on his buff coat. They grabbed what they could of their booty. 'Bring her,' the captain said to Lukas, pointing at the girl. 'I may take my use of her at the camp.'

Lukas pulled the girl to her feet and she immediately broke away from him and ran to Götz. 'Where is my sister? What have you done with her?'

Götz clasped her hands. 'Calm yourself. She's seated on a bench in the workshop, good as gold, praying for God's mercy.'

Captain Sadeler watched this exchange with displeasure. He turned to Lukas. 'You'd best keep that bitch on a leash, Weinsburg. She seems inclined to stray.'

Lukas grabbed her and began to drag her through the workshop towards the front door of the house. The child was seated, as Götz had said, eyes closed, head bowed, for all the world as if she were in church. Lukas could smell the smoke now. It might have been night in the street beyond the door, there was so little light.

'Elsbeth,' the girl shouted, trying to wriggle free of him.

'She may make her own escape,' Lukas said. 'We've no time to wait for her.'

The girl continued to twist away from him as he dragged her through the doorway and into the street. The roof of the house opposite was ablaze, and the air was swimming with ash. As Götz came outside the girl said to him, 'Please, sir, my sister hasn't the wit to save herself.'

Götz stared at her, then ran back into the house. *Stupid*, Lukas thought. He'd get himself killed for a simpleton child. They made their way out into the main street, but it was barely recognisable. Half of the buildings were on fire, and both soldiers and citizens were doing their best to flee. Lukas pulled out his short sword and used it to fight his way through as best he could with the girl encumbering him. He sliced at any citizen who blocked his path. Some had fight in them yet, and seemed more determined to slaughter the Emperor's men than to save themselves. Others had run quite mad. He saw a merchant dash into a burning warehouse shouting something about gold. As he passed another house he saw faces at an upstairs window, staring out but making no move to escape. In some ways he was glad of the chaos – it gave his conscience no opportunity to make its voice heard.

He could no longer see Captain Sadeler and Baxandall. They must have broken away, unburdened as they were. For a moment he considered letting the girl go. She might as well die here of the flame than be passed through the company. Still, Captain Sadeler had ordered him to bring her back, and a broken order might mean a flogging. He tightened his grip on her arm and marched her on. In truth, she was no longer dragging her feet. The flames were consuming the city, and terror of them seemed to have put all notion of resistance from her mind.

At last they reached the remains of the city wall. There was nothing left of it but rubble, and Lukas took a firmer grip on the girl to stop her tripping on the tumbled bricks. They pushed on to the bridge and Lukas forced his way into the crowd pressing over it. The wood creaked and groaned. Like as not the whole damn thing would fall and throw them into the river, but the tide of people carried them forward. Some were in the water already, those who could swim, or any who feared the flames more than death by drowning. Lukas saw that he was not the only one carrying a woman. Many of the soldiers judged a girl as good a battle-prize as loot. Perhaps the fire had interrupted their pleasure, and they were unwilling to be denied.

The bridge held, and they tumbled off onto the far bank. Lukas pulled the girl clear of the crush and stood still until his heart had steadied. He tried to take a deep breath, but the air was bitter with ash. The fire was roaring through the city behind him. He didn't dare look back. 'Are you fit to go on?' he shouted to the girl. She nodded. Her face was drained of colour. Even her lips looked white. 'Come along then.'

As they walked through the camp Lukas let go of her. He didn't think she would run away. Her steps were slower and he had to slacken his pace to let her keep up with him. She winced each time she took a step. 'What's wrong with you?' he said.

'My feet are giving me pain.' She stopped and lifted the hem of her skirt. They were dark with blood and dirt and her shoes hung in rags of leather – they had not been made for crossing a ruined city but for indoors.

Lukas felt a terrible weariness. He wanted nothing more than to lie down in his tent and sleep until morning, but he knew that hunger would not permit it. The effects of the drink he had taken in the city were long gone. At least he had some treasure in his pockets, and a spare musket to trade, but how would he have peace to do that with this girl to guard? The sooner he could pass her on to Captain Sadeler, the sooner he would eat and sleep. He rubbed his eyes with one hand to chase the weariness from them. 'I'll carry you,' he said.

'No.' She flinched away from him. 'Thank you, but no. I will try to walk faster.' Her face set in a tight grimace, and she began to walk again.

The path back to the company's tents was lined with sutlers who were offering what food stocks they had in return for a share of the loot. Lukas found one willing to trade him bread, *Bratwurst* and beer for the good cloak he'd taken from the girl's house. When they reached his tent he bade the girl sit and offered her the beer. She hesitated, and he fought the anger he felt. Who did she think she was to scorn his kindness? At last she took the jar and drank. He then broke a piece of bread for her and she took it in her hand but did not eat it. She was looking across the river in the direction of the city. He sat down a little way from her and sliced off a chunk of the sausage. By God it tasted good. The flavour of the meat blended with the smoke in the air around him. He followed the girl's gaze. Where he had been used to seeing the city there seemed only to be flames. The air was so black that he couldn't tell what time it might be. Why was it burning so? Magdeburg was to be their treasure trove, their larder. Their orders had been to force a surrender, not to raze the place.

'Is this Judgment Day?' the girl said.

'I don't think it.' Her question vexed him. He had seen more cities fall than she might imagine. He pointed to the untouched bread in her hand. 'You should eat.'

She nodded and chewed a piece of crust. When she had swallowed it she accepted some more beer.

As the day wore on the men of the company returned to the camp. Some brought women with them, others whatever treasure they had laid their hands on. Some did not return at all. Lukas kept his eye on the tent beside his. It was better-looking than his own, the property of the Blickle brothers from Munich. If they were killed he might take possession of it for they had no friends. It was late when Captain Sadeler was carried back. He had taken injury during his escape, when a house had collapsed close by, splintering him with shards of roof-slate. Baxandall helped bring him into the officers' tent, then walked over to where Lukas and the girl sat. 'I'll take her in your tent now,' Baxandall said. 'The captain won't be fit for her awhile yet.'

'You've a wife in the camp,' Lukas said. 'What need have you of this one?'

'I'd have taken her in the city, wife or not, had the flames not prevented it.'

'But Captain Sadeler was to have been next after me. You may wait your turn until he's mended enough.'

'Give her here, you bastard.'

Lukas struggled to his feet and placed one hand on his sword hilt. He was so weary he could barely stand straight. 'His order was that he would have her next after me. You'll not take his place unless he commands it so.'

Baxandall spat on the ground close to the girl, but he had no more strength for a quarrel than Lukas did. He staggered back to his tent. His little wife was standing in the doorway. Lukas wondered how much of their dispute she'd understood.

Still the city burned, as if there would be no end to it. Lukas and the girl sat, unable to turn their faces away from its heat and light. Once he suggested to her that she should go into the tent and sleep, but she shook her head. He would have lain down himself, but he was afraid that she would creep off.

Lukas didn't see Götz return. He must have fallen into a sitting-doze, because he jumped awake to find Götz standing next to the tent, and the girl close to him. She appeared to be listening intently, but Götz was speaking too quietly for Lukas to hear what was said. Eventually she nodded. He heard her say, 'Thank you.' Götz made a small bow and turned to walk away.

'Wait, Götz,' Lukas called, climbing to his feet. 'Here, take some food and drink.'

Götz stopped. 'I'll find my own,' he said, and walked on. Lukas watched him disappear into the dim, torch-lit paths of the camp.

He turned back to the girl. 'What did he say to you?'

'That my sister is safely carried to the cathedral. General Tilly was persuaded to allow sanctuary there.' She held a hand over her eyes. 'I think I should rest now, if you'll permit it.'

'Aye, go ahead.' He hesitated. 'I'll not trouble you.'

'What about that other one?'

'You're safe for tonight.'

The girl nodded briefly and crawled into the tent. Lukas sat down again close to the entrance. He continued to eat and drink. The food had no taste for him now, but he knew if he didn't finish it before the weariness took him, he would wake to find it stolen from his hand.

Eleven

IT WAS MIDNIGHT, BUT NO ONE knew it. The smoke from the city swirled grey against the night sky, hiding the half-moon. Those soldiers who were living and still able to walk had found their way back to the camp. If they could not find their own tents in the dark they lay on the ground, curled round whatever sparse booty they had scavenged. Some were dead drunk, and would not have been roused had an eighteen-pounder cannon blasted beside them. Others, like Lukas, fell quickly into a deep soldier's sleep, but jumped awake when any slight sound came near them.

Christa had not expected to sleep. When she closed her eyes she had the sensation of being a stone on the bed of a river in spate. There was cold turmoil all around her, but she was dead, inert. She lay down in the little tent, with its alien, sour smells, and she did sleep at last.

Down at the river the water flowed strongly on. The bodies of those who had drowned in their efforts to flee the city were carried downstream. Three miles away, where the river narrowed and trees overhung the water, some became tangled in the weed, like fish netted by the river-men. By morning the river would have formed them into a dam built of limbs and bone, and the dead would gather there, washed clean of their names and places and all the words that had formed their lives. Karl Rothkrug, night watchman; Johannes Störmann, labourer; Rolf Pfeiffer, cloth merchant; Gerhard Kiessling, Imperial soldier; a dozen more; a hundred more; a thousand more. As the dead made their last journey through the water, they became again what they had once been — naked, nameless, unknown.

And the city was still in flames. Flakes of ash the size of bedsheets danced up through the air. In the printers' quarter the roof beam of Paul Henning's house crashed through the burning floorboards of the bedrooms. Across the close the Schwarzes' house was already gone, leaving only a mound of smouldering brick where it had stood. Nearby, the west tower of the Johanniskirche crumpled into itself with a gasp of smoke and soot. The flames made a funeral pyre for those who had died in the fight for the city, and who lay where they had fallen, on barricades, on the streets, in blind alleys where they had been cornered by the invaders. Wolfgang Höss, tapster; Georg Blarer, garrison soldier; Ingrid Müller, seamstress; Jörg Schwarz, printer; Hannah Schwarz, printer's wife; a dozen more; a hundred more; a thousand more.

The flames pronounced a sentence of death on those who had not found a way of escape from the city. The staggering soldiers, too drunk to find their way to the walls; the cowering women, saving their virtue in attics and cellars; the wealthy men, who could not bear to leave without one last pocketful of treasure; they all were made to lie down and sleep by the flames. Soft hair that had once been caressed burned away with a crackle; brains that could calculate a profit as fast as a blink boiled and burst in the cauldrons of their skulls. Helmar Holl, banker; Barbara Günzburg, baker's wife; Katerina Günzburg, baker's daughter; Anna Günzburg, baker's daughter; Otto Blickle, Imperial musketeer; Thomas Blickle, Imperial musketeer …

The living were gathered in the cathedral. They huddled in the darkest corners, fearing that the doors or windows might crash in on them. Their enemy now was the fire, and those who could prayed to

God to preserve them. One woman, near death from a cut to her belly caused by a dragoon's sword, lay looking up at the gracious vault of the cathedral roof, and fancied that its curve was the palm of the Lord's hand, sheltering her from evil. Perhaps she was right. The flames came close, and painted the outer walls black, but they could not catch hold of the stone and slate. The cathedral was a dark spot of hope in the glowing field of death that Magdeburg had become.

And the list of the dead grew longer. Jacob Städel, goldsmith; Heinz Städel, apprentice goldsmith; Klaus Varrelman, apprentice printer; Gottfried Helmholtz, pastor ...

The fine palaces that lined Gelsenkirchenplatz were gone now. The gold and silver had melted in the vaults of the banking houses. The bolts of close-woven wool were turned to ash in the cloth merchants' warehouses. In the *Rathaus* the flames ate up volume upon volume of Magdeburg's story. Deeds of Ownership, Agreements of Indenture, Proceedings of the Court, the Almanac of Misdemeanours and Their Penalties, Marriage Contracts, Covenants, Wills and Testaments, maps of the city boundaries, Certificates of Fishing Rights, the city census of every decade from 1540 to 1630, applications for patents, Bills of Divorce, Declarations of Guardianship, all were gone, every word of them.

Helmut Steinhausen, sexton; Rosina Sitzinger, needlemaker; Paul Henning, printer ... After a time the detail became tiresome, the names blurred, a meaningless litany. The dead and the dead and the dead. They were already halfway to being forgotten. Albrecht Baier, tapster; Wolfgang Hoffmann, ostler; Maria Schopper, maidservant; Ursula Obernitz, merchant's wife; Dieter Henning, apprentice printer ...

A dozen more; a hundred more; a thousand more. Nameless or named, loved or neglected, rich or poor, wise or foolish, saints or sinners. Twenty-four thousand. Too many to remember. Too many to record.

Twelve

WHEN CHRISTA WOKE IT WAS LIGHT outside. The day before seemed like a dream, but she knew it had been real, just as this tent was real, and the voices of the men talking in low voices outside it. It was tempting to lie a while longer. There was safety of a sort in here. The man with the scarred face had given her his promise that he would not come near her. She wasn't sure if she could believe him, but her hiding in here would not change anything.

Her belly ached, and she felt pain between her legs where the man had hurt her. Was this what happened between a man and a woman? Were these the doings that had put Klaus's child in Gertrude's womb? She forced her thoughts away from her friends. From them it was only one remove to her family, and she knew she could not allow herself to think of them. If she weakened, even for a moment, she might be lost. The sights she had seen yesterday as the man dragged her through the city seemed like the worst of nightmares, but she knew they were all real. She had seen lives ended on a whim. The man himself must have killed near half a dozen, with as little concern as she would have swatting a fly. Those images were burned on her mind, and somehow seemed more real, more terrifying, than the thing the man had done to her. He could have killed her, had the notion taken him. Even now he might. If she annoyed him she could be cut down like all those others. She must be brave then. There was nothing to do but face it. Face him.

She crawled out of the tent and stood up. Her limbs were stiff, but she did not dare stretch to ease them. The scarred man was sitting on an empty brandy barrel, his bare feet splayed on the grass, his head drooping. He looked up at her, then away. She glanced around the tents. A small bonfire was burning, and a soldier was heating a pot on it. Others were standing, rubbing at their shoulders and staring at the place where the city had been. Christa didn't dare turn her head towards it.

'Here, I've saved some bread for you,' the man said. He held out a crust to her.

Be brave, she thought, *do not vex him*. 'Thank you.' She took it, looking quickly at his face as she sat on the ground. The scar seemed different in daylight. She could see now that it ran deeper than she had thought, twisting the flesh beneath his eye. As she chewed the hard crust she realised he was staring at her, and felt a flutter of fear, but there was no anger in his face. He looked bleak. Exhausted.

'You are very young,' he said.

'I am fifteen years old, sir.'

'Fifteen. My God.' He rubbed one hand over his face.

Another man walked towards the tent. It was the dark-haired one — only a boy, now that she saw him in daylight — who had taken Elsbeth. The scarred man rose from his seat on the barrel. 'Götz,' he said flatly. 'Have you seen to that wound on your arm?'

The boy — Götz — ignored him and Christa. 'I have come to take my things from the tent. I will find some other place to rest my head.'

'For God's sake, Götz,' the man said, anger and pleading mixed in his voice. 'Don't let us fall out over this.'

'You have broken the laws of God and man.'

'This is war. You live too much in those books you've read. Real life is different.'

'The nature of sin does not change.'

The man stood abruptly, toppling the barrel as he did so. 'Ach, for fuck's sake, Götz. The last thing I need is for you to act the priest.' He walked off, pushing his way through the tents, half knocking some of them down in his temper.

Götz hunkered down beside Christa. 'How do things go with you?'

She noticed how he blushed now that he was speaking directly to her. He seemed younger than ever. 'I am ...' she began. Which words could she use? 'I am alive.'

'God be praised.'

'Amen.'

He tilted his head and considered her. 'What do you wish to do now?'

'Find my sister, and be with her.'

'You would go back to the city?'

Christa nodded. She steeled herself to look down towards the river. The towers of the cathedral still stood, but she recognised nothing else. Smoke was rising across what was left of Magdeburg. She was trembling and thought she was going to be sick, but she took a deep breath and steadied herself. There were those other men, the captain, and the one who had tried to come to the tent last night. 'I think I would be better there than here.'

'Aye. It is not a good time to be a woman.' He stood, and muttered, almost as if he was afraid of being overheard, 'I'll take you to the cathedral, if you wish it.' He held out his hand to her.

Perhaps this was a trick, and he was taking her to those other men. Well, they would find her sooner or later. She had little choice but to trust him. She took his hand and got up. 'If anyone asks us where we are going, I shall say that we are in search of food.' He noticed how cautiously she walked. 'Have you shoes? No? Never worry. There's a man in the camp sells boots.'

'I have no money.'

'I have booty I can trade.'

They found the boot-seller, and Götz traded him a gold chain for a pair of boys' boots that fitted Christa. 'Come now. We should make our way to the cathedral.'

Christa's feet were still paining her, but it was better now that she was properly shod. 'How do you think that man came by all those boots?'

Götz hesitated. 'Most likely they belonged to the fallen.'

'He steals from the dead?'

'We soldiers steal from the dead, and we sell what we steal to the likes of him.' He glanced at her, as if he sought her approval. 'It would be a sin to waste their belongings, don't you think?'

They walked on a little further. 'What would happen to you if the captain and the others knew you were helping me to be away?'

He paused. 'I don't know.'

Christa thought he knew well enough. She felt a tremor of gratitude that here at least was a good man. 'Is the bridge passable?'

'Aye, it still stands, I believe.'

'You should leave me there.'

'Very well.' He was unable to hide his relief.

They didn't speak again until the ground sloped down towards the river. Götz searched inside his jacket and pulled out a silver buckle. 'Here,' he said, handing it to her. 'You can sell or trade it. Here's some bread too.' He gave her a baked roll no bigger than an apple.

She took the buckle and tucked it into her skirt, out of sight, and slipped the little loaf into her pocket. 'Why are you helping me?'

He seemed nonplussed by her question. 'It is my Christian duty,' he said, but the words sounded stale. For a moment he seemed to be fighting some strong emotion. 'What happened yesterday …' He stopped.

Christa pitied him, for all that he was her enemy. 'I'll away, then.'

'Aye. On you go. God bless you.'

Christa walked down towards the river. The sky was an unvarying white that made it hard to tell how far on the day had gone. It was impossible to see where one cloud ended and the next began. The air felt empty, although it still carried the smell of burning. There was no breath of wind. Every face she saw wore the same blank look she'd seen on the scarred man. She couldn't find the words to explain it to herself. It was as if everything was ended. The soldiers looked up at her as she passed, but only one or two called to her. Even their crudity sounded worn out.

The river looked different somehow. She couldn't tell why. As she got closer to the bridge she saw that the water seemed thicker than it should. It looked ... clotted. A man was walking at the edge, picking his way carefully through the mud. He had a scarf tied round the lower part of his face, and was carrying a stick that he used to support himself. As Christa came closer he stopped and poked it into the water. Something was floating there, and it dipped in the water as the man prodded at it. At last he ducked and tugged at it with his free hand. He must have sensed Christa's eyes on him, because he turned suddenly. He eyed her, then returned to the thing in the water and tugged again, finally pulling free what looked like a piece of cloth. It hung in his hand, dripping. Again he looked at Christa. 'It's mine,' he said, his voice muffled by his scarf. 'Find your own booty.'

Christa walked faster, scared by his ferocity. She stepped on to the bridge, taking care to find safe footing on the splintered wood. Slowly she began to understand why the river was different. The dark surface wasn't flowing, not in the way it always had. It was thick with the bodies of the dead. She held up a hand to cover her nose and mouth, although she knew the slain could not be rotting, not so soon. Only yesterday they had been alive. The strange motion of the water was drawing her eye. She tried to stare straight ahead to the other bank, but something about the river kept pulling her gaze. They were down there. Not yet swollen. That would come in a day or two. Dipping up and down. She glanced through the broken slats beneath her feet. It was too dark to see anything under the bridge. She looked up again, focusing on the cathedral. Forward. She had to go forward.

At last she reached the far side of the bridge. There were more scavengers on this bank. They glanced up at her, their faces hungry. Christa was aware of the loaf in her pocket, and wondered if they could sense it. She held her arms down, hoping they wouldn't notice. For a moment she thought of finding some quiet place to eat it quickly. If it was in her belly no one could steal it. She pushed the thought away. If she found Elsbeth she'd need feeding. And the others ... Perhaps she'd find her father and Dieter. They might only be injured. She hesitated, allowing herself that brief glow of hope. For a strange moment she felt as if she was watching herself. It was almost as if she had stepped away from her own mind. She could recognise this other her, this fearful girl who was foolishly letting hope flower in her heart. Impossible. She looked at the ruined walls of the city. What man could have survived? Father was likely dead. Dieter too. She made herself repeat the words inside her head. The only one who was living was Elsbeth. Götz swore he had delivered her safe to the cathedral. She didn't think he had been lying.

Two of the scavengers had moved closer to her. They were eyeing her, looking her up and down for anything worth taking. She walked quickly away from them, closer to what was left of the Fürstenwall gate. Rubble was piled around her like a little mountain range. She stepped carefully. The ground beneath her feet was warm, as if the fires still raged deep beneath the surface. There were no proper buildings left between her and the cathedral, and no streets either. She passed an old man sitting in a stone doorway with its studded oak door intact. The house it had belonged to had vanished. All that was left was the door, and its arch, and the old man sitting there with puzzlement on his face.

As she got closer to the cathedral a group of three soldiers appeared from the ruins of a shop. Christa flinched. She couldn't tell if they were Tilly's men or from the garrison, and she wasn't sure that it mattered. She'd seen what soldiers could do when they had the battle-rage on them. 'Hey, *Mädchen*,' one called. 'Have you food?'

She shook her head and hurried on, stumbling on the loose cobbles. The cathedral was dead ahead of her now. She slowed as she saw the soldiers standing guard at the main door. Surely the rules of sanctuary would be respected. Götz had told her this was a safe place. Were these soldiers no more than thieves guarding their booty, or were they protectors defending the innocent? She wondered about the women inside, the lucky ones who had not had done to them what the scarred man had done to her. Why had they escaped it when she had not? Perhaps it was a punishment. She considered the sins of which she was guilty. There were so many, probably more than she even knew of. She forced herself to take a step closer to the cathedral, to the soldiers. And then another. Where else could she go? She had no choices. Another step. And another.

One of the soldiers on guard duty had noticed her. He called to her: 'What do you want here?'

Christa's mouth felt dry and bitter. 'I'm looking for my sister.'

The soldier came closer. He was old, she realised. As old as her father. 'There's no food in there. No water either. You've seen the river? No clean water to be had.'

'I just want to find my sister. She was brought here yesterday.'

The old soldier looked at her coldly. 'And where have you been since then, *Mädchen*?'

It seemed to Christa that the word twisted in his mouth. *Mädchen*. He knew it was a lie.

Christa was afraid she would cry, and she didn't want to, not in front of this man. It took her a moment to steady herself. When she looked back up at him his expression had changed. It wasn't compassion, more … what? Shame? She had been about to tell him bluntly, *I was taken to your camp*. Now she saw there was no need. He banged his fist on the door. A few moments later it was opened by a Papist priest. 'Yes? What is it?'

'This girl seeks her sister,' the soldier said, dipping his head respectfully towards the priest as he spoke.

The priest glared at her. 'We are starving in here. How would we keep you?'

'You need not keep me. I want only to look for my sister.' She was aware of the bread in her pocket. She could use it to trade her way in, but she didn't trust the priest or the soldier. One sight of the bread and they might snatch it from her, and give her nothing in return. She wondered if she should plead with the priest, tell him Elsbeth was only eleven, tell him how Götz had promised to bring her here, but some sense told her that female prattle would not impress the sour-faced man. Instead she stayed silent, looking him in the eye, waiting for his decision.

'Come in, then,' he said at last. 'But I warn you, things are not good here.'

Christa followed him into the cathedral, and waited while he secured the door. There were soldiers standing guard inside as well. She had been expecting the cathedral to be lit by its usual soft glow, but it was in near darkness. When she looked up at the windows she saw that they had been blackened by the smoke and would admit no light. The stench was so powerful that for a moment she could barely breathe. It was not the smell of death. The cathedral was rank with life — human waste, sweat and spew. Groups of women and children had set up camp, of a sort, in the alcoves and side chapels. 'You may search as you please,' the priest said, 'but if I catch you taking anything I'll turn you over to the soldiers.'

'I'll take nothing but my sister, if God has spared her.'

She walked slowly past each group, looking for familiar faces. Some of the women glanced up at her, but mostly they ignored her. As she approached one group she noticed a woman crouched on the ground beside a half-naked child. He was convulsing, his pale limbs flailing as if he was tossed about by some invisible force. Suddenly he was still, flopping as Elsbeth did when the Holy Ghost overpowered her. The woman made a choking sound, as if she was fighting for breath. For one confused moment Christa thought she must have some dreadful ailment of the lungs, but then she realised that the child was dead. That choking was the sound of a woman whose child had died before her eyes. The others in the group looked on, but none moved to comfort her. Perhaps they hadn't the energy for grief. *And neither have I.* For some reason the thought brought no shame. She turned away and walked on.

There were many women walking as she was, searching the faces for those they wanted but could not find. Others seemed driven to walk by some different impulse. One girl, perhaps a year or two older than Christa, walked like a blind woman, although her eyes were clear and staring. She had somehow come by a kitchen knife, and was hacking at one of her plaits as she walked. When she had cut through it she cast it onto the floor and set to work on the other. *Should that be me?* Christa asked herself. *Should I be cutting off my hair to show how I've been shamed?* She knew she would not.

As she moved further away from that one group she became aware of how quiet it was in the cathedral. There must have been three or four hundred people there, but apart from the occasional wail of a baby there was little sound. 'Elsbeth!' she called. 'Elsbeth? Are you here? It is Christa.'

A woman shushed her.

'Hold your noise,' somebody said. 'If you wake the children they'll only cry with hunger.'

Christa walked on through the cathedral, fearful of calling Elsbeth's name again. The priest would need little excuse to cast her out. When a voice spoke her name she froze. She knew in an instant that it wasn't Elsbeth — it was too old, too hoarse. But it was familiar. 'Miss Christa,' she heard again. A woman was limping towards her, her arms held out. Her dress was soiled beyond recognition, and her face puffed and dark with bruises. But that voice ... 'Is it you, Lotte?' she said uncertainly.

'Why, yes, Miss Christa. Praise God that you're spared.'

'And praise God that you are too. Have you any word of the Schwarzes?'

Lotte was beside her now. She grasped Christa's hands. 'Only poor Miss Gertrude is still living,' she whispered, 'but she's bad hurt.' She stopped and took a few deep breaths. 'I doubt she'll live long, my poor wee girl.'

'Can I see her? Is she here?'

'Yes.' Lotte paused, and her grip on Christa's hands tightened. 'The soldiers were cruel to her. Do you understand? They even … I mean … me? Still, I suppose if they hadn't had their sport they would have killed me.' She searched Christa's face. 'Pray God they didn't get their hands on you, Miss Christa.'

Christa tried to speak, but her throat felt as if it had closed. She wanted to deny it. It didn't seem real. Even the pain she still felt could almost have belonged to someone else.

Lotte seemed to understand. 'Ach, no,' she said, and raised her hand to touch Christa's hair. 'Were there many?'

'One.'

'Just the one? Well, that's not so bad, is it?'

Again Christa struggled for words, but none came. She felt as if some great weight was pressing on her, crushing the air out of her lungs in a sob.

'There now, there now. It's over,' Lotte said, putting her arms round her shoulders.

Christa found her voice at last. 'Lotte, please don't tell anyone.'

'Of course I won't, poor girl. And no one would know. You look right as rain, apart from a little bruise on your cheekbone. We may pray he hasn't left his mark, but a few weeks will answer that question, eh?'

Christa rubbed her sleeve across her eyes. 'Will you bring me to Gertrude?'

'Yes, of course.' Lotte began walking very slowly towards the Ernst Kapelle.

'Here, take my arm,' Christa said.

Lotte did so, but could not move any faster. At last they reached the chapel. Lotte beckoned her to a figure lying close to the wall. The light was dimmer in here. 'Here, Miss Gertrude,' Lotte said softly. 'I've found your friend Miss Christa.' She beckoned Christa forward. 'I doubt she'll know you. There's little sense coming out of her, poor thing.'

Gertrude was lying curled on her side with her face turned to the wall. Christa sat beside her. 'Gertrude. Here I am.' She touched her friend's shoulder. Gertrude flinched and groaned. Christa glanced at Lotte, who was watching anxiously. 'Did I hurt her?'

'She's sore all over, the wee soul. She took a fair battering.' Lotte lowered her voice. 'She tried to fight them off, pleaded her belly and all, but they weren't listening.' She paused. 'She might have been better off just letting them.'

'Is the child in her yet?'

'It is. I felt it move last night. God help the poor thing. What a world to be coming into, if it comes at all.'

Gertrude struggled to turn on to her back. Lotte and Christa helped her. Christa gasped. Gertrude's face was like a grotesque mask, distended to twice the size of any normal human's. The eyes were hidden in two mottled puffs of flesh, like some kind of fungus ripening on a forest floor. Her mouth, too, was swollen. The lips were split and black with dried blood. Once, just yesterday, Christa would not have believed that men could do this to a girl. She knew better now. 'Can she eat? Drink?'

'I don't know. There's been little enough food since we've been here.' Lotte lowered her voice again. 'I've a drop of water about me. It's stale, but it's more than a lot of the ones here have. I give her a taste of it when I can. I wouldn't want anyone else to see it.'

Christa thought of the bread hidden in her pocket. She could break it now, share a little with Lotte and Gertrude, but then how would she feed Elsbeth? What she had wasn't enough for herself. If she shared it, as she knew was her Christian duty, she and Elsbeth might starve. Gertrude would die anyway — Lotte had said as much. And Lotte was an old woman, not even kin. Christa felt cold. Satan was inside her heart. She closed her eyes to pray, but the chill filled her. For a moment she was terrified that her goodness would return, and drive out the Deceiver. *Stay*, she whispered inside her head. Dear God, was this what she was becoming? A girl who would pray that the demon of low selfishness would take root in her soul? Who wouldn't even try to fight him off?

'Lotte,' she said quietly, 'have you seen Elsbeth? She was brought here yesterday before the fire took hold of the city.'

Lotte shook her head. 'I haven't, Miss Christa. I don't like to leave Miss Gertrude, except to find a bite of food or a drop of water. I'm that afraid she'll go when I'm not with her, and no poor soul should die alone, should they?' She covered her face with her hands and rocked to and fro. Gertrude lay very still, but the breath still rasped in and out of her swollen mouth.

'I have to look for Elsbeth,' Christa said, 'but when I find her I'll come back.' She couldn't tell if Lotte had heard her, but she got up and made her way on through the cathedral. A priest was standing at the altar, looking down on them all. She wasn't close enough to tell if he was the same man who had let her in, but she kept to the shadows to avoid being seen. A nun approached the altar, crossed herself and beckoned to the priest. There was something striking in the way she gestured to him. She had an air of authority, as if she were used to people doing her bidding. Christa couldn't remember seeing any woman behave in such a way to a man. She wasn't surprised when the priest stepped down from the altar to confer with her. He appeared to listen to her carefully, nodding. She seemed satisfied with his response and turned away, moving quickly towards the door that led to the cloister. The priest walked briskly to the front of the church.

Christa waited until he had passed her, then ran towards the cloister. She knew a little about nuns. Her father had printed dozens of pamphlets cataloguing their vices. They were prone to avarice, unnatural practices and lustful relations with priests and monks. In spite of all this, Christa recognised in the woman a strength she had not seen for what seemed now a long time.

The cloister was full of children. Christa looked from face to face, but they were all so dirty and ragged it was hard to tell the girls from the boys. Some were so grimed with soot that they resembled blackamoors. Two nuns were moving among them, offering a sip of some drink to each one. The nun who had been talking to the priest noticed Christa watching and approached her.

Christa felt herself bristle at the woman's demeanour. She appeared to expect her to retreat.

'Be off with you. There's no water for you here. These little ones need it more than you.'

Christa returned the nun's glare. 'I'm looking for my sister. Her name is Elsbeth Henning, and she is eleven years old.'

The nun waved one hand towards the children. 'Do you think I have time to take a register of every child here?'

'So I will look for her myself.'

'I do not permit all and sundry to come into the cloister.'

'I am not under your rule, madam.'

The nun's face paled and she drew herself up even straighter than before. For a moment Christa thought she would strike her, and clenched her fists to defend herself. Then the nun blinked rapidly. 'I do not believe we have any girls of your sister's age. Most of these children are younger, as you can see.'

Christa looked again at the sorry gathering of youngsters, none of whom were more than seven or eight. Many were nursing toddlers and babies on their laps. Their own little brothers and sisters, or just other lost souls clinging to another for comfort? Christa couldn't tell. The dirt hid any signs of family likeness. 'My sister is slight for her age.'

'You may look, then. But if you find her she is yours to feed and water.'

Christa walked along the north side of the cloister to begin her search. Many children peered up at her. One little fellow held out his arms to her. He must have mistaken her for his mother or nurse. As she walked past him he began to cry. She supposed she could have pretended he belonged to her, persuaded the nun that he was a young nephew or cousin. He would grow up never knowing his loss. But no. She remembered the tiny loaf of bread, and how Elsbeth and she would share it. Only her kin mattered now.

Once, twice, three times she walked round the four sides of the cloister, but Elsbeth was not there. Could Götz have lied? He might have disposed of her to save himself.

She felt a hand touch her arm and turned. It was the nun. The expression on her face was less stern now. 'Child,' she said. Christa wondered at this new gentleness. 'I can show you those who have died today.'

'Are there many?'

'Only a dozen or so. Mostly infants. But there are some older children too. The weak ones. Was your sister frail? You said she was small for her age.'

'I wouldn't say she is frail. She has lived this long, so she must be strong enough.'

'Well, then, I pray that she lives yet.' She crossed herself. 'So, do you wish to see?'

Christa followed the nun through the archway into the cathedral garden. They'd come here sometimes, she and Dieter, Gertrude and Klaus. There was little grass to be seen now. One half of the ground was freshly turned. Two lines of small bodies were laid out in the lee of the west wall. The tiny ones were wrapped in lengths of grimy cloth, but the older children were uncovered. She forced herself to look from face to face. There was one girl of about the same build as Elsbeth. Christa felt as if she had frozen, as if the world had stopped, but then she saw that the dead child's hair was dark, and longer than Elsbeth's. The world began to turn again.

'We have been burying them as quickly as we can,' the nun said, 'for fear of disease.' She looked at the sad bundles closest to her. 'This ground will be full by tomorrow. I do not know what we will do then.'

'My sister is not here.' Christa felt the panic rising inside her. 'I have looked everywhere for her.'

'You are sure she was brought here?'

'I was promised she was.'

The nun made a noise that might have been an expression of doubt or pity. She straightened her shoulders again. 'I have work to do.'

'I will leave you, then. If you see a girl-child, light-haired, quiet and godly…'

'I doubt there will be more children brought here now.'

Christa nodded, and walked back into the main body of the cathedral.

'Miss Christa!' a familiar voice called. She turned, and saw Helga limping towards her.

'Helga …' Christa wondered if she should embrace her, but even now she recoiled at the thought. 'Are you hurt? Your leg …'

'Twisted my ankle. You see what they've done to our streets.' She stopped suddenly, looking Christa up and down. 'You're weary, Miss Christa.' Her mouth twitched with the hint of a bitter smile.

'Have you seen Elsbeth?'

'Not I. I'd have thought she'd cling to you, Miss Christa.'

'We were parted. What of my father and Dieter? Have you seen them?'

'No.' Helga's mouth tightened. 'You don't ask after Andreas. I suppose you wouldn't concern yourself with the likes of him.'

Shame coloured her face. 'I'm sorry. I was thinking of my kin. What of Andreas?'

'I've seen nothing of him either, and he was the best of the lot of you.' Helga stared hard at her. 'There've been wild tales of what the soldiers did. I trust they didn't get hold of you, Miss Christa?'

Hate rose in her like bile. She clenched her fists. She wanted to punch Helga's cunning, lazy face. She swallowed hard, fought to steady her voice. 'They didn't touch me.'

Helga tilted her head to one side, raising an eyebrow. Christa met her gaze steadily. 'If you say so,' Helga said at last.

Suddenly Christa could bear Helga's presence no longer. She had to end this conversation. 'The house is gone. My father and

Dieter ...' Christa's mouth dried. 'It's all gone. So we have nothing to do with each other.'

'I'm owed wages.'

Christa wondered if this was Helga's idea of a joke, but saw from her face that it was not. 'Goodbye, Helga,' she said, and walked away.

It was near nightfall. Even through the smoke-blackened windows there was a sense of the day ending. Christa had searched the cathedral from one end to the other. When she saw a familiar face — someone who attended the Johanniskirche, perhaps, or a regular customer from the market — she asked if they could recall seeing Elsbeth. One or two thought that, yes, they had seen her somewhere, but in the turmoil of the last day they could not recall where or when. She had made herself speak to one of the priests, who remembered a young girl carried in by a soldier. 'She was fallen into a faint,' he said, 'and when she roused she was babbling in a language we none of us knew.' But that was all he could remember. Some of the nuns, who were wise in the ways of these afflictions, had taken her.

Christa could barely stand from exhaustion. She found her way back to Lotte and Gertrude in the Ernst Kapelle, and sat down beside them. Gertrude seemed no better than before, and Christa felt a jab of guilt at the thought of the piece of bread she had concealed in her skirt pocket.

'Have you eaten today?' she whispered to Lotte.

'Not a bite, Miss Christa. There's no food to be got here.'

Christa checked that the women closest to them were not watching. She reached into her pocket and broke off a piece of bread. Slowly she withdrew her hand. 'Maybe you could wet it with your water? She'll hardly be able to chew it, will she?'

Lotte nodded, her eyes fixed on the bread. She drew a small flask from the folds of her skirt and scattered a few drops of water on the dry crust. 'Do you want a sip yourself?' she said reluctantly.

Christa's mouth watered at the prospect of a drink of water, stale or not. 'No, Lotte. You save it for yourself and Gertrude. I'll find my own.' She hesitated for a moment, thinking of her own hunger, then broke off a piece of bread for Lotte.

'Bless you, Miss Christa,' Lotte said, and hid it in her skirt. The demon of selfishness had been defeated, for now, and Christa thanked God for it. She was not entirely lost.

She leaned back against the wall and watched Lotte coax Gertrude to eat. The old woman spoke to her as if she was a little child, encouraging her and stroking her hair gently. The sound of Lotte's voice was soothing; Christa closed her eyes and allowed herself to be lulled by it.

She must have slept, and jumped awake to see a dark-clad man walking past. The swish of his robes must have stirred the air. There was something familiar in—- It was Pastor Ovens! How had he contrived to find sanctuary here? What had become of his grand scheme to attach himself to Falkenberg? She felt her heart pound with shock. That he should have lived when so many had died ... Perhaps he might offer her protection. Then she remembered what the scarred man had done to her, and was filled with shame. How could she speak to Pastor Ovens now? How could she look him in the eye? She did not call to him.

Lotte was sitting just as she had been this last hour in the same place beside Gertrude. Christa looked round the cathedral. Soldiers still stood guarding the doorways, and priests slunk from shadow to shadow. They were, she realised, the only men there. She scanned the huddled groups of survivors again. Women and children. No men — apart from Pastor Ovens, of course, and she could no longer see him. 'Lotte,' she said, 'what has become of the menfolk?'

Lotte shook her head. 'Perished or fled, Miss Christa.'

'Do you think any of ours escaped?'

'None of my household. I saw it myself.'

Christa held her breath, forcing away her memories of Herr Schwarz and Klaus. 'What of my father and Dieter? Did you see them?'

'No, Miss. I doubt your father would have fled without you.'

That was true. He would never have gone without her and Elsbeth, not even to save his own life, but there was a chance he was lying injured somewhere. What about Dieter? Dieter would surely have grabbed any chance for escape without a second thought. Her mind was in turmoil. The idea that he might yet be alive was so sweet she could hardly bear to consider it, while at the same time she felt consumed by anger with him. Would he have fled and left her to suffer what had befallen her? She found that she was trembling. In truth, she didn't know what he might have done. It seemed to her now that she had hardly known him at all.

Thirteen

LUKAS HAD SEEN MANY STRANGE WEDDINGS in his time as a soldier, never any as ramshackle as these. Fifty or more couples were being married at the same time. Captain Sadeler's company had been summoned, with all the others, to stand witness to the ceremony. One of the bridegrooms, a half-witted pikeman from their company, was so drunk he had to be held up by his friends. Some of the others seemed sick with the after-effects of drink. The brides were an odd collection too. Several looked well on in years, the kind of women you might make a grab for in the dim light of a tavern and let go twice as quickly when you saw them in daylight. The greater number were young girls, some with bruised faces and their gowns ripped.

Lukas looked around for Götz, but couldn't find the lad anywhere. These past few days Götz had turned away whenever he had seen Lukas approach, and had avoided all conversation. Lukas had moved his own belongings into the tent that had belonged to the Blickle brothers, since it was clear they would never return from the city. He'd had some hope that Götz would come back to this better accommodation, but he had not. He didn't know where the boy had been laying his head.

He was angry with Götz for prolonging their estrangement, and his anger was as good a way as any of distracting himself from the shame he still felt at what he had done to the girl. The lad was an innocent. Every soldier must run off the leash from time to time. It was allowed for. Yet here was this sorry gathering of brides and their grooms, dragged together for marrying on the orders of General Tilly. For the last day there'd been arguing about it throughout the camp. A squad of priests had overrun the place, haranguing those soldiers who had kept hold of the women they'd taken. Lukas was sick of the sound of the priests' voices, with their monotonous litany of penance and reparation. He was glad now that Götz had helped the girl run away. He'd no wish to be forced to turn husband like these other poor fools.

The priest rhymed through the wedding rites, and the brides and grooms mumbled their responses. Lukas glanced up at his face. The man was as stern as a hanging judge. He uttered the words of dismissal, then sighed deeply, as if this day were confirmation of all he thought worst in the world.

As they tramped away from the wedding field and back to their tents Lukas stared across the river at the ruins of the city. 'Weinsburg!' Captain Sadeler called to him. 'Stop dreaming and ready yourself for work.' Lukas jogged over to where a group of men had gathered. 'We must take our turn with the dead-carts,' Captain Sadeler said. 'Order yourselves in fours or sixes, dependent on your strength. And tie a kerchief round your face for fear of plague.' The captain's injury was mending, but his face was pale and moist. A mild wound-fever, Lukas thought.

They marched in loose formation down to the bridge, tying their kerchiefs over their noses and mouths as they went. The bodies were flowing freely through the water now. There had been a bad day or two when there was a log-jam of them downriver, but General Tilly had dispatched some powder-men to it yesterday, and they had blasted the river clear.

Within the jagged stumps of the city walls they were met by another party of soldiers who had been carting bodies to the river all morning. They changed places with curses and crude jokes, but their laughter sounded hollow to Lukas's ear. He found himself by Götz's side, but the terrible task of pulling the dead clear of the rubble and casting them onto the cart pushed aside any notion of talking. Some of the corpses were ripening now, and Lukas did his best to lift them by their clothes, so that his hands would not touch their skin. The worst were those that had been stripped naked. There was nothing for it but to grab them by the ankles or, worse, under their arms and heave them onto the cart. Lukas's gut twisted, and the spew rose in his throat as his fingers dug into flesh that was as soft as a plum on the turn.

When the cart was full, they hauled it down to the riverside and tipped it until the bodies tumbled into the water. Then it was back up the slope to the city for more. They worked stolidly, ignoring the cathedral bell that tolled the quarter-hours. There was something reassuring in the sound, the sense that order was coming back to this patch of hell, but they knew that the bell signalled no relief for them. They would work until another party was sent, and when no one thought to send fresh troops they worked until nightfall.

They trudged back over the bridge, and Lukas was assailed by a terrible loneliness. He needed a companion, someone to share a bottle with, and words perhaps. He searched out Götz and walked alongside him. The lad glanced at him and, for once, did not move away. Perhaps he had only enough energy to get him back to the camp. 'Shall we be friends again?' Lukas said awkwardly.

For a long moment Götz didn't reply. Lukas was about to fall back when the boy finally spoke. 'It grieves me that we are broken apart.'

'And me.'

Götz appeared to be fighting for breath. Lukas hoped it was the struggle of the walk after the long day — he didn't want the lad crying like a woman in front of all the company. 'You did a wrong thing to that girl,' Götz said at last.

This old rhyme again, Lukas thought. 'What's done is done. I'll make confession and stand right with God.'

'You'd do better to repair the harm, like those other men today.'

'I'd hardly find her. She's likely fifty miles away by now.'

'She was headed for the cathedral. That's where all the women are, the ones who weren't carried back to the camp.'

'Sweet Jesus, Götz! Can you not let this rest?'

'Don't add blasphemy to the list of your sins.' Götz's voice was flat.

Lukas turned the idea over in his mind. Was this the price of restoring their friendship? It seemed so. Was it worth paying? He'd no wish for another Katherine. Then again, the girl might be dead by now. Hadn't they been bringing bodies out of the cathedral by the dozen? Even if she lived and he was forced to wed her she'd likely run away at the first chance. He'd be rid of her and his sin wiped clean. 'I'll go to Captain Sadeler in the morning,' he said. 'Seek his permission to find her, and make things right. Will that give you satisfaction?'

Götz nodded.

They walked on in silence. Even if the girl were living, she might take payment in return for her dishonour. He'd do his best to turn his booty into cash before he went looking for her. Better to be poor and free than a well-fortuned husband.

Captain Sadeler listened to Lukas's petition, then dismissed his lieutenant and servants. When they were alone he spoke: 'You're a fool, Weinsburg, to seek trouble in this way. You know nothing of the girl.'

'I ruined her, Captain, and I must set that right.'

'If I was you I wouldn't pay so much mind to what the priests say. What do they know about the taking of a city?'

'In all conscience, sir, I am persuaded that amends must be made.'

'Ach, well, you may pray she'll take the offer of money. Her type put a price on everything.' The captain made out a pass for him. Now that order was restored General Tilly had required that the men should no longer roam the city ruins as they pleased. 'I suppose

I should be grateful that you let her run off, Weinsburg, although I thought to have you flogged for it when first I heard,' he said, as he placed his seal on the pass. 'I've one wife already in Munich, and she furnishes me with more expense than I would wish.'

It was mid-morning when Lukas and Götz made their way to the cathedral. The soldiers on sentry duty spoke to them briefly, then let them in. They stood in the transept, and waited for their eyes to become accustomed to the gloom. The place was in tumult. A group of soldiers were raising a statue of the Blessed Virgin into a niche close to the altar. It was twice the size of a grown man, and they had fashioned a pulley with ropes to hoist it up. A priest — he was as bald as an egg — danced round them, flapping his hands and shouting orders in a reedy voice. Smaller statues of saints were being placed in the side chapels. The women and children of the city were gathered near a side door, with nuns shooing them like sheep. Lukas approached one of the nuns. 'Where are these women being taken?'

She seemed irritated at being distracted from her task. 'We are removing them to our convent, now that it's safe to leave.' She took in his scarred face and commonplace attire. 'What business is it of yours, anyway? These poor creatures have had enough distress from the likes of you.'

Lukas bristled at her tone, but his anger was muted by guilt. He walked back to where Götz was waiting for him. 'This is impossible. How will we ever find her in this press?'

'You've barely tried,' Götz said, with a reproachful look that made Lukas feel more wretched. 'I'll find someone with position to ask.'

He left Lukas and crossed the nave to where the bald priest was still supervising the positioning of the Virgin. Lukas watched them confer. The priest pointed across the cathedral, and Götz walked away. The women were still milling about. For each one the nuns got through the door another would fall back. Some seemed unwilling to go, while others could not manage the weight of the frail or injured they were carrying.

As the crowd shifted Lukas caught the odd glimpse of Götz. He was in conversation with another priest and an upright nun. The two holy ones looked in Lukas's direction, and shame burned on his face. The nun laid her hand on Götz's arm and pointed into the throng. Götz nodded. She made her way into the crush and drew out a girl, followed by a tall, stout man dressed in the dark clothes of a pastor. Lukas couldn't bear to watch. He turned towards one of the side chapels. No one had yet placed a sacred statue in it so there was only a small altar, with a plain wooden cross. The Lutherans liked their churches so, he'd heard, as dull and joyless as they were. Still, there was something comforting about its soft darkness. No sad-faced Virgin to remind him of how fallen he was.

'Lukas,' Götz said quietly, behind him.

He took a breath and turned. His friend stood there, with the nun, the priest, the dark-robed man and the girl. The other women were still being driven from the cathedral. Some strained to see why one of their number had been pulled aside, but the nuns chided and chivvied them through the door.

Was this girl really the one he had taken? Lukas's memory of that day was so clouded he could not tell.

The nun squeezed the girl's arm and spoke gently to her: 'Are you certain this is the man?'

'I remember the scar on his face.'

The nun turned to Lukas. 'You have agreed to make honourable reparation for the harm you did her?' There was no gentleness in her voice now.

'I have, and may God forgive me.'

'Amen to that. You offer her marriage?'

'Aye. Or if she would rather, I can give her a sum in compensation for — what she has lost.'

The nun turned to the girl. 'What say you?'

She took a deep breath. 'What would my standing be if I took payment instead of marriage?' She looked at the pastor. 'What say you, Pastor Ovens?'

The clergyman puffed out his chest. 'In the fifth book of Moses it is written that if a man lay hold of a virgin who is not betrothed, and lie with her, then he must wed her and pay her father fifty shekels of silver.'

'But what of this circumstance? Can I, with honour, take compensation, and not marry the man?'

'There is no reference I know of to such. Not in the Book of God's Word.'

'My father ...' She stopped, and took a few deep breaths. 'My father taught me that where the Word of God does not give clear instruction on any matter, I must turn to my own conscience and pray that the Lord will illuminate it.' She looked from the pastor to the priest, but neither made any comment. 'I believe that only marriage will wash away the stain of my dishonour.'

Lukas felt as if there was no air in the building. She would have him. He was a done man.

She spoke again, turning to the pastor. 'Pastor Ovens,' she said, 'I have no wish to be married to this Papist.'

So she wanted a husband to mend her broken honour but she didn't want him. The little bitch. The pastor said nothing. Lukas noticed how determined the girl seemed, how controlled.

'You should be grateful he will have you,' the nun said. 'If you would wed him, say so now. Father Pius can't wait upon your whim.'

'Pastor Ovens,' the girl said again, 'there was a time when you seemed to admire me. Would I not make a sound wife for you? We are of the same mind, and I have managed my father's house this last number of years.'

Pastor Ovens adjusted his robes as if he had the itch. 'Christa ... Fräulein Henning ... I regret that I cannot marry you.'

'I need to stay in Magdeburg. Elsbeth is here somewhere, and for all I know my father and Dieter could be injured or captive.' Now she addressed Götz. 'You promise me that you brought my sister here safely?'

'I swear it, on all that is holy,' Götz replied.

She turned back to the pastor, holding out her hands to him like a beggar. 'So you see, Pastor Ovens, I must stay in Magdeburg. You know Elsbeth, what a gentle soul she is. She has no one else now. And I must be married for the sake of my good name.'

The pastor was edging away from her. 'I cannot marry one such as you.'

'What do you mean?'

'You are ...' He scratched his neck. 'You are spoiled.'

That gave her pause. 'Not through my own fault,' she said at last.

Pastor Ovens laughed, in the way that a man might before delivering bad tidings. 'Well ... where are your bruises? I see not a scratch, not a mark upon you.'

The girl lifted her hand to her cheek, and Lukas remembered the slap Baxandall had given her. Any bruise that had caused was gone now. She must be quick to heal.

The priest touched Pastor Ovens's arm and whispered in his ear. The pastor flinched at first — perhaps he did not like to be so close to a Papist — but attended to the man's words and nodded.

'Young woman,' the priest said, 'how is it that your gown is not torn, or even badly soiled? And why do you show no sign of pain? Did this man not force you onto the floor?'

The girl glanced briefly at Lukas. The expression on her face chilled him. 'He told me to lie down.'

'And you complied without resistance?' The priest left the question hanging.

She made to speak, but the pastor interrupted her. 'So you see, Fräulein Henning, I really could not demean myself ... and, of course, you have no dowry now.'

Lukas saw her resolve leave her. It was as if the flame had gone out in her soul. 'I've little choice, then,' she said, her eyes now fixed on his. 'It seems I must wed you.'

'Aye.'

'Well, let us get on with it, shall we?' the priest said, all bustle now. 'It can be done quickly enough in this chapel.' He indicated the one Lukas had been looking at not ten minutes earlier.

They made their way to the plain altar, led by the priest. 'You, boy,' he said to Götz, 'are you old enough to stand witness to your friend?'

'Yes, Father, and gladly.' Lukas felt a pang of gratitude at Götz's reply. The lad had forgiven him.

'And you, sir, will you be the girl's witness?' he asked Pastor Ovens.

The pastor made a solemn bow.

Götz stepped forward. 'I beg your pardon, Father, but I think he's not a right witness.'

The priest's mouth opened and closed. They all stared at Götz. Finally Pastor Ovens spoke, his voice trembling with affront: 'Why do you say such a thing?'

'It falls to kin or a friend to be witness. You are not of her family, and you have not behaved like a friend to her this day.'

There was something implacable about Götz, Lukas thought. He had the makings of a priest, to be sure.

The girl was gazing at the boy with a strange expression in her eyes ... What was it? Lukas felt uneasy, as if he had stumbled upon some private business. Pastor Ovens puffed out his chest again, and seemed about to speak, but the nun cut him off. 'In the name of all holy things, I will stand witness for the girl! Now let us speed this business to an end, for I have more to do than I know how to tell.'

The priest began the ceremony. He spoke in Latin, and nodded at Lukas and Christa when he required a response from them. It seemed he had taken the nun's words to heart, for he rattled through the missal in haste, and all was done before five minutes had passed. 'There will be a Mass here tomorrow,' he said. 'You should attend. It will place the final seal on your marriage.'

'Mass?' the girl said. 'Here?'

The priest's mouth twitched. 'Yes, child. Tomorrow this place will be returned to the true faith.'

The nun and the priest strode back to persuade the last of the women out of the cathedral. Pastor Ovens crept away. Lukas and

Götz stood with the girl. She straightened and turned to Lukas. 'What is your name?'

'Lukas Weinsburg. A musketeer in Colonel von Breuner's battalion.'

'How many years have you been a soldier?'

'Fifteen, near enough. I joined as a boy.'

'And do you have rank?'

Lukas was becoming irritated. 'I am a private soldier.' He waited for her to comment, feeling the flame of anger in his gut, but she said nothing.

'He was a sergeant,' Götz butted in. 'His being a private now … it was over a misunderstanding. He'll be raised up again before you know it.'

Lukas knew Götz meant well, but his words increased his annoyance. 'We should be going back to the camp. Come.' He stalked to the main door of the cathedral, not waiting for them.

They walked in silence until they got to the bridge. It was Götz, of course, who started the talking again. 'Your name is Christa?' he said. He sounded shyer now.

'Christa Henning.' The girl paused, then went on, 'I can cook, sew, launder linen, mind children, tend invalids, run a market stall … I will be a useful enough wife, I hope.' Her prattle had a brittle, nervous edge, and grated on him. He wondered how he would endure her.

Fourteen

CHRISTA WOKE BEFORE DAYBREAK. IN THE moment between sleeping and waking she thought she was at home, but before she had opened her eyes she knew that the warm body beside her was not Elsbeth's, but Lukas Weinsburg's. She said his name again in her head. Whatever the circumstance, this was the name that had repaired the dishonour done to her. In the eyes of God and the world she was restored to virtue. She clung to that thought.

This was a better tent than the little one she had slept in after the city's fall — how many nights ago was it? She had lost track. Her mind seemed in an odd, frozen state. Almost as if she had simply stopped. For so long she had struggled — running the house, caring for Elsbeth, worrying about Dieter — and now it was all over. In some other part of her mind she felt sure they were still there, hiding in a secret untouched courtyard in the city. If only she could find her way to them. Even last night, walking through the camp, she had seen a man who, for a wild moment, she had thought was her father. Then he had turned and she had realised her mistake.

When had she last prayed? Not for days, it seemed. *Dear Lord, forgive me my neglect of You ...* Had she forgotten to pray in these last terrible days? Perhaps that was why all this had been visited on her.

Lukas turned over beside her. She held her breath, wondering if he was about to stir, but his breathing settled again. Soldiers, she had discovered, slept in their clothes. So, it seemed, did their wives. Her petticoat and chemise must be filthy after so many days' wear, but she did not know how to remedy it. She had no other clothes, and no means to wash the ones she had. The river water was still rank with all that had been thrown into it.

The sun must be rising now. Christa could see the entrance to the tent outlined in light. She slid from under the blanket and quietly searched for food. There was a cup of split peas, the stump end of a *Bratwurst* and a drop of stale beer in a jug. She lifted them all, along with a little pot she found at the front of the tent, and slipped outside.

Others were up, even at this early hour. They were mostly soldiers, although there were one or two women as well. Some looked at her, but no one spoke. One or other of the early risers had lit a fire. Christa hung back, until she saw that all were making use of it to heat their breakfast. She mixed the peas, beer and *Bratwurst* together in the pot and set it on the fire. Water would have been better than beer, but there was none clean to be had. She shook the pot. There wasn't even a stick to stir it with. What this stew might taste like she didn't dare imagine. But it was food, and that was all that mattered in the end.

Order was being restored to the camp. The men were summoned to drill. Lukas left her with instructions to look through the loot he had gathered on his journey through Magdeburg. 'You might find some attire for yourself,' he said.

'She may search through my booty as well,' Götz said, with a smile at Lukas. 'You and I have little use for petticoats.' He pulled a bulging knapsack from his tent and set it in front of her.

He'd meant the joke kindly, she supposed, but when she took the knapsack inside the tent and emptied it out she was almost undone. Here were her own best stockings; a good lace collar that had belonged to her long-dead mother, a shirt of Dieter's. There were other items that had not belonged to her household. Fine clean linen of a size that would fit her, God be praised. She could not help but wonder what had happened to the girl these clothes had belonged to. They seemed brand new, and unworn. From a wedding chest, perhaps. She felt a pang of grief and forced it down. *Harden your heart*, she told herself. *You'll make better use of it than she can.*

She folded the garments that would not fit her, and went to place them back in Götz's knapsack. There was something heavy at the bottom that had not tumbled out when she had first emptied it. She reached in. What was it? A book? She pulled it out, and looked at the binding. Fine calfskin of a quality she recognised. When she opened it she found it was in English. *The Works of Homer, Prince of Poets, in His Odysses, Vol I. Imprinted at Magdeburg by Paul Henning, 1631.* She remembered it. It had been a special order, made before the siege took hold, and never collected by the diamond merchant who had commissioned it. She held the book in her hands, running her fingers on the uncut edges of the pages. It was tempting to start reading it. She might find a little blade and cut the pages. Strange to think that the printed words she could see on the title page had been set in place by her father or Andreas. When she laid her hands on those words, she was touching them, nearly. But she had no leisure to sit reading. What would he think, that Lukas Weinsburg, if he returned to find her in such a fashion? She could not risk it.

She went through Lukas's loot, and garnered another petticoat for herself, and a gown of almost the right size for her. This time she had no weakening thoughts of their first owner. She changed her clothes. It would have been more pleasing to have had some water to wash herself, but that would have to wait. Lukas himself had changed into a fresh shirt this morning. He had left the soiled one folded beside his bed. Christa picked it up with her own dirty linen.

Outside a few women were occupying themselves with shaking

out the bedding from their tents. Christa asked one if there was anywhere to wash linen. She was met with a quizzical stare. 'There's a stream in the forest beyond the camp, but no sensible girl would go near the place,' the woman said. 'You may content yourself unless you can persuade your man to come with you and stand guard.'

'Perhaps I will, when he gets back.'

'We'll hardly see much of them today.'

The woman seemed disinclined to say more, and Christa had no hunger for talk. She carried the dirty clothes back to the tent, and wondered what to do next. There was no tidying to do. Lukas had few possessions, it seemed, and what he had was neatly ordered.

When the men finally returned they seemed in better spirits, and sat down in the afternoon sun. Some of the other women ran off at their order and came back with pitchers of beer. Christa stood close to their tent. 'What is the reason for all this merriment?' she asked one of the other wives.

'We're to leave this cursed place,' the woman said, cradling the beer-jug with both hands. 'The day after tomorrow, at daybreak, we'll be on the march, thank God.'

'I cannot leave here,' Christa said. 'My sister is in the city somewhere, and I am all she has.'

The other woman shrugged. 'The army is your family now.' She walked off, bearing the beer to her man.

Christa knew she must speak with Lukas, and persuade him that she could not leave the city. She walked over to where he sat beside Götz. 'I cannot leave with the army until I have found my sister,' she said. She was aware of laughter and coarse words from some of the other men. Lukas was mellow with drink, but she noticed irritation cross his face.

'Give me peace, woman.'

'I cannot leave until I have found her. I will not.' Anger filled her and she felt strong — stronger than him.

'Keep your voice down. Don't make a show of me before the whole company.'

The other men and some of their women had stopped their chat and she sensed them eyeing her.

'Weinsburg, she has you well nagged already,' Baxandall called. The men standing closest to him laughed approvingly. 'You need to show her who is master.'

Christa wheeled round to face him. 'Like you do to that poor child?' she shouted, pointing at Baxandall's wife. The girl was startled, and looked up at Baxandall with a mixture of fear and need on her face. He, however, kept his eyes on Christa, and she realised she had gone too far. The same terror that had gripped her on the day the men had come to the house took hold of her again. Her anger was gone, replaced by fear.

'Hold there,' a female voice called. The crowd parted to let through a young woman on horseback. She trotted her pony closer to them, and looked from Christa to Baxandall's wife. 'I'll tolerate no fighting between you whores.'

It was a moment before Christa realised the woman was talking about her. The shock of being given such a name stunned her at first, but then her anger flared back to life. She took in the woman's green velvet gown and the smear of red on her cheeks. 'I am a wife, not a whore,' she said. She had not sounded as measured as she had intended.

The woman sneered. 'It was a Magdeburg marriage, was it not?' She glanced around the crowd. 'Who does this girl belong to?'

For a moment no one spoke. 'He's ashamed to own her,' Baxandall said.

'She is mine,' Lukas said at last.

The woman in the green gown walked her pony towards him. 'Then you had best teach her manners. Like this.' She lifted her riding crop and brought it down hard on Lukas's back. The crowd laughed nervously. Lukas had not flinched at the blow, but he looked as if he could gladly have ripped the woman's heart out. She smiled tightly at him, then turned her pony and trotted away.

Lukas turned to Christa. His face was drained of colour, except for the raw red of his scars. 'Go into the tent.'

She ducked through the entrance and sat on the stool. How bad would this be? She remembered Gertrude lying in the cathedral, her face swollen from the beating she'd received. The men outside were still calling and laughing. She heard Baxandall shout words she didn't quite understand. Things quietened. Still Lukas did not come. Christa picked at a splash of soup on her skirt. She remembered all the stories she had read of brave Protestant martyrs, defiant in the face of brutish Papists. Why could she not be like them? *You are a coward*, she thought. But, no, that wasn't quite right. The martyrs gave their lives for the faith, knowing they were going to be with God. Elsbeth needed her to be alive. If Lukas beat her, killed her, even, that would be little comfort to Elsbeth.

There was movement at the entrance to the tent and Christa stiffened, relaxing a little when she saw Götz.

'He's gone to walk off his anger.' The boy stood awkwardly, not moving closer. Christa realised they had never been alone together in here. 'Be careful with him. I would not like to see you harmed.'

'What will he do to me?'

'I don't know.' Götz paused. 'He's not like Baxandall. He tries to be a good man.'

'Who was that woman in the green dress? How was it that she could speak to my husband so easily?'

'I do not like to say it.'

Christa felt a sudden pang of compassion for him. 'You will not offend me,' she said softly.

'She is … They call her the Marshal of the Whores.' He kept his eyes downcast. 'She is employed to keep good order among … the women of the camp.'

Christa nodded. 'I see.' So her honour was not restored. To these people around her she was no better than a ruined maiden. She closed her eyes and focused her mind on Elsbeth again. 'Advise me, Götz. How can I persuade my husband to let me look once more for my sister? Without provoking him, I mean.'

'I could speak with him in the morning, perhaps suggest that I go with you.' He wiped his mouth with his hand. 'Is that what you would have me do?'

'Thank you, yes. Are you thirsty? There's a little beer here.'

He lifted the jug from the table and drank. She could sense his disappointment that there wasn't more. 'I should go.'

Suddenly she was fearful. It had been her hope that a husband would offer her protection, but with the mood that was upon Lukas she had no faith in that. 'Are there many men outside?'

'No, they are about their business in the camp.' He hesitated, seeming now to understand the meaning behind her question. 'Baxandall has gone to play dice.'

The tension inside her eased a little. 'I will be well here now. There are things I must be doing. You go.'

By nightfall the sky had clouded and a soft rain was falling. It drove everyone into their tents. Christa set Lukas's little pot outside to catch some rainwater for drinking, then sat by the table, waiting for him to return. There was a clay lamp, with oil enough and a decent wick, but she had no means of lighting it. The rain had been the death of the fire outside. She peeped out through the gap in the tent door. There were lights glowing through the canvas of some of the other tents, but she was shy of going to ask for a flame.

Eventually she saw Lukas and Götz dawdling through the camp. They walked as easily as if it were a fine summer's day, unconcerned by the rain that had plastered their hair to their skulls. Götz was unsteady on his feet. She pulled open the canvas to let them in. They seemed to fill the tent, Götz laughing as they dripped rainwater onto the floor. When they shrugged off their wet coats the smell of drink rose off them. Lukas hunted out his tinderbox and fumbled with it. 'Damn it,' he said, when he couldn't raise a spark. 'The damp has got into it somehow.'

'I'll borrow a flame from our neighbour,' Götz said, lifting the lamp and slipping outside.

Lukas set the tinderbox carefully on the table. 'We may hope for fair weather tomorrow to dry it out.'

Christa thought to speak. She could say, *God willing*. But no. He might think she was being overly pious and she understood now the danger of vexing him. But she must reply or her silence might anger him more. 'Aye,' she said at last.

He reached for his satchel and pulled out a loaf of black bread and some cheese. 'There's food here. Götz has a bottle, naturally.'

'Hold the door there,' Götz called, from outside. Lukas lifted the canvas and he came in, cradling the lamp in one hand, and shielding the flame from the rain with the other. He set it on the table, and Lukas fastened the door flap against the weather. The three sat down to eat.

The food was all gone, but there was a little drink yet. Christa had been persuaded to take her share of the liquor. It was stronger than anything she had tasted at home, and left her thirstier than before. For all that, it had warmed her and taken the edge off her misery. She stood up to discover that the ground shifted beneath her feet. The two men were watching her. 'Have a care, Christa,' Götz said. 'We don't want you tumbling.' His voice was kindly enough, but she felt ashamed to be so unsteady. Lukas said nothing. His face was flushed and sullen.

'I'm going to fetch in the pot,' she said. 'There may be water enough for drinking, and my mouth is parched.'

'Götz will reach it in to you when he leaves now,' Lukas said, and stared hard at his friend.

Götz nodded vaguely, then caught Lukas's look and rose. 'Aye, I'd best be away. We'll have much to do tomorrow.' He went out, pausing to hand the pot of rainwater in to Christa through the tent opening.

Christa offered it to Lukas. He drank half of its contents, and gave the remains to her. When she had finished, he pointed at the bedding. 'Lie down.' He had that dark look on his face, and she understood now what it signified. She did as she was bade.

Lukas snuffed out the lamp with his fingertips. She heard him move cautiously across the floor towards the bedding and felt him ease himself down beside her. For a moment she thought she had been wrong, that he would turn over and sleep, but then he put his hand on her face, holding her steady while he pressed his mouth against hers. His beard was rough against her skin, and his lips were dry and flaked. She tried to turn away as he pushed his tongue inside her mouth, but he held on to her so tightly that she thought she might suffocate. Finally he stopped. 'Don't turn away from me when I want you, do you hear?'

'Yes,' Christa said, forcing herself not to flinch at the sour smell of liquor on his breath.

She sensed him fumbling with his clothes. Then he reached over and pushed up her skirt and petticoat. 'Come now,' he said, 'you must play your part in this.' He rolled on top of her, and forced her legs apart.

It was worse this time than it had been before. She did not understand how this could be so. Last time she had lain on the floor, with Baxandall and the captain jeering, and she had not understood what was being done to her. So why was this now worse? It was hurting more. She cried out, and her pain seemed to urge him on. At least he couldn't see her tears in the darkness.

When he had finished he lay gasping on top of her, then pulled himself away and lay down by her side. When he had caught his breath he said, 'Are you crying?'

'Yes.'

'Good.'

Good. So this was her punishment, because she had opened the way for Baxandall to mock him today? She felt him turn over so that his back was towards her. Within moments he was asleep.

The voice entered her dreams. It was a man shouting. He seemed in terror of his life. Christa raised herself on one elbow. Lukas slept beside her. Perhaps it had been a dream. The cry came again. It was almost a scream this time. It was coming from the tent next to theirs. Götz's tent. She shook Lukas awake.

He grunted and cursed her, but sat up and listened. 'The night terrors,' he said. 'I'd best attend to him.' He left the tent and Christa lay down again. She heard Lukas talking to Götz. His voice was so soft that she couldn't make out what he was saying, but she recognised the tone of consolation and reassurance. It was how she had spoken to Elsbeth when she grew agitated. The thought of her sister pierced her with such a sharp pain that she could barely breathe. What if Elsbeth were waking from a nightmare in some unfamiliar place? Who would soothe her? She pushed the thought away. It could do nothing but distress her, and such misery would benefit no one.

Lukas came back into the tent and lay down beside her. 'How does he?' she said.

'Awake now, and afeard to go to sleep again.'

'Can we do nothing for him?'

'What's to be done? I entreated him to bring his bedding in here. Company can keep the night terrors away. But he's shy of intruding.' He turned away, as if he had done talking.

'Is it because he is new to soldiering, do you think?'

'Go to sleep.'

She couldn't tell if Lukas had fallen asleep. She suspected he was as wakeful as she was. He was very still, but there was no ease in his body. There were no more cries from Götz.

The next morning they were up early, the whole camp in a bustle of preparation. Christa observed Lukas's mood as he took his breakfast. He made no mention of the happenings of the previous day and night. His eyes seemed a little red with the drink and the broken sleep, but that was all.

Götz came to call upon them after they had eaten. He wore his restless night more easily than Lukas, but Christa could smell the liquor on his breath. He must have breakfasted on it. Still, he seemed steady enough. He signalled to her that she should move away, so she went on the pretext of seeking bread. There was none to be had, of course, so she returned empty-handed. She loitered within sight of Lukas and Götz, unsure whether the subject of

Elsbeth would yet have been broached. They were both occupied with cleaning their muskets, but Götz must have spotted her for he waved her over. Lukas polished the barrel of his weapon with a rag, not watching her as she walked towards him. 'So,' he said, 'Götz tells me I should allow you to go seeking for your sister.' He glanced up at her. 'I have little need of another belly to fill, but he persuades me it's my Christian duty.'

'Sir … husband … it is my belief that my sister is still living. If I could find her it would be a great consolation to me.'

'We have orders to march.'

'Not until tomorrow.' Christa steadied herself. She must not become shrill. 'If I could but go today to the convent where the women were taken and search there for her …'

'And what if you search and do not find? The Emperor's army will not wait upon your concerns.'

'I know that. But I would have done all that was within my power.'

Lukas looked at Götz. 'You'd be as well to get permission from Captain Sadeler. And don't be all day about it.'

Christa hardly dared to believe what she was hearing. 'We can go?'

'Aye, you can go.'

After the chaos of the camp the convent seemed like heaven, Papist as it was. The main entrance was guarded by soldiers, but within it was hard to credit that they were in a fallen city. The cloister was quiet as they walked through, following a young nun. They climbed a staircase, and at the top she stopped. 'There are many fewer now than were in the cathedral. The fever, alas, has taken a great number. You say the child is eleven years of age?'

'Yes, but she is slight. Fair hair, blue eyes. Most devout.'

The nun nodded. 'I cannot think that any of the girl-children could be her. But let us look and be sure.'

She led them into a long room with narrow beds running down both sides. They walked slowly along, looking at each child. 'Was she quite well when you left her at the cathedral, Private Fuhrmann?' the nun asked. Christa noticed how he hesitated before he replied.

'She had fallen into a faint, so I carried her. She weighed almost nothing.'

'My sister was prone to … faintings,' Christa said. 'The Holy Spirit came upon her.'

The nun turned to her. 'Truly? She was visited by the Holy Spirit? How was this manifested?'

Christa felt a bristling of resentment, but the nun seemed well intentioned. They were not to be trusted, she knew, but still … 'When she prayed, most particularly when we were at holy service, she would be overpowered by God's love, and tumble down.'

'And did she speak?'

'Aye, but with a strange babble no one could comprehend.'

The nun looked thoughtful, but made no further remark as she led them through to another room. Christa felt a heaviness in her body. Elsbeth was not here. She knew it. She was weary, and wished she could link arms with Götz to support herself.

In a bed at the far end of the last room they found Gertrude, with Lotte at her side. Gertrude was sitting upright. The swelling of her face had subsided, but her bruises had darkened into a horrible pattern of ink blue and jaundice yellow. Christa ran to her. 'Dear Gertrude,' she said, but could find no other words. She had almost forgotten her friend in her concern to find Elsbeth.

Gertrude laid one of Christa's hands on her swollen belly. She felt the child stir. Gertrude tried to smile, but her mouth was stiff with scars. 'Do you see? He knows you are to be his godmother.'

Christa leaned forward to kiss her, but Lotte reached over and held her back. 'Best not to, Miss Christa.'

'Why?'

Lotte looked away, as if she had been caught out in some wrongdoing. The nun spoke. 'Because of the fever, of course. It's as well not to be embracing with so much disease about.' Christa caught a grateful glance from Lotte to the nun.

'Will you visit us again soon?' Gertrude said. Her voice was hoarse and she sounded like an old woman.

Christa stood. 'The army moves on tomorrow. I must go with it.'

Gertrude frowned, not understanding, but Lotte smiled sadly at her. 'Pray God you will come back here some day.' She glared at Götz.

Christa felt a powerful wish to correct Lotte, to make her know that Götz was not the one who had wronged her, but she felt so tired. Explanations were beyond her today.

They had been through the convent, but there was no sign of Elsbeth. The same nun led them back towards the door, but when they reached it she asked them to wait, and strode away. Christa and Götz stood in silence. She would gladly have spoken to him, but her mind was empty. All the normal doings of her life had gone. There was little now to be made into light conversation between acquaintances. He seemed to feel likewise constrained. The more lacking in ease the silence grew, the more impossible it was to break it.

At last the nun returned, accompanied by a much older woman who walked with the aid of a staff, although her bright eyes hinted at a lively mind. 'Sister Mathild,' the nun said, 'this is the girl who is seeking her sister. Tell her of the child you tended.'

Sister Mathild looked at Christa. There was an air of excitement about her. 'She was in a dead faint when she was brought to me. I let her lie so for a time. It's as well not to stir a body in such a state — that's what I've found.'

'But was it Elsbeth?' Christa said.

'All that you said of her matched with Sister Mathild's remembering. More than that we cannot tell,' the younger nun said.

'Where is she now?'

Sister Mathild seemed impatient to continue with her story. 'When her spirit revived she woke and talked in some strange tongue, praying, I should say, for she called out Our Lord's name over and over, and then this odd babble of words, but all the time with such holiness on her face. You would have thought she was shining.'

Christa felt her chest tighten and fought for breath. This must have been Elsbeth. That glow she had about her when she fell into her rapture — how many other children would have shown such signs? Christa tried to speak, but the words would not come. She felt Götz's eyes on her.

'Sister,' he said, 'what became of the child?'

'I was coming to that,' Sister Mathild said, glancing at each of them in turn. 'A fine lady had come in to help us in the cathedral. Well, when I say help, she was a little too grand for that, but she encouraged us, and paid for some Masses. A very pious lady.' Sister Mathild paused, and for a moment Christa thought she was in need of another prompt, but at last she continued: 'This lady said she would take the child, and find a safe haven for her. And so she carried her off.'

Christa found her voice again. 'But where? Where did they go? Do you not know this lady's name? Why did you not ask these things of her?'

Sister Mathild laid her hand on Christa's arm. 'Dear child, we had little enough food and water. You saw how things were in the cathedral, did you not? It was an answered prayer to have one less mouth to feed. The lady was well attired, and I believe her intentions were good. We had little reason to oppose her.'

Götz stepped forward. He held out his arm to Christa, as if he was afraid she might fall. 'At least you know that she is living, and likely to be well sheltered.'

'But she is not with me. We are all that is left of my family.'

'There's no remedy for it. We march tomorrow.'

Christa closed her eyes and prayed silently. *Lord, let me bear this.* When she had calmed herself she opened her eyes again, and thanked the nuns for all that they had done. She and Götz left the convent and made their way back towards the camp.

Lukas had been at work, preparing for the company's departure. He looked hot and irritable when he saw them. 'You took your time,' he grumbled. He made no enquiry as to their success. 'We must take down the tent now, and stow it on one of the wagons.'

'But where shall we sleep tonight?' Christa said.

'On the ground, under a blanket.' He spoke as if it was the most natural thing in the world to sleep in the open, as if they were livestock.

They worked together to pack their belongings into Lukas's knapsack, and wrap everything that could not be fitted there inside the fabric of the tent. 'Smooth it out flat,' Lukas ordered. They stood, one at either side of the rough square of canvas. Lukas laid the supports like a bundle of firewood and tied them together with a strip of cloth. 'Come here and we'll roll it up together.'

'Why, Lukas,' Götz said, watching them struggle, 'you were better off when you slept in this humble tent.' He patted the compact package he had made of it.

'Don't be standing there when you could be helping us.'

Götz set his own belongings down and joined them in rolling the larger tent up, then tying it into a long parcel. 'Is it right what they say in the camp, Lukas, about the King of Sweden?' he said, pulling a tight knot.

The shock Christa felt on hearing this stopped her short. 'The King of Sweden? Is he coming?'

Lukas shot Götz a warning look. 'Enough gabble. Let's get this done and be off to the cathedral.' He glanced up at Christa. 'It is being rededicated today, to Our Lord's Blessed Mother. The city is being renamed.'

'How can it be called anything but Magdeburg?'

'A victor may do as he pleases. General Tilly has ordered that it now be known as Marienburg, in honour of Our Lady.'

Christa helped the two men finish binding the tent. Her heart was pounding with anger and hope. If the King of Sweden was nearly here there was hope for Germany and for the faith. Perhaps he would restore the city, and give it back its proper name. General

Tilly's vanity might be short-lived. But then she looked over the river at the ruins, and hope withered as quickly as it had blossomed. The King of Sweden was too late for her. The city might as well be called Marienburg. The place she knew had gone. Magdeburg was dead.

Most of the men of the company, and a good number of the women, had gone to the cathedral for the rededication. Christa remained behind, sitting guard over Lukas and Götz's knapsacks and weapons. She had been in the camp only a few days, but she had grown used to the little settlement where the company had bided. Now that it was dismantled and loaded into the wagons she felt the lack of it. The ground seemed naked, and she felt more lost than she had before.

She studied the muskets. It was the first time she had seen such a weapon at close quarters. How strange it was that such a simple device could rob a man of his life. Still, she supposed that a knife was simpler yet, and many fell at its touch.

The bells of the cathedral rang out, and the cannon fired time after time. The two sounds, so ill met, seemed to hang in the air, reverberating for a long moment after both had ended. A soldier came back into the patch of ground that had been the company's camping place. It was Baxandall. He was carrying a jug of beer and had his arm round his young wife. She looked little older than Elsbeth, but Christa saw now that her belly was swollen with child. Most of the other camp women moved freely about the place, attending to the business of cooking and mending, but this girl had rarely peeped outside her tent. Christa noticed that her eye was blackened and there were bruises on her arms.

Baxandall signalled for his wife to sit down where their tent had been. He walked towards Christa and looked across the river at the city. 'Aye, the Papists are all there, crowing their victory.'

'Are you a Protestant, then?'

'I am, thank God.' He returned her gaze with an intensity that made her feel uneasy. 'You are not alone here, you see.'

There was movement by the pile of Baxandall's belongings. Christa saw the girl crouched there, watching and listening. Baxandall followed her gaze and barked something at the girl in a tongue Christa did not understand. The girl tried to reply, but Baxandall shouted her down.

'What land is she from?' Christa said.

'No land.'

Christa found herself wishing that Lukas would return. If he were here Baxandall would not be talking to her, edging closer, as he was now. 'I must be going.'

'Where to? There's no requirement for Protestants to be anywhere today.'

'I'll go to the sutlers while the place is quiet.'

'Let me accompany you.'

Christa wished she knew a way to deny him. The cathedral bells began to peal. *Please, God, let them return soon.* Baxandall extended his arm to her. She shook her head. 'My husband would not wish me to take the arm of another man.'

'You will insult me if you refuse.'

She sensed the danger in him, but recognised also an answering anger in herself. How dare he treat her like a woman of no decency? She would show him – show them all – that she was as worthy of respect as any properly wed woman. 'I fear my husband's fury more than your hurt pride.'

Baxandall let his arm fall, but his eyes burned into her. 'Don't act the prim little wife with me. You forget I saw you with your legs spread open on a floor in Magdeburg.' He grabbed at the front of her skirt. He had such a firm grip that she could not release herself. 'I've seen all those pretty parts of you, and I'd have known them better had not the town been fired.'

Without stopping to think Christa clawed at his face, scraping his cheek with her fingernails. It barely gave him pause, and he slapped her so hard that her head rang. What was that question the priest had asked her in the cathedral? *And you complied without resistance?* It had not been so much a question as an accusation.

'Help here!' she shouted, not knowing whether the few people who were left in the camp would regard Baxandall's doing as sport or infamy. Fear had her in its grasp now, and she knew it would paralyse her, just as it had on the day that Lukas had robbed her of her innocence. Baxandall's words seethed in her mind. She tried to scratch him again, and this time his response was to hit her mouth with the flat of his hand. *No one can say I did not resist this time*, she thought. Her lip throbbed as if she had been stung by a dozen bees, and she could taste blood leaking between her teeth.

There was a movement behind Baxandall, and suddenly he was away from her, staggering like a drunkard and clutching his head. His little wife had an iron pot in her hand, and her chest was heaving with anger and exertion. 'You bitch!' Baxandall screamed at her. 'You near had my brains dashed onto the ground.'

The girl shouted back at him in her own tongue, and soon their two voices were combined in a yelling match that could not have been comprehended by anyone. Christa backed away, but the girl was screeching at her now, as if she were somehow to blame. A few stray men had returned from the cathedral and gathered to be entertained by the fight, but one of Captain Sadeler's lieutenants was among them, and he stepped forward to quieten the girl. 'Keep this one in order, Baxandall,' he said, taking her by the hair and shaking her. 'And keep your cock in your breeches too.' Then he spoke to Christa: 'If you'd changed your ways to follow the true religion you'd have been safely in the house of God with your husband, instead of asking for trouble here.'

Christa swallowed her fury. She was minded to argue with this ignorant man, but the memory of Lukas's anger yesterday silenced her.

When Lukas returned from the cathedral she saw him take note of her swollen lip. 'What happened to you?' he said.

She hesitated, fearful that he might blame her, as the lieutenant had. And even if he didn't, he might feel obliged to pick a fight with Baxandall. It was wrong to lie, she knew, but she was too weary to bear the consequences of the truth. 'I tripped and fell,' she said.

'The ground is uneven here. You must watch your step.'

That night they lay huddled together under their blankets. Christa was glad of Lukas's warmth for the air was cool. The ground was too hard for peaceful sleep, though. In the dead of night she lay awake, listening to the river flowing. She had never noticed the sound of it before. And now another noise was breaking the night's silence. Some man was grunting, and each grunt he made was answered by a responding gasp from a girl. Christa's face warmed as she recognised the sound — it was the animal noise that Lukas had made last night. The girl yelped in pain, and spoke in a strange tongue —Baxandall's child-wife. He was doing to her what Lukas had done to Christa the night before.

Fifteen

CAPTAIN SADELER'S COMPANY WAS TAKING A day's ease in a village tucked in the low hills of Harz. Now that summer was at its ripest, with crops to be harvested, they found the villagers less inclined to flee at the sight of them. No farmer would willingly let the wheat wilt in his field, so the villagers had little choice but to make terms with the captain and his men and trade what food and shelter they could offer in return for preserving their homes and lives.

These last weeks the company had shifted from place to place, depending on where the spies told them the King of Sweden was expected. They would march to the south for five days until, on some contrary intelligence, they would change direction and march north-east. None of it mattered much as long as they could find food and a place to lay their heads. The losses in the company had benefited many. Captain Sadeler had seen fit to improve Lukas to the rank of lance corporal, which meant he and Christa were permitted to take possession of a billet in a humble cottage, although they were obliged to share it with two other junior officers. Baxandall was in a better house, promoted now to corporal, and Lukas was glad enough to have some distance from him.

Baxandall's wife had died a month south of Magdeburg, when the child could not be got out of her. His loss of her had not improved his temperament, or calmed his lust.

Lukas left Christa making ready their bed for the night. The room was frugal enough, but there was fresh straw to put on the floor and a fine sheepskin rug to lay on top of it. He felt warm at the thought of the comfort to come. Tonight he would take his husband's rights, but for once it would be on a soft bed. He knew that she took no joy in it. The memory of Katherine came to him again, as it often did on these late summer days. That way she had of laying her hand on his belly when they were abed, and how she had curled in against him after their loving was done ... There was none of that with Christa. She was a sound wife, now that she had settled, but she was not Katherine.

Out in the village he met Götz, walking along in conversation with the local pastor. 'Have you no work to do?' Lukas said good-naturedly.

'I have a bag of provisions,' Götz said, raising the bulging sack he was carrying, 'most of them kindly given by this good man.'

'Little choice I had in the matter,' the pastor said sadly.

'You have your life and health,' Lukas said. 'There's many would be thankful for that.' Götz was inclined to be too friendly towards these people, and took little heed of Lukas's advice to stay distant from them.

'I am indeed thankful, and bless the Lord for sparing me thus far,' the pastor said.

'Amen to that,' Götz said, and patted his arm.

'You might be better to bide in your house than to wander about the place with our company here. They're not all as civilised as young Private Fuhrmann.'

'The pastor is keeping me company while I carry this food to the captain,' Götz said, 'and then he is to show me his library.'

'I have thirty-two books,' the pastor said, straightening as befitted a man of such learning.

'Perhaps Christa might like to come with me,' Götz said. 'She is

231

so fond of books, and has none but that one volume that came from her father's house.'

Lukas felt as if the day had cooled. A sour heaviness came inside him every time he encountered Christa with her head bent over the book — or, worse, when she and Götz passed an evening in discussion of some passage or other from Götz's New Testament. Once Götz had offered to teach him to read, and he had burned with such anger that he had not been able to look straight at the lad for a week. But what reason could he give to forbid Christa? None that would not make him look more of a fool than he already felt. 'Aye, if it pleases her you may take her with you,' he said. 'I'll come with you to the captain. He'll likely hope that some of his men will do a bit of real work while it's light. If we all waste our days on book-learning we'll be a long time in winning the war.'

When his tasks were done Lukas walked back through the village. A good number of the men had gathered in the tavern, and were busying themselves with drinking it dry. The smell of the beer gave him a thirst, and he joined them. Baxandall was slouched at a table and called him over. Lukas found room to sit down and asked the tavern keeper to bring him a fresh jug of beer. He filled Baxandall's empty tankard, then his own. 'We'd best enjoy this before it's gone,' he said. He had no wish to be drunk, and less to be with Baxandall, but he supposed that as they were comrades they should endeavour to be civil.

Baxandall watched him warily as he drank. His eyes were bloodshot. 'Fortune favours you again, Weinsburg,' he said. His voice was hoarse with liquor.

'Does it? You still outrank me.'

'Aye, but your wife lives and breathes, while mine is meat for worms. Your bed is warm, while mine is cold.'

'You'll find another woman soon enough. Aren't we bound for Leipzig? There'll be hundreds for you to pick from there.'

Baxandall drained his tankard and pushed it towards Lukas for more. 'I miss her. Stupid little bitch. She fought like a cornered rat the first time I had her.' He rubbed the tears out of his eyes.

Lukas refilled their tankards. 'We'll drink a toast to her memory.'

Baxandall tapped his tankard against Lukas's. 'To all the women we've had, and the ones we've still to enjoy.'

It was dark by the time Lukas made his way back to the billet. He was not falling-down drunk but in that fine state of mellowness that comes when food and drink are in good supply. He had left Baxandall snoring in the tavern. For once they had not quarrelled.

The little house was near dark, apart from one lamp on the table. Christa was seated there, mending a stocking. The others who were billeted with them were already asleep. Lukas could hear their breathing drift from the other room. She laid down her work and stood to bring a plate of food to the table. 'Would you like some bacon fried?' she said. 'There's enough heat in the fire yet to do so.'

Lukas sat down. 'This will do. Have you eaten?'

'Yes.'

He watched her as she sat down again and resumed her needlework. She was a little wan, but that might be the lamplight. Still, there was something different about her manner. A brightness he had not seen before. 'Did you spend your time agreeably today?' Lukas heard the catch of jealousy in his voice, and hoped she had not noticed it.

'There was much to do, with the washing and mending. It's hard to keep clothes clean on the march, isn't it?'

'It was not all work, though. You and Götz were at your studies, were you not?'

She smiled. He thought he saw something closed and secretive in her face, and felt a pulse of anger.

'Aye, and I spent too long at that when I should have been at this. Stitching is better done by daylight.'

Lukas ate his food quickly. The thought of that warm bed was in his mind. She seemed well disposed tonight, and he must try to keep his ill-feeling in check. He took a drink of water. 'Finish off that mending now, and we'll to bed.' He looked intently at her so that she would understand him.

He saw her colour. 'I am ... I cannot.' She twisted the stocking in her hand.

'What do you mean?' There it was again, the anger.

She struggled to find words. 'There is blood coming from me.'

Lukas gave a sharp laugh. 'Your monthly time, you mean?'

'Yes.'

'You have not had this time before, not since we were married.'

'No.'

'It means there is no child in you. Did you know that?'

She nodded. 'When I'd gone so long without I was afraid I might be with child, but one of the other women said such disorder is not uncommon when there's hunger and upset.'

'I'm glad enough of it. This is a bad time to be born.'

'I am glad too. It is a thing I fear. My mother died in childbed, when my sister was born.'

Lukas thought again of Katherine, torn apart by his baby daughter, and felt a terrible sadness pour over him, like a river in flood. This girl was right to fear it. Thank God they had both been spared this time.

The garrison at Pleissenburg fort put up a stout enough resistance, but they could not withstand the might of the Emperor's men. The fort had not been properly repaired after an attack on it a year or more ago — the war had sucked up all the materials that might have seen it fast again — so now the Imperial cannon made short work of its walls, and the garrison was routed. Lukas and Götz chased a clutch of fleeing soldiers through the gun-smoke. Götz brought one down with his musket. Lukas would not have wasted a ball on an enemy who was running away, but Götz was finding his own way of soldiering. It was not for Lukas to undermine him now that the lad was acquiring a taste for battle.

They approached the felled soldier cautiously. Lukas could see that he was not dead and there was always the risk of a bite from a dying snake. Götz walked forward more boldly and looked down at the man. 'There's no fight left in him,' he said. 'That wound has done for him.'

'Take care, Götz. He may be play-acting.'

'Not with that bleeding from his guts.' Götz hunkered down beside the soldier. 'You'd have been wise to strap on a cuirass, my friend,' he shouted down at him. 'You might have lived long enough to run away.'

'Don't torment him, Götz. We'll take what we can and move on.'

Götz began to work quickly through all that the soldier carried with him. He tossed the satchel to Lukas. 'Take a look in there. I've these buttons to cut off, and I can feel a coin or two in his coat-lining.'

Lukas opened the satchel. The soldier had bled onto it, and the fastenings were supple with blood. There was bread and a spare bag of shot to be pocketed. He left aside a shirt. It was stiff with old dirt — even Christa wouldn't be able to scrub that out. At the bottom of the satchel he found a small book. The binding was stained with blood, but when he flicked through the pages they seemed clean enough. 'Here, Götz, what's this?' he called.

Götz left his looting and took the book. 'It's by the heretic Martin Luther,' he said. '*The Small Catechism*. I think the Protestants use it in their homes.' He handed it back to Lukas with a smile. 'I'd have little use for it. Father Tomas used to keep a small library of such items, better to know the enemy, but he said it was as well to be properly learned in the true faith before risking infection from heresy.'

'Do you think Christa would like to have it?'

'Christa?' Götz seemed to consider the proposal. 'I suppose she might. Although ...'

'What?'

They jumped as a musket made fire in the smoke ahead. 'This fort is not won yet,' Lukas said, slipping the book into his pocket. 'We must go and earn our booty.'

Once the fort was theirs the wagons and camp followers were called forward, and they made camp as best they could in and around the shattered buildings. Lukas and Götz decided to raise only the larger tent. There was room enough for three in it, and it would save work when they struck camp on the morrow.

The company grew merry that night, full of the wine they'd looted from the cellars of Pleissenburg. Lukas and Götz drank away the weariness of the day's action. Götz had found a flask of brandy and fortified his wine with it so he became drunk more quickly than his fellows. Lukas decided to take him back to the tent while he could still walk.

They staggered through the camp, tripping over so many times that they hardly knew whether to curse or laugh. They tumbled into the tent and landed in a heap in the darkness. 'Get a light here, for God's sake,' Lukas shouted. He heard Christa rise and feel her way to the table. She made a spark from the tinderbox and lit the lamp. From where he was lying she was like an avenging angel, standing there gazing down at them. The lamplight gave her hair a halo of gold it did not possess in the daytime. When she pursed her lips he thought, for a moment, she would scold them, and sniggered like a schoolboy.

'What is so funny?' she asked.

Götz was giggling as foolishly as Lukas. 'You look very stern.'

'I hope your wits will be clear for your work tomorrow. Leipzig will hardly fall to a battalion of fools nursing sore heads.'

Götz's laughter faded and he laid his head on the ground. 'I am so tired. I think I will sleep for a little while.' He yawned and belched at the same time, then closed his eyes.

'No,' Christa said sharply. 'I won't have you sleeping on the ground like a dog.' She shook him roughly and pulled him up by the arm.

Götz struggled to his feet and allowed himself to be led to his bedding. Lukas got up and sat at the table, watching as Christa made Götz lie down, then covered him with a blanket. She straightened and looked down at him.

'Did we waken you?' Lukas said.

'I was not sleeping deeply. There's too much revelry in the camp tonight.'

'You have the knack with him. I'd likely have let him sleep where he lay.'

'My brother used to come home in that state. I'm well used to it.'

She fell quiet, and the silence hung heavy in the air. He knew she was thinking of her brother, and all the other people she had lost. Suddenly he remembered the book in his pocket. 'I found this today,' he said, pulling it out and handing it to her. 'Götz tells me it's for your sort of people.'

Christa took it and opened it, turning the first pages slowly. 'This is for me?'

'Yes.'

'Where did you find it?'

'Among the belongings of a dead soldier.'

'I suppose it's of little use to him now.'

'Do you ... like it?'

'Thank you, yes.' She closed the book and packed it in her little bag of possessions.

Lukas stood up. 'If you're for bed now I'll quench the light.' He watched her walk to their bedding and lie down. 'Your monthly time is past now, isn't it?' Briefly a curious expression swept across her face. Not resignation exactly ... He didn't understand what it signified. For once he was not angered but saddened. He had hoped the gift of the book might soften her a little, or at least ease the guilt he could not be rid of. It had done neither. He put out the lamp.

Sixteen

THE EMPEROR'S MEN MARCHED THROUGH THE west gate of Leipzig, followed by the wagons laden with their women and all else they had gathered on their march. The citizens stared as the cart on which Christa was seated rolled towards the marketplace. She wished there was some way of announcing that she was not one of the invaders, and that her heart ached for all good people who saw their city taken. Deeper inside her, though, she envied these men and women. Their city was occupied, but it still stood, and they still lived. The citizens of Leipzig had taken heed of the fate of Pleissenburg and decided that surrender was the best course. This might have been the destiny of all those she loved, if only there had not been so many diehards in Magdeburg – and she had been among them. Had her stubbornness made the fate of her own city more certain?

Thank God she was only a woman, and a young one at that, to whom no one had listened. But how must a man feel when his arguments had doomed so many? For the first time in months she thought of Pastor Ovens. He had shown little sign of regret when last she had seen him. His certainty was like armour on him. She wondered how he had fared, and prayed hard to suppress the uncharitable thoughts that filled her head.

Once the wagons had stopped, Christa stayed where she was, guarding Lukas and Götz's possessions. Lukas had told her also to mind Baxandall's goods, now that he had no wife to do the job for him. She hoped he would not be billeted close to them. The other women on the wagon chatted excitedly about the prospect of a real bed, or at least a proper floor to sleep on. Christa did not join in. She had remained apart from them. Doubtless they thought she was haughty, but it was not pride that kept her quiet in their company. Some of them were crude, rough girls, and many were not properly wed to the men they lived with, but she was less apt to pass judgement now. No, she could not feel easy with women because the companionship they shared made her feel her loss more keenly. These last couple of weeks, when food had been more plentiful, she had found herself remembering her father's house and her family. Strange that when they'd all been half starved she had had no thought of home. Elsbeth was always in her thoughts. Sometimes at night when she could not sleep she would try to still her mind, hoping that God might send her sight of Elsbeth. She had read of such things: of a mother whose child had been lost in the forest, and in the night a vision had come to her of a particular grove, so she had risen and found the child to bring him home. Christa prayed in vain for such a vision.

Lukas and the other men arrived back, drawing her from her thoughts. 'We have decent enough lodgings with a baker and his wife,' Lukas said, lifting most of his belongings from the cart. 'Can you carry that sack? Götz and Baxandall will manage their own baggage.'

Christa jumped off the wagon and slung the bag over her shoulder. Lukas was already pushing his way through the throng, and she ran to catch up with him. 'Are Baxandall and Götz billeted with us?'

'Aye, and two others also.'

'I hope you won't come home singing. The baker will need his sleep.'

Lukas made no reply and they walked on in silence.

The baker and his wife greeted them warily. They had clearly no wish to give houseroom to soldiers. Lukas took him aside and spoke to him quietly. The man seemed moved to argue, but gave way and signalled to Christa to go with him. Lukas nodded at her to comply, so she followed him up two flights of stairs to a small bedroom. She set her bag on the bed and a puff of what she thought was dust rose into the air. It made her sneeze, and she realised by the scent that it was fine flour. 'Is this your room, sir?' she asked.

'Mine and my wife's.'

'Thank you.'

The baker muttered something, but Lukas was coming into the room and Christa did not hear what he said. He stepped around Lukas's belongings and went back down the stairs.

Lukas lay on the bed and closed his eyes. 'It will be good to sleep in a real bed again.' He patted the space beside him, and a haze of flour-dust rose. 'Lie down beside me for a minute.'

Christa did as she was told. She prayed he would not want his pleasure here and now, in the daytime with all the house in a bustle, but he made no move to turn towards her. She, too, closed her eyes. A door banged near by. Baxandall cursed and another man laughed. There was Götz's voice. Outside in the street there were the usual noises of a city. This place sounded no different from Magdeburg, yet she would have known it was not home.

Lukas sighed and sat up. 'I should be away. We're to muster for battle practice outside the gates.'

'I'll rise too,' Christa said. 'I wouldn't want the woman of the house thinking me slothful.'

'We'll have time enough abed tonight.' Lukas gave her the look she had come to understand. It was more of misery than lust, as if his desire were a burden to him.

The next morning Christa helped the baker's wife with her work, fashioning dough into little bread-cakes. The woman had been stiff and unfriendly at first. She and her husband were Calvinists, and as ill-disposed towards Lutherans like Christa as they were towards the Papists. However, as she saw Christa's usefulness she thawed a little. The baker came in for a mouthful of beer. His face was grey with flour that had stuck to his sweat. When he spoke his face seemed to crack and flakes showered off him. 'By God, you and your man were making good use of our bed last night.' He nudged his wife. 'Weren't they, Mother? It was creaking that much I thought it would break.'

'Shut up with such talk,' the wife scolded. 'Can't you see you're shaming the poor girl?'

The baker laughed and went back to his oven in the yard behind. Christa worked on, not daring to look up. Her face burned with humiliation.

'How long have you and your man been wed?' the baker's wife said gently.

'Since Magdeburg fell.'

The woman worked on for a few minutes. 'Does he treat you badly?' she said at last.

'No, thank God. I am lucky, I suppose.'

'There are others here from Magdeburg. They fled here after it was taken.'

Could Elsbeth be among them? Christa put down the dough she was working with and rested her hands on the table. She thought she might faint. 'Where are they? In what part of the town?'

'Sit yourself down before you fall.' The woman led Christa to the settle and eased her into it. 'Take a drink. You're all of a quake.'

Christa sipped the beer she was offered. She swallowed, and tried to calm herself. 'It's my sister. I think she is still living, but I lost sight of her …'

'Let me tidy up here, and leave this bread to rise. When that is done I'll take you to where they are.'

'We call this part of the city Little Bohemia,' the baker's wife said, leading her down a wide road that led off the marketplace. They walked along a covered alleyway. It was so dark that Christa struggled to find her footing. The baker's wife must have noticed, for she took her arm to reassure her. 'All our poor brothers and sisters fleeing the tyrant come here. It's not everyone who welcomes them — God have mercy on us for our hard hearts.'

The alley opened into a small square lined with shabby houses. Most of the occupants seemed to be running some manner of business from their front door, but there was little sign of the order and prosperity Christa remembered in Magdeburg. They stopped outside a house that was also a tavern. 'I would not be going into such a place in the normal way of things,' the baker's wife said, 'but I find a tavern is the best place for news.'

The tavern tattlers directed them to a house where a group of women sat stitching. When the baker's wife introduced Christa to them they rose and embraced her, crying out that they remembered her, or thought they did. Christa struggled to recognise them, but they seemed to be everyone and no one at the same time. She questioned them about Elsbeth. One woman recalled a fainting child in the cathedral, but no more than that. The rest told her of houses where she might find other refugees from Magdeburg.

Christa and the baker's wife spent the next hour going from house to house. Always there were embraces and tears, the same doubtful claims of recognition but no one had any firm news of Elsbeth. Christa sensed that the baker's wife was growing impatient. No doubt she had work to do, and her husband would be expecting his meal.

They were halfway through the covered alley on their way home. The light at the alley's end darkened as a man turned into it. Christa could see he was lame and leaning on a crutch. 'Hold there, sir,' the baker's wife called. 'Let us make our way out first, and then you'll get through more freely.' He made no reply, but retreated.

When Christa and the baker's wife emerged from the alley they turned to thank the man for his patience. He did not wait to speak with them and pushed into the alley as quickly as he could. Christa caught only a glimpse of his face — and thought her heart might burst. 'Andreas?' she called. 'Is it you?'

The man stopped dead, and leaned his free hand against the alley wall. He turned slowly. It *was* Andreas. He tried to speak, but no words came.

Christa and the baker's wife supported him to a bench outside the makeshift tavern. 'God be praised!' the baker's wife said. 'Is this your brother?'

If only it was Dieter... It was a cruel thought. 'Andreas, is ... was my father's journeyman.'

The baker's wife attempted to find a suitable response, then made her excuses and left them. Christa was glad to let her away. She bought a tankard of beer and gave it to Andreas. Now that the first shock had left him she could see he was sorely changed. It was not just his injured leg, although it was bad enough, twisted into an unnatural shape and of less use than no leg at all. His face was gaunt, and there were dark patches under his eyes like bruises. His eyes — those shifty eyes she had so disliked — were bleak and dead. He drank some beer and set the tankard on the bench between them. Christa saw that his hands were trembling, but it was not like the drink-tremor that afflicted Götz in the morning. 'Thank God,' he said at last. 'Thank God in His mercy for sparing you unharmed.'

My wounds cannot be seen, she thought. 'Andreas, I must ask you ... my father and Dieter?'

He shook his head.

'Are you certain? Might they not have got away?'

'They are dead, Miss Christa.'

Christa was silent for a moment. Andreas's words were confirmation of what she had, in her heart, already known. It was hard, though, to have the spark of hope extinguished. She forced her attention back to Andreas, and pointed to his wasted leg. 'How is it that you survived such injury?'

'I suppose I must call it a miracle.' He covered his eyes with his hands, as if he was trying to gather his memory. 'I woke up among the dead. I don't know when it was. There were maggots in me.' He gagged, but held one hand over his mouth and did not spew. 'I thought I was dead and rotting in my grave. And then I knew I was not. I did not dare cry out, but when it was dark I crawled away and found a safer place to hide. I don't know how I survived. Then some good Christians found me, and carried me here.'

'And how do you live? If you need money …'

'I have work, thank God. With a printer.' His mouth twitched with the trace of a smile. 'Some things do not change, eh?'

He closed his eyes, and Christa could see how weary he was. There were so many questions she must ask him, but it would be unkind to make him answer now. 'Do you lodge here?'

'Aye. I am back now to sleep. I have not the strength I used to have.'

'Please God it will be restored to you in time.'

'Amen.' Andreas hauled himself to his feet, but brushed away her efforts to help him. 'Will you come again?'

'Tomorrow, if I'm able.'

'Come at this hour. My new master lets me away. He knows I'm good for nothing by this time of day.' Andreas grimaced as he found his balance on the crutch. 'You must think me rude, Miss Christa. I have not asked after you, or how you have fared since the city fell.'

'We'll talk of that tomorrow.'

Christa hurried back to the baker's house, fearing that Lukas would have returned and be angry at her absence. She need not have troubled herself, for there was no sign of the men, save the baker. He approached her with contrition. 'I apologise if I spoke too freely to you this morning,' he said, with a small bow. 'My wife has put me right, as wives must do with us men.'

It was night-time, and Christa sat up alone reading her *Small*

Catechism by lamplight. The baker and his wife — she knew them now to be Herr and Frau Ackermann — had retired to bed. Herr Ackermann was obliged to rise before dawn to prepare his ovens.

There was little noise in this back room of the house, apart from the soft hiss of the fire. The street outside was quiet, but Christa could hear revelry from other parts of the city. Nowhere could be peaceful with such a great army visiting. She turned the page, grateful for this moment of solitude, and for the familiar, comforting words of Luther.

Footsteps approached along the street and stopped at the front door. Christa tensed as the latch was raised. The door had been left unbolted so that the men could get in when they returned, but she realised now that any stray drunkard could walk in. The door swung open and Götz peered round it. He smiled when he saw her, and swayed in, leaving the door open.

'Ach, you are drunk again,' Christa said lightly, getting up to close the door.

'Not as drunk as the others,' Götz said. He stayed where he was until she sat down, then pulled a chair close beside her. 'We work hard, and we play hard.'

'More battle drills?'

'Aye. They say the King of Sweden is nearly upon us. We will meet his army in battle in a day or two.'

So it was true. She had not expected it to be so soon. 'I will pray for your preservation.'

'Will you?' He looked down at the book in her hands, and touched the open page with his fingertips. 'Does it comfort you?'

'It does. I am so weak, and it gives me strength.'

'I do not think you are weak.'

The fire settled, and Christa's eyes grew heavy in the heat. 'I should go up to bed.'

Götz laid a hand on her arm. 'Will you tell me something … to ease my mind?' His voice sounded strained.

'What is it?'

'It disturbs me at night.' He stopped, and it seemed he would not speak again.

'I don't understand you, Götz. What is it disturbs you? Bad dreams?'

He shook his head. 'I can hear when ... when you and Lukas are ...'

Christa flushed. Her eyes fell to the book lying in her lap. 'I have no choice.'

'I know that.' Another hesitation. 'Does he hurt you? That's what troubles me.'

Christa could hardly form the words to reply. 'I do not think I can talk about these things. It is not right.'

'I'm sorry. Ach, God,' Götz buried his head in his hands. 'Forgive me for asking. It's the drink making a fool of me.'

She stood and moved quickly away from him. 'Goodnight, Götz,' she said softly.

When he looked up, his expression made her want to weep. Yes, he was drunk, dear God, yes, but there was such sorrow and tenderness in his eyes. No man had ever looked at her like that.

Christa jumped as Baxandall stepped forward out of the shadows. She had not even heard him enter the house. How long had he been hiding there, listening?

'Now there's a sweet scene,' he said, his voice thick with drink. The front door of the house banged to. One of the other men shouted, only for Lukas to hush him.

'Are you not upstairs yet, wife?' Lukas said, as he lurched in. 'I'd an idea you'd have warmed that fine bed for me.'

'Aye, off to bed, you lovebirds,' Baxandall said, never taking his eyes off Christa.

She hooked her arm into Lukas's and helped him upstairs.

He had taken a great deal of drink, that was clear, and she had hopes that he would fall straight to sleep, but when they had lain down on the bed he took her face in his hands. It was too dark to see him clearly, but she could smell the beer on his breath. 'I have scarcely had a kiss from you in all the time we've been wed,' he said.

It was true. She'd been grateful that whenever she'd been obliged to comply with his wants, he had rarely forced his mouth onto hers in the way she saw the other soldiers do with their women. 'Do you wish me to kiss you?' she said.

'Aye.'

She leaned closer to his face, pressed her lips to his and moved away. Perhaps that would content him.

'You must tarry a little longer than that, Christa. And don't keep your mouth shut tight like a sprung trap, eh?' He pulled her back towards him and kissed her again, darting his tongue into her mouth. She forced herself not to push him away. That might anger him.

After a few moments the kissing no longer contented him, and he pushed her skirts up in the customary manner. She had devised a way now to endure this. Inside her head she would sing a song she had known as a child, 'All My Clothes Are Green', and hope that by the time she reached the end he would be satisfied. Tonight, though, was different. As the bed creaked beneath her she recalled what Götz had said. Somewhere in the house, at this moment, he was listening. He was thinking of her, imagining what Lukas was doing to her. The thought caught her off guard, and she gasped. Lukas gave a little laugh in the midst of his thrusting. In all the time she had been with him she had never understood why men — and some women — were so driven to this deed. What was there in it that was worth imperilling your immortal soul for? Now, for the first time, she wondered how it might be if the man she lay with was someone she cared for. *Götz*. She gasped again, disturbed by the turmoil in her body.

'Put your arms round me,' Lukas said hoarsely.

She did as he bade and he finished his pleasure. He did not immediately roll off her, but lay with his head resting on her shoulder. She held him, listening to his breathing calm. When he finally moved away from her she thought he would turn over and fall asleep, but instead he lay on his back. 'We leave tomorrow,' he said, after a long silence.

'For the battle?' Götz must have known he would be leaving the next day. Was that why he had regarded her with such emotion?

'Aye. They say the King of Sweden has more than twenty thousand men.' She sensed that Lukas was staring at her in the darkness. 'If you're widowed, make sure to keep hold of all that was mine. It will be yours by right.'

'You won't die.'

'We all must die some day.'

They lay quietly, and she was glad now that she had put her arms round him. For all the wrong he'd done her, it would be uncharitable to let a man go to his death feeling that he had no one in this world to care for him. She could not lie to him, and pretend affection she did not feel, but at least she could open her heart to pity him. *Blessed are the merciful*, the Lord Himself had said. She reached for his hand in the darkness. He tensed for a moment – puzzled, perhaps, by such tenderness – and then curled his fingers around hers. Neither of them spoke again, but lay hand in hand long into the night.

It was still dark when she heard him get up and go downstairs. There was a low murmur of men's voices for a time, and chairs being scraped back on the stone floor. Then the front door creaked open. Christa got up quickly and opened the shutters to watch them leave. They were gathered in the street outside the baker's house, laden with their weapons and accoutrements. The sun had not yet risen, and the sky was the mournful grey of early morning. The men formed themselves into a loose line with Baxandall at the head and Götz at the rear. At a signal from Baxandall they began to march away. Götz paused, looking up at the house, and Christa stepped back, suddenly shy, but he had already turned away and was marching out of the street. The thoughts she'd had the night before seemed now like nothing more than a dream.

Seventeen

LUKAS HADN'T SEEN SO MANY MEN together since the battle at Höchst nearly ten years before. He'd not been much older than Götz then, although he'd a good deal more soldiering to his name.

The order that came down the line was said to be from General Tilly himself. March out from the city until the enemy came into view, they were told. 'So it's true, then?' Götz said, as they formed into rows. 'The King of Sweden is near upon us?'

'It seems so.'

'He'll take one look at our force and turn tail.' Götz swaggered as he spoke.

'You think so?' Baxandall said. 'He's been sent by God to crush the Emperor.'

'It must be a dark day when you're turning pious,' Lukas said.

'Keep your mouths shut!' Captain Sadeler roared, from the head of the line. 'Save your breath for battle.'

They marched steadily, taking a road that led to the village of Breitenfeld. A bold wind had got up since they'd left Leipzig. It cooled the sweat on them, and made the standards flutter prettily enough, but it gave Lukas a sick feeling in his gut. A wind like this had been blowing on the day they had taken Magdeburg. It felt like an omen of ill-fortune.

The sun was at its highest when the march slowed. Word came down the line that the enemy was sighted, and they were to move forward at an easy pace and follow orders as to where they should place themselves. Other word came down the line with it, of the sort whispered by one soldier to another. *Twenty thousand of them; no, thirty thousand, if the Saxons joined with them; closer to forty thousand* ... Lukas watched Götz's eyes widen with each report. 'What think you now, young Götz? Do you still believe the King of Sweden is for running?'

'Can he really have so many?'

'The only ones you need worry about are those within range of your musket. Keep this in your mind. If they're in your range, then so too are you in theirs. One man or forty thousand matters not. It only takes one shot to end your troubles.'

They shuffled forward. General Tilly's order was for the infantry to be arranged in a wide line, pikemen to the fore, musketeers behind them. The cannon were established a hundred yards further back. The cavalry was split into two forces, one on either side of the infantry. As they drew into position Lukas caught his first sight of the King of Sweden's force. They were far enough away that their great number was clear to see. Their position was inferior — they would be fighting up the slight incline of the land — but from where he stood Lukas could see nothing but enemy soldiers and the bright colours of the standards. He realised that a powerful silence had fallen on the men around him. A few were kneeling, but others had closed their eyes and clasped their hands in prayer. 'Götz,' he said quietly, 'utter a prayer for us all.'

'I'm not a priest.'

'You'll do just as well.'

Some of the men around them were attending to their conversation. 'Aye, say a prayer, lad. It will comfort us.' Even Baxandall was joining in the encouragement.

Götz seemed uncomfortable. 'We could all say the "Hail Mary" together,' he suggested.

'The last rites would be more fitting,' Baxandall muttered.

Götz closed his eyes, as if he were considering the matter in his soul, then opened them and nodded. 'If I were a proper priest I would gladly say the words, but I dare not. Still, since our souls may be in peril I hope God will permit me to say the Prayer for a Happy Death.' He folded his hands together and began. *'Da, quaesumus Dominus, ut in hora mortis nostrae...'*

The rest of the men mumbled along with him. As he ended, Baxandall cried, 'Christa?'

'What?' Götz was flustered.

'You said "Christa" instead of *Christum*. *"Per Christa Dominum nostrum."*' Baxandall looked at Lukas. 'You heard him, Weinsburg. He said your wife's name, did he not?'

Lukas stared hard at Götz. The boy's face was as white as a shroud. What had he said? Christa or *Christum*? And did it signify if he had slipped? Lukas felt the old snarl of jealousy, remembered from all those evenings Götz and Christa had spent in dispute about their theologies. How he had burned to hear them use words he didn't know, showing off in front of him.

'A strange mistake for a priest-to-be, is it not?' Baxandall said, scenting blood. 'Or maybe not. You Papist priests dance to the same tune as other men, no matter what you say.'

Lukas steadied his mind and turned his anger away from Götz. He was inclined to direct it at Baxandall, but there'd be other battles to win before this day was over. He'd save his fire for them. 'It matters not what he said.' He spoke quietly, the better to contain his fury. 'Let it rest.'

The other men accepted this and turned to face the enemy. Götz moved into the line beside Lukas, with Baxandall the next man down.

'He's a liar,' Götz whispered to Lukas. 'I said *Christum* — on my own life I swear it.'

'Hush now, I believe you,' Lukas said. But he didn't.

At first Lukas did not realise the Swedes were moving towards them. They came forward so slowly and steadily. The only hint of movement was the flapping back and forth of their standards. The wind was blowing hard, whipping up the soil from the parched fields all around him. The sun was at his back, and must be shining full in the face of the enemy. It caught on the Swedish weaponry, so that the whole field glittered with sparkles of light.

When it became clear that the Swedes were advancing the order came down the line that they were to make ready their muskets. Lukas did so, watching Götz out of the corner of his eye to be sure the lad made no mistake. For all that he was well able now after so many months on campaign, this was his first full battle. A young man's nerves could get the better of him at such a time. But Götz had it right. His lock was filled with powder, and the shot-ball pushed home into the depths of the barrel. Götz must have sensed him watching, for he glanced over and gave him a little smile. Lukas did not smile back, but he nodded to show his approval.

Now that the Swedes were closer Lukas could see that they were strangely ordered in small cohorts. Although their standards were fine and bright the men beneath them looked ragged and half starved. Lukas imagined he and his comrades looked just as unkempt. The only real splendour was in a party to the far end of the field. From their standards Lukas thought they might be Saxons.

The order came to make fire until countermanded. The pikemen stepped back to let the musketeers take their aim. Lukas fired and reloaded with the speed he had learned over the years. He did not pause to see if his shot found its target, but some part of his mind registered that men were falling at the front of the Swedish line. Load, make fire ... load, make fire ... He continued, aware too that the Swedes were returning fire with a frequency that seemed impossible. The pikeman by his side was hit and tumbled down. The wind, which had dropped for a short while, was blowing again. What with the dust and the smoke it was all but impossible to see the enemy in front of them.

Captain Sadeler came galloping down behind the line, and ordered them to cease fire. 'We're to make after the Saxons, lads,' he shouted. 'They're untried and we'll take the weight off their feet easily enough.'

Lukas slung his musket over his shoulder and jogged along with the rest of the company towards the wing. Some of the cavalry were riding with them too, but Lukas kept clear of them. He didn't trust those arrogant bastards of dragoons. They'd swipe your head off just to boast how sharp their sabre was.

Götz was at his elbow. 'How are you faring, boy?' he shouted. His voice was already cracked dry with the dust and heat of the day.

'Very good, thank you,' the lad replied, as if he were a fine lady at a feast.

The Saxons were disordered by the time Lukas and the rest of the company reached them. Their numbers seemed thinned, but there were no more bodies on the ground than was normal, so it was likely that many had turned tail and fled to their homes.

'Attack with a fury!' Captain Sadeler commanded them, and Lukas ran forward. He had loaded his musket again, but once he had made fire and taken down a flaxen-haired man in a gentleman's coat he flipped the weapon over and used the stock to batter the head of the next he encountered. A few of the Saxons stood and fought, but the best part of them ran. The gunners abandoned their cannon, and Captain Sadeler screamed down the line for their own bombardiers to come forward and make use of them. This was no longer a battle, it was a rout, and the Saxons were quitting the field as if the hounds of hell were nipping at their ankles. Some men of Captain Sadeler's company chased after them and cut down those they caught, but Lukas, Götz and Baxandall took their ease for a moment, enjoying the brief respite victory had bought them.

'Did I do well enough?' Götz asked, eyes bright with excitement.

Lukas saw the lad's need for his good opinion, but Baxandall's poison was seeping through his mind. 'I was too intent on my own work to take notice of yours,' he said. He felt a pang as he saw the hurt on Götz's face, and regretted what he had said.

'You're alive at any rate,' Baxandall said heartily, slapping Götz on the shoulder as if they were old friends. 'Please God the battle is as easily won as its opening parry.'

Their gunners had taken possession of the Saxon cannon, and had swiftly turned them about to face the Swedes. All conversation ended as the cannon fired at their new target, and the smoke hung like a cloud between the two forces. Lukas made ready his musket again, to be prepared against the moment when a Swede might run at them out of the smoke. The wind was no longer at his back but blowing into the side of his face. With all the dust, he could not see where the sun was in the sky. Either the wind had changed direction, or they had turned on the battlefield. Lukas felt a niggle of worry flutter in his gut. It was not good for an army to let its position drift, and he had heard no order to turn. The cannon ceased firing, and the word came down the line that they were to attack as soon as the smoke cleared. 'It's a slight enough company in front of us lads,' Captain Sadeler shouted. 'The cannon have cut them off from their comrades, so let's send them to meet St Peter this fine day.'

The wind was full in Lukas's face now, and as it blew away the smoke the sun shone into his eyes. He squinted at the enemy. A small crew, as Captain Sadeler had said. On the order, they raised their muskets and made fire. No sooner had the shot left his weapon than a volley of fire crackled back from the Swedes, more than should have come from such a modest company. Lukas saw that some had fallen, and felt a thrill of triumph that the Imperial musketeers had laid them low. As he watched, there was movement from the Swedish line. The wounded and dead were ignored, while fresh men appeared from the gaps between the small cohorts. Each time a man fell, another would step forward to take his place. Their own line was disordered by comparison. Lukas looked from left to right. Götz and Baxandall were still at work, but a number of men had dropped alongside them.

Captain Sadeler still rode up and down behind what was left of their line, shouting orders in a voice so hoarse that Lukas could not understand him. The captain lashed his horse onwards. The poor beast's pelt was flecked with foam as thick as curds. A lieutenant rode up and handed his officer a flask. He drank quickly, and found his voice again. 'Take the fight forward, lads,' he shouted. 'Shot's no good for this crowd. The sword and the cudgel's the only medicine will cure them.'

Lukas pressed forward. He stumbled where the ground became unexpectedly rough, and felt a sharp pain in his ankle. Damn it. There'd be no running for him this day. He hobbled on, falling behind the rest. Götz was just ahead. He saw the boy look round, then turn back. 'Are you hit, Lukas?' he shouted, his face pale in spite of the sweat that dripped off him.

'Not hit, just lamed.'

Götz ran back to him and gave him his arm. 'Come. You'll forget your pain when you see the Swedes close to.'

Götz had barely finished speaking when Lukas felt as though the ground had risen up and fetched him such a punch that he was flying through the air. At the same moment his ears rang so that he could hear nothing. For a strange time he was falling in silence, with his comrades beneath him and his enemy before him. Then he hit the earth hard, and lay, unable to move.

He felt a hand grasp his own, and raised his head. It was Götz, lying on the ground close to him. He, too, had been tossed through the air. Götz was speaking, but Lukas could not hear him. Götz spoke again, moving his mouth slowly and deliberately. What was he saying? *Cannon?* 'They have no cannon that I can see,' Lukas said, although he could not hear his own words.

Götz shrugged, with puzzlement on his face. The boy must have been deafened as thoroughly as he had been, Lukas thought.

Lukas struggled to his feet, and helped Götz up. Two other men were lying on the ground. One was dead, his head twisted at an odd angle. The other was living, but would not remain so for long. A fragment of the cannon ball had struck him in the guts, spilling his inner parts before him. Lukas could not hear if he was screaming, but he doubted it. The man's chest moved up and down as he fought for breath, as if his lungs did not comprehend their labour was in vain.

Götz had lost his musket, and was searching for it on the ground. Lukas realised that he was in the same position. He still had all his accoutrements, so he picked up the first weapon he found. It mattered not if it was his own. The silence in his ears had been replaced by a low ringing. Before long, he would hear as well as any man.

The ground shook as another cannon ball landed not half a field's length from where they stood. Lukas looked backwards, up the hill, and saw the smoke rising from under the Imperial standards. *Their own cannon!* Didn't those bloody fools know they were falling short? He ran to Götz and shook his arm. 'Go forward!' he shouted, pointing with his weapon.

They ran together to rejoin the line. As they went they met some of their comrades heading the other way. Lukas shouted at them for explanation, but no one answered. When they reached the line it was a line no more. The company was in disarray, hurling itself at the Swedish cohorts, and being cut down just as quickly. Lukas saw Captain Sadeler, still on horseback, and headed towards him. Some of the Imperial standards were fluttering from the middle of the Swedish cohort, which must mean they had been captured, but their own company standard was still with them, held at a slant by one of the lieutenants. He was on foot now, and struggling to defend himself with his sword arm. Baxandall was by his side, assisting him.

Captain Sadeler glanced about to see who was left to him, then pointed his sword at a small clump of trees. He spurred his horse forward, and the rest followed. Lukas ran, despite the ache in his ankle, outstripping Captain Sadeler's weary mount. The captain himself seemed to take note of this, and abandoned the horse to the enemy. They ran until they reached the trees, and struggled to reorder themselves.

Lukas was breathing in sharp gasps. He forced himself to take in the air more deeply and slowly. There were perhaps twenty of them. No more than thirty, to be sure. Götz was close by him, and Baxandall not far off, both intact, yet exhausted beyond believing. Any who had wounds had not achieved the safety of this thicket. One man lay on the bare ground before them, less than twenty paces away. He was endeavouring to rise, but whatever hurts he had taken made it impossible. Two of the Swedish cohorts had turned towards them and were advancing. 'If any of you would run, you should do it now,' Captain Sadeler croaked. No one moved, except to make ready their weapons.

A small squad of Swedes was approaching. Lukas watched as they came first to the wounded man. A Swede pulled out his short sword and made ready to dispatch him. Lukas raised his weapon, but did not make fire. They were just too far away for him to be certain of his aim. He must save his shot to preserve his own life. 'Mercy,' the wounded man cried. The wind had dropped, and his voice carried through the still air. 'In the name of Christ, mercy, *clementia*.'

The Swedish swordsman paused and said something to his comrades in his foreign tongue. The only word Lukas recognised was *clementia*. One of the Swedes stepped forward and spoke to the wounded man in German. 'We will show you mercy, friend. The same sort you showed at Magdeburg.' He nodded to the swordsman, who sliced the wounded man's throat.

Lukas felt a cold heaviness where his heart was. Magdeburg mercy. They could expect no better here.

The Swedes made ready their weapons and came closer. As soon as they were within range someone in another part of the thicket made fire, but his aim was awry. The Swedes returned it, and Lukas was half deafened again by the cracking of muskets from the enemy before him and the company alongside him. The smoke shifted like a summer mist, and at moments he could see that the Swedes seemed to be growing greater in number. He recharged his weapon with powder and reached into his shot-bag for a ball. There were but three left. He loaded and waited until one of the Swedes was nearly upon him, then fetched him down with a shot that took him in the neck. At this it seemed the whole front line of a cohort charged forward, and his last two shots were made before he had time to think. That was it. He was done. There was nothing but his sword between him and the Judgment Seat.

Lukas kept his eyes on the enemy, but his ears heeded the sounds from the men around him. There were fewer and fewer shots now. They must all be exhausting their ammunition store. The Swedes could not fail to notice that there was no more fire from the thicket. Slowly, steadily, they walked closer. *Merciful Father, forgive me my many sins*, Lukas prayed. *Save my soul, dear Lord.*

Someone on the Swedish side gave a battle-cry, and they rushed forward into the thicket. Lukas scrambled backwards until he had a tree behind him. He felt the hilt of his sword slip in his hand. It was so greased with sweat he could barely keep hold of it. Two Swedes came towards him. One had slung his musket over his shoulder, and brandished a dragoon's sabre. The other had his weapon loaded and ready to fire. Lukas remembered the soldier in the house in Magdeburg, and how he had shot him clean in the face after promising him quarter. *Blessed Father, let me not plead for mercy from my enemies. Let me die like a man.* There was a clash of metal on metal from another part of the thicket, and then a man's scream. A Swedish officer rode into the thicket on a fine fresh horse. He called something to his men and they stepped back. The two who had Lukas at their mercy moved away from him, but their eyes never left his face. The one with the loaded musket kept it pointed at him.

The Swedish officer spoke in German: 'You men have fought bravely. Good soldiers are welcome in the army of King Gustavus Adolphus. Surrender to us now, and you may have your lives and a place in our force. If this plan is not to your taste only say so and my men will gladly take the weight off your feet for all eternity.'

Lukas looked around to see who was still living. There was Götz, crouched behind a blackberry bush with his dagger in his hand. Baxandall was pinned to the ground by a young Swede armed with a sword that was nearly as big as he was. And there was Captain Sadeler. It was for him to decide. Fight and die, or surrender and live?

Captain Sadeler stepped forward. 'I am a captain in the Emperor's army, and of prosperous enough stock. I hope you will show due respect to me.'

'Have you friends who will pay for your freedom?' the Swedish officer said.

'I have, but let the price be fair.'

The Swede nodded. 'That will be discussed by and by. What of your men here?'

Captain Sadeler shrugged. 'None has a *Taler* to his name, apart from the loot they left in Leipzig. They may shift for themselves.'

'We'll bring them to the recruiting sergeant then, unless they prefer to die?' The Swede scanned them. Each man put his weapon away and stood up. When it came to Lukas's turn, he did the same.

Slowly, the bedraggled remains of the company made their way out of the thicket. The sun was setting, and fog was creeping over the land. Lukas tried to work out where they had stood at the start of the battle, but it was impossible to tell. The whole field was crowded with scavengers piling carts with trophies. There were so many that he could not even see the bodies of the dead. He felt a hand touch his arm. Götz and Baxandall were beside him. 'Well, Götz, this is a turn of events,' he said.

'What can we do?'

'What all soldiers must. Endure. Obey orders. We may pray that before long we'll be restored to the Emperor's force.'

'Perhaps the King of Sweden will pay better than the Emperor,' Baxandall said.

Some man behind them muttered, 'He could hardly pay worse.'

Baxandall was smirking.

'What have you got to be cheerful about?' Lukas said. 'Aren't you mourning that booty gathering dust in Leipzig?'

'Ach, there'll be more by and by.'

'I don't know how you can smile when you're a prisoner,' Götz said. 'Are we not the lowest of the low?'

'You might be,' Baxandall said, 'but not I.' He gave them a sly smirk. 'I'm with my own sort now. It's you Papists who are in the dirt.'

Eighteen

WITHIN A WEEK OF THE BATTLE it was clear to Christa that Lukas would not be returning. She raised the matter with Frau Ackermann as they worked together one morning. 'You may stay with us,' Frau Ackermann said, but Christa thought she could detect hesitation in her voice.

'I must pay you a proper rent,' she said, 'and let you and Herr Ackermann have your bed back.'

Frau Ackermann brightened. 'I suppose your man left you plenty of booty to live off.' She was a sharp-eyed one, that was for sure.

It was agreed Christa would have the second bedroom, but first the room had to be cleaned and put to rights. It had been occupied by Baxandall, Götz and the other two soldiers, and they had left it as squalid as a pig-pen. Frau Ackermann set about restoring it, and asked Christa to do the same with the room she and Lukas had shared. She stripped the linen sheets from the bed, turning her eyes away from the stains Lukas had left on them when he had lain with her. It unsettled her to think he could be lying dead on the battlefield, while his mark was still here, the living proof of him.

Leipzig settled. Those soldiers who had survived the battle soon thought it wise to move on. Now that their numbers were so few they could not bully their way about the place. They gathered up their loot and women and went on their way. Some would doubtless find their path back to General Tilly and his army, but one soldier's wife whispered to Christa that she and her man were slipping away in the hope of finding some other way of living. By many accounts they were not the only ones to do so.

Christa's heart was in confusion. When she knelt to say her private prayers she could not find the words. Should she pray that Lukas was dead? She knew that Andreas did. When she had told him that she had been made to marry a soldier he had ranted about the evils of an Emperor who wished Papist seed to be planted in Protestant bellies. She had not, of course, told him of all that had preceded her wedding day.

Still, it did not seem right and proper that she, a Christian wife, should pray for her husband's death, in spite of the wrongs he'd done her. But to pray for his safe return would be the worst kind of falsehood, and surely God despised liars. And then there was Götz. When she thought of him she did not know how to pray at all. She stayed kneeling by her bedside for a long time each night, not praying, not even inside her head. She knew God could see the deepest thoughts of her heart and words were not needed, but she wished she had them at her disposal. If only she could frame her turmoil in words she might be less tormented.

Christa moved into the small bedroom and paid her rent, but she still felt ill at ease in the Ackermanns' house. She did all she could to assist Frau Ackermann in her household tasks, but she felt the older woman's discomfort. 'Rest yourself, child,' she would say. 'I have my own way of doing things, and your help will only double the task.' Frau Ackermann was pleased enough to take the rent money from her, but it seemed she wanted neither company nor aid.

As Frau Ackermann had noted, Lukas had left Christa well

provided with war loot. She did not like to live off it — to her mind it was blood-tainted — but she knew she could ill afford the luxury of such scruples. It was all she had and it would be gone quickly enough if she could not add to it. Her father had always cautioned against spending capital. She could imagine him advising her now: 'Put it to work, and live off the interest,' he would say. Wise words, if the world had been as it should be, but whom could she trust here? She would as likely be cheated as prosper, and then where would she find the money for her rent? 'Money is like wheat-grain,' his voice whispered in her head. 'Grind it for flour and you'll eat bread tomorrow. Sow it in good soil, and when the harvest comes you'll have bread every day.' He was right. The money should be held back. A time would come — she had to believe it — when she might find the means of planting it. The idea of Lukas's money — her money now, she supposed — melting like snow from a ditch troubled her. She must find the means to preserve it.

Andreas's new master shook his head. 'I have little enough work for him, and in truth I only keep him out of Christian charity. I could find no reason to engage a girl like you.'

Christa burned on Andreas's behalf. He himself said nothing, but continued his work setting the type for a new run. He must have heard his master's words, though, and Christa knew how his pride would smart. She tried a different tack. 'What of the other printers in the city? I was reared in this trade, sir. There must be some employment to be had.'

The printer scratched his chin. 'There's old Schumacher. He might be worth a try. His maidservant died of the plague.'

Andreas leaned on the edge of the press for balance. 'Christa reads and writes both German and Latin. A little English too. She's able for more than mopping up after old Schumacher.'

'Don't trouble yourself, Andreas,' she said. 'I will take any respectable work I can.' She had no appetite for acting the maidservant, but she was afraid that Andreas would raise a quarrel with his new master. If he lost his position it was doubtful that he'd find a new one. For all the knowledge of the trade he carried in his head, any master printer would see only a cripple.

Herr Schumacher was a foul-smelling old man, who appeared to have dismissed the idea that a godly one should wash the ink off his hands at the end of a day's labour. His skin seemed stained with many years' worth. Christa had to force herself not to turn away from his reek as he peered closely at her. She wondered had it really been plague that his last maidservant had died of. Perhaps the poor woman had absorbed some contagion from his sour breath. He offered Christa a *Taler* a week for her labour, and she countered that the least she would take was a *Gulden*. They parried back and forth until they met in the middle, and came, at last, to agreement.

His maid had been dead only a month, so the house was soon put to rights. Christa was glad enough to be busy, and there was satisfaction to be had in bringing order and cleanliness to the place. It was comforting, too, to be close to a printing press and all those other objects that meant home to her. Paper, ink, the cabinet of type with its little drawers — their familiarity both grieved and welcomed her. Each day, as soon as she had finished her tasks about the house, she would find an excuse to be in the workshop, and watch Herr Schumacher go about his business.

For all that he was old and rancid, Herr Schumacher was well able for a day's work. There was strength still in those arms, and he worked the press with the vigour of a man in his prime. It was as well that he was quick with it, for he was slow as forgiveness when it came to composing the type. One day, as she swept the floor of the workshop, Christa watched him squint into his cabinet of type. He picked a piece out and felt it with his fingertips. It seemed to Christa that he was trying to read it by touch. She laid aside her broom and stepped closer. 'What word is it you're making?' she said. 'I'll find the letters for you, quick as a blade.'

'There's more to it than knowing your letters,' the old man huffed.

'Which typeface do you want? Schwabacher or Fraktur?' She let this evidence of her knowledge sink into his mind. 'I would propose Fraktur for the title. Are you in agreement?'

Old Schumacher scowled at her. 'You're a bossy one, aren't you?'

'My father said I was sharp-tongued, but he thought it was as well in these times.' She swallowed her grief at speaking of her father in the past tense. *Lord, let me be strong.* Götz had said she was not weak. But there was no purpose in thinking of him.

'The word I wish to make is "devotions". Pick the letters out for me.' Herr Schumacher turned half away as if he had no interest in what she was doing.

Christa chose them and lined them up on the platen. 'There. The title is done, and hardly a breath drawn.'

Schumacher ran his fingers over the type. 'You have them all coggledy.' He pulled a soft hammer from his pocket and tapped the type down. 'You're not so smart as you think, eh?'

'So, I will pick out the letters, lay them down, and you can perfect them. You'll still work ten times faster than you are now.'

Old Schumacher twisted his mouth as if he was chewing something sour. Christa knew by now that he would never admit she was right, but she thought he was nearly persuaded. He pushed the text towards her. 'Just as long as you won't be expecting any more pay out of me,' he said, not meeting her eye.

It became a custom with them that when the work demanded it Old Schumacher would call upon her to assist him. He did not trouble himself with making books, but instead turned out song-sheets and rhymes. As he had no skill in the marketplace he sold his work to traders who would instruct him in what wares they required. One day he might be printing a run of prayers for the King of Sweden, and the next a saucy ballad about a sausage-maker's wife. There was an occasion when a gentleman called with a handwritten page of accusations against a lewd woman now living in Leipzig who was said to have married and cheated men from Munich to Hamburg, and had lately tried these same tricks on a local cloth merchant. That pamphlet was printed with neither author's name nor printer's mark. Both the mysterious gentleman and Herr Schumacher might have found themselves before the judge for libel if anyone had discovered that they were its progenitors.

Christa's life took on a new pattern. She would work from early morning at Old Schumacher's and return to the Ackermanns' at the end of the day. Sitting at table with them in the evening, she was conscious again of their discomfort in her presence. There was little conversation. She came to dread Sundays, when she had no work to escape to, only church and perhaps an hour or two spent with Andreas and the other Magdeburg refugees in Little Bohemia. 'Schumacher would give you lodgings,' Andreas said. 'His dead maid had her own room.'

'It would not suit me.' Christa could not tell him her real fear. The idea of lying down for the night with only herself and the old man in the house was too much to bear. Old as he might be, she would not sleep easy. He was a man, when all was said and done, and she knew better now than to trust one. At least at the Ackermanns' the man of the house was safely tucked up with his lady. There seemed no mending of her circumstances.

It was laundry day. The tub was filled with boiled water and Old Schumacher's soiled linen. Steam misted the kitchen windows and hung in the air. She welcomed its heat. The winter was turning bitter, and washday was the only time her hands were warmed. She knew she'd pay for it later, when she went back into the chill outside, but for now she revelled in it.

'Come here, milady,' Old Schumacher called from the workshop.

She wiped her hands dry on her apron and walked through from the kitchen. 'The laundry's not half done yet. If you want a clean shirt for the Lord's Day you'd better not detain me.'

'Clean shirt be damned. We've a useful commission here, but the customer wants it turned out post-haste.' He handed her a sheet of paper covered with neat script. 'There's a good enough woodcut here to enhance it.' He already had it set on the platen.

Christa read the sheet of writing. *The Settling of a Score, or how King Gustavus Adolphus and his armie have lately sacked the City of Erfurt. Vengeance is Mine, I will Repay, Sayeth the Lord.*

'Is your heart not glad to read it?' he said.

'I am happy that the King of Sweden has had another victory.'

'But it is vengeance, too, for the hurt done at Magdeburg, and that is sweeter, is it not?'

Christa gave her thoughts to this. Did it soothe her to know that a Papist city had suffered as Magdeburg had? Was her anger sated, or her pain resolved? She could not say it was.

They worked quickly, she picking out the type and placing it roughly where it should be, then he fixing it in place. By the time they had finished her hands were nearly as stained as his. 'Look at me,' she said, holding her hands in front of herself. 'Your shirts will be black as sin if I can't scrub this off.'

'You may let them soak a bit longer. I'll need you to pin the pages to the line as they come off the press.'

By the time Christa returned to the laundry tub the water was as cold as stone. She steeled herself to it, and managed to get the linen rinsed, wrung out and hung on the stand in front of the kitchen fire. The day was already dark, but even had the sun been shining, the air was too cold now for anything to dry outside. Herr Schumacher called that he was going out to fetch a jug of beer. She rushed on with her work. It was not that she had any wish to be sitting down in silence with the Ackermanns, but neither would she enjoy a late journey home through the dark city.

She was laying the table for Herr Schumacher's supper when he returned with his jug of beer and Andreas. 'I found this fellow huddled by the fire in the tavern and remembered him by his wounds,' Old Schumacher said. 'I offered him a bite to eat here, and a first look at that new handbill we printed today.'

Andreas took a seat at the table, and Christa set a place for him. He was wan in the lamplight, but he was not as starved-looking as he had been when she had first seen him in Leipzig. Perhaps he was mending at last. When she set down some bread and sausage he ate as heartily as she did. It frightened her sometimes how quickly she had become accustomed to having a full belly after so long a hunger as she'd known while Magdeburg was besieged. How would she fare if she had to face such want again? Old Schumacher watched them with a look on his face that suggested he regretted his hospitality. Christa resisted the urge to reach out for more bread. It would be best not to torment the old skinflint. 'I shall put these leavings away for the morning,' she said, rising and taking the remains of the supper to the larder.

'Fetch in a copy of that handbill, while you're on your feet,' Old Schumacher said, pouring the smallest drop of beer into Andreas's mug.

Christa went into the workshop. It was near dark in there now, and she had not liked to lift the lamp from the kitchen table. She could see the handbills, though. Pale in the gloom, they appeared to be floating in the air. Carefully she touched her lips to the closest one, to be sure that it was dry. Fingertips would smudge wet ink, but the delicate touch of lips would not. Christa found she could tell by the smell of the air round a sheet of print whether it was dry or not, even before she tried her lips on it. This one was ready, to be sure. She unpinned it and carried it into the kitchen.

'Read it, sir,' Old Schumacher said, laying it before Andreas.

Andreas pulled the lamp closer and pored over the flyer, his lips moving as he did so. When he had finished he leaned back and was silent. Old Schumacher looked at him so eagerly that he seemed obliged to speak. 'Aye, well, they reaped what others sowed.'

'Indeed they did.' Schumacher banged his fist on the table. 'Your friend there,' he pointed at Christa, 'was filled with compassion for them.'

There was no hint of softness in Andreas's face. 'Has this world not burned the kindness out of you yet?'

'I wouldn't want any others to suffer as we have done.'

'What of those who did us such harm? Do you feel so kindly towards them?'

Christa's face warmed under the men's stares. The easiest thing would be to busy herself in the last tidying of the day, but her thoughts were in such disorder that she felt she must frame them in words. It might be the only way to still them. 'I lived with them for more than a quarter-year. I came to know them. Some were wicked enough, it's true, but they were not all devils.'

Andreas's face was flushed now, and his mouth trembled with rage as he spoke. 'They were all devils the day Magdeburg fell. You didn't see it, hidden away as you were.' He pulled himself up and fumbled for his stick. 'I saw it. If you'd witnessed what they did to your kin you wouldn't be so free with your mercy.'

Christa felt that if she stayed a moment longer her mind might fall to pieces and never be put together again. The room closed in around her, and she could not bear the sight of Andreas, his face twisted with anger. It put her in mind of the way Lukas, Baxandall and Captain Sadeler had looked that last day in Magdeburg as they prepared to ruin her. She ran through the house to the door, not pausing to lift her shawl or take off her apron. Out she went into the dark street. Andreas was calling out to her, but he would never catch her, not with his injured leg. She ran as carelessly as a child, crying now.

Eventually common sense told her to stop and take her bearings, even though her distress could have caused her to run to Prague and back. She paused and looked about her. There was the tavern they called the Sun Rising. She was already nearly halfway to the Ackermanns'. A drinker reeled outside and mistook her tears for frailty. When he laid his hands on her waist she roared at him with such fury that he stepped away in shock and tripped over his feet. She left him lying on the dirty ground and went on, walking now, but still with the turmoil boiling inside her.

The Ackermanns were already in bed when she got there. Frau Ackermann had left some bread and cheese for her, wrapped in a cloth for freshness. Christa had no appetite for the food, but was loath to cause offence by leaving it. For a moment she was tempted to dispose of it in the fire, but such sinful waste would have lain heavy on her. How could she cast away food when so many across the land were dying of want? She forced herself to eat, washing it down with the weak beer Frau Ackermann had left.

She felt better when she was done, but although her breathing was calmer she felt a fierce strain where her heart lay, as if a trap there was ready to spring shut. The words Andreas had spoken repeated themselves in her head. *If you'd witnessed what they did to your kin you wouldn't be so free with your mercy.* Try as she might she could not silence the words, or turn away the pictures that offered themselves to her imagination. Damn him for opening this door in her mind. She had done her best not to wonder how it might have been with her father and Dieter. When any thought of it came to her she had pushed it away. She had seen some of what Tilly's men could do since she'd become Lukas's wife. She'd seen men die quickly and slowly, and had persuaded herself that for her father and Dieter it would have been swift. So swift, perhaps, that they had not known anything about it. But now Andreas, *damn him*, had robbed her of this scant consolation. *Damn him. Damn him. Damn him.*

Christa slept badly. It was still dark when it was time to rise from her bed. She could have lain on readily enough. There would have been no pleasure in such idleness, it was just that the prospect of facing the world made her want to weep. As she readied herself for the day her limbs felt heavy as death, and her head too. Frau Ackermann asked her if the fever was on her, but she said no. The older woman watched her fearfully. She wanted no fever in her house.

That day Christa was listless in her work. If Old Schumacher was dissatisfied with her, he must have thought it wisest to say nothing. She worked and worked, forcing herself on, clamping her teeth together to keep herself going as she ironed the old man's clean shirt for his church-going. Her melancholy reminded her of how she had felt on her first morning in the Imperial camp. That had been different, though. The terrible new world had been strange to her, and buried deep beneath her numb shock there had been fear. She felt no fear now. That evening the Ackermanns watched her closely as she ate. Perhaps they still worried that she was succumbing to fever. The idea was beguiling. To lie down and never rise again. She would be blessed indeed.

The next day Andreas sought her out at church. He looked ill, as if he also had a fever working on him. 'Is it too cold for walking?' he said. His voice sounded forced and unnatural.

'Are you fit for it?'

Annoyance — or perhaps injured pride — swept over his face, but he took a breath and said, 'If I tire I will stop.'

They walked through the pleasanter parts of the city. It was cold, bitterly so, but she had no wish to rush back to the Ackermanns'. She had to slow her pace so that she did not outstrip Andreas but, even so, he wearied quickly. They sat down on a stone bench in the marketplace. There was no trade today, naturally, but the younger people of the city were there in number, meeting friends and enjoying the short hours of daylight.

At last Andreas spoke: 'If I caused you distress by my words the other night I am sorry for it.'

'I know you are.'

'I spoke in heat. It was unjust. But yet ... this world seems so easy for you women. You suffer little, and therefore are more ready to forgive.'

Christa could think of no reply. Was he right? Were her tribulations petty compared to his?

Andreas glanced at her awkwardly. 'I would be grieved to lose your friendship over this quarrel.'

'We are still friends.'

They sat on in silence. The chill in the air was making Christa's bones ache.

'You have landed well here in Leipzig,' he said. 'Better than I have.'

This was more like the Andreas of old, always full of complaint.

She decided to keep that thought to herself. He would hardly thank her for sharing it with him. 'Perhaps you'll find a better master, by and by.'

'I'll not find one to equal your father.' He clasped his hands together.

He was trembling and her heart ached for his pain. She could not trust herself to speak.

'I'm sorry if talking of him brings your sorrow back upon you,' he said.

She shook her head. 'I'm glad to hear him spoken of with kind words. Sometimes I wonder if our life before was just a dream.'

'There are people still, in Magdeburg, so I've heard. They live in the ruins.'

Christa tried to imagine how the city might be now. She could not see it — there was no image in her head. It was the same when she thought of her father and Dieter. She could not bring their faces to mind. 'Would you go back there?' she said.

'I have not the strength.'

'But you are stronger than you were.'

Andreas was staring at her. 'You wish to return. I can see it in you.'

Christa let his words settle in her. She had not thought of it clearly before, but now that she did she knew she could not go back. 'I would have too much fear of the journey.' She had seen it often enough as she travelled with Lukas and the rest of the Emperor's men. More than once some poor band of travellers had crossed their path and been persuaded to part with all they possessed. Those who had dared to oppose the soldiers had lost more than property. No, she would not quit Leipzig until the country was at peace.

The feast of Christ's birth was past, and the merrymaking as forgotten as the memory of summer heat. One day, in the cold heart of January, Christa returned to the Ackermanns' at the end of her day's work to find a package awaiting her. It was rectangular, with the longer edge the length of a child's forearm. It looked to Christa the same shape and size as the books her father had sometimes received from the great printing cities. 'It was carried here by a messenger,' Frau Ackermann said. 'The impudent lad wouldn't go until I paid him three *Taler.*'

'I will repay you,' Christa said. She was tempted to carry the parcel away to her room, which would torment poor Frau Ackermann beyond endurance. There was little point, though. She would likely go looking for it the very moment Christa left the house. Anyway, she had no lamp in her bedroom, and the candle there gave off only a poor light.

She found a paring knife and cut away the seal and twine that held the wrappings in place. It was soundly parcelled. There were four layers of covering on it to protect it during its journey. 'Was there no note to tell where it came from or who sent it?' Christa said. She could feel her heart beating hard in her chest. If Lukas had survived the battle, it might be from him. Or Götz.

'The boy seemed to know nothing.' Frau Ackermann seemed more interested in the wrappings than in the contents. Perhaps she thought she might sell them for a *Pfennig* or two. 'He didn't seem quite right in the head, which seems a flaw in a messenger.'

Christa opened the last layer of wrapping, and saw that the parcel indeed contained a book. The binding was cheap — mere board covered with brown linen. She opened it and read the title page. It was the fifth volume of the book Götz had taken from her father's house. The paper was smooth, and of a decent weight. She checked the name of the printer — Kleinschmidt of Mainz. Perhaps they had produced it unbound. Some customers liked to have their books bound to their own particular taste. It was a puzzle why it had been so cheaply finished. Maybe its first owner had been low on funds when the book was delivered, and been forced to settle for this.

'A book?' Frau Ackermann said. 'Not scripture, I fear.'

'No. It's the tale of an ancient hero called Odysseus. Do you know of it?'

Frau Ackermann stiffened. 'Indeed I do not.'

'This is the story of his return from a great war, and all the trials he faced in his efforts to go home.'

'Pagan nonsense.'

'I suppose they could not help but be pagans, for our Lord Jesus had not yet come for our salvation, had He?'

'I'd rather not have it about the place.'

'I'll keep it in my room.'

'There is only one book I will permit under my roof.' She nodded at the Bible on the far shelf.

Christa fought down her irritation at Frau Ackermann's narrowness. These Calvinists prized their ignorance, and refused to distinguish between a strumpet-song and the finest philosophy. 'I will take it away with me in the morning. Herr Schumacher will be glad to examine its workmanship.'

Frau Ackermann did not look satisfied with this, but she could scarcely force Christa out into the night to carry the book away.

Christa lit her candle and took it upstairs to her room. She sat on her bed and waited for her heartbeat to steady. Lukas or Götz. Which of them was it? She turned the pages carefully. Although the candlelight was weak, it was enough that she might see any note among the pages. There was none. A red ribbon marked a page close to the end. It might well be from Lukas. Had he not given her that *Small Catechism*? And he could not write his own name, so he would hardly scribe a note to go with his gift. But why would he send her such a thing? He had no care for her, although he had been less hard on her than some of the other soldiers had been towards their wives. Her mind was unsettled. She had grown accustomed to thinking of him as dead. If he wasn't ... Dear God, her stomach tightened at the thought of him returning to take possession of her once more.

But perhaps he was dead and the book was from Götz. They had talked together of Troy, and he had told her of all that had happened there. That tale had given her a strange comfort. To know that Magdeburg was not the first city to suffer such a fate, and to know that the name of long-fallen Troy still lived on the tongues of scholars — these things had made her feel less hopeless. She examined the book again, squinting at its words. Her skill in reading English had grown rusty these last months, but gradually she began to understand it. *All the survivors of the war had reached their home by now and so put the perils of battle and the sea behind them.* Was it possible that she could do as Odysseus had done? Could she find her way home?

It pained her eyes to read in the poor light. She closed the book, put on her nightgown and got into bed.

Nineteen

AS USUAL, LUKAS HAD TO SHAKE Götz awake. The lad had drunk more than his share of the convent's wine last night, as he had every night of the month the company had been billeted there. He stirred when Lukas shook him, but pulled his blanket over his head and would not rise. The dormitory was already half empty, the men seeking food to break their fast or readying their weapons for inspection.

'Get up, damn you. We're to start our exercises before the next bell. They'll tolerate no slacking.' There was no response from Götz. Lukas knelt beside the makeshift bed and pulled away the blanket. His stomach heaved. 'Dear God, you smell worse than an old he-goat.'

Götz tried to grab the blanket back, but when Lukas would not let him have it he covered his face with his hands. Impatience swelled in Lukas; fear, too. Their new masters were sticklers for order. Of the remnants of Captain Sadeler's company that had been pressed into the Swedish service two had already been hanged, one for looting, one for rape — and all but Baxandall and Lukas had been flogged for small failings. Even Götz had not escaped. He had grown neglectful since Breitenfeld, and the drink he took so freely made him worse.

Lukas left Götz and walked out of the dormitory. For all that the boy infuriated him, he didn't want to see him beaten again or dancing at the end of a rope. He made his way to the chapel. It was the time of morning between the offices of Terce and Sext. He hoped to find the old priest who conducted the Mass. Perhaps such a man might persuade Götz where he could not. The priest, however, could not be found. A frail nun was at prayer before the crucifix. She was on her knees, her face turned up to Christ on the cross, her arms spread apart in imitation of the Saviour. Lukas watched her from the back of the chapel. She did not move or alter her stance. He wondered at such quiet strength, and admired it.

He must have made some sound as he backed out, for the nun turned and saw him. She got stiffly to her feet, and he bowed in apology. 'I was seeking the priest,' he said.

'He is gone away until tomorrow,' she said. 'Did you wish to make your confession?'

'No.' Lukas hesitated. He had no real wish to talk of his and Götz's business to a woman, nun or not, but he feared that delay might bring more trouble to Götz. 'My friend is plagued by the melancholy. I cannot rouse him from it. He seeks forgetfulness in strong drink, but that will not cure him. He is a godly lad, and I thought …'

'Would you like me to pray with him?'

'Yes. Thank you, sister.' His worry might be carried a little way on another's shoulders, Lukas thought, and felt lighter.

The nun clicked her fingers, and an older nun appeared from the transept. She must have been waiting there while the first was at prayer. Lukas had noticed that the nuns of this convent made sure they were not alone, with so many men about the place.

The three walked towards the dormitories where the soldiers were billeted. 'My friend and I were with our blessed Emperor's army,' he said, so that she would understand him. 'Alas, we have fallen into the hands of our enemies.' He glanced at her. She was not especially old, but her skin was as dry and flaking as willow bark. 'I hope these heretics do not put you out of ease.'

'We were fearful at first, but they have shown us some civility. I am told they respect our devotion to our faith. They feel it mirrors their own steadfastness.'

Lukas pondered this. It was true that the Swedes seemed fonder of their religion than the Germans, but they were bloodthirsty in a skirmish.

They found Götz still curled in his bed. There were only a couple of other soldiers still in the dormitory. 'Here are some of the good sisters come to speak with you,' Lukas said.

Götz forced himself to sit up. He smoothed his hair, which showed some care for appearances, but his eyes were downcast. He settled his hands on his knees, rubbing his breeches in a way that suggested he was ill at ease.

The nuns gestured that Lukas should move away and sat beside Götz. Lukas walked to the furthest window, and looked out at the country beyond the convent. Mistletoe was still flourishing in the willows that grew down by the river. It put him in mind of last spring. Dear God, the world had changed since then. He could hear the soft murmur of the nuns' voices, and Götz's halting replies, but he could not make out their words. A drum and a bugle sounded from the front of the convent, to summon the men to the morning's exercises. Lukas walked back past Götz and the nuns. He looked towards them, to see if Götz was for stirring, but the nuns waved him away. He would have to make excuses for the lad, say he was ill and in the care of the sisters, then hope that would suffice to spare Götz more punishment.

He found Götz later at prayer in the chapel. A few others were there too — even some of the Swedes, he noticed.

He waited for Götz at the door. The boy smiled at him sheepishly. 'Well, are you mended?' Lukas said.

'I am a little strengthened.'

'Let's take some food, then. That will strengthen you even more.'

They made their way to the refectory. The food was plain, and not so plentiful as it had been at the beginning of their stay, but it sufficed. Baxandall had quipped that he'd never heard of a priest or nun dying for want of food, and while his gibe rankled, Lukas acknowledged to himself that there was truth in it. The thought of Baxandall soured his appetite. That bastard had prospered in the Swedish service. He was a sergeant now, and had found himself a new little wife from among the camp followers. She seemed to his liking, and he to hers. She trailed after him everywhere, gazing fondly at him like a puppy at its master. Lukas forced his thoughts away from Baxandall and looked over the table at Götz. The boy was eating well, and not taking overmuch of the beer. 'Will you be able for this afternoon's drill?'

Götz nodded. 'With God's help, yes.' He took another piece of bread and chewed it slowly. When he had finished he looked up at Lukas. 'The sisters were telling me a strange thing.'

'What was that?'

'They said they'd heard that in the convent of Our Lady of Pity in Hedersleben there is a saintly child who has the cure for melancholy.'

'Hedersleben? I don't think I know of it.'

'It is two or three days' journey south-west of Magdeburg.'

The city's name hung in the silence between them. Lukas drank the last of his beer. 'That's a fair distance from here. I doubt the King of Sweden's plans will take us near it.'

'I know I cannot go there. Please God I will be cured through my own prayers and those of the good women here.'

'So you'll have no need for this child in Hedersleben.'

'The sisters said the girl is known as the Child of Magdeburg. She survived the city's fall, and was blessed with the gift of healing.'

'Well, that's a miracle and God be praised for it, but what has it to do with us?'

Götz's eyes were bright now. Lukas hadn't seen that spark in him since Breitenfeld. 'Don't you remember how Christa's young sister was lost? I took her to the cathedral, to safety, but then she could not be found again. Christa and I went looking for her in the convent at Magdeburg, but she was vanished.'

Lukas could recollect nothing about the child. He could scarcely remember Christa. Hearing her name now was like a daytime echo of a dream long forgotten. 'I don't recall it,' he said, hoping that Götz would allow this theme to lapse.

'I should perhaps send a letter to Christa in Leipzig, if you would allow it.' The colour rose a little in Götz's face. 'It might give her hope that her sister is still alive.'

'You'd be wasting your effort and money. There'll be no post getting through the country in these times.'

Götz blushed deeper. 'Much of it gets to its destination, I believe. There's not a week goes past that a messenger doesn't arrive here with a pannier of letters.'

The rest of the men were rising to prepare for the drill, and Lukas stood. 'Do you know for certain that this girl in Hedersleben is Christa's sister?'

Götz looked deflated. 'No.'

'If ever you confirm it, you may write to her. Until then, keep your silence.'

They were in the habit of conducting their drills and other exercises on the flat ground that lay before the main entrance to the convent. At some time in its past flat stones had been laid to form a smoother path for wagons to come and go. In peace time the convent was famed for a restorative liquor they distilled, as well as the more usual harvests of wine and beer. The war had killed the trade. Such goods being carried to market rarely reached their destination untapped. The only wagons that rolled in and out of the convent now carried soldiers and their belongings. Still, the paved path made a solid, if uneven, foundation for musket and cannon practice. They had taken to referring to it as the parade-ground.

The air was calm today. The trees were near enough in full leaf now. In the breaks between drills Lukas watched a pair of collared doves dance through the air. While the world went on as usual for the humbler of God's creatures, mankind destroyed all it could see.

The pleasantness of the day was dimmed when Baxandall took charge of their exercises. He stalked back and forth as they followed the orders hammered out by the drummer boy, swinging his shoulders to show off the new coat he'd had made to order by the nuns. Along with his new rank and wardrobe he had acquired a grinning corporal, who followed him on the parade-ground, and laughed at all his jokes. Götz was positioned a row in front of Lukas. Thank God the boy had pulled himself together since his conversation with the nuns.

Baxandall stopped pacing and ordered them to present arms. This they did. He ordered the man immediately before him to drop the ramrod into the barrel of his musket. The man did so. The ramrod slid home smoothly. Baxandall turned and walked along the row to where Götz stood and gave the same order. Lukas held his breath. He had helped Götz put his musket to rights that very morning. He hoped no grain of dirt had clogged it in the time since. Götz held the ramrod above the mouth of the musket barrel and dropped it. It rattled down unimpeded. Lukas breathed easy again. Baxandall didn't move. 'What is your name?' he said. Götz did not reply, wondering no doubt why Baxandall should be asking his name when they had fought side by side for the best part of a year. 'Answer me!' Baxandall shouted.

'My name is Götz Fuhrmann, sir.'

'And where are you from, Götz Fuhrmann?'

'I was reared in Saalfeld. Sir.'

'What was your father?'

Again Götz hesitated. 'I believe he was a soldier, sir.'

'You believe? Do you not know for certain?'

Götz's face was flushed with embarrassment, and Lukas burned with rage at Baxandall. He was angrier still to see the young fool of a corporal laughing along with his master's joke.

'You don't answer me, Private Fuhrmann,' Baxandall continued. 'Are you deaf? I said, do you not know for certain what your father was?'

'No, sir.'

'What was his name, then?'

'I don't know, sir.'

'Perhaps your mother didn't know either.'

The corporal grew merrier still. Baxandall smirked at him, then turned back to Götz. 'Do you hope to advance in the Swedish service, Private Fuhrmann?'

'If it's God's will, sir, yes.'

'I will keep you in mind, then. If I become dissatisfied with any of my junior men here,' he glanced coldly at his corporal, 'I may be looking for a replacement.'

He was cunning, Lukas had to give him that. The young corporal now resembled a dog whose master had beaten it. No doubt he'd be scurrying around doing whatever he was bade for the next week. Lukas hoped Götz was not taken in by Baxandall's slyness.

The inspection continued. Baxandall and the downcast corporal worked their way through the rest of Götz's line, and moved to the one in which Lukas stood. When Baxandall reached him he stopped. 'And what is your name?'

The old anger uncurled in Lukas's belly. 'You know my name.'

Baxandall brought his face so close that Lukas could smell the lunchtime *Wurst* on his breath. 'I do not recall it.'

'Don't try your tricks with me.' Lukas gripped his musket firmly as he spoke. His hands were trembling with the urge to wring Baxandall's throat.

'Have a care, soldier,' Baxandall said. 'The Swedish service will not tolerate insubordination. Tell me your name.'

Lukas kept his mouth clamped shut, and stared straight ahead.

Baxandall shifted so that they stood eye to eye. 'You've kept your back unmarked so far, soldier,' he said quietly. 'I'll be glad to be the man to put stripes upon it at last, and watches you piss yourself with the pain of it. Still, I'm a Christian man, so I'll give you this last chance. What is your name?'

Lukas was in torment. He did not want Baxandall to win this

battle, yet he would be a pig-headed fool to sacrifice himself for the sake of pride. He thought of the humiliation of being half stripped before the company and tied down like an animal. Pain he could bear, but not such humbling. 'My name is Lukas Weinsburg,' he said at last.

Baxandall cocked his head to one side. 'Not such a man as you thought you were, Lukas Weinsburg.' He did not wait for Lukas's response, but continued down the line.

There was little revelry to be found in the convent. The presence of so many holy women had a crushing effect on merriment. With no tavern close at hand the men had made one of the dormitories an informal beer cellar. After the day's work was done, and the last meal eaten, they would gather there to sup quietly, and perhaps enjoy a crafty game of dice. Some were fond of tobacco, and the room was hazy with it.

Lukas took no pleasure in either gaming or smoking. He sat on a window ledge where the air was clearer, drinking a mug of beer and watching a game progress. Götz was at prayer, and Lukas had no wish to converse with any other companion. This time of year provoked a restlessness in him. He itched to be on the road again. With luck they'd encounter Imperial troops, and he might slip over to his own side. He and Götz had talked often of it, during the long nights of the winter. A man could always find a way to switch allegiance if he was minded to, but it took care and skill to pull it off without earning a hanging. Baxandall would likely stay where he was, since he'd advanced so well. It would be best if he did stay with the Swedes: then Lukas might one day have the pleasure of filling him with lead shot.

Just at that moment Baxandall's half-witted corporal came into the dormitory. He stood looking at the assembled men with his mouth hanging open. When he spotted Lukas he approached him. As he walked he attempted an imitation of Baxandall's swagger. 'Sergeant von Baxandall requests you attend him in his private quarters,' the youth said.

'Sergeant *von* Baxandall?' Lukas couldn't stop himself laughing at Baxandall's affectation of a nobleman's styling. 'He was plain Ernst Baxandall when I first knew him.'

If the corporal understood this he made no show of it, but stood waiting for Lukas to accompany him. Lukas drained the last of his beer and put the mug down. At least he had drunk enough to take the edge off his anger. God alone knew what mischief Baxandall was at now.

Officers of the rank of sergeant and above had each been given a nun's cell for their living quarters. Life was cramped for those who were accompanied by their wives — the narrow bunk was not designed for either ease or pleasure — but at least it was a private place. That was luxury enough in the eyes of any soldier.

Baxandall's room had even less space than usual for he had placed in it two fair-sized trunks, which stood side by side on the floor and left little room for anything else. When Lukas arrived, led by the corporal, Baxandall was standing on one of the trunks, peering out of the small window set high in the outer wall of the cell. He turned. 'I thought you might refuse my invitation, stubborn bastard that you are.'

Lukas did not reply. He stood in the doorway. The corporal was closer to his back than was comfortable, but although instinct would have caused him to move away from the lad, caution kept him where he was. He didn't trust Baxandall not to be planning some malice.

Baxandall jumped off the trunk. 'The weather is fine, is it not? We'll be on the road again soon enough. Onward to more glory, eh? Come in, for God's sake.' He waved Lukas into the room, but held up his hand to stop the corporal following. 'Clear off. I've no more need of you now.'

He closed the door and shook his head, like an exasperated father. 'That boy's an idiot. I only advanced him as a favour to the captain. That's how it goes, sometimes. Sit down, sit down. The bed will do.'

Lukas sat, not taking his eyes off Baxandall. He mistrusted him all the more when he was pleasant. Some twist in his character made him play with people: sweet one day, bitter the next. 'Why did you summon me here?' Lukas said.

'Ach, you're too plain-spoken, Weinsburg. You must learn a little finesse.'

'Like you, *von* Baxandall?

Baxandall laughed, but Lukas thought he detected annoyance in him at the mockery of his improved name. 'The war has changed our world. We can be what we want to be. A man may be born dirt poor and end up a colonel, with a rich wife and a fine manor house.'

'You have not explained why you wanted me here.'

Baxandall nodded. 'It is time to bury our differences. We are old comrades, are we not? That little wife of mine is gone to fetch some liquor, and then we can drink ourselves into friendship, eh?'

At that moment she tapped on the door. She was carrying a bottle in one hand and a pewter jug in the other. The jug was evidently well filled, for the girl's arm trembled with the strain of holding it upright. Baxandall took it from her. 'What's this you've brought us? Wine as well as brandy?' He set the jug on one of the trunks and chucked her under the chin. 'What a clever little thing you are.'

She smiled up at him and gave him the brandy bottle with a curtsy, then twisted a loose strand of hair between her fingers. She was wearing a great number of gold bangles on each arm that clattered together as she moved. There was a pair of mismatched goblets on the shelf, and she lifted them down and set them on the trunk beside the wine jug. She glanced at Baxandall and mimed the act of pouring.

Baxandall nodded, and watched her dispense the wine. 'We understand barely a word of each other's tongue, but that's no bad thing,' he said to Lukas. 'At least I don't have to listen to her prattling. Not like you and that Christa one, eh?'

Lukas tensed at the mention of her name. It had been the same when Götz had babbled about the child he thought might be

Christa's sister. Lukas wanted nothing more than to forget the whole business, but he seemed cursed with comrades who would not let the past fade. Baxandall was watching him, waiting for a response, so he said, 'She knew well enough not to tax me with too much talk.'

Baxandall handed him a goblet. 'I suppose she got enough from your young friend Fuhrmann.'

Lukas did not reply, but drank the wine in one gulp. He felt the slow, steady pulse of anger, but could not tell whether it was against Baxandall or Götz. The memory of the morning of Breitenfeld came back to him, and Götz's stumbling prayer. Had the boy really said *Christa* when he should have said *Christum*?

Baxandall uncorked the brandy and half filled Lukas's goblet. His wife topped it up with wine, then sat on Baxandall's lap, laying her head on his shoulder. 'See how she adores me?' Baxandall said, feeding her wine from his goblet. 'She loves her finery. These trunks are packed with the pretty things I've plundered for her. Don't you think she's the daintiest sweetmeat you've ever seen? Doesn't she make your mouth water?'

'She's a little young for my taste,' Lukas said, and drank some more.

'It must be months since you've had a woman,' Baxandall said, 'unless you've persuaded one of those nuns to open her legs for you.'

Lukas' felt as if the blood was thundering through his heart, but he held himself back from punching the lecherous grin off Baxandall's face.

'No?' Baxandall said. 'By God, Weinsburg, you're as good as a monk. What of young Fuhrmann, though? The sisters seem taken with him. He has a way with these serious women, doesn't he?'

'His mind is solely on prayer.'

Baxandall laughed. 'Jesus, you're an innocent, for all you've seen and done.' He paused, letting the girl drink some more of his wine. 'Götz was close with that wife of yours. I tell you this as a friend.'

'They read their holy books and argued about the true interpretation of them.'

'Ah, no.' Baxandall shook his head sadly. 'There was more than that went on.'

Lukas knew this was a game Baxandall was playing, but he could not stop himself probing. 'What opportunity would they have had for wickedness? Götz was rarely away from my side in the daytime, and she was with me at night.'

'That last night in Leipzig — do you remember it? We went out carousing and were all divided in the crush of the taverns.'

Lukas thought back. His memories of the evening were fuddled, what with the drink he had taken then, and the distance of time since. But it was true, now that he recalled it. The taverns of Leipzig had been in uproar, packed with soldiers drinking away what might be their last night on earth. They had all been parted, but it had not mattered. He had drunk his fill, and wandered back to his lodgings when the mood of the city turned from drinking to fighting. 'I remember that, but …'

'Young Fuhrmann returned home a while before you. He cannot hold his drink as well as we old warhorses, can he?' Baxandall pushed his wife off his lap and motioned for her to refill their goblets. He watched her as she did so, and the expression on his face made Lukas's stomach turn. It was not affection, or even plain lust, but something darker for which Lukas could not find a name. He drank quickly from his replenished goblet. The liquor was pounding in his head, as was his anger, so that he could not tell which was which.

Baxandall's wife completed her serving duties and staggered a little as she straightened. Lukas realised she must be tipsy. Baxandall had probably been filling her with drink half the evening. She giggled, and sat on the bed beside Lukas, close enough that her skirt was brushing his leg. He tried to edge away from her, but she hooked her arm in his and laid her head on his shoulder, as she had with Baxandall.

'She's an affectionate soul, isn't she?' Baxandall said.

'I think she's taken too much drink.' Lukas could smell the girl's hair, a queasy mixture of perfume, grease and sweat. She relaxed against him, and her breathing became louder and deeper.

Baxandall laughed. 'Dear God, she's asleep! How I'll mock her for this tomorrow, and she won't know a word of what I say.'

Lukas eased her onto the bed so that she was lying on her side, facing the wall. She muttered in her sleep, but did not wake. He stood up. He realised that he too was drunk. The floor tilted beneath his feet, and he took a moment to steady himself.

'Don't go so soon,' Baxandall said. 'Here, this brandy is near done. We might as well finish it off.'

Lukas swayed. He could stumble for the door, or sit on the bed. If he sat, he might have trouble rising again. He had no wish to remain, yet he sat once more. Baxandall emptied the last of the brandy into the goblets, giving the greater measure to Lukas.

'Why did you want me here?' Lukas said. He was shamed to hear his words slur.

Baxandall scratched his beard. 'I see how you worry for young Fuhrmann. You fret over him like an indulgent father.'

'And what if I do?'

'No man likes to be made a fool of. Especially by the lad who has put the cuckold's horns on him.'

'The boy couldn't hide something like that from me. I'd have smelled it off him.'

Baxandall leaned back against the wall, and put his feet on the bed, close to his sleeping wife's head. 'Poor Weinsburg. You're unlucky with the women, aren't you? There were your wife and your dearest comrade making hay while you were drinking your worries away ...'

Lukas struggled to his feet. 'You're a liar.' He swayed back and forth.

Baxandall was grinning up at him, his greasy face red as any devil's. 'She was generous, though. To me she gave special privileges, on account of us both being the same faith.'

Lukas laughed at that. He knew there was no truth in it, but still he felt sick at the idea that he might unknowingly have shared a woman with Baxandall. 'She wouldn't have given you anything unless you pinned her down and took it.' Even as he spoke, he remembered that day in Magdeburg, and how he had made Christa lie down on the floor of her father's house.

Baxandall leered up at him, and Lukas knew he was recalling the same moment. The sergeant opened his mouth to speak again.

It seemed to Lukas that the world had slowed. Baxandall's mouth opened, slowly, slowly. The time had not yet come for him to speak again, but it was on its way. Lukas could not bear to hear what he would say next. He saw his own hands stretch forward, slowly, slowly. Baxandall's mouth continued to open. His eyes were open wider too. Lukas's hands were on Baxandall's neck, stopping the words. The anger that had been brewing inside him had surged with a rush into his hands, and he dug his fingers hard into Baxandall's neck. He was on top of the other man now. They were lying as close as lovers. He knew that Baxandall's fingernails were digging into his hands. He could feel his skin tear, and knew that this should hurt, but it did not. Baxandall had such strength. His legs kicked, his heart thudded against Lukas's, and his neck muscles seemed to writhe beneath Lukas's hands. Lukas closed his eyes so that he could not see Baxandall's face. In the darkness of his mind he remembered the little Croat — what had his name been? — the one he'd given the mercy to. How he had struggled, his dumb body fighting for life when his mind must have known it was hopeless.

Lukas did not know how much time had passed. The cell seemed a little darker. Baxandall's little wife still snored drunkenly on the bed. The sergeant himself lay beneath him, quite still. The air smelled of shit and piss. Lukas realised his hands were still round the man's neck. He leaped up, away from Baxandall. Dead. No doubt of it. Lukas felt sober now, in spite of all he'd drunk. There was no escaping this.

He glanced at the girl on the bed. She was in the deepest of slumbers. No danger that she'd wake. It would be morning before Baxandall was discovered. If he could get away somehow …

Baxandall's body was lying on the trunk where he'd been sitting. The other stood beside it. Lukas opened it. It was filled with garments — gowns of silk and velvet, mostly showing signs of damage. Perhaps their previous owners had not given them up easily. Lukas pulled them out and shoved them under the bed. At the bottom of the trunk were two leather pouches. One was half filled with coins, the other with necklaces made of gold and coloured stones. Perhaps they had not pleased Baxandall's little wife so he had secreted them here. Lukas stuffed both bags inside his jacket.

The trunk was all but empty now. He slid the body into it, bending the dead man's limbs to fit. Thank God the rigor of death had not yet stiffened him. Lukas stood for a moment, looking down at him. It was the right end for such a bastard, and Lukas could not find it in himself to repent, although he knew that his soul was condemned. There would be time enough for repentance, with God's grace, but he was damned if he would go to the gallows for one such as Baxandall. Lukas checked once more that the girl was still asleep. She would wake in the morning with a sore head and assume that her husband had gone to his duties. Lukas could be the best part of a day away from here before the truth was known. He took a last glance at Baxandall, crossed himself, and closed the trunk lid.

Twenty

THEIR FIRST SIGHT OF MAGDEBURG CAME when the barge rounded yet another bend in the river Elbe. Most of the little group of passengers stretched to catch a glimpse of the cathedral's towers between the willows that lined the banks. Andreas moved more slowly, gripping the gunwale to help his balance. Only Christa stayed where she had been, sitting close to the boat's cargo. The vessel was carrying pepper spice to Hamburg. The river was the only safe way to transport such a precious load, and even by that means it was close to a miracle that it had got so far unmolested.

She saw Andreas turn to look at her. He was wondering, no doubt, why she showed no hunger to see her native city again. It had been she, after all, who had determined to return, in spite of her fears. This was not like the melancholy that had afflicted her last autumn in Leipzig. It was something deeper. That misery had weighed on her heart. Now her very bones felt as if they were made from lead.

The barge sailed steadily on, the flow of the river rippling like muscle beneath it. Christa kept her eyes on the willows. The towers of the cathedral were there, she could detect the dark shape of them, but she would not look at them directly. This was not a new feeling. She remembered it from somewhere, but could not place it.

They had left Leipzig early on a fine April morning, with five others who had fled from Magdeburg and were now minded to return there.

Christa's preparation for the journey to Magdeburg had been simple. She spent a number of weeks selling off the booty Lukas had left for her, turning it into coin. It had taken her that time, as she had not wished to let the traders see that she needed to be rid of so many goods in haste. They might offer her less for it. Worse, the word would be out that she was a woman with gold, and she might find herself robbed. So, each week she would take some part of Lukas's treasure and sell it, complaining about the cost of her lodgings and the price of bread. Back at the Ackermanns' she would stitch the coins into the seams of her skirt. Easter was past before she was done. The only things she did not sell were a fancy pistol, two daggers and her books — Luther's *Small Catechism*, and the final volume of *The Odyssey*. She had also made a purchase from Old Schumacher before she left his service — a set of Blackletter type, packed carefully in a wooden case.

She knew the journey would take the best part of a month. All the advice was to avoid the roads and travel by boat. The armies of the Emperor and the King of Sweden were in the west of the country now, but stray packs of men roamed the entire land. Some were deserters, others mercenaries in search of a new paymaster. Many had been decent enough men until the war had destroyed their homes and livelihoods, but whatever their beginnings, they were all a danger to the innocent traveller.

Well, God had preserved them, and they had survived the journey. True, one young woman had lost her nerve before they'd got the length of Halle. She had disembarked at the first opportunity, with her disgruntled mother. But now the remainder of the party were nearly home. The Elbe was carrying them closer with every moment that passed.

As they drew nearer Christa forced herself to look. There was the cathedral. It seemed sound enough, with its roof still on, although the windows were empty of glass. All the other church spires that had graced Magdeburg were gone. Those parts of the city walls she could see from the river had been reduced to rubble. She breathed in deeply. There was no smell of burning, just the damp air of the river, and the faintest tang of pepper from the barrels on the deck. Andreas made his careful way back to her. She stood up, so that he wouldn't have to stoop to talk to her. 'Are you not well?' he said. 'You are pale.'

Christa took a moment or two to gather herself before she replied. 'I had forgotten how injured the place was.'

Andreas nodded. 'We must play our part in bringing her back to health.'

'Yes.' In her heart she did not believe it could be done.

The old wooden quays had gone, but whoever was now living there had rigged up a rough jetty from whatever pieces of timber they could find. It was a ramshackle construction, but sound enough for the barge to stop at and unload its human cargo. Christa and Andreas disembarked, each with a satchel containing food and belongings slung over a shoulder. Andreas struggled to keep upright on the rough surface of the jetty. The stick he used to support himself had a tendency to catch in the gaps between the planks. Christa would have offered him her arm for support, but she knew he would be mortified.

One of the other women in their party ran forward until she was on solid ground, then knelt and kissed the stones of the quayside. The sight made Christa tremble. This *was* home.

'Where should we go? Your father's house must surely be gone.'

'We must go there anyway.' Even as she spoke the words, Christa wondered if she would have the strength to do her own bidding. 'Let us see what remains.'

The Fürstenwall gate was only a stump now, but the ground to one side of it had been cleared to make a thoroughfare of sorts towards the back of the cathedral. Now that they were closer to it

Christa could see that the lower parts of the walls were pocked. Many of the fancy stone curlicues were damaged in the same way. They came round by the Paradise Porch, but the entrance was boarded up. There were huddles of shabby dwellings in the cathedral square. Some were little more than ragged tents, but others were more weatherproof, constructed from scavenged doors and fragments of wood.

The residents of this shanty village looked out warily at the new arrivals. Christa kept close to Andreas, but she would not let herself feel afraid. These were her fellow citizens. They bore the marks of hunger, and she realised how lucky they had been in Leipzig, with employment, food every day and a proper bed at the end of a day's work. She could not help but look from face to face, in the hope of finding one she knew. It was possible … No, she reminded herself, it was not. And yet she could not help but imagine it.

Now that she had returned, every young girl reminded her of Elsbeth. There was even the thought, buried as deep as she could keep it, that one of the men huddled over their scant fires might miraculously be her father or Dieter. Never mind what Andreas had said. He might have been mistaken. But even as she thought it, she knew it was she who was in error. The city had disordered her thoughts. She felt as if she could no longer distinguish dreams from waking truth.

Andreas's hand was on her arm. 'We should not tarry here,' he said.

Christa realised she had stopped walking and was standing dumbly in the cathedral square, staring down at a girl of about Elsbeth's age. She shook her head, as if to acknowledge her foolishness, and let Andreas lead her on.

They passed the convent. Christa slowed again. 'I left Gertrude there. I doubt she lived long after I went.'

'What of the child?'

'Unborn when last I saw her, but stirring in its mother's womb.' Her eyes stung. She pressed her hands against them as if that might stop the tears. Why now? She had scarcely shed a single tear in all this time. Why should the notion of Gertrude's child move her more than anything else?

'I could go to the door, if you like. Enquire for you.'

'No. Later, perhaps. But not now.'

They walked on through the city. There was less rubble than Christa had expected. The streets had been cleared. Along Breiter Weg builders were at work. The house they were reconstructing was a good deal more modest than the grand residences that had once lined the street, but surely it was a symbol of promise. The tapping of their hammers followed Christa as she and Andreas continued to the old market.

And here again there were signs of hope. Trestle tables were folded against the shell of a building. A broken chicken cage lay beside them. Three half-starved cats fought over a small pile of fish innards. 'The market must be back in business,' Andreas said, sounding as amazed as Christa felt. 'Can it be? Are there people enough here to be buying and selling?'

'It seems so. We will come back in the morning, and that will give us our answer.' Christa felt a wild joy inside her. If there was trade, then Magdeburg was alive. 'I wonder are there printers yet,' she said, half to herself.

'Are you thinking to find us work?'

'I am thinking that we will be printers again.'

Her mind was on fire with ideas as they got closer to where the printers' quarter had been. Less clearing up had been done there, and they had to pick their way carefully across the ground. Andreas's face was grey with fatigue. It hurt to curtail her thoughts, but compassion for him left her no choice. 'I am weary,' she lied. 'Would you mind resting here awhile?'

'I'd be glad enough to stop,' Andreas admitted. 'Perhaps if you took some food it would revive you.'

They found what appeared to be the front steps of a house, and sat down to eat. Christa watched him discreetly. His colour improved once he had swallowed some bread and wine from their supplies, but his face gleamed with sweat. She would have to ensure he had somewhere dry to sleep tonight, for fear of him becoming ill with the fever.

When she felt sure he had strength enough to go on, they rose and walked further. The break in their journey had dampened her excitement. The notions she'd entertained of reviving her father's business were cast down by what she now saw. The Johanniskirche was gone. There was no trace of the covered alley that had led into their close. Yes, there were piles of charred bricks as high as three men, but precious little else. The ground beneath their feet was grey and slippery, thick with paper ash. 'Ach, God,' she said. It was all gone.

Now it was Andreas's turn to tend her. He took her arm and led her away from the ruins, back to the house steps where they had rested earlier. 'Look, do you see where there's a decent bit of wall still standing? We can rig up a shelter there. The weather is settled, thank God. Let us make some accommodation for ourselves. We'll be better able to face tomorrow when we've had a night's sleep in our own city.'

Christa's months on the road with the Imperial force had taught her to catch her rest in any circumstances, but the next morning, although she had slept, Andreas seemed less refreshed, and she worried once more that the fever might be working on him. They had lain close to each other in the lee of the wall, just as they had on the boat from Leipzig. She knew that Andreas would do her no harm, and thanked God for men such as him.

They made a modest breakfast from their supply of food. It was badly reduced, and in another day or so Christa would need to unpick some of the coins from the seams of her skirt. At least there would be food for sale in the market, from what they'd seen yesterday. The prices might be another matter. As they ate, a bell sounded from somewhere nearby. It did not chime like a church bell – in any case, all the churches were gone, along with their bell towers — yet it was something more than a cowbell. It clanged a steady repeat, just as a church bell might on a Sunday morning.

'What day of the week is it?' Christa said. She had lost the run of the calendar since they'd been travelling.

'I don't recall.' Andreas grasped his stick and pulled himself up. 'Can it be the Lord's Day?'

They followed the sound of the bell in the direction of the marketplace. There were other people about now, and they, too, were walking towards the chiming. When they got close to the place where the Johanniskirche had stood they found a small group gathered. The bell was hanging from a low gallows. A well-muscled old man was striking it with a wooden hammer. A pastor was standing beside him, with his head bowed and a threadbare Bible clasped in his hands. His thoughts seemed to have made him oblivious to the sound of the bell. Christa did not recognise him. She looked around her at the other faces. Some were a little familiar, but she could not put a name to any.

The old man stopped striking the bell, and the pastor began to read from his Bible. Christa tried to keep her thoughts trained on the sacred text, but she could not help wondering how the service would progress, and them all without a hymn book or a copy of the catechism. The pastor himself must have been industrious in the past because he knew most of it by heart. The congregation, if they could be called such, were also familiar enough with its form to make their responses when they should. Their hymn singing was sad, though. They did well enough with the first verse of 'A Mighty Fortress Is Our God', but faltered thereafter. The melody petered out into humiliating silence before the end of the second verse.

Christa counted the number gathered here. Near enough thirty souls. Perhaps a third might have the wherewithal to purchase a penny hymn-sheet. Ten *Pfennigs* would not cover the cost of paper and ink, but if there were ten other such congregations across the remains of the city, a printer would at least break even, with a few *Pfennigs* left over to plough into the next job. Christa looked again at the people in the crowd. This time she was not studying their faces but their hands, seeking the tell-tale ink stains that could not be washed out, not even for church-going. From what she could see the hands of many were dirty, but none was besmirched with ink.

Two days later Christa and Andreas approached the *Rathaus*. This was no longer the grand old building that had looked down over the marketplace for all the years she could remember. It had been turned to ashes, like so much else. The new *Rathaus* was a wooden structure with only one storey, but its purpose was much the same. The fine men of the council who had bribed their way out of the city before its fall were back now, keen to reassert that this wasteland was still theirs to order.

Christa had done her best to make sure that she and Andreas looked as respectable as they could. It had not been easy. They had carried only the most necessary clothes with them from Leipzig. In truth, neither they nor their garments were as clean as they might have been, but if the *Bürgermeister* and his friends did not like the smell they would have to hold their noses.

Even in the new humble *Rathaus* there was a room where petitioners were kept waiting. 'Some things don't change,' Andreas muttered. Christa had to agree, although she wished he would not expend so much of his strength on grumbling.

When they were finally shown into the meeting room Christa found that the city council was not what it had been. The *Bürgermeister* had either lost his finery in his flight from the city or had deemed it politic not to dress too grandly. He was clad plainly, as were the other four councillors seated on one side of a trestle table.

The *Bürgermeister* requested Andreas to make his petition. Andreas glanced over at Christa with confusion on his face. 'If you please, gentlemen,' he said, sounding half choked, 'it is Miss Christa who will make the petition.'

Christa watched the councillors' faces as they received these tidings. Two appeared bored, while one frowned with the appearance of disapproval. Another leaned towards the

Bürgermeister with a leer and muttered something that might have been lewd. Whatever was said did not seem to find favour with him — he waved away his colleague with a scowl. The joker seemed chastened.

'Well, then,' the *Bürgermeister* said, 'speak, girl.'

Christa took a breath, and glanced at the notes she had made on a blank leaf torn from the small catechism Lukas had given her. 'My father was Paul Henning, a master printer of this city, as were his father and his father's father. Some of you good men may have been present when my father made petition to you for the granting of rights to print a weekly newssheet, the only one of its kind in Magdeburg.'

The councillor who had leered nodded. 'I recall it. Is your father still living?'

Christa tried to answer, but the words would not leave her mouth. She shook her head. One of the men before her sighed, as if he were bored with this business. 'I am all that is left of my father's household, and I would petition you good men that I should inherit the rights you granted him.' She consulted her notes again. She had known by heart everything written there before she had walked into the room, but now her mind was as empty as the marketplace at midnight. 'He was granted the right that for five years only he or his inheritors could print a weekly newssheet in Magdeburg. One year has passed since then, so I humbly request that I may continue with this right for another four years.'

The councillor who had been yawning scratched his armpit. 'It is uncommon for a daughter to inherit her father's place in the Guild.'

'But not unknown, sir, begging your pardon,' Christa said. 'Some of you will recall a goldsmith's widow who took her husband's place in their Guild.'

The leering councillor nodded again. 'Yes. Frau Hinkelmann. I remember her.' His mouth twitched with a smile.

The *Bürgermeister* puffed out his stomach, which seemed unusually substantial for the hard times in which they were living. 'Are you handy with a press, my dear? You do not look as if you would have the strength for it.' Everyone knew that printing a run took muscle. He looked Andreas up and down. 'This man can hardly be your husband, since he gives you the speaking rights.'

'This is Andreas Ritschel. He was my father's journeyman, and near enough a master printer when the city fell. It is our intention to be partners in this resurrected venture.'

'He does not look fit for much.'

At this Andreas spoke out: 'My injuries were earned in defending my city, so I cannot regret them. My skills as a printer are undiminished.'

His voice was stronger and more determined than Christa could ever remember hearing it. She longed to say more, to talk of how the city could be rebuilt, not just with new houses but with words. She and Andreas would print more than news: they would print hymns to gladden the hearts of the citizens, and Bible verses to strengthen their faith, improving tracts, children's primers and bawdy songs. But although she longed to speak out, she could see that the councillors were now at the point of consideration, and she knew that to say more might damage their chances.

The *Bürgermeister* and his four colleagues leaned together in conference. After a few minutes more they sat back in their seats. 'Very well,' the *Bürgermeister* said. 'Your petition is granted. Come tomorrow and all will be signed and sworn. Please God that these small steps towards order will make our city great again.'

'Amen to that,' Christa said, and every man in the chamber echoed her words.

Christa and Andreas stood outside the *Rathaus* for a few minutes, enjoying the sunshine. 'You did well,' Andreas said.

Christa smiled. 'So did you.'

'We have no workshop.'

'True.'

'Nor a press.'

'But we have type. There's no shortage of scrap wood to fashion a press frame.'

'What about paper? And ink?'

Talking with Andreas was like meeting a raincloud on a fine day.

Magdeburg marketplace was not what it had been. The few stalls had evidently been hammered together from salvaged timber, and many traders simply laid out their wares on the ground, like gypsies. At first Christa's spirits were lowered — it was so different from the bustling, orderly prosperity she remembered. But here and there she saw little signs that cheered her. Some days countrywomen would be present, selling a small number of eggs or early vegetables. If the farmers had spare produce to sell, the land could not be in complete ruin. More to the point, there were customers in the marketplace. None were living in luxury, but they had a few coins to put food in their children's bellies. A pastor's widow had set up a little school in one corner of the market, and would teach a child for a *Pfennig* a week or goods in lieu of payment when the parents had no money. Most days she had half a dozen scholars, and the sound of them reciting their numbers and grammar was like balm to Christa: it was the music of innocence.

And today, for the first time in what felt like eternity, Christa was behind her own stall in the marketplace. She and Andreas had laboured hard, making sufficient shelter for themselves in the cellar of a ruined building, roofing it over, then constructing a small press frame from wood they found among the debris. The shortcomings in their materials and strength limited them in the goods they could produce. Christa decided it would be best to restrict themselves to simple, cheap wares: the newssheet, of course, containing whatever tidings she could gather from travellers on the barges that stopped at the river quay; a hymn-sheet, compiled in consultation with the pastor who preached every Sunday by the ruins of the Johanniskirche; and a woodcut of Martin Luther. This last had been another of those little miracles that helped to sustain Christa's spirits. Andreas had found the original amid the wreckage they had cleared from their cellar, and brought it to her. She applied her mind to recalling some of the wise sayings of Luther that her father had been fond of quoting, and together she and Andreas fashioned a worthy, but not costly, memento of the great man.

So, now the stall was laid out, and all that remained was to see if the citizens would part with their money for something they could not eat. Christa was alone behind it. Andreas was as ill fitted as ever for market trading and, besides, they both feared to leave the press and their rough-built workshop unattended.

The shoppers walked past, looking but not buying. Christa had spent a good deal of the gold she'd brought with her from Leipzig on paper, ink and other necessities. If business went on like this ... Fear tightened her throat. She made herself swallow it. It never did to look needy: her father had taught her that. A sudden memory overcame her. She had been standing on this very spot, with him close by. He was pretending not to watch her as she talked a customer through their wares, but she had known he was taking in what she said, hoping she had heeded his lessons in the art of trading. She blinked away tears. He would not have approved of her weeping there. Who would buy anything from a snivelling girl?

A woman approached the stall, holding a basket with a dozen eggs in it. She stood to read the newssheet. Christa felt a prickle of anger. 'I could not eat your eggs without first buying them,' she snapped, 'yet you take my news without paying a *Pfennig*.'

The woman cringed, and Christa repented her sharpness. 'If I threw my money away on reading matter my man would beat me,' the woman said, and Christa could tell from the fear in her eyes that this was no lie invented to placate her.

'Here, then,' she said, lifting one of the woodcuts of Martin Luther, 'take this, and may God send you a better man.'

'I'd rather God sent me no man at all, but bless you for your kindness,' said the woman, lifting the woodcut and tucking it into her basket. She leaned closer to Christa. 'You'd best not be so kindly to every comer, or you'll be starving before midsummer. Here, have this.' She handed an egg to Christa. There was still a trace of warmth in it. It must have been laid that morning.

After that more customers approached. Many were able to pay in coin, and from the others she gathered up the makings of two half-decent meals for her and Andreas. It would take them another week to produce sufficient wares to bring to market again, but at least now they had the means to buy more raw materials. Christa realised the fear had lifted from her. She could still do this. Her father had taught her well.

As she was packing the few unsold hymn-sheets she saw an oddly familiar couple walk slowly across the marketplace towards her. Her heart lurched when she recognised the woman as Helga, although she was no longer clad in servant's dress. The gown she was wearing must have been grand when it was first stitched, but it was faded now and none too clean. It had obviously been made for a smaller woman: the hem danced well above Helga's ankles, and there were panels of plain fabric let in to the bodice to allow for her greater girth. 'Why, there's Christa Henning!' Helga shouted. For some reason Christa found the familiarity less jarring than the resentment in Helga's voice when she had addressed her as *Miss Christa* back in the old times.

'Helga, how are you?' Christa replied. She kept her voice light, but deliberately chose the informal *you*.

'I am married, Christa Henning. What do you think of that?' Her hand was hooked into her companion's arm, and now she swung closer to him with a giggle.

Christa took a closer look at Helga's husband. He must have been at least thirty years his bride's senior. There was something in his appearance that Christa remembered. His face was red and his nose more so. Yes, it was him — the argumentative customer who'd haggled with her one day in the market. The man she'd seen taken on a charge of witchcraft. She wondered how he had escaped his gaolers. Perhaps when the city fell the prison gates had tumbled open. As she stared up at him she saw in his eyes the fog of confusion. He did not recognise her.

Helga must have taken note of Christa's scrutiny of her husband, for she spoke in a more defensive tone that made her voice sharp: 'My dear spouse is a most important merchant. Why, he traded from Hamburg to Munich until this current trouble did such harm to the markets.'

'These are hard times for all of us.'

'But still he's better off than most. We are here to gain satisfaction on some outstanding debts, and then we shall remove to Hamburg. He has property there. Fine property.' Helga simpered up at him. He did not appear to notice her efforts. 'I am indeed blessed that a prosperous man has found me acceptable. No more sweeping of other people's floors.'

Christa was tempted to remark on how little sweeping Helga had done in the past, but she did not want to turn a good day bitter. 'I wish you joy,' she said. God help the poor man. He must have been badly fuddled to take on Helga.

Helga seemed offended by Christa's blessing. Her eyes narrowed. 'I suppose you are unwed, Miss Christa?' In her unkindness she had forgotten that she no longer had to address Christa with deference. 'No decent man will take on a ruined girl.'

Christa felt the old hatred flare up in her, but exerted herself to keep her voice calm. 'I have a husband. He provides well for me.'

Helga raised her eyebrows, and turned away. 'Oh, Helga,' Christa called after her. 'Andreas survived. Isn't that a miracle? We are partners in business now.' She took a certain pleasure in watching the mixture of expressions on Helga's face. No doubt her grand catch of a husband might seem a little less delightful.

The ill-matched couple walked away, Helga directing the old man's steps. His clothes were as shabby as hers. Christa wondered how much of his wealth was left.

She packed up her little stall, which Andreas had fitted with rope straps so that she could carry it on her back. It was not unduly heavy, but its shape was awkward. She gathered up the unsold hymn-sheets and the food she had been given instead of coins. The money was already safely stowed in her pocket. Thus burdened, she made her way from the marketplace to the workshop — she did not feel able yet to call it home. It had been a good first day's trading. She only wished it had not been soured by Helga's appearance.

Andreas seemed only to half listen to her tale of the day's trading. At first she thought it was the dark mood that came upon him now and again, when the memories of all he had seen and endured reared up to trouble him, but she soon realised that this was something different. He was agitated, not cast down. She said nothing, and prepared their meal.

He took more drink at the table than was his custom, and for the first time she felt the bite of anxiety. This was Andreas, she reminded herself: for all he was inclined to complaint and bleak thoughts, he was an honourable man. He would do her no harm. And yet, deep inside, there was fear. She had seen how men could be with drink in them and their temper up. Now she was alone with him, the long night ahead, and not a living soul to protect her.

When the meal was done he cleared his throat. 'Miss Christa,' he said. He coughed and shuffled in his seat.

'Are you in pain?' Perhaps his injuries were preoccupying him. She began to hope it might be so, although it was not a kindly hope, she knew.

He looked surprised by her question. 'No more than usual.' He reached forward for his tankard, but stopped short and let his hand rest on the table. 'I am a hard-working man, Miss Christa, for all that I know I am damaged. Our business will prosper, I hope, with God's help.'

'Amen to that.'

'Do you not think it might be as well for us to wed?'

Christa looked away from him. *No.* That was what she wanted to tell him. *Never.* But she must think of his pride. 'I have a husband already,' she said simply.

'It was a forced marriage, and has no standing.'

'I consented to it, Andreas. It seemed the only course open to me. The ceremony was carried out by a priest – a Papist, it's true, but an ordained priest nonetheless – in our own cathedral here in Magdeburg.'

'Whether or not it was a proper marriage, you have seen neither hide nor hair of your husband since the battle at Breitenfeld. He is most likely dead.'

'I cannot assume that unless I have evidence.' She felt as tainted as a lawyer, twisting the facts to her own advantage.

Andreas picked at an inky scab on his thumb. 'It seems you have a grand supply of reasons not to wed me.'

How could she tell him what was truly in her mind? That the notion of lying down with him made her feel sick. That the very idea of him doing to her what Lukas had done was unbearable. She knew that what he was proposing was prudent. There would be some safety in having a husband, and perhaps as Magdeburg became a proper Christian city again there might be a need to order their household better. But, no, she could not. 'It is too soon,' she said. 'I am sorry, Andreas. My husband has been lost to me for a little more than half a year. It would not be the act of a good woman to remarry in haste.'

'I may ask you again, then, when more time has passed?'

Christa nodded, even though the prospect appalled her. She prayed he would not ask again too soon.

Christa took a deep breath and knocked on the door of the Convent of Our Dear Lady. After a time a young lay sister admitted her. Christa told her what her business was there, and the woman bade her wait. Then she scuttled off down a cloister and ducked out of sight through a doorway.

It had been more than a month now since they had returned to Magdeburg, but this was the first time Christa had ventured to the place where she had last seen Gertrude. Guilt weighed on her, especially when she passed the convent on her way to the quayside to gather news. She made excuses in her own mind. There was little time for such visiting, what with the work she and Andreas were at, but she knew it was not the true reason. It was fear that had kept her away — fear that she would go there and find that Gertrude was dead. She was not sure she had the strength to encounter more death, particularly not now, when her life was beginning to flower again.

But the time for excuses was past. In the dim hall of the convent, she steeled herself for whatever tidings she might hear.

A nun approached from the direction that the lay sister had gone. As she came closer it became clear that she bore the scars of smallpox on her face. Her skin was so deeply pitted that it was hard to tell her age. She told Christa to follow her. They walked back along the cloister, and turned into a little doorway that led directly to a narrow stone staircase. At the top the nun paused, and waved Christa into a room equipped with a table and two chairs. A large statue of the Virgin and Christ-child stood in one corner, but otherwise the room was unadorned.

The nun sat behind the table, and gestured Christa to a chair. Christa scrutinised her face for signs of what she was to be told. 'Your friend is living, as is her child, thanks be to Our Lord and His Gracious Mother.'

Christa felt a slight easing at this news, but a coda was still to come, she was sure. 'And what of Lotte, the servant who attended her?'

'Dead, alas. Last winter was merciless on the old.'

Still Christa felt that something had not yet been revealed. 'Are mother and child both well?'

The nun lowered her eyes. Christa noticed how fine her bones were. She might have been a beauty before the smallpox had destroyed her skin. 'The child, thank God, seems well. We are caring for him in our orphanage. His poor mother, alas, is very weak.'

'May I see her?'

The nun hesitated. 'We do not know what afflicts your friend. She has suffered fever after fever, and the child's birth was hard on her. At one time her poor body was badly racked with sores. We feared it was ... a certain disease ... but the physician said not.

Still, we treated her with mercury, and an elixir distilled from the bark of a tree called the holy wood, but I cannot say she benefited from it.'

'Holy wood is costly, is it not?' Christa said. When the nun seemed surprised at her knowledge, she explained, 'I am a soldier's wife, and I have travelled with his company. I have heard much talk of that disease.'

'I may speak plainly with you, then. We do not know what ails your friend, and we are fearful that it may be some noisome thing that might pass from her to others. At first she understood this, even when we would not let her embrace her infant, but now that she is so much worse she may forget herself.' She looked directly into Christa's eyes. 'There may be danger to your health in visiting her. For me,' she pointed to her face, 'it matters not. If the Lord wishes to call me home, then so be it.'

'I will trust in God to protect me.'

As they approached Gertrude's room Christa felt her resolve waver, and prayed hard for strength. What if she fell ill? The business would not survive without her. And what if she brought whatever sickness afflicted Gertrude out of the convent and into the city? The people were weak and prone to ailments. Still, she could not show cowardice in front of this Papist who seemed to care nothing for her own safety.

The air was smoky and scented with herbs, but another smell underlay these fragrances. Christa recognised it as the same stench that had clung to everything as the days had passed after the city had fallen. It was the smell of rotting flesh. The nun took two muslin cloths from the sleeve of her habit and handed one to Christa. 'Hold this over your nose and mouth. It is impregnated with oil of rosemary.'

Christa was glad of the rosemary's sharp tang. The nun opened the door to a tiny room. Gertrude was propped upright on a bed no wider than a side-table. Smoke was drifting from a small stove in the corner. Christa looked at her friend through the haze.

Gertrude's face was unblemished, but wasted, and her eyes were closed. 'Is she asleep?' Christa whispered.

'It may be that she is.' The nun stepped closer to the bed and leaned over it. 'Gertrude, my dear, here's a friend come to visit you.'

Gertrude opened her eyes and looked up at the nun with an expression of malevolence that seemed too powerful to have come from her weak frame. 'I have no friends in this world,' she said. Her voice was hoarse, like an old woman's.

'Gertrude?' Christa said. She did not dare approach the bed. 'It is Christa. Do you remember me?'

At this Gertrude's eyes opened wide and she lifted her hands to her chest. Christa saw that her arms were wrapped with bandages and dressings. As she moved, the smell of corrupting flesh grew stronger. 'Ach, Christa. It *is* you,' she said.

Christa took only the most shallow breaths. Neither the rosemary oil on her muslin nor the herbs burning on the stove were strong enough to disguise the stench of disease rising from Gertrude's body. She turned to the nun. 'How long must she endure this?'

'I cannot tell. She is young so her body fights against its dissolution, even though her soul longs to quit its tainted habitation.'

'Christa,' Gertrude rasped. 'Come closer.'

The nun touched her arm. 'Not too close.'

Christa held the muslin over her nose and knelt on the floor beside the bed.

Gertrude's eyes were full of rage. 'Do you still keep the true faith, Christa?'

'Of course.'

Gertrude glared up at the nun, then looked at Christa. 'They have my child, my boy Jürgen,' she said, so quietly that Christa had no choice but to move closer to hear her.

'Jürgen? A beautiful name.'

'Never mind that. These ones will raise him as a Papist. That's their way you know, to catch them young.'

'Are they not kind to you, Gertrude?'

'Don't trust them. They're cunning.' She stopped, exhausted beyond speech.

The nun stepped forward. 'I fear your friend is tired. Perhaps another day ... ?'

'No!' Gertrude said, clearly summoning all her strength to have her say. 'I wish my friend to take my boy and rear him in my faith.' She reached for Christa's arm.

Christa flinched, and was immediately ashamed. The nun touched her shoulder and helped her to her feet. 'Are you willing to take the child? Have you the means to keep him?'

'Of course,' Christa said, without thinking.

'There are procedures. Papers to sign.'

'Then let us not delay.' She knelt again beside Gertrude. 'You have my word. I will care for your baby as if he were my own.'

Gertrude turned away her face and did not speak.

'Come now,' the nun said. 'Let her rest.'

Christa was surprised to find the nun leading her back to the main door of the convent. 'Should I not take the child?' she said, fearful that the nun had been practising some deception to placate Gertrude.

The nun raised her eyebrows. 'Is your home prepared for the infant? A wet nurse engaged and the various necessities laid in?'

Christa blushed. 'No. I had not thought.'

The nun patted her arm. 'Come again tomorrow and I will advise you on what you will require. When all is ready, you can take the child home.'

She had never seen Andreas so angry. 'It is madness,' he repeated. 'We've scarcely money enough to feed ourselves.'

'Babies don't eat much.'

Andreas limped across the cramped floor of the workshop, banging his stick down angrily as he went. 'Is he weaned, or will we need to throw away money on a wet nurse?'

'We will need a wet nurse, but they are not so very costly.'

Christa felt her own anger rising. She had agreed too quickly and thoughtlessly to Gertrude's plea, she knew. And Andreas, of course, was ill disposed towards her since she had declined his suggestion of marriage. 'What would you have me do, then? Refuse my friend, and her in the terrible state she is?'

Andreas leaned against the doorframe. 'Will she not mend?'

'No.'

'I do not know how we will manage. We have not even a cradle, and you'll be out at market half the day. Am I to be his nursemaid at the same time as running the press?'

'He's a boy, Andreas. He may be a burden now, but before long we can make use of him in the workshop. Look at the parents he had — he'll have printer's ink running in his veins.' She saw that he was considering this. 'You'll be the master, and he'll be your apprentice.'

'Ach, Christa. You will have your way as always.'

Christa felt a pang at his words, even as she savoured winning him over. *You will have your way as always.* How many times had she heard her father or Dieter say that? Suddenly grief overwhelmed her, so powerfully it seemed to knock the breath from her body. She gasped, and wondered what the terrible sound was that howled in her ears. Andreas was speaking, but she could not understand him. His face was in front of hers, but she could scarcely see him for her eyes were raw with tears. She felt him take hold of her and guide her out into the air, then ease her down so that she was sitting on the ground. She sat with her knees bent up close to her chest, still struggling for breath. That sound, she realised, was her own sobbing. Andreas was crouched beside her. He said nothing, but let her weep.

When it was over Andreas fetched her some wine mixed with water. He helped her to her feet, using his stick to balance as he gave her his hand. 'Was that the first time you have properly wept?' he said.

Christa nodded, too raw for words.

'Lie on your bed now. You must sleep.'

Their beds were in opposite corners of the workshop. Andreas had hung a bolt of old cloth around Christa's, for decency's sake. 'There,' he said, drawing it back. 'Rest now. Once you've slept you will feel better for having a proper mourning.'

Christa lay down and pulled a blanket over herself. Andreas let the cloth drop back into place. She could hear him start to go about his work at the press. He had been interrupted by her return, with the tidings of Gertrude and the child. She closed her eyes, which were swollen and sore. Was Andreas right? Would she feel better for this weakness? Whether she did or not mattered little. Such grieving would not put food in their bellies. It was a luxury she could not afford.

The next day, after she was finished at the market, Christa returned to the convent to claim Gertrude's child. The nun who had been her guide the day before led her to the orphanage. Jürgen was confined in a room with a number of other infants, who, like him, were discovering their talents for sitting and crawling.

'You must have care that he does not hurt himself in your home,' the nun said. 'The fireplace is a particular peril.'

Christa studied him, wondering at her wisdom in taking on this additional burden. Andreas had been right – it was madness. Jürgen was staring at her with frank curiosity. 'What shall I do if he will not come with me happily?'

The nun smiled. 'Why not pick him up, and see what sort of beginning you make with him?'

Christa reached down and lifted the child. He was sturdy, and his warmth and weight in her arms were comforting. To her relief he made no objection to being held by her. She rested her cheek against the fine gold of his hair. For a fanciful moment she imagined his baby smell was the very scent of life and hope.

'I have prepared a bundle of garments for him,' the nun said. 'We have little to give, but it will be a start.'

'You are very kind.' Christa remembered Gertrude's hard words against the nuns, and felt ashamed on her behalf. 'Should we take him to see his mother before I leave?'

'I think that might cause her more pain, not less.' She hesitated. 'Your friend is sinking fast. Her Calvary will soon be ended.'

Christa saw the nun again less than a week later, in the marketplace. The demands of her life had given her reasons not to return to the convent to visit Gertrude. Now she watched the nun approach her through the crowd, and could tell from her face the tidings she brought.

Twenty-one

LUKAS WAS CAUGHT NOW, AND NO mistake, even though he'd drawn his dagger the instant he was discovered in the farmhouse kitchen. The farmer was armed only with an ancient arquebus that would likely blow up if he tried firing it, but the end of the barrel was close enough to Lukas's face to stop him moving. As ill luck would have it there were soldiers billeted here too. A half-dozen infantrymen had sprung from the dark corners of the farmhouse, and they had him cornered. 'You picked upon the wrong sorry soul to rob, my friend,' the farmer said, keeping his gun steady.

'I can see that,' Lukas replied. 'It was only hunger drove me to it. I've found nothing but hawthorn leaves this last week. There's little fruit ripe yet.'

'You have the manner of a soldier,' one of the infantrymen said. 'Who do you serve?'

'I have fought under the Emperor and the Swedish king.'

The infantryman considered this. 'Why do you live this life? A soldier should be able to find a place in these times.'

Lukas forced himself to think before he spoke next. He could not tell which army these men served. The one who was doing all the talking was German, but that meant nothing. 'I thought I was done with war. I had served out my contract, earned my booty, and was headed home.'

'A lucky man, then,' the infantryman replied. 'So what ill fortune brought you to this?'

'I was robbed on the road, which is nothing new.' Lukas saw some of the soldiers nod ruefully. 'But when I reached my home I found it burned, and my wife and children dead.'

'God have mercy on them.' They were all silent for a moment, and Lukas felt a twinge of guilt that they were mourning a wife, family and home that had never existed. Even his tale of being robbed was false, but he had long since spent the treasure he'd taken from Baxandall.

At length the infantryman roused himself. 'What is your skill? Musket? Pike?'

'I was a musketeer.'

'There's all sorts of law in this land. We could drag you to the magistrate at Jena, and he'd give you a civilian's trial. We could have let this good man here dispense his own justice to you, and you'd now be full of lead and cooling in a ditch. But instead we'll give you a soldier's trial. As soon as the sun is up we'll go outside and see if you can hit a target at fifty paces. If you can, we'll take you to our captain and see if he'll take you on. We're in need of good musketeers.'

'And if I miss?'

'Then we'll leave you to the farmer's justice.'

Lukas considered this. It was a better result than he might have hoped for. 'My aim will be better if I have some food in my belly, and an hour or two's sleep.'

The infantryman smiled as if he understood Lukas's cleverness. 'A good point, my friend. What is your name, since you'll likely live?'

'Schmidt,' Lukas said quickly. 'Johann Schmidt.'

'Well, Schmidt, sit down here and let this good man offer you some food.'

The farmer looked none too pleased at this turn in the night's events. He banged around in the kitchen for ten minutes while Lukas sat waiting, the hunger cramps twisting his gut. At length the farmer slapped a pewter dish of cheese and *Wurst* on the table in front of him. This was joined by a mug of beer. Lukas forced himself to eat and drink slowly. It had been so long since he had tasted proper food that it might injure his stomach if he bolted it. When at last he had finished the farmer showed him to a corner of the kitchen where some blankets had been thrown down for him. 'I'd be more comfortable in the barn,' Lukas said, thinking of a warm and prickly bed in the last of the winter hay scattered there.

'You might more easily slip away,' the infantryman said. 'It would not be just to let the accused man escape before his trial.'

Lukas managed snatches of sleep in his makeshift bed. When he closed his eyes his head whirled. It was not through any fear of the other men. If they'd meant to kill him they'd hardly have fed him first. He had slept badly since he'd run away. Forests and hedgerows were not conducive to a restful night, and it was hard to sleep with the hunger on him. Yet on this good dry floor he was wakeful. He would plummet into sleep, and wake just as abruptly. Sometimes it seemed that every moment of fear he had ever encountered and beaten down came back to him in those first moments of waking. So his head would whirl and he would lie in the dark until sleep grabbed him again.

His last sleep of the night was the best, and it was the lightening sky outside the window that woke him, not the night terror. He sat up and saw the infantryman sitting at the kitchen table watching him. 'You sleep uneasily, my friend,' the man said.

'Aye.'

'Let us go outside and you can reacquaint yourself with a musket.'

The soldiers had requisitioned the farmer's scarecrow and leaned it up against a trestle. 'We've been kind to you, Schmidt, and had little Löwe pace out the distance for you.' He pointed at the shortest of his comrades. The other men laughed, but Lukas noticed their weapons were primed and loaded, in case he took any wild notions when he had a gun in his hands.

He took the musket the infantryman gave him, and set himself to cleaning it. When he was satisfied there was no dirt to spoil his aim he loaded it, then took a moment to tuck it under his arm and remind his body of its feel. That done, he touched the slow-match to the fuse, took aim at the mid-body of the scarecrow and made fire. It had been many months since he'd felt the recoil of a musket punch him in the ribs, but the sensation was as familiar as his heartbeat. His aim was a little awry. The shot blasted away the scarecrow's shoulder, but left it standing. No gun barrel was entirely true, Lukas knew, and so did these men. He did not wait for their comment, and reloaded as quickly as if he were on a battlefield. This time he made adjustment for the gun's deviance. The shot hit the scarecrow soundly in the belly, and it fell away from the trestle, collapsing into two parts. He lowered the weapon and turned to the soldiers. 'Will I do for you?'

The infantryman nodded. 'Well enough. Our company has been scattered about here while the captain's wife was poorly, but we had word yesterday that since she's in no rush either to die or be cured we'll leave her in the village and be on our way back to Erfurt.'

'Whose men are you?'

The infantryman raised his eyebrows. 'Does it matter to you who you serve?'

'I'd like to know who my master will be.'

'We serve the King of Sweden.'

This was a blow, but there was little Lukas could do about it. There was always a chance that some of the regiment at Erfurt would know him. He had grown his beard, and was leaner than he had been back then, but the scars on his face would name him to any who had ever laid eyes on him. He could only pray that the tides of war had swept the men with whom he had fought to some other part of the country.

The days on the road to Erfurt were unexceptional. Lukas found his place among the company, and kept to himself. There was a certain comfort in being back in the world he knew best, but he had an edge to him that had not been there before. He was weary too.

Erfurt was still in ruins, but it made for a gathering point, and the river water was clean enough. They were to make camp until another regiment should join them, and then they would head back towards Leipzig. It was rumoured the Swedish king was hungry for another battle to better Breitenfeld.

Lukas did not wander far from his tent and the men of his new company. The ration of bread and beer was brought to them each day, and he made do with it. When a week had passed the ration stopped, and the men had no choice but to buy their own supplies wherever they could. There was no one Lukas would trust with the little loot he'd gathered on the road, so he followed his comrades about the camp in search of food. It went well enough the first day; he saw no one who knew him, and he was glad to taste a slice of *Wurst* again. The next was the same, and the fear in his gut eased its grip. And the day after that he was discovered.

Of all the people to undo him, who should it be but Baxandall's little wife. He was haggling with a sutler over a cut of cheese when he froze at the sound of a woman's scream. It seemed the whole camp turned to see who had let rip with such a screeching. Lukas could hardly help but turn too, and saw her directly in front of him. Her finger was pointing at his face, and her mouth was shaped into an ugly grimace as she howled. Some of the soldiers were laughing, taking her for a scorned whore, but then she spoke out, in strangely accented German: 'Killer! He is killer!' She turned to the man by her side, poking him in the arm and urging him to speak out for her. Lukas recognised him as Baxandall's witless corporal.

'She speaks true,' the corporal called. 'He murdered her husband, Sergeant von Baxandall of Isenburg's regiment. Seize him.' His voice quavered, as if he were uneasy to be shouting orders.

Lukas reached for his sword, but strong hands grabbed his arms.

He felt himself lifted so that the soles of his boots skimmed the ground as he was carried forward. His captors had closed round him, and the smell of the sweat of so many men was strong enough to taste.

They brought him before a captain, who sent him to be held until the colonel's men could gather a court fitting for such a trial. Lukas found himself locked into a closed carriage with chains binding his ankles together. He sat in the dark, and immense weariness overcame him. There was fear, of course, boiling deep inside him, but at heart he was exhausted. Yet he felt no relief that the race was nearly run, for the terrible prospect before him could not be denied. It was hard to think that after all the many ways he might have ended, all the bullets and cannon cheated, he had come to this.

Now and again, as the hours passed, he considered that he might be lucky. So much depended on the temper and disposition of the colonel. Some would hang a man for stealing a chicken, while others would declare that all violence committed in drink was the devil's crime and not the man's. Lukas knew his chances of finding such a pliable colonel were slim, particularly among these Swedes, with their name for good order. He bowed his head and prayed for bravery, that he might make a good show. He prayed that the colonel and his men would not believe Baxandall's woman, and that he would, miraculously, walk free. He prayed for forgiveness for all his many sins, but he knew that this prayer was in vain. He could not repent the killing of Baxandall, and where there was no regret there could be no forgiveness. He was only sorry to die for it.

Baxandall's grieving widow appeared to have transferred her affections to her dead husband's deputy. She clung to his arm as she came into the large tent that had been set aside to hear the case, and wept so violently upon his chest that the fighting men gathered there were made to feel most uncomfortable.

The colonel and four of his officers were seated at a long table.

Lukas was brought before them. The colonel's secretary unrolled a paper. 'This man, believed to be Lukas Weinsburg but latterly claiming to be Johann Schmidt, is accused that in March of this year, in the convent at Bamburg, while serving under Captain Hastfer of the Isenburg regiment, he did murder by strangulation Sergeant Ernst von Baxandall, who was his superior in rank, and immediately thereafter did desert his company.'

The colonel looked at him coldly. 'What is your true name?'

'Lukas Weinsburg, sir.'

'And did you indeed murder Sergeant von Baxandall?'

Lukas hesitated. He could lie, and hope that he would be believed. Then again, sometimes an officer would give a man credit for truthfulness. He tried to assess what sort of man the colonel was. Plain-spoken, he thought. A favourer of honesty. 'I killed him, yes, sir.'

'You murdered him, and then ran like a dog?'

In spite of his fear the anger stirred in Lukas, but he bit back the retort that was in his mouth and simply nodded.

'And why should you not be hanged for it?'

Lukas tried to gather his thoughts. 'I recall that Baxandall invited me to his quarters, which was strange. We were not friends, for all we'd been comrades this last five years and more. He gave me brandy and wine there until we were drunk. His wife fell asleep due to the liquor she'd taken. Then he fell to taunting me.'

'And how did he taunt you?'

Lukas closed his eyes. He could see Baxandall's face in his mind's eye, that leering, crafty face. 'He defamed my wife's good character, sir, and claimed she had made me a cuckold. He also said that he himself had had the pleasure of her, sir.' Lukas opened his eyes again, and looked straight at the colonel.

The colonel raised one eyebrow. 'Did he speak the truth?'

Again Lukas felt the pulse of anger, but this time it was towards Baxandall. 'I do not know.'

The colonel bade him stand aside, and addressed himself to the others who had been called in the case. Baxandall's little widow sobbed so loudly and made to faint so many times that the colonel ordered the corporal to slap her about the face until she was persuaded to speak sense. When this was achieved she pointed at Lukas and said, 'He kill my Ernst.' This seemed sufficient to satisfy the court.

After that came the infantryman who had captured him at the farm and compelled him to demonstrate his skill with the musket. All he could confirm was the false name he had been told, and his own belief that Lukas had been at loose for two months or more, judging from the state of his apparel and the look of hunger on him.

There was a ripple of movement in the crowd of soldiers standing in the doorway to the tent. Lukas had not realised that it was so tightly packed. This must be the day's great entertainment. A young officer stepped forward and requested permission to approach the colonel's table.

While the senior officers conferred, Lukas looked towards the doorway, his eye caught by a familiar face. It was Götz. His young friend was watching him, his face pale as a shroud. When he caught Lukas's eye he nodded very slightly and looked away. Lukas felt the sourness of disappointment. The lad did not wish to acknowledge him. Lukas could not blame him. There was danger in being associated with such as he.

The young officer finished his discussion with the colonel, who summoned his secretary forward. The scribe listened and wrote a note on his scroll, then turned to the room and called, 'Götz Fuhrmann, step forward.'

Lukas watched as Götz pushed his way through the men standing in the doorway. When he was before the colonel he straightened and stood with his hands behind his back.

'What is your purpose in coming before this court?' the colonel said.

'To stand as a witness to the good character of Lukas Weinsburg, sir.'

'And what are you?'

'I am lately promoted to lance corporal, sir, under Captain Roerkohl.'

'How did you win your promotion, Fuhrmann?'

Götz hesitated, and Lukas saw a slight blush colour his face. 'The previous lance corporal died of the scours.' Some of the men in the tent laughed at that, and Götz blushed still redder.

The colonel was smiling too. This day's work would make for amusing talk over his dinner table tonight. Lukas wished them all in hell. 'Tell me then ... um ...' The colonel looked to his secretary for a prompt.

'Fuhrmann,' he hissed.

'Indeed. Tell me why we should not hang your comrade for his crime.'

'He is a fine soldier, sir. Brave in battle, steadfast on the march, and a good man in any kind of skirmish.'

'He is your friend?'

'Yes, sir. He taught me how to be a soldier.'

The colonel made no response. He turned to his fellows at the table and looked at them steadily in turn, as if he were reading their faces. When he looked back he seemed irritated to see Götz still there, and waved him away. At that the soldiers who had been standing guard over Lukas urged him forward. He stood once again before the colonel's table. 'You have confessed your guilt. The murder of a superior officer is a most grievous crime,' the colonel said. 'If I show mercy to such as you, then there would be disorder in the ranks before the month's end. You must be hanged, for the betterment of the army's good standing.' He turned to his secretary. 'What hour is it?'

'Near noon, sir,' the secretary said.

The colonel turned back to Lukas. 'You will be hanged at six this evening, before sunset. That will give you time enough to be shriven.'

Lukas heard the colonel's voice pronounce the sentence as if he were speaking through a winter fog. He was cold now, in spite of the heat in the airless tent. The guards had taken his arms, and he was glad of it, for he would have despised himself had he tumbled to the floor.

Götz came in to him after the priest had done with his confession. The cleric had offered to stay until the end, but Lukas had said he would rather see his friend. This did not appear to please the priest, who flounced away, like a petulant girl, from the closed carriage that was to serve as the death cell. The door was closed and locked, and for a time Lukas feared that Götz would not come, or that the guards would not admit him. But now, as the clock struck four, the carriage door opened and in stepped the lad, followed by a soldier who was to sit with them as guard. There was just enough light for Lukas to see by. Götz looked calm, but he sensed that the boy had fought hard to compose himself.

'So,' Lukas said, 'how goes the war with you?'

'Well enough. I have missed your company.'

'You'll find better friends.'

'No.'

Lukas felt his eyes sting, and rubbed them with his sleeve. 'And what of your own spirits?' he said, steadying his voice. 'Are you still afflicted with the melancholy?'

'At times. I pray for the strength to overcome it, and God listens to my prayers.'

They sat in silence. Lukas pitied Götz. He knew the poor lad would be agonising over what next to say. That was the way with these scholars. They thought too much before they uttered a word. The guard shifted in his seat. Lukas knew that if they were silent too long the man would conclude that their meeting was done. He did not want Götz to leave.

Götz, too, seemed to realise that something more was needed. 'Has the priest been in to you?'

'Aye. I've made my confession.'

'That's good.'

'I still fear I'm damned.' He found he was shaking.

Götz reached out and took his arm. 'No. No. Not that. No. If you have made your confession and been absolved you have nothing to fear.' His eyes were bright with pain and fervour.

'I have not your faith. And I have tried to be sorry for killing Baxandall, but in my heart I am not.'

'I am sure you are sorry. Sometimes repentance is hidden so deep that only God can see it.'

Lukas considered this. Could it be true? Götz was more learned in these matters than he was. He turned to his friend again. 'Are you still minded to be a priest some day?'

Götz was taken aback. 'It has been a long time since I thought of it. But since you ask it, yes. It is my dream.'

'Then I would ask a promise of you.'

'Anything.'

'When you are a priest, will you say a Mass for me? I hope I can face death like a man, but I am so afraid of how God will judge me. Promise me you'll say a Mass for the relief of my soul.'

Götz clasped his hands around Lukas's. 'Of course.'

Lukas nodded and pulled away. He needed to compose himself, and the boy's passion would be of no help to him in that task.

'It is heavy on my mind that in the next world I will meet those I have wronged.'

'You are a soldier, Lukas. God will not condemn you for the lives you took in battle. Don't you remember? The priests absolved us in perpetuity.'

'It's not that. There are others. Katherine. The child. The child is likely dead too by now, and I never even gave her my name.' Lukas felt a sick sweat break out on his face. 'I cannot remember what Katherine looked like, and yet I glimpse her in my memory. When I *try* to bring her face to mind, there's nothing. It's as if when I turn to see her she vanishes. Is it her spirit, do you think?'

'Her spirit is with God, Lukas. It is perhaps your own troubled conscience that makes her appear in your mind.'

'And how can I ease it?'

'Prayer is the only salve for these secret guilts.' Götz picked distractedly at the ragged skin around his thumbnail. 'The child may be living yet. That was the last word I had, that she was taken into the orphanage at Saalfeld.'

'She'd be better dead and out of this cursed world.'

The time had come. The priest had returned, as if determined to be granted his place, and made the guard send Götz away. Now Lukas's arms had been bound tight against his sides and he was led out of the carriage, with the priest stalking along before him reading aloud from his missal. Lukas kept his eyes focused on the back of the man's head. His hair was thin and grey, with just the odd remnant of the red it must once have been. Lukas felt an odd resentment towards him. He seemed to revel in his role.

From the hiss of whispers surrounding him he knew that a good-sized crowd had gathered. There were no jeers, not yet. Soldiers were not like the common populace in that way. They rarely bayed like a pack of hounds at the extinction of one of their own. Perhaps they saw so much death that it had lost its novelty. The colonel would probably have compelled them to witness this, in order for them to learn by example.

As they walked across the *Platz* Lukas struggled to calm his breathing. His feet carried him forward, but he could not feel the ground beneath them. Up ahead, he knew, stood a wooden frame with a rope tied to the crossbeam. He could tell it was there, even though he was not looking at it. His heart hammered in his chest, and with each beat he feared he would spew. *How many beats more?* he thought, and quickly pushed the thought aside. It was his soul he should be thinking of, not his body. *Father, forgive me*, he said, over and over again. He stopped when he discovered he was muttering the words out loud, like a half-wit.

They were nearly at the gallows. A high bench had been placed beneath it, and a ladder was propped against one of the side beams. 'God bless you, Lukas,' a voice called from the crowd.

Lukas turned and saw his young friend. The lad was standing at the front of the crowd, with two boys of twelve or thirteen at his side. Lukas tried to smile at Götz, hoping they might both pretend courage. One of the boys looked at his companion with panic on his face. Without warning they darted back into the crowd. Lukas saw Götz's face grow even paler than it had already been, and he shouted something after the boys.

Now Lukas and his guards were at the gallows. The ladder was set against the bench, and the first of the guards climbed up it. When he reached the top he took hold of Lukas's shoulder, steadying him as he came up. The other guard kept a hand at his back, pushing him. Lukas's foot slipped on the ladder, but the guards held him in place. *The mercy*, Lukas realised. That was what the two young boys had been in place for, Götz must have arranged it, but they'd taken fright and run off. His heart was beating so loudly now that even if the crowd had been roaring he'd not have heard them. He gasped in what air he could, but he felt as if a great weight was lying on his chest. One of the guards placed the noose over his head and tightened it so that the rope chafed against his neck. He wished he had a hand free to scratch away the discomfort. While the guards scrambled down the ladder he scanned the crowd for Götz's face, but his eyes were strangely clouded, and he could see nothing but a blur.

At one moment the bench was beneath his boot soles and then it was gone. He fell, and his body leaped as the rope snapped tight across his throat. His head pounded as if a cannon was thundering … terror … no air … redness before his eyes … unending terror … and suddenly the grip of arms around his waist … Götz's voice calling words he could not hear … *the mercy* … and, at last, the coming of night.

Twenty-two

THE FEAST OF FIRST FRUITS WAS only a week past and the summer at its hottest. Not a breeze drifted up from the river Elbe to cool the citizens of Magdeburg. There were rumours of plague in Braunschweig, which was less than two days away. Christa was thankful it had not discouraged the farmers' wives from travelling to the market to sell the produce of their husbands' land. Fresh food brought in the customers, who might then be persuaded to buy a hymn- or newssheet.

Trade was brisk, but the heat was draining. Christa's head ached. Her discomfort was made worse by the constant hammering of the builders all around the marketplace. The city was being remade. Nearly every day the river carried boatloads of bricks, fresh from the kilns of Wolmirstedt. There was a lack of timber, and the woodcutters had to travel far to find forests that had not been turned to fuel for the armies. Each morning a queue of citizens waited at the makeshift *Rathaus*. They were establishing their claims to the ground where their houses had once stood. As soon as they had their assurance, the building would begin. The councillors themselves had caught the building frenzy. A new proper *Rathaus* was under construction, on the very spot where the old one had stood.

Christa sold another hymn-sheet and made herself exchange pleasantries with her customer, in spite of her headache. She touched the moneybag at her waist. It was pleasingly heavy, but that made her anxious. There had been strangers about these past weeks, drifting round in ones and twos. They looked like fighting men, but showed no sign of allegiance to either king or emperor. It unsettled her to have men like that around the place. In the same way the building work disturbed her. On the one hand, her heart was glad to see Magdeburg coming back to life, but the war was not yet over. What was built up could so easily be torn down.

The crowd began to thin, and Christa's unease increased. She quickly tidied the remaining stock, ready to be gathered and carried back to the workshop. When she looked up she saw a man standing at the drinking fountain across the way from her. His hat was pulled down so far that she could not see his face, and he was well wrapped up in spite of the heat. She felt her heartbeat quicken at something about him that was familiar. His stance was so like Götz's, and yet … She could not say for sure. There had been too many times this last year when the breath had nearly left her as she saw – or thought she saw – a face she knew. He seemed to be staring at her now, although his eyes were hidden in the shadow cast by his hat brim. Very slowly he began to walk towards her. It *was* Götz.

He drew nearer. It was strange, she thought, how a person could be recognised by the way in which they moved. As he came closer she could see the lower part of his face. It was dark with stubble and his mouth was harder than before. He hesitated, and for a moment she wondered if Lukas was here too. Her heart quickened in terror, but she remembered that she was no longer alone and undefended. This was her home, and no one would force her from it again.

Although she felt unsteady she came out from behind the stall and went to meet him. 'Here you are,' she said, and could think of nothing else to add.

'Christa.' He looked around furtively, then took off his hat and smoothed his hair. 'I thought you would likely return to Ithaca.'

'Ithaca?'

'You do not recall then, the tales of King Odysseus, and how he found his way home at last?' Some fleeting expression crossed his face – disappointment?

She cursed herself. The volume of *The Odyssey* was hidden in the bottom of a chest at the workshop. She had scarcely had a moment's leisure to read it since she had returned. But she had another, more immediate concern. 'Are you alone?' she said.

'Aye.' He peered closely at her, then seemed to understand her question. 'Lukas is dead.'

'Did he fall at Breitenfeld?'

Götz hesitated. 'No. Later.'

She felt a bitter thrill of triumph — *I am alive and you are in the ground* — though knew she should offer words of comfort to Götz. Lukas had been his friend. But she could not bring herself to say anything soothing, even though Götz's face bore all the marks of grief. 'It was kind of you to bring me word of this.' She felt a sudden fear that the armies might be bearing down upon Magdeburg again. There had been no word of such in this part of the country, but still … 'Is your regiment near here?'

'I've had a parting from the army.' He pulled his hat on again.

Christa lowered her voice. 'You've deserted?'

'Aye.'

'Are you not afraid of what will be done to you if you are caught?'

'Germany is full of deserters. There isn't rope enough to hang us all.' He rubbed at his mouth. 'I'm parched.'

'There's good water in the fountain.'

'It's a proper drink I need.'

'Come to my house. I'll fetch a jug of beer and you can drink that.' Christa piled up the stock and handed it to Götz while she dismantled the stall. He offered to carry it, so they exchanged their burdens and walked home.

She had not yet asked him what had brought him to Magdeburg. She did not dare.

Christa led Götz down the rough lane towards the workshop. 'We were not always so humble,' she said, stepping round a crack in the ground, 'but we have had a small workshop built, and it does us well for living quarters too.'

'Is this the place where your father's house was?'

'Yes.'

'I would not have known it again.'

Of course, Christa thought, *you have been here before.* That day seemed like another life, yet it was only a little more than a year ago. She began to think about how she should introduce Götz to Andreas.

The door to the workshop stood open to let in the air. Christa indicated to Götz that he should stay where he stood, and stepped inside. Andreas was setting out some type in a frame, while baby Jürgen played in a little pen built to keep him safe from both press and hearth. The child reached up his arms to Christa and called her name. She set down the unsold stock and lifted him up. 'Good day, little one. How goes it?' she said, holding him high above her until he gurgled with delight.

'How was trade today?' Andreas asked.

Christa settled the baby on her hip. 'Brisk enough. Here, untie my moneybag, will you? I don't want to set this rascal down just yet.'

Andreas left his typesetting and came over to do as she had asked. He weighed the bag in his hand and nodded with satisfaction. 'I'll leave out two *Taler* to buy tomorrow's food, shall I?' Christa agreed. He set two coins on the shelf, then placed the bag in the strongbox tucked in the corner of the room.

'I met an old acquaintance in the marketplace,' Christa said, rocking from side to side to keep the baby placid. 'He's outside now.'

Andreas looked past her into the doorway. Götz was staring at them, his face unreadable. 'You have a child,' he said flatly.

Christa realised that, to Götz's eyes, she, Andreas and the baby must look like a little family. 'Jürgen is not my own. He's the child of my friends. They are both dead now and in God's care.'

'In truth?'

Christa did not understand his manner. 'Yes. Of course.' She was conscious of Andreas by her side, glaring at Götz. 'Götz Fuhrmann, this is Andreas Ritschel, my partner in this enterprise. Andreas, Götz was a friend of … my husband.'

'A friend of your husband?' His voice was thick with anger. He rested one hand on the press for balance and pointed the other at Götz. 'So were you here when our city was destroyed?'

'I was,' Götz replied.

'You should be put to the sword for what you did that day.'

'I did what any soldier must, which is obey his order.' Götz's face was stony and pitiless. 'If you had ever been a soldier you would know this.'

Andreas seemed too overcome with fury to speak.

'He saved Elsbeth,' Christa said weakly, but neither man appeared to hear her.

'I will go,' Götz said to her.

'No! Come in for a drink.' She could not bear him to leave so soon. She turned to Andreas. 'Can't you see he's travel worn? What kind of Christians are we if we will not give him refreshment?'

'You'd entertain one of those monsters?'

'Götz is not a monster.'

Andreas swung away from the press and lifted his crutch. 'It's well enough for you to say so. You suffered little harm at their hands. Don't ask me to break bread with him.' He scooped the two *taler* off the shelf and pushed past Götz on the way out of the door.

After he had gone, Götz said, 'How can he say that you suffered little harm?'

'He does not know the truth of what befell me. I only told him I had been made to marry after the city fell. Nothing more. I could not … He has troubles enough of his own, without knowing of my shame.'

'I am sorry to have brought dissension to your home.'

'What has brought you to Magdeburg, Götz? Was it to bring me tidings of Lukas's death?'

Götz blushed, and no longer looked the hard-bitten soldier. 'I have some matters to attend to.'

'And how long will you stay?'

'However long is required.'

'I would offer you a corner of this place for your lodging, but ...'

'I'll find somewhere.'

'Take some food at least. Andreas will likely drink his anger away. He'll not be back this good while.' The baby grizzled, and Christa spoke soothingly to him. 'Bring a coin out of the strongbox and I'll go out to get you some beer.'

'Shall I not go, if you want to mind the child?'

'I should do it – you might encounter Andreas. I'll put Jürgen in his little pen. Are you fit to watch over him?'

'I've little knowledge of such matters. What should I do?'

'Talk nonsense to him.' Christa set Jürgen down. He pulled himself up and shouted after her. Götz would scarcely have heard her speak over the noise, so she smiled and ran out to fetch the beer.

Jürgen had settled by the time she returned. Götz was dangling a broken necklace of brightly coloured gemstones in front of him, and the baby was reaching out for it with delight. 'He likes this new toy,' Götz said.

'Let him hold it, then, while you drink and I gather some food.' Christa saw how thirstily Götz eyed the beer.

He allowed the necklace to fall into Jürgen's outstretched hands, and sat by the small table that served for dining, reading and writing in this modest household. Christa poured him some beer, and he drank it quickly. 'The child is so like you,' he said, as she refilled his mug. 'I was sure he must be yours.'

'I don't know how he could be like me. He's the son of my friends Gertrude and Klaus.' She looked down at Jürgen, who was shaking the necklace in both hands. He seemed utterly absorbed in his task, but he must have felt her gaze on him, for he glanced up at her, his eyes full of mischief.

They ate, and Christa mashed up some breadcrumbs for Jürgen. He was weaned now, and it was a relief to both her and Andreas that they no longer had to find money for a wet nurse. It meant they could save a little more, which would be used in time to build another room onto the workshop. Then it would start to become a proper home.

Götz said little as they ate and drank. When the beer was gone he opened his satchel and took out a flask. 'I have some brandy here,' he said. 'Will you share it with me?'

'Thank you, no. My head aches. Brandy would hardly improve it.'

She left Götz drinking his brandy while she settled Jürgen for the night. Her bed and the baby's were in one corner of the workshop. The nuns at the convent had sent her a cradle for Jürgen after she had taken him away. He would soon be too big for it, but when the winter came he could share her bed and they would both be the warmer for it. She tucked him into his cradle and sat on her bed rocking him until he drifted off to sleep. There was little noise from the workshop beyond, just the occasional sound of more brandy being poured, or the mug being set down on the table. She felt at peace with Götz there.

When Jürgen was sleeping she went back to the table. Götz tipped the last of the brandy into his mug and drank it. 'There is something I must tell you,' he said.

Christa waited for him to continue, her heart pounding. It was plain from the look on his face that he was troubled, and she could not imagine what he might say. She remembered that last night in Leipzig, and the tender look he had given her before Baxandall had burst into the room, but she did not think there were such soft thoughts in his mind now.

Götz took a deep breath and clasped the mug firmly, as though he wished it were full to the brim with strong drink. 'I have found your sister.'

Christa could not reply. She could barely understand his words. The room seemed suddenly bright and airless. Every detail was clear, from the grain of the wood in the tabletop to the dark circles under Götz's eyes. 'Alive?' she said at last. Götz nodded. 'Where is she? Is she well? How did you find her?' She waited for his answer, afraid to let the joy blossom in her soul.

'Last winter I was billeted in a convent in Bamburg. I heard tell from the nuns that their sisters in Hedersleben had given refuge to a pious young girl, and she was becoming known as the Child of Magdeburg because she had survived the city's fall.'

'It could be any girl. Others survived.'

'I have seen her. I sought her out. Her name is Elsbeth Henning. I could not recollect how she might look, for I only saw her on that day when — when I took her to the cathedral. But I asked her did she have a sister called Christa, and she said she did.'

The room swam round Christa, and she wished Götz had saved some of his brandy to steady her. 'My God,' she said. 'He is merciful, isn't He?' She pressed one hand to her mouth, fearful that she would cry out. Götz reached across the table and took her other hand in his.

They sat like that for a while. 'You will want to go to her?' Götz asked.

'Of course. Can it be safely done?'

'The roads are dangerous, but if you dare to travel I would see you there and back, and defend you with all my might.' He gave her a small smile. 'I am a hardened fighting man now, not the innocent I was when first we met.'

His smile chilled her. He had changed, no doubt about it. There was something cold about him, as if the war had killed part of his soul.

Andreas returned very late, drunk and surly. In spite of this he rose at his usual hour the next morning and went about his work. Christa left for the marketplace without speaking to him. The wonderful news about Elsbeth remained unspoken. She would save it until he was more civil.

When she returned he seemed recovered, and received the news thoughtfully. She was less content. Götz had not appeared in the market today. What if he had slipped away? There was a restlessness in him now that she had not noticed when she had known him before. If he had gone, who would bring her to the place where Elsbeth was?

Andreas ate the meal she had prepared for him with appetite. She suspected he had felt too queasy for food earlier. Afterwards he wiped his mouth and gripped the table. 'Did your friend bring you any word of your husband?'

She felt sick at heart. 'My husband is dead.' He went to reply but she hurried on to prevent him: 'I have no wish to marry again, Andreas. I am only sixteen years old.'

'When we spoke before ...'

'It would be madness to marry, with our business just begun, and little Jürgen to rear.'

'Are you saying never?' There was a tremor of anger in his voice.

She could not bring herself to give him hope with a lie so she said nothing.

The morning they set off from Magdeburg was overcast and stifling. Andreas had bade her a sullen God speed. She knew that at heart he was fearful for her safety but that, being Andreas, he would not say so. Instead he had grumbled at being left to work on alone, and forced to tend the child, which, as a man, he was hardly fitted for.

Götz had hired a piebald horse for the journey. She did not ask where he had acquired the money to pay for it. At first she sat side-saddle in front of him. He smelled of liquor, although he showed no sign of drunkenness. She wondered how much drink he needed to begin his day. He did not seem confident in the saddle — she supposed he was more used to marching than going on horseback — and she clutched the animal's mane for fear of falling off. Götz was encumbered with his satchel, a musket and short sword. Once they were on the road, with no one near, he suggested she might feel safer if she rode astride, as he did. As if to help her make up her mind the horse stumbled on a loose stone. She gathered up her skirts and swung her leg over. 'What shall I do if we meet other travellers?' she said.

'Say good day and ride on. If they stare at you, let them. Are you so timid of the opinion of strangers?' This was the new, hard-hearted Götz, yet she felt safe with him. As she tired she leaned back against him. There was comfort in his warmth. Even as she revelled in it she was afflicted with guilt: she should be concentrating her thoughts and prayers on Elsbeth.

The journey would take two days. Götz's plan was that they should stay the night at an inn in a village on the way, but as they drew close to it they heard men's voices raised in drunken shouting. Every moment or two a shot would be dispatched, followed by wild laughter. 'We'll keep clear of this place,' Götz said. 'Whoever they are, their blood is up.'

'Where will we stay?'

'I still have my little tent. We'll find a good spot out of sight of the road. Have you forgotten how to live like a soldier's wife already?'

While there was still some light in the sky they followed a stream into the woods and made camp. When the tent was pitched Götz took the horse to drink, then tethered it where the grass was lush. The two of them sat down in front of the tent and ate their bread and cheese. Götz drank freely from his flask. It was not brandy he had this time, but some other liquor he had bought from a Pole in Magdeburg. It grew dark, but they did not light a fire. The night was warm, and they had no wish to attract the attention of any night-wanderers.

'We should sleep,' Götz said. His voice was less clear than it had been earlier.

'Aye,' said Christa. She was suddenly very conscious that she was alone with him, and that they must sleep side by side in the little tent. If he had been the Götz she had once known she would have had no fear of him, but this was a man made sharp by the war.

'You know I would not harm you,' Götz said, as if he had heard her thoughts. 'I'll place my musket between us, and may God strike me dead if I lay a finger on you.'

They crawled into the tent and lay down. Its smell took Christa back to her life as Lukas's wife. She remembered the first time she had lain in this tent, the night the city had fallen. Götz turned away from her. Before long she heard his breathing slow into sleep. She lay for a while, listening to the noises of the forest beyond the canvas. At last she, too, slept.

The convent of Our Lady of Pity was directly before them and the horse lurched up the path to the gate. Christa had resumed her demure side-saddle way of sitting but her mouth was dry. Götz was sure that the girl here was Elsbeth, but what if he were mistaken?

When they reached the gate they dismounted, and Götz went to explain their business to the gatekeeper. An elderly man was summoned to lead them to the part of the convent where the Child of Magdeburg had her quarters. 'Aye, they're coming from all over to see her, but the sisters turn most away. The child has not the strength for it.' He led them to a high-ceilinged corridor and bade them wait.

When she was sure they were alone Christa whispered to Götz, 'Why do so many come to see her?'

Götz shifted uneasily. 'It is said she has the cure for melancholy.'

Before Christa could respond to this a nun appeared. She looked at Christa gravely. 'You claim kinship to the child?'

'I am her sister.'

'Then follow me.' She glanced at Götz. 'And what of you? You have visited here before, have you not?'

'I am well mended.'

The nun raised her eyebrows. 'Then God be praised.'

She led Christa along the corridor then turned through a door into a walled garden. 'We have given the child two rooms that look into the garden. One is her private chamber. The other is where she receives those in need of her cure.'

'How did she come to be here?'

'A pious lady, a great benefactor of this place, discovered her in Magdeburg after the city fell and saw a godly light in her, so she brought her to us. We have been spared the worst of the war, thanks be to God, and pray that we will stay safe.'

As they came closer to the garden rooms it seemed to Christa that her spirit was not wholly in her body. The ground beneath her feet felt insubstantial, and there was a strange glare in the light of the overcast day.

'Wait by the door,' the nun whispered to her. 'The child is frail, and I should prepare her for your coming.'

The nun walked inside, leaving Christa by the open door. She heard a murmur of conversation, then the nun returned and beckoned her in.

Elsbeth was standing to greet her. Christa searched her face. Yes, it really was Elsbeth. Taller than she had been — nearly as tall as Christa now — but thinner than ever. She permitted Christa to put her arms round her, but did not reciprocate. Christa pulled back and studied her sister's face. 'God be praised,' she said.

'Amen,' Elsbeth replied. She smiled sweetly, as she might have done for any visitor.

They sat down and Christa tried to engage Elsbeth in conversation, but she did not appear to listen. 'Elsbeth, dear sister, I have made a little home for us in Magdeburg. Andreas is there. You remember Andreas? And Gertrude's baby.'

Elsbeth smiled, her eyes downcast, and said nothing.

Christa looked at the nun in despair. 'You can come home now, Elsbeth. Back to Magdeburg. You do not have to stay here any longer.'

The expression on Elsbeth's face changed from serenity to distress. 'No, Christa. Please, no. Don't make me leave here. The world is so very wicked. Please, dear sister, please ...' She cringed away from Christa and began twisting her skirt in her hands.

'Of course I won't make you leave, if you do not want to.' Christa was filled with an agony of guilt at causing Elsbeth such upset. 'You must stay here, sweetheart, if that's what you want.'

Elsbeth nodded. Christa longed to hug her again, but feared she would be repulsed. She did not think she could bear the pain of that. The nun stepped closer and touched her shoulder. 'We should leave the child in peace.'

The nun brought Christa into a private parlour and ordered wine and sweetmeats. 'They will restore you, my child. You are paler than parchment.'

'Why would she rather be here than with her family? She is my only living flesh and blood.'

The nun thought for a moment before she replied. 'When first she was brought here she did not speak. She lay in a kind of paralysis for the best part of six months, and we thought she would surely die, for she could barely be persuaded to take a mouthful of food each day. Whatever shock her poor soul sustained on the day your city fell, it has filled her with a terrible fear of the world. She feels safe here.'

'But is anywhere truly safe?'

'That is in the hands of the Almighty. But your poor sister *feels* safe here. This is a place where she may prosper in spirit.'

'Then here she must stay, I suppose.' A sudden bitter thought entered Christa's mind. 'Do you mean to convert her to your faith?'

'I confess we have tried, but we have failed. For all her docility, your sister is a most intractable Protestant.'

Christa hid a smile. Elsbeth was not entirely lost to her. That was some consolation.

She could not find Götz, so she waited close to where the horse was tied up. At last he appeared. He asked her no questions about Elsbeth, so she guessed he must have been told what had taken place between them.

They rode until evening was close. This time they found a quiet village with an equally quiet tavern. The tapster offered them the one bedroom. Götz accepted it for Christa, and said he would sleep in the stable. The tapster's wife brought them bowls of good turnip stew, and Christa ate hers hungrily.

They sat at the table, with the last of the bread and beer. There were no other customers. Götz was quieter even than before. He drank the beer steadily, long after Christa had finished. 'I will go to my bed now,' she said, and stood.

'Wait a moment,' Götz said. He looked at her, then into his tankard. 'I saw your sister today.'

Christa was perplexed. 'After I had seen her?' Götz nodded. 'But why? I thought you had no need for her cure.'

'The melancholy ... Sometimes I think it has gone, and then ...' He covered his eyes with his hand, but Christa could tell he was weeping.

She sat down again beside him. Only once in her life had she seen a man cry – her father, that morning long ago on the walls of Magdeburg when she was a little child. She put her arm round Götz's waist and let him lean against her, sobbing. If she could have thought of wise words she would have said them, but she could construe nothing that might ease his pain. She was conscious of how starved he felt. His ribs were plain to the touch as she rubbed his back. After a time he quietened, then straightened. 'I thought the war had turned your heart to stone,' she said.

He shook his head. 'I wish it had.'

'Did Elsbeth ease your melancholy?'

Götz smiled wryly. 'You have cured me better than she did.' He studied her face. 'What would you think if I stayed a while longer in Magdeburg?'

'I — I should like that. But how would you employ yourself?'

'I have been a teacher of the young. That was how I earned my keep at the seminary in Saalfeld.'

'And would that content you?'

'A man must learn to turn his hand to all manner of occupations.'

She went up to bed then, but found it hard to sleep. When she did drop off her rest was troubled by dreams. She would wake from each one struggling to remember the details, but they were always gone. In her last dream before daybreak she was in darkness with the smell of the little tent in her nostrils, and a man's chapped lips pressed to hers. She woke with a start, and for a moment afterwards she could still feel the weight of him on her, the rough bristles of his beard scratching her face.

Twenty-three

'BE CAREFUL WHERE YOU SET THE paperweight,' Christa said. 'There's little point in stopping the pamphlets blowing away if no one can see what their subject is.' She was teaching Götz the business of being a market trader, since he had found few students yet to teach. He had learned well in the days since they'd returned from Hedersleben, although he was shy with the customers. It was useful all the same to have him with her on the stall. The strangers who drifted about the marketplace would be less inclined to steal from her when Götz was at her side.

They sold a fair number of hymn-sheets early on as it was Saturday, and people were preparing themselves for tomorrow's church-going, but by mid-morning there were few buyers. Christa was worried about the business. A new family had taken residence in the ruins of the printers' quarter, and had done as she and Andreas had – fashioned a shelter and constructed a small press. The husband claimed to be a cousin of one of the other printing families who had traded from there before the city fell. Christa was glad that the quarter was being restored to life, but their new neighbours were competition.

Around noon Götz became restless, and excused himself.

Christa knew he would seek out a tavern where he would drink until the market was closing. She had never seen him incapably drunk since he'd come to Magdeburg, but it was plain that he could not go half a day without liquor.

She sat down on a low wall close to the stall. There was confusion in her mind. When Götz had first declared that he would stay in Magdeburg she had been happy, and also a little fearful. She was sure she was the reason for his delay. What it might signify she did not dare to speculate. Andreas, though, was immovable. He would not be in the house at the same time as Götz. To add to that, the business did not make sufficient profit to pay a third worker. Andreas did not stint on reminding her of that fact.

Christa allowed her anger with him to divert her from another truth: Götz was discontented. This was not the life for him. She tried to persuade herself that if only Andreas would be more agreeable things might be different, but in her heart she knew that they would not. The time had come for her to address the problem.

As the market emptied of customers Götz returned. His face was flushed with drink and the September heat. They tidied the stock and Christa readied her words. 'Götz, we are friends, are we not?' she said.

He was clutching a bundle of pamphlets and looked as guilty as a thief. 'Of course.'

Christa took a deep breath. 'You are not as happy here as you thought you might be. I believe you wish to be away.'

'I am not sure what would content me. Some days I wish I was a soldier again, and others I yearn for Saalfeld and my old life. There are times when I am sure God means me to be a priest, but within the hour I am filled with doubt. And then … there are promises I have made, and I cannot keep them by staying here. A man should honour his promises, should he not?'

'If he can, yes.' Christa wondered what the promises might be. Did he have a sweetheart somewhere? Or even a wife? It seemed doubtful. Any time a girl came near him he blushed as pink as sunset. She was the only one he seemed at ease with.

'But I said also that I would stay here in Magdeburg.'

She understood now that he would only go if she gave him permission to do so. If she did not, he would stay – discontented and unsettled, but he would stay. 'I think you would be best to go, or you will always yearn for the paths you did not walk.' she said, and the words tasted bitter in her mouth.

Götz handed the bundle of pamphlets to her. 'Thank you,' he said at last.

'Where will you go? Saalfeld?'

'I have some business there, and some wrongs to beg forgiveness for. And then ... I shall find the Emperor's men to join them and fight on while this present trouble continues.'

'You would return to the war?'

'I'm fitted for little else. And it's a way for a poor man to make his fortune.' He glanced shyly at her. 'You will never leave Magdeburg again, will you?'

'I'd die first,' Christa blurted out, and was embarrassed by the fervency of her words. She was not sure that they were true. It was easy to make such declarations here in the peaceful city, but in reality she would do whatever was needed to save her life, or little Jürgen's. Still, she prayed that she would bide there for the rest of her days.

'I'll leave tomorrow morning,' Götz said at last.

They carried the stall and stock back to the workshop. Andreas had taken a break from his labours and was playing with Jürgen outside in the sunshine. He was seated on a bench and helping the baby to stand. The sun was shining down on them. Andreas was smiling and talking fondly to him, although he looked weary in the bright light. Jürgen's face shone with health. The sunlight made his hair gleam like red gold. Christa stopped short, struck by recognition of that hair, those mischievous eyes ... No, it was impossible. She pushed the idea from her mind.

Andreas looked at them, and his smile vanished. Götz nodded to him, and carried the stall into the workshop. Christa followed him, arranged the stock on the shelf, and bade him wait there a moment.

She went back outside and sat beside Andreas on the bench. 'Götz is leaving tomorrow morning,' she said. 'I would like to offer him the hospitality of a meal tonight.'

'Then I will find my victuals elsewhere.'

Christa struggled over what she should say next. In truth, she would rather Andreas was not there this last evening, but she knew that was an unkind thought. 'It would please me if you could find it in yourself to sit down at table with him.'

'I'll leave such nonsense to you.' Jürgen was sitting on the ground now, piling shards of broken brick, one on top of another. 'You're a fool, Christa Henning,' Andreas hissed, 'for all your cleverness.'

'What do you mean?' Christa was taken aback by his venom.

Andreas glanced back into the workshop. 'I've seen how your eyes follow him. Is that what you want? To be nursemaid to a drunkard? You'd turn away from a decent man in favour of a Papist sot? And now he's going, you'll be left behind like a ruined servant-girl pining for her soldier-boy.'

Christa was too angry to reply. She stood up and went back into the workshop. 'Come and sup here tonight, Götz,' she said, as steadily as she could.

He searched her face, perhaps made uncertain by her manner. 'Very well,' he said. 'This evening, then.'

After he had gone she stood alone in the workshop. She prayed that Andreas would not come through the door. The thought of him with her was unbearable, but there was nowhere for her to go. One cramped room was all they had, and no hiding place.

She prepared the meal. There was a jug of Rhine wine, and a pot of stew she had made with *Wurst* and barley in an onion stock. She was spitefully pleased to see how Andreas gazed longingly at it as it bubbled, its savoury smell filling the room. But he still refused to join them. She could not bring herself to reply to his farewell as he left for the evening. It was a blessed relief to be without him. Jürgen was playing happily on the floor, and she sang to him as she laid the table.

When Götz arrived he seemed in low spirits, and Christa felt her own pleasure in the evening drain away. They ate and drank in silence. Jürgen crawled to her and endeavoured to pull himself up onto her lap. She lifted him and let him have a crust of bread to try his latest teeth on. His childish contentment made her own melancholy hang all the heavier on her.

Götz cleared his throat. 'You know I hope to be a priest some day.'

'Aye. Or else you'll be a soldier, or a schoolteacher, or whatever other notion takes you.' Christa had intended to sound light-hearted, but Götz seemed irritated.

'It is clear you think I am unsteady. It's well for you. You have always known what you are, and what your place is in this world.'

'I'm sorry if I offended you.'

'A priest is a soldier of God. I *will* be a priest, but I am poor. If I make my money in this war it will ease my way into the priesthood.'

Outrage flared in Christa, but she kept her voice soft so that she did not unsettle the baby. 'Is this the will of God? That only the rich man may be a priest?'

'It is the will of the world.' He poured himself more wine and sipped it thoughtfully. 'I am not so arrogant as to think I can challenge centuries of tradition.'

'You think it is arrogant to have the conscience to challenge a tradition that is wrong? That is not arrogance. That is wisdom and courage. It is not me who is arrogant, Götz, it is your church. You are blinded by its errors.'

'Listen to yourself. You repeat the ideas of those who reared you.'

His words stung. 'And do you not do the same?'

'Aye. But I am in the right, and you are in the wrong.'

Their argument acted like a lullaby to Jürgen. He grew sleepy, relaxing into the crook of Christa's arm. She carried him to his crib and tucked him into it. She was angry at Götz for bringing disagreement to the table. Why had he allowed this dispute to flourish on their last night of fellowship? 'We cannot both be right,' she said, more lightly than she felt. 'At least we'll not have to tolerate each other in the afterlife, for one of us will be saved and the other damned.'

'The destination of your soul is nothing to joke over.'

'Don't be so dour. You're worse than a Calvinist.' Christa came back to him and poured another drop of wine into his cup. Götz didn't lift it. He simply stared at the table. She took a deep breath. 'You've changed since first I knew you. I'd rather have you as my friend than my preacher.'

'I hope I'll always be your friend.' He took a sip of wine and handed the cup to her.

She reached out to take it with both hands, and their fingers touched. His skin felt rough, as if these last months had weathered him like wood. 'If you abandoned the errors of Rome, we could be friends in heaven too.'

'I'm afraid we'd be in hell, if I followed your path.' She could feel his eyes on her as she drank. 'This earthly life is the only time we'll be together.'

The little house was very quiet now. The fire had died down, and the child breathed softly in his crib. There was no sound from the close outside. Christa wondered when Andreas would return. The moment would soon come when Götz would rise to leave. She reached out and laid her hand over his. 'Then let us remain friends while we can.'

He curled his fingers round hers. Christa wished they could stay like that always, in the peaceful room, in harmony with each other, but after a time he released her and stood up. 'I must be on my way.'

She stood too, and walked with him to the door. 'Farewell, then,' she said. Her voice was unsteady.

Götz touched her face. 'Until we see each other again.' She

lifted up her hand and laid her fingertips on his cheek. His skin was warm, heated with the drink no doubt, and she could feel the coarse rasp of his stubble. He moved towards her, brushed his lips lightly against hers, then drew back. They stood like that for a long moment, his hand on her face, and hers on his, and she thought that if God Himself were looking down on them He would think them perfectly met, like two entwined parts of the one whole.

After he had gone she sat down at the table and put out the candle. She waited for her eyes to adjust to the darkness. The baby slept on peacefully. What a gift innocence was. Christa wished she was a child again, sleeping in a safe world where no harm could come. She doubted she would fall asleep this night, but her body and soul were weary. Carefully she made her way to her bed, edging past the crib. A little later she heard Andreas return. He seemed to stand for a long time in the room, then made the door fast before he limped to his bed.

Jürgen woke her with his customary early-morning babble. She propped herself up on one elbow and watched him. He had a new trick of kicking his blanket off and grabbing his feet with his hands. Christa had slept ill, but the sight of his game cheered her. She wondered if Götz was on his way yet.

All that day she and Andreas behaved charily towards each other, as if they knew it would take care to mend the fabric of their partnership. They attended the service by the ruins of the Johanniskirche, and ate cold stew for their meal, with every show of politeness.

That evening was pleasantly warm, and they sat outside on the bench, watching Jürgen play. Their new neighbours watched their little daughter toddle about. The wife smoothed her gown over her swollen belly. Perhaps she would give birth to a son who would be a friend to Jürgen.

Andreas cleared his throat, and shifted on the bench as if he were uncomfortable. 'I am sorry to see you in sad heart,' he said.

His compassion was harder to bear than his anger, but still it touched her that he had noticed her pain.

'Your soldier boy may come back some day,' he added.

'I think not. He's away to make his fortune and then turn priest.'

Andreas shook his head. 'Sometimes what we dream of is not what we want.'

'That seems deep philosophy for a practical man like yourself.' When Andreas made no reply she changed the subject. 'I have much to be thankful for.' Jürgen looked up at her as she spoke, and smiled. 'This little fellow for one thing.'

'Aye,' Andreas agreed. 'In two or three years I'll train him up to be useful about the workshop.'

'You *are* a practical man.' She watched Jürgen again. That red-gold hair ... 'Who do you think the boy is more like?' she said, as lightly as she could. 'Klaus or Gertrude?' She glanced at Andreas and saw that he was blushing, his eyes as shifty as they had been in the old days.

'I cannot say,' he mumbled.

'Do you think he resembles his father? Is that an easier question to answer?'

Andreas remained resolutely dumb. Christa looked down at Jürgen. Yes, it was absolutely clear now. It was not simply that he had the red-gold of Dieter's hair, but also the curve of his eyebrow, and the shape of his eyes when he smiled. Wicked, wicked Dieter, God bless him. She thought of her dead brother and dead friends. Sweet, reckless Dieter; foolish, lying Gertrude; poor, deceived Klaus. How strange that such sin could result in the blessing of this child. A consolation from God. Her own flesh and blood.

Twenty-four

WHEN CHRISTA WAS A LITTLE GIRL her father had lifted her from her bed on a dark winter morning and carried her to the city walls, meaning to make an end of them both. His tormented mind had conceived that it would be an act of love to spare her from the sorrows of this world. Now, sitting in the evening sun outside the workshop, she understood that he had, in the end, made the braver choice, and dared to live.

For the first time since the city's fall she sensed his presence. This was no ghostly visitation. He was here. His bones lay in the dust and ashes beneath her feet. His blood pulsed in her veins. Past and present were met in her.

It seemed that those she loved most would always be just beyond her reach: her father and Dieter, hidden among the multitudes of the dead; Elsbeth, spinning herself a filigree cage of prayer to protect herself from the world; Götz, travelling away from her, seeking a path he might not recognise even when he found it. She must love them all, and trust that she would meet them again.

Yes, past and present were met in her, and the future too. She watched baby Jürgen play. Life lay before them, with all its terrors and delights. Anything was possible.